COFFEE DATES

COFFEE DATES

Megan Becker

LUMINARE PRESS
WWW.LUMINAREPRESS.COM

Luminare Press
442 Charnelton St.
Eugene, OR 97401
www.luminarepress.com

LCCN: 2023909111
ISBN: 979-8-88679-296-6

For Mom—
You've taught me so much

like life is short and meant to be enjoyed
and the minutes need to count
and to love books
and how to be a mom
and, and, and…

Enjoy the campfires.

ONE

The rain slows, and a hint of sunlight peeks through the clouds visible between distant high-rises. A steady stream of commuters and tourists flows past the window next to me.

"I'm fine, Mom," I say into the phone pressed against my left ear. To block out the noise of the milk frothers and other patrons, I squish my right tragus into the ear canal. I only know the word 'tragus' because my sister is one of those cool people who pierced hers to fight off migraines, and now she looks like a badass. Or at least a badass as far as her fellow accountants are concerned.

Mom's chirping something about being safe on the subway, but I can only make out every other word. I nod like she can see me and begin to pack up my things, hoping I can make it out in time before the fresh batch of dark clouds rolls in with more storms.

"Mom, it's fine. I've been here before. I know how to get around, and I know how to be careful." In hindsight, and thanks to the sideways glances of the nuns at the table next to me, I realize that hearing only *my* side of the conversation might make it sound like I'm looking for something I am definitely *not* in town to find.

My cheeks flush and I mouth *sorry* to the nuns as I gather my papers into a neat-ish pile and slide them into my backpack. Its waterproof material and the short line are all the convincing I need to get one more latte on my way out. If I get stuck in the next storm, at least my papers will stay dry and I'll have coffee to warm me up.

"Gotta go, Mom. I promise I'll call you when I get back to Lindsey's apartment." If she argues, I don't hear it.

The barista raises an eyebrow as I approach the counter for the third time this morning. "Napkins are that way," she says, pointing to the end of the counter.

I plaster a smile on my face. "Thanks, I'm good. Could I please get another caramel vanilla latte, though?" Hiding my already jittery hands behind my back, I confirm that, yes, once again I would like the largest possible size. My heart ricochets inside my chest from caffeine and excitement and nerves. I pay for my coffee and wait, tightening and loosening my backpack straps like I did every middle school morning while waiting for my school bus. The sky beyond the windows is darkening again and I'll probably get drenched on my way to the subway station, but it's worth it for espresso and sugar.

I'm lucky to be here. Lucky that Lindsey is willing to lend me her spare room for two months while her boyfriend spends time back home with his ailing father. It feels weird to say I'm lucky that my life is in shambles, but if that's led to me spending time in New York, seeking inspiration and sharing time with my best friend since middle school, then sure, I'm lucky that I was fired from my job and dumped for a cat.

"Caramel vanilla latte for...*Hellary*?"

I swear the nuns cross themselves. Maybe they hear me curse at the mix-up under my breath, or maybe they feel the name really fits the person they think I am from that phone call earlier. I swear some people become baristas just to mess with the rest of us because sure enough, when I look at the cup, the "i" sure as *hellary* looks like an "e."

I plaster on that smile again and yell, "Thanks Candy!" to that initial, eyebrow-raising barista, whose nametag totally says Mandy.

There—karma for Mandy, I laugh to myself. I take a sip and look behind me as I walk to the door, just in time to catch Mandy's annoyed eyeroll.

I'm two feet from the door when karma comes back for me.

A man—inexplicably not watching where he's walking in a coffee shop in the most crowded city in America—collides with me and sends my latte spilling down my jeans and onto the floor. *Karma.*

He kneels at the same time I do to try to clean up the mess. And he is the hottest man I have ever laid eyes on. *Luck.* Or maybe this is karma, too.

"I am so, so sorry," he says in a voice that's kind and genuine. "Let me find some napkins."

"I'll grab some," I say, rising. "I know exactly where they are."

TWO

Even if my Old Navy jeans hadn't been splatter-painted with my delicious latte, today is not a great day for me, appearance-wise. The moisture in the unseasonably warm air outside has turned my bob into a frizzy, wavy mess. If I hadn't chopped my hair off in a moment of redefining-myself-insanity, I could at least opt for a ponytail on days like this, but instead I look like some taller, less confident version of my twelve-year-old self. On the bright side, since a pigeon pooped on my raincoat the second I stepped out of the building this morning, I'm wearing a super cute blazer as a jacket. I even threw on some mascara, which totally helps to hide the fact that I haven't slept well in months. I hope it does, anyway.

So here I am, haphazardly casual, mopping up coffee from the floor beside a perfectly coifed Adonis in tailored pants and a button-up shirt that shows off the broad shoulders and trim waist of someone who spends a lot of time at the gym.

I'm also sweating. First-impression superstar, here.

"I am so sorry," he repeats, and I believe him.

"No problem—happens all the time," I say in a borderline-chipmunk voice. I clear my throat to stop the squeal and swipe the hair off my sweat-sticky forehead with the back of my hand. He stops cleaning and looks at me.

"Really? You make a habit of bumping into strangers, or…"

My cheeks flush again at his hazel eyes and friendly smirk.

Shit. He's gorgeous and nice. And talented. I'm not sure the 'stranger' classification works for a celebrity whose career I've followed for a decade, but I don't want to come across as a teenage fangirl and I'm too socially awkward to say *If I remember correctly, you bumped into me* in a way that sounds flirty and not mean, so I just say, "Sorry."

His smile widens just as Mandy arrives with a towel that will actually absorb the mess instead of just pushing it around the floor. She kneels dangerously close to him and I'm pretty sure she's arching her back and using very deliberate arm placement to enhance her cleavage through her polo shirt with every swipe.

She lets out a shrill "all done" for his benefit and shoots me a dirty look before smiling at him and walking back to her position behind the counter.

"Her technique was certainly… interesting," he says, stretching out a hand to help me to my feet.

"It certainly was. Maybe that's part of some specialized OSHA training I've never been privy to." I swear he snorts at the joke, and I try to hold back the newest rush of red to my face.

"So, I owe you a replacement coffee. What were you drinking?"

"Thanks, but I'm good. If she has to help me again, I think she'd probably just wring out the towel into a cup for me."

"Now, *that* OSHA would most certainly *not* approve of," he says, and now I snort. I'm pretty sure that doesn't fall under OSHA's purview, but the comment's still funny as hell. He whips his face toward mine and the corners of his eyes crease as he smiles.

"If you've got time, there's a great little place down the street that would absolutely not serve you floor towel coffee."

The outside world looks gray again. I'm going to get rained on either way, so I agree.

Mandy has not taken her eyes off of us since she returned to her station, and I take great joy in seeing her disbelief as I walk outside with Mr. Perfect.

Under the layers of scaffolding that frame the sidewalks, he apologizes once more, and my dad-joke loving self makes it weird.

"Hi, Sorry, I'm Hillary. Nice to meet you."

He smiles again and shoves his hands into his pockets. "I'm sorry if my manners bother you," he says. "You must be a New Yorker."

"Ha! No, not quite. And your manners *don't* bother me. You just don't need to apologize anymore. I think three times was plenty for an accident."

"Fair enough."

Without apologies, we have little to talk about. We stop at the end of the block, and he points across the street, four storefronts from the corner. "That's where we're headed." We dart across the road and turn left, dodging puddles as we go. He holds the door open for me, and now I'm standing in the quirkiest café I've ever seen.

Bright yellow and teal stools, occupied by young adults with laptops and ear buds, line a countertop by the window. There's a bicycle mounted to the wall and oversized sketches of coffee cups behind the counter. In the far corner an electric fireplace emits a warm glow, and arts-themed graffiti adorns the wall next to it. Plush, worn armchairs litter the floor, ranging from bright orange and hot pink to navy blue and black; wooden tables, glass tables, reclaimed tree trunk tables, and one with a pineapple-shaped base add to the unconventional decor.

I sense magic in this room of misfit things and know, instantly, that this is my new favorite place on the planet.

Even if present company was not present.

"Pretty cool, huh?" he breathes dangerously close to my ear as he literally spins past me, matching the lighthearted, free-spirited atmosphere of the surprisingly empty café. My heart leaps in a caffeine-unrelated way.

"It's really unique."

"Mmhmm. And their coffee is excellent. Also, it's in a cup." He shrugs playfully and motions me forward to the counter where a smiling barista with a sparkling purple nose ring greets us.

"Welcome to Eunoia," she says, effortlessly cool beneath a mess of turquoise and purple curls piled on top of her head. She beams her cheerful and not-at-all starstruck gaze at him and asks, "The usual?"

"Actually," he says, drumming his fingertips on the counter. He turns to me. "What are you drinking? Caramel vanilla latte?"

I nod, impressed or flattered. *Idiot. He's not flirting with you. He's replacing your coffee. Calm down. Not gonna happen.*

"Great," he says, ordering two. He nods toward the barista. "Jolie and her wife, Shan, own the place."

"Yeah, and your friend here is our number one customer," Jolie smiles, passing two steaming mugs across the counter.

"Oh!" I let slip as he passes one to me. Somehow he intuits that syllable perfectly.

"Is it okay that they're for here? I can ask for to-go cups, or..."

"No, it's good. I just wasn't expecting..." Neither of us can finish a sentence, apparently, but he still manages to figure out what's in my head.

"Ah, yes, sorry—I don't mean to insert myself into your day. I'm sure you've got things to do. I can get them to go."

Okay, he *sorta* manages to figure it out.

He steps toward Jolie, who has journeyed to the other end of the counter to collect used mugs. Instinctively I reach out, my fingers landing on his bicep. A very toned bicep on a very attractive man. They linger there a moment as he turns, and I retract them, suddenly very aware that I just touched a semi-stranger who happens to be way out of my league.

Coffee sloshes up the walls of my mug and nearly spills down the sides. "I have time. I'm just going to park in that chair over by the fire and relax for a bit." I jerk my head toward the pink chair by the graffiti wall and fireplace. "If they have sippy cup lids, that may be a good idea if you're going to be joining me."

His smile creeps back and a laugh escapes his lips. It's deep and bright and fills the room, but no one seems to hear or mind. "So help me, if I spill this cup too, I will just have to try again a different day to buy you a coffee."

There goes my heart, dancing at the thought of seeing him again.

He follows me to the corner and lowers himself into a dark leopard-print chair. He hesitates and blows on his coffee before taking a sip and nods slowly as he sets the mug on the tabletop. "Okay, okay, not bad."

I follow his lead, sipping the latte, thinking maybe the coffee won't be as good as he's promised, but it's amazing. "*Not bad?* This might be the best latte I've ever had."

"I'm just not normally a latte guy."

"Ah. Iced black coffee, right?"

He leans in for his mug but stops and snaps his head toward me. "Yeah. How'd you know?"

Instagram. "Lucky guess." This could actually be fun, this knowing-things-about-him-without-him-knowing-I-know-things-about-him game, if I didn't feel that twinge of guilt.

"Do you run a coffee psychology firm? Is that a thing? I think that could be a thing. Everything's a 'thing' now."

"Yes, and this session will cost you seven hundred dollars. Insurance likely won't cover it unless you've got the platinum plan."

He raises his eyebrows and shakes his head. Something like a smile tugs at the corners of his lips. "I definitely do *not* have that."

"*Mmm.* Lucky for you, today's session is discounted to the cost of one replacement coffee."

"Lucky for me," he repeats.

Without apologies or mindless banter about coffee we're stuck in silence again, which I don't mind, but I'm also trying *really* hard to not stare at him. *Creation Appreciation,* my high school youth pastor called it, whenever we talked about all the boys we thought were cute back then. I am definitely appreciative but don't want to be creepy. I take in the sights around the café instead.

"So, you said you're *not* from here?" he asks, sinking back into the chair and crossing his legs, ankle over knee.

"One hundred percent, not from here or anywhere *like* here. Is that not obvious?"

He shrugs. "The city's home to so many types of people. Are you just visiting?"

"I guess you could say that. How about you? Are you from New York originally?" I can answer my own question. "Not originally, no. Been here most of the last decade or so. I moved here for work."

I stop myself from asking what he does because I don't want this bubble to burst. I like this feeling of being two strangers, this even playing field. "So where did you move here from?"

He rests his elbows on the arms of his chair, further settling in and all but abandoning his latte. "It's a small town in the tiny sliver of West Virginia that sneaks in between Pennsylvania and Ohio. Spent my summers working at an amusement park, trying to scrounge together the money to get a car to impress Gina Thompson." His cheeks turn pink at the memory and I'm afraid he feels he's overshared.

"Coolwater Springs?" When his head perks up, I ask again, "The amusement park you worked at—was that Coolwater Springs?"

One side of his mouth curls. "Yeah—how'd you know?"

I inhale, aware that a certain response could brand me mildly dorky, but I go for it anyway. "I'm a big amusement park fan. And I'm only a few hours from there."

"Very cool. Not many people know that area."

He's right. "That's what I love about it. It's so unknown, like a hidden treasure. No frills, but great rides, good food, and short wait times."

His smile widens and he leans into the conversation. "Can I tell you a secret?"

You can try, I think. *But I know so much about you.* "You mean, other than your crush on Gina Thompson?"

The pink in his cheeks returns, borderline red now, but he laughs and continues. "I actually hate roller coasters."

"Really? I love them. I can't do anything that spins, but I'll ride coasters all day. As long as it's not too hot, I can take breaks between them, and I have something for my motion sickness."

"Seems like a lot of 'ifs' in there," he laughs. "I actually *love* anything that spins, but I can't do coasters. I hate heights."

"Oh, me too. The hating heights thing, I mean." My hand brushes across the top of the backpack next to me; coming to New York to chase my dream has the same fear-inducing, knee-weakening effect on me as a hyper-coaster does.

His gaze falls to my hand and bounces back to my eyes. "So where is home for you?"

"Only about three hours away, a place called Lemming, in Pennsylvania."

"Never heard of it."

"Well, we can't all be from a booming metropolis like Greentree, West Virginia."

He arches a brow and leans in, folding his hands. "I never told you I was from Greentree."

My stomach flips and I do my best to play it cool. I'm terribly uncool, as a rule, so this should be interesting. "Oh, are you? I was guessing, since that's where we stayed when we visited Coolwater Springs."

"Mmm."

I can't tell if he's buying it or not at first, but when he nods and eases his posture, I feel somewhat safe. Then he opens his mouth, and I feel like I'm in shark-infested waters with a fresh papercut.

"What did you say you were in town for?" He's still friendly, not fully accusatory. That's good, I guess.

I lazily reach for my mug and shrug, because how do I put into words the exact chain of events that have led to this moment without ending up sobbing incoherently, curled up on the floor in the fetal position? When I weigh my options, a filtered version of the truth wins out, and I take a sip to drown back the lump in my throat. "For… self-discovery. For inspiration."

"Cheers to that," he says, raising his mug to mine. When he takes a drink, his face sours. "God, that's awful."

"I can fix this."

Ignoring his objections, I approach the counter and order his regular. Jolie asks, "For here? Or to go?" and I feel stuck between seeming presumptuous and seeming like I'm trying to get rid of him.

"Um…here? I guess?"

The coffee is in front of me before my payment is processed.

"You didn't have to do that," he says when I return, but he accepts the gift and happily sips it, and it's well worth the four dollars I spent.

"Trust me, I did it for me. I can't stand to see someone cringe at their coffee like that. I feel like that Sarah McLachlan song should be playing in the background."

He laughs again, loud enough to draw Jolie's attention to our corner, then sobers, his index fingers tented together and tapping his lips in a very theater teacher kind of way. "So, what inspires you, Hillary? And for what do you seek inspiration?"

My lips part, then purse, trying to hold back the torrent of secrets and shame that threaten to spill out. I avoid meeting his eyes and tilt my head backward. With that motion I see the bicycle, the graffiti, the young artists-or-students at the counter, and the vibrant barista. "Art inspires me. In all its forms." It's a safe answer, and I dare to return his gaze. He's nodding, slowly, thoughtfully. "Well, you're in the right city for that. Which form speaks to you most?"

I curl my legs up beside me on the chair, unable to sit still or straight when I talk about art. "Honestly, my favorite is musical theater." The words tumble out before I can think to restrain them.

The left side of his face smiles, creasing the skin around his lips and eyes. He may sometimes play a teenager, but I see his so-graceful-it-should-be-illegal aging. "Really."

Though the left side smiles, the rest of his face does not. His practically-marble jaw tightens; his hazel eyes disappear as he surveys the floor. His free hand rakes through his swoopy, chestnut hair.

My words have clearly upset him, but I spew out more anyway. "Yeah, I was really involved in music growing up."

That seems to do the trick. His eyes rise again, and he swallows more coffee. "What all did you do?"

"What *didn't* I do? Church choir basically from birth, school choir from sixth grade on. Concert band starting in fifth grade and marching band all four years of high school. I was in every musical we did in high school and college."

"That's quite the resume."

I feel my cheeks burn. Here I am, telling *him* about *my* stage credits. Like he's actually interested or impressed.

"Do you have a favorite? From all the musicals you did?"

And now I'm gesturing wildly, describing the dance solo I had once, when I had to play Boy Number Three in a production of The Music Man because our girl-to-boy ratio was off, and I happened to be tall and flat-chested and therefore asked to play a boy. Maybe it should be weird to reveal that tidbit, but he's so easy to talk to that it just comes out and I'm not embarrassed or ashamed the way I had been when I was sixteen.

"On the bright side, I felt very at-home in a marching band uniform, so that big eleventh-hour number was right up my alley."

There's something freeing in being around him, in being with someone who knows nothing about me apart from what I choose to share. In knowing I can share it all because the coffee shop will close, eventually, and he'll need to get back to his life and we'll never see each other again. In being honest and not feeling judged. In being *me*. Unapologetically.

I wonder if he feels it too. He seems easy, carefree, like he gets to be who he wants to be and not who the world expects him to be.

A pang of guilt stabs at my ribs as I consider my lie of omission. If he knew that I know who he is, we wouldn't be sitting here right now. He chose a seat with his back to the door, probably so people wouldn't see his face. He's telling me about his fear of heights and Gina Thompson because *he thinks I don't know who he is.*

Or maybe, my heart suggests to my brain, *he likes talking to you and he doesn't care if you know who he is or not.*

Thunder rolls in, long and slow, and rain spatters the window.

"I love thunderstorms."

We say it at the same time, but his words come out as a longing sigh, a love song breathed in five syllables. I snap my head back from the window and our eyes meet. His half-smile crescendos then fades in an instant, and he adjusts his hair again.

He clears his throat and slaps his hands against his thighs. "I'll be right back," he says and disappears.

When he returns, I'm daydreaming, watching the rain. "*Hillary?*" When his hand touches my shoulder, I worry I was basically unconscious. "You okay?"

"Oh. Sorry. I'm not sure where my mind wandered." In reality I know exactly where it went: a covered porch, the smells of a vanilla pipe and sawdust and new hardcovers mingling with a faint whiff of earthworms as raindrops fall above and around us.

I shake the thought free and accept the glass of water he offers to me.

"If you prefer another coffee…"

"No, this is great. Thanks." I extend the glass back to him. "Did you want my lemon?"

He's already squeezing his own lemon wedge into his glass but nods and lifts the wedge from the rim of mine, too. "Thanks. I drink a lot of lemon water. Helps my voice."

We both realize he's said too much, and he stiffens, though he doesn't know that I know he's said too much.

"I never liked the taste, myself. It either needs about eight lemons and a cup of sugar or it needs to be just pure agua."

"That's quite the recipe for lemonade." I read cautious relief in his expression.

I shrug and take a drink. "Don't quote me on that compound."

We talk, much longer than we should, but there are whole lives to share. It was eleven this morning when I basically hung up on my mom; now it's two thirty. My stomach growls but I quiet it with water and my long-cold latte.

I hear more of the story of Gina Thompson and that first car—a Dodge Neon that was not impressive to her despite the fact that he'd saved enough to buy it outright and had no debt from the purchase. Responsible Hillary approves of that tidbit.

I share the story of my first date with a guy with a nice car: he'd picked me up in his convertible, but after a long shift at work that day and a bajillion hours of Lord of the Rings during our local theater's Two Dollar Tuesdays special on older movies, he was sound asleep in the theater when the film ended.

"*No!*" Deep, joyful lines form around his mouth and in his forehead as he laughs out loud, uninhibited and free. A few heads turn from the patrons who have snuck in as the storm lingers over the city.

"I swear. So there I am, sophomore in high school, and the average age of the other people around me has got to be sixty-two, and I'm trying to wake him up without him *realizing* he fell asleep on our date, and—"

"Excuse me," a voice interrupts as a hand appears between our faces, and three girls who can't be old enough to drink are standing across from us.

He turns his head reflexively and the girls shriek. The one in the middle, wearing cut-off jean shorts over black leggings, a white crop-top, oversized flannel button-down, and black combat boots has her arm extended from her initial interruption and begins fanning her face. "Shut *up*," she squeals, drawing the attention of others around us. "It's really you! I can't believe I'm standing here talking to Dalton Tremaine."

When he turns back to me, his wide eyes tell me everything I need to know: this is exactly what he was hoping would *not* happen today.

The bubble has burst.

THREE

"You handled that really well."

"Ha, yeah."

"I'm serious. I can't imagine what it's like, not being able to go out in public without people approaching you when you're trying to mind your own business." Actually, I *do* know what that's like. That's Lemming, every damn day. And that's why I'm not there right now.

"Is that a dig?"

I look at him, confused.

"Because I have now trapped you for..." he checks his watch. "Holy shit, *four hours?*"

"Technically you didn't approach me, and it's not a dig at all. Today's been great. Even if we had to pivot a bit with that interruption from the sexy wannabe-lumberjack and her posse."

He throws his head back and laughs, the first time he's looked up in the five minutes since we left Eunoia. A raindrop rests on his eyebrow.

"Can I ask you something?" I stop abruptly in the middle of the sidewalk, and after one more step, he pauses and turns. Annoyed commuters bump into my shoulder as they pass.

"Uh, sure?"

"Where are we going?"

In our haste to escape his safe haven, eight autographs and twelve selfies later, we failed to name a new destination. Instead, we hide in plain sight in the sea of umbrellas and bodies that converge downtown.

He pulls me out of the way to the edge of the sidewalk, his elbow dangerously close to a speeding cyclist in the bike lane. "Are you hungry?"

"Always."

"Great. I owe you dinner."

"You owe me nothing."

"I owe you an explanation. Which I think you'd rather have over dinner than out here in this storm."

"Don't be so sure," I say, smiling wide. Rain gives me this *joie de vivre*. Maybe it's the memories of vanilla pipes and books or maybe it's the idea of cleansing and renewing, but rain is my favorite. I stretch out my arms, forgetting the crowds, and twirl in the downpour. Immediately my arm collides with a stranger's, and I recoil, overcompensating and throwing my weight too far in the opposite direction. I'm toppling over and my foot slips off the curb into the green paint of the bike lane.

"Look out!" I hear his voice over the panicked dinging of a bike messenger's bell. His arm wraps around my waist and he pulls me to him just before the messenger passes.

I'm pressed against Dalton Tremaine's chest, enveloped by one arm with a comforting and surprisingly strong hold on me. One of our hearts is thumping, but we're so close I can't place whose it is. *Of course it's mine,* I know. But deep down I really hope it could be his, too.

His free hand is wrapped around a *No Parking* sign; I hope he's had a tetanus shot recently. When he exhales into the semi-sticky and wet spring air, it's just puffs of steam.

"Thanks," I say, barely above a whisper. I'm afraid to open my mouth too much because I know I have terrible coffee breath and because our mouths are incredibly close to each other. Since I haven't eaten all day, I'm not sure I'd have the energy to keep myself from kissing him if given the chance. That's how these encounters are supposed to go, right? *Am I in a real-life meet-cute?*

His eyes rise to meet mine. Their perfect shade of hazel sends a flutter through my stomach. "You okay?"

"Yeah. Thanks."

I let myself be swept up in his arm—and the moment—for two more seconds and then press off gently against his chest. I repeat another "thanks" and understand why he apologized three times earlier for spilling my coffee—it's easy conversation when other words won't come out.

"Anyway," I say, avoiding his eyes because I'm embarrassed that he had to save my life from a bicycle.

"Did you want to grab dinner somewhere? Will you spontaneously combust if you sit down at an actual restaurant or is that a safe option?"

A yellow cab drives by, directly through a pothole. The puddle that's formed inside is displaced, and we're close enough to the street that we're now soaked in pothole water from the waist down. He looks at his perfect pants, now drenched, appalled. I laugh.

It starts out mild and light but pretty quickly progresses to full-belly, squeeze-my-legs-together-so-I-don't-pee-myself laughter.

He eyes me, jaw dropped and locked, before his expression changes completely and now he, too, laughs at the this-day-just-keeps-getting-better circumstances.

"Not sure I'm dressed for a restaurant. Can I interest you

in a street cart hot dog instead?" I ask through fits of giggles. The green in his eyes brightens and he asks through hearty laughter, "Will it be better than floor towel coffee?" He grasps my hand, half-dragging me as we both waddle uncomfortably down the sidewalk. If our fingers were interlocked it might feel romantic, but right now I feel like a curious toddler being pulled along by a mom on a mission. In this case, though, the "mom" is really the eighty-third most gorgeous person in America, per a two-year-old issue of a magazine I'd picked up before a flight home from a work conference.

The magazine was long gone, each page ripped out and burned as campfire kindling, but not before I saw the restrained, tight-lipped smile of an incredibly debonair-looking Dalton Tremaine, dressed in a tux on a red carpet, eyes afire with passionate reticence. Then Peter saw the list of gorgeous people, mocked them, called them something inappropriate, and stole the magazine because I wasn't tearing out pages fast enough for his liking.

A chill runs from my toes to my fingertips at the thought of Peter, something like cold electricity that causes my feet to stumble and my hand to contract around Dalton's. He looks at me, his concern obvious, and slows.

"You alright?"

"Yeah, I'm fine. Sorry." I realize I've been three paces behind him the last two blocks, my mind elsewhere entirely and my body moving at a small-town pace. I shake Peter from my mind when I realize I'm wasting my present on the past. Instead of living in the moment, I'm stuck back in Lemming. But isn't the point of being in New York to live in the moment—to seize the day and live my life selfishly and authentically for two months? So I decide, here and now, to be fully present. *Carpe the damn diem.*

His hand releases mine and I match his pace now, far enough downtown that the crowd is thinner and we're not at risk of losing each other. At least not until tonight, when I'm back at Lindsey's apartment and he's lounging in, I suspect, a modern loft somewhere.

We acquire two soft pretzels pretty quickly, though "soft" might be a gross mischaracterization, and the rain has nearly stopped. Strands of hair are plastered to my face, and my jeans will no doubt be soaked for days.

Dalton leaves the change from the pretzels in the tip jar and waves politely to acknowledge the "thanks man" from the vendor. Somehow things have changed since that initial response to the taxi incident, and though we wordlessly hoofed the seven blocks south, we're still in no hurry to speak. Instead, he gestures toward an abandoned bistro set, one of many sitting vacant and very, very wet in an open plaza. I lower myself into a seat that faces an archway at the far end of the park

As he chews his pretzel, a smile crosses his face.

"What?" I ask, suddenly self-conscious.

He extends his legs and shakes his head. "It's just nice to see people looking up for a change. That's all." He slides his chair around to my side of the table so he can take in the arch, too.

I shrug. "How can you not? The architecture in this city is incredible. The Empire State Building, Chrysler Building…"

"Radio City Music Hall."

Of course he names the most famous theater in New York. "Mmm."

"Look, Hillary, about earlier."

I hold up a hand to stop him. "Hang on, are we talking about spilling-my-coffee earlier, or showering in street water, or…"

I'm trying to keep the conversation light, but his expression is serious. "Is it weird," he asks, "that that happened?"

"The lumberjack?"

He smirks. "Yeah. The lumberjack."

"I mean, it's not something that happens in my normal day-to-day, if that's what you're asking."

He sighs and drums his fingers on the heavy iron table, like he's deciding what to say.

"It's really not that big of a deal," I offer, trying to ease his tension.

"You looked terrified."

It's probably true. I hate crowds that I can't move through, which is why I feel fine trudging along the sidewalks of New York, swept up in the hustle and bustle of people walking with purpose, but I hate a crowded day at Disney World when people are just *there*. The group that clamored for his attention definitely bordered on 'New Year's Day at Magic Kingdom' territory, if not in size, then in oppressive proximity. "I don't like crowds."

"I'm sorry we were interrupted. I was really enjoying talking to you."

I make a show of looking around, craning my neck like I'm searching the whole plaza for someone, and then meet his gaze again. "Wait, *me*? If only we were still able to talk to each other. Maybe in a serene outdoor setting with great architecture all around us, or something."

His expression sours, and he turns—I can't believe I'm using this expression to describe *the* Dalton Tremaine— *gruff.*

"I don't like the crowds either, and I especially don't like them in my favorite coffee shop, making a scene. And I *really* don't like them scaring my new friend."

"'My new friend' sounds like how a divorcee introduces a future stepdad to her kids."

One loud laugh leaves his lips. "Sorry, that did sound weird. But this whole afternoon has been weird. First I spilled your coffee all over you, then we were bum-rushed by a lumberjack and her minions." After a deep sigh that captures his shoulders and chest, he asks, "Do you ever just wish you could have a do-over?"

A moment passes, and I turn and extend my hand to him. "Hi, I'm Hillary."

A smile creeps into his lips as he regards my hand and shakes it, eyes locked on mine. "Hi, Hillary. My name is Dalton. Dalton Tremaine."

"Well, that sounds like a very fancy name. What do you do, Mr. Tremaine?" I've taken on the character of a southern, star-struck tourist, accent and all. It was not initially intentional, but now I commit.

"I am an actor," he says, slowly and deliberately, like he's unsure if that's an admission he wants to make.

"Oooh like Tom Hanks? I love Tom Hanks. Do you know him?"

He plays along, embracing his answers to my southern belle questions. "Yes, sort of like Tom Hanks, but much less famous and significantly less talented. I don't know him, unfortunately."

"Shame, really. I'd love to meet him."

He ignores the attempt at a joke and offers another admission. "I'm also a singer."

"So, you do it all, huh?"

He shrugs. "Try to."

I open my mouth to tell him I know it all, when he continues, suddenly serious.

"I don't usually tell people. I try to keep a low profile. Sometimes people get a little weird around me, like they're afraid to be themselves and they're just putting on an act. And it's hard to know who wants to be around me for me, or who wants to be around me for *themselves*, if that makes sense."

I realize my whole torso has been nodding along with him, from stomach to shoulders, neck to nose, like some hippie turtle. "It does make sense."

I decide not to tell him the whole truth at this point, partly because I don't want him to doubt that I've fully enjoyed this day regardless of the fact that he is an award-winning stage actor whose rare Instagram posts always get a "like" from me, and partly because my cell phone vibrates in my blazer pocket repeatedly.

"For what it's worth, I find it very easy to believe that people want to be around you for *you*. I've really enjoyed today." Hopefully the genuineness of the sentiment shines through as I fish my cell from my pocket. Notifications fill my lock screen and my stomach sinks.

Where are you?
Why aren't you calling me?
Hillary, are you OK?
HELLOOOOOO?!?
Call me ASAP.
Hillary…

I promised Lindsey I'd join her for dinner, but the sun is yielding to the evening now and I've somehow missed a million texts from my friend.

"I am so, so sorry, but I have to go." I stand, already texting Lindsey back.

"Oh," he replies, rising with me. "Can I give you a lift anywhere?"

"Nah, I'm good. I just need to hop on the A train and I'm good to go."

"So—" he says, just as my phone rings. Lindsey's name appears on the caller ID.

"It was really nice to meet you," I smile, fumbling my phone, pretzel, and wallet to shake his hand.

"Likewise. Thanks, Hillary."

"Thank *you*, for the coffee, the pretzel…and for a wonderful conversation. It was great meeting you—great talking to you today." I absorb the last glimpse of him that I can. I don't want to do it, but I turn my back on Dalton Tremaine and make a beeline for the station at Fourth Street. This is not the way my once-in-a-lifetime encounter with him is supposed to end.

The station is warmer than the street level air, and other trains *woosh* through, ushering a breeze that reeks of garbage from the abyss of the city.

I board the A train and melt into a seat, grateful that the train is empty enough for me to sit and close my eyes, replaying snapshots of today over and over in my head with the resolve to burn each one into my memory forever. After all, soon I'll be back at Lindsey's apartment and this day—the puddles and coffee and company—will be a story that I tell and retell just so I remember that it happened and I didn't just create it. I'll have to write down all the details after dinner tonight.

I bolt upright and grasp the edge of the seat. My backpack, with my laptop and journal and completed pages—the whole reason I came to New York—is missing.

FOUR

"You mean to tell me you were on a date with Dalton Tremaine and you left him there just because I called?"

"It was not a date," I say, my face flushing. "And the point is, I lost my backpack somewhere in New York City."

"No, you left your backpack behind, somewhere between that coffee shop and the Fourth Street Station, and I hardly doubt you just set it down on a curb when you were reenacting 'Singing in the Rain' with a Broadway star."

"Right." Now I'm pacing the floor like an amateur sleuth. "So likely it was Eunoia. I don't remember having it after that." I've already tried calling the number listed on their website. Unfortunately, they're closed for the night. No voicemail option, either.

"Looks like I'm starting tomorrow out with some coffee. Maybe they'll have it pulled aside in lost and found or something."

"Maybe," Lindsey shrugs. "Worth a shot, for sure." She curls her legs up onto the couch and clutches a pillow in her lap. "Sooo? How was it?"

"How was *what*?"

"Um, duh, a day with Dalton Tremaine."

The mention of his name sends heat to my cheeks again. "I mean, it was awesome. He's pretty cool."

"Pretty *hot*, you mean?"

"Okay, that too." I inhale one of the first relaxing breaths I've taken all day. The air that inflates my chest carries the comforting aroma of something savory, and I realize that I'm famished. "That smells delicious, by the way."

"Thanks," Lindsey smiles. She loves to cook and bake and hopes to eventually open her own bakery and café in Brooklyn, *because it's cooler and a little less expensive than Manhattan*, she always says. "Dinner should be ready in about ten minutes, but I'm going to need you to fill that time with more details about your day. 'Pretty cool' is not going to earn you shepherd's pie."

I fill her in on the coffee shop, the nuns, the freaking out from my mom—*note to self: call Mom ASAP*—and the chance encounter. "And I get him wanting to replace the coffee. I really do. What I *don't* get is him spending half his day with me."

She opens her mouth to interject, but I don't let her. "Come to think of it, I think I did that. He ordered the coffees, but I think I'm the one who sat down with him. He probably wanted to drink in peace, and I'm the one who actually inserted myself into *his* day, not the other way around."

"Or—and stay with me here—he bumped into a beautiful, independent, *kind* person who captured his interest with her smile and her sense of humor, and he wanted to enjoy his coffee with someone who wouldn't spend an hour asking him for tips and tricks to making it in the biz or if he could set them up with an audition or something."

For a moment I let myself consider that *maybe* Lindsey is right, that I—*beige*, personified—have somehow charmed him by being a total departure from his normal life. But the insanity passes quickly, and I shake off the notion.

Lindsey probes again for more information. "So, is he as good-looking as all the pictures make him out to be? Or is there a lot of editing on his social media?"

"Haven't you seen him on stage?"

She waves off the question. "Yeah, a few times, but it's far away, and there's makeup involved. I want to know if he looks that good in the wild."

"Yes, he definitely does," I confirm.

Just as my cheeks redden for the twenty-third time today, the timer on the oven beeps and Lindsey jumps up. "Time for dinner!" her voice rings out, filling the entire apartment, despite the fact that I am right next to her.

My eyes follow her to the kitchen area (it's a New York City apartment, so it's about five feet from the living room) and my stomach rumbles at the sight of the browned edges of the whipped potatoes that peek out from the au gratin dishes she takes out of the oven.

Because space is limited, and because Lindsey and Marco are casual and cool, there's no dining table. Instead, I spread out floor pillows on opposite ends of the coffee table and uncork the bottle of the pink Moscato I bought for $9.99 at the wine & liquor store back home, pouring two glasses a little fuller than I should. But the evening ahead calls for dinner, a phone call to Mom, and a movie, so we'll end up finishing the bottle before the night is over, I'm sure.

We talk about Lindsey's favorite places in New York—to eat, to visit, to experience life at its fullest. If I do everything she loves, I will fill every moment of the next two months. We talk about life back home, avoiding the sore subjects she knows about (work, dating, nosy people) and focusing more on common interests (our alma mater's spring musical performance, confirming suspicions about former classmates based on cryptic Facebook posts, other random gossip).

I call Mom after dinner and keep things as brief and upbeat as possible. I let her know I'm settling in fine, that Lindsey and I have an exciting week planned, that we're safe. "Gotta go, Mom. Lindsey and I are about to watch a movie and I want to be respectful of her time, since she's got to work tomorrow morning."

I realized long ago that if I announced that I was respecting someone else or doing something unselfishly for a friend, I had her full support. If I was doing something just for me, different story.

Yet here I am, in New York City, doing everything just for me. Living. Writing. Lying to Dalton Tremaine. I push the idea and the guilt from my head. It doesn't matter, since I'm never going to see him again.

When I hang up, I rejoin Lindsey in the living room. She raises her eyes from her cell phone, her face illuminated in the bright light. Evening has settled on the city, and the high-rises around us have blocked the remnants of the sunset.

"Everything alright?" she asks.

No, I think. "Yep!" I say.

"Great! Movie's cued up. Wine glasses are refilled. Are you ready to watch the best movie ever made?"

"I'd love to…but I don't think that's what's about to happen." I wink at her. She whips a pillow at me.

The TV displays the title screen for *Love Actually.*

"This is a cinematic masterpiece."

"It's British *He's Just Not That Into You.*"

"Au contraire," she says, playfully wagging a finger. "This beauty came out years earlier. And what's not to love about an awkward encounter leading to a glorious romance?"

"It's great, except it never happens."

"Tell that to David and Natalie," she says, hitting play on the remote.

FIVE

Eunoia opened at six o'clock, but I was definitely not waking up at five to get there when they unlocked the doors. Not after movie night last night and half a bottle (okay, fine, two-thirds of a bottle) of wine. Not after lying awake for hours replaying my time with Dalton.

Instead, I walk in at eight o'clock, desperate and cautiously optimistic that my backpack is still there, somewhere. I look around first at the bold chairs where we sat before the teenage girls accosted us, but there's nothing there but other patrons who scowl at me over their newspapers and teacups.

"Sorry," I mumble and scan the rest of the café for my bag, only to see the nothingness I'd anticipated.

I join the line behind a man in a navy suit. Despite not yet having caffeine I'm already jittery, shifting weight from one foot to the other. It probably just looks like I need to pee.

When it's my turn to order, a familiar heap of bright curls stands in front of me. "Jolie!"

Her head snaps up from finalizing the last sale on an iPad. "Um, hi?"

I tuck my hair behind my ear, and it falls back to my face. "Hey. Hi. I'm sure you don't remember me, but I was here yesterday, and I—"

"Oh! Yes, you were with—" she lowers her voice to barely a whisper and leans toward me. "Dalton."

"Yes! Okay, so I think I left a backpack here, and I was wondering—"

She waves a hand and cuts me off. "Let me go grab your stuff."

Holy crap. How am I so lucky that someone turned in my backpack? This is a win for New York, in my book.

Jolie reemerges from the Employees Only area and holds out an envelope.

"What's this? I'm looking for my backpack?" I repeat, like maybe she didn't hear me. Behind me there's a sigh, and I can see the line has grown by about four people; the woman directly behind me checks her phone and taps her foot.

"He picked it up this morning. More like, we gave it to him when he came in at seven, I guess. Weren't sure if you'd be back for it, but he said he'd get it to you and left this for you just in case." Jolie slides the envelope toward me. "I need to move on to the rest of the line though, hon, so can I get you anything?"

I pick up my dropped jaw and the envelope. "Um, yes—a hazelnut latte please." I swipe my card and apologize to the woman behind me for making her wait. Mom would be proud.

Coffee—and mysterious envelope—in hand, I leave Eunoia and head northwest into a perfect almost-springtime breeze. The air is comfortable, perfect for leggings, slip-on shoes, and an oversized sweater. When I reach the High Line, stop number one on the list of Lindsey's Favorite Places in New York, I climb the stairs and search immediately for a bench. There's one nearby in a little alcove, and I rush to it.

I sip the latte to steel my nerves, then set it next to me and open the envelope. Inside, a note is scribbled in blue ink:

Hillary—

Thanks for a great talk yesterday. Sorry it ended ~~the way~~ ~~it did~~ so quickly (if you can call 4 hours quick?) but it was great while it lasted. To get your backpack back, stop by the address below between 11 and 1, if you can. Google it first, so you know I'm not a deranged killer luring you into a trap. (That's weird. I'd erase it if I could.) Tell the guy at the door your name and that you're there to see me. Text me if you have any trouble.

—Dalton

PS—Enjoy your latte!

He includes a cell phone number and an address at the bottom of the note, and I save his number to my contacts. I start to text him, then delete everything—a process I repeat three more times before messaging Lindsey instead.

You will never believe the morning I've had.

I'm surprised to get such a quick response considering she's covering the breakfast shift at the restaurant where she works. Oh? Tell me more.

I reply, Dude took my backpack. I'm supposed to meet him later to get it back.

Like a hostage situation? Or…

The laugh I feel in my chest escapes as a snort. Maybe. Seems a little off-brand though. And he'd be the worst criminal ever, unless the number he gave me goes to a burner phone.

I take another sip of my coffee and enjoy the city view as I wait for Lindsey's reply. From here I can see the Hudson and escape the street-level steam that emanates from manhole covers and subway grates.

After a few moments, another text comes through.

Definitely not a burner phone.

I respond, How can you be so sure?

Because for what they charge for these things, this is my sidekick for life.

I gasp and drop my phone, reaching for it as it skids along the concrete. I look closely at the recipient and the texts and send one more. I am so sorry—thought I was texting my friend.

I can tell. 😄. All good. Are you able to meet later?

Can't, sorry. I text back. I think I've died of embarrassment. Can you bring my backpack to my funeral?

I may have to go through it first to get notes for my eulogy.

Don't you dare! I'm relieved that it seems he hasn't begun a self-guided tour of its contents. Also, my eulogy will be sung by Ed Sheeran, TYVM.

He sends a GIF of a pouty child and I respond with a simple haha.

Then, Yes, I can meet you later. Is 11 OK?

Perfect. See you then.

I tuck my phone into the side pocket of my leggings. Sitting still, the chilly air makes me shiver, but the coffee feels good when I hold the cup in both hands. Maybe it doesn't warm me. Maybe I'm feeling melty and content from the act of just holding the cup, like an emotional accompaniment to the muscle memory of this position.

Up until a few months ago, my coffee dates were almost exclusively with Peter. Once upon a time we'd spend Saturday mornings at the local farmers market, picking up goodies from a local café's stand. Or we'd run to a coffee shop, then walk to my favorite bookstore, browsing stacks of new releases together. Peter hated coffee, and he hated the farmers market, and he hated browsing. He'd complain about the price, that coffee was gross and I could make it cheaper at home, and I could buy books cheaper online, and I'd roll my eyes and savor the aroma and the rich, creamy latte as my fingers grazed crisp, colorful spines.

"You don't have to come if you don't want to," I'd told him once, meaning that we could hang out later in the day. I didn't want him to be miserable, or for me to be miserable when he interrupted my sacred Support Local Businesses Saturdays with his deep sighs or verbal complaints.

Apparently, "you don't have to come if you don't want to" roughly translates to "please stop putting in any effort whatsoever" in Peterese, and things went downhill after that.

So here I am, a stranger in a strange city, doing the thing that always grounds me and makes me feel good: holding an overpriced coffee that puts a smile on my face. And this time there's no Peter, but there's *me*, and I'm enough.

I've got about two hours until I need to be in Midtown to meet Dalton. I already have a favorite New York coffee shop; now it's time to find my favorite New York bookstore. According to a quick search, there's one opening in less than ten minutes, about four blocks south. I'll have about an hour and a half to browse before I have to—*get to?*—meet Dalton.

After one more sip of coffee, I open a new text message and verify Lindsey's name appears at the top. Again, I type, You will never believe the morning I've had.

SIX

"**H**oly shit," Lindsey says.

"Holy shit," I repeat.

My curling iron is plugged in and resting on her coffee table, and she's got a full palette of makeup spread out like a MAC smorgasbord in front of us.

A calf-length blue dress hangs off a bookshelf across the room—my second non-food New York purchase, right after the book I grabbed this morning on my way to meet Dalton. Right after Dalton handed me two tickets to his show tonight. I mean, technically, he handed me one, at first. But when I told him that Lindsey and I had planned to spend the evening together again, he disappeared, returning a minute later with a second ticket so we could both come. *Because he wants you there so badly*, Lindsey had said when I told her about it.

"The dress is too much, right?" I ask aloud. "Like I'm trying too hard or something."

"I think it's the right amount. It looks great on you."

"Thanks." The cerulean hue caught my eye at the boutique where I found it—mostly because it was the only non-black article hanging from the clearance rack where I figured my shopping would need to be focused. The silk dress feels polished and flirty and is definitely something I'd never wear back home.

Lindsey dabs gold shadow on my other eyelid. "This will really make your eyes pop," she says. "They're such a pretty blue."

"They're gray."

"They're color-changing, like mood eyes. Maybe when you got here two days ago they were gray, but today they're blue, babe." Under her breath she adds, "Wonder why?"

I scrunch my face, and she playfully pushes my shoulder. "Um, excuse me, the artiste is working here."

"Right, sorry."

"So he just had you show up at this club, where he's singing tonight, to give you back your backpack?"

"Yup."

"He totally wants to impress you," she says, and her breath is warm on my face as she takes a pencil to my eyebrows to fill them in. Apparently, women have to apply all eye makeup with their mouths open, whether applying it to themselves or to their friends.

"Or, and I know this sounds crazy, but maybe he just didn't want to go out of his way to meet somewhere else. Maybe after being attacked yesterday, he just wanted to lay low, hide a little."

"*Or*," she counters, "he's bummed you left so abruptly yesterday and is just looking for excuses to see you again and show you who he is a little. I mean, he's a pretty amazing performer."

"I know that." It comes out harsher than I intend it to.

"But *he* doesn't know that you know that," she says. She shrugs and pulls back, eyeing my face to make sure my brows are even and there are no mascara clumps in my lashes. "Anyway, unrelated. What would he have done if you hadn't shown up? If he'd taken your backpack from Eunoia and never saw you again?"

I had asked him the same question earlier. He'd shoved his hands into his pockets and dug the toe of his boat shoe into the burgundy carpet just inside the club's front door, "I was just really hoping you'd show up, I guess. And if not, I was just going to have to knock on every door in Lemming until I found someone who could help me get it back to you."

"Like Cinderella." As soon as the words came out, I'd regretted them. My cheeks flushed and I was grateful for the dim lighting in the club.

His mouth curled into a crooked smile and his eyes flashed. "Like Cinderella."

I leave out the part about Cinderella in my retelling, but Lindsey shrieks when I tell her about Dalton coming to Lemming to find me. "Hillary!"

"It's *nothing*!" I say, now wagging my curling iron at her.

She rolls her eyes. "He is crushing on you, hard."

"We just met."

"Yeah… but it was a meet-cute, so it's destiny at this point. This is the stuff of cheesy made-for-TV movies."

She changes in her room while I finish my hair. She reemerges in a crocheted lavender crop top and ripped skinny jeans. A star in her belly button catches the light overhead.

"You still have that thing?" I don't mean to laugh, but it definitely sounds like I'm mocking her belly button ring.

"Of course! Till I *die*, Hillary. It hurt so bad; I need to get my money's worth from it."

"Makes sense to me. Would love to see the reactions in the retirement home, decades from now."

I examine the dress again. It's way too fancy to wear tonight, or maybe I'm afraid I can't pull it off, or I'll look like I'm trying too hard, especially next to Lindsey's more casual look. Instead, I dig through my suitcase and pick a pair of black paper-bag waisted pants and a form-fitting fuchsia shirt with sheer sleeves.

Lindsey nods her approval with a wink when I step out from the spare room. "It's no blue dress, but that looks good, too," she says.

After a quick check in the full-length mirror, we grab our jackets and head out the door. My heart races already, though the show doesn't start for another hour. Outside, the frosty air greets us and I shiver, though whether from the excitement or the cold I'm not sure.

··············

Our seats are along the outer edge of the club, near the door to the kitchen, so a good amount of the concert was interrupted by swinging doors and indiscernible chatter from the staff. That's what Lindsey says when it's over, anyway, though I hadn't noticed.

What I *did* notice was that the show, from start to finish, was incredible. He performed mostly covers, a few numbers from various shows he's been in, and brought some friends up on stage to sing with him, including Samantha Darling, an actress he's worked with a few times and who the audience loved.

The audience is gone, but Lindsey knows a few of the servers here and she's deep in conversation with two of them while I lean against a pillar, staring at my phone and trying to decide whether or not I should text Dalton. Not wanting to seem ungrateful, I send a very platonic Great show! Thanks for the tickets! message, realizing too late that I probably didn't need both exclamation points.

Finally Lindsey finishes her conversation, and we slip into our jackets to leave before getting any more side-eye from the manager.

"Excuse me! *Yoo-hoo!*" We hear the trilling voice behind us but only realize it's meant for our ears when a petite hand falls on Lindsey's shoulder. We turn, surprised to see the exasperated face of Samantha Darling.

"*Finally,*" she says. "I've only been trying to get your attention for five minutes."

Lindsey and I exchange confused looks and she speaks for both of us. "Sorry, Samantha. You—you wanted to talk to *us?*"

"Yes. I was hoping to get a cup of hot tea to go, please."

"Um, okaaay," Lindsey replies. "Let me see if someone can get one for you." She cranes her neck to find one of her friends and heads toward the kitchen.

Samantha buries her face in her cell phone, disregarding me completely.

"You were excellent tonight."

"*Mmm,*" she almost says, ignoring me. An awkward minute later she asks, "What do you think is taking your friend so long?"

I'm surprised by her rudeness, which is so unlike her public persona as the newest, well, *darling* of Broadway and cheesy TV Christmas movies. "Oh! Um, she's probably finding one of her friends who can make that for you. Plus, I'm not sure they have anything ready to make hot tea, since it's so late and they closed a while ago." Also, it's a bar, and do bars even serve hot tea?

Her eyes narrow when she spits out, "Well, can you just go check on my tea, please?"

"Everything okay?" Dalton thankfully interrupts, taking a sip from a reusable water bottle.

"Just waiting on my tea so we can get out of here." She crosses her arms and checks her watch.

Dalton doesn't seem to notice her annoyance and instead asks me, "Did you enjoy the show?" He runs a hand through his damp hair as he takes another drink.

"It was excellent." I choke back my nerves, certain my face is tomato red. Suddenly Lindsey is next to me again.

"Someone should be out with your tea ASAP. My friend Prita had to hunt down all the supplies since they'd closed up for the night."

I wouldn't call it an eyeroll, but Samantha gives a long blink, looks to the ceiling, and sighs.

Ignoring her, I change the subject. "Dalton, this is my friend, Lindsey."

He extends a hand to shake hers. "Nice to meet you. I hope you had a great time tonight."

"Sure did! Right up to the very end of your performance," Lindsey replies with a pointed glance at Samantha, who glares in return.

"I don't mean to be rude," Samantha interjects, definitely being rude and seemingly okay with it, "but wouldn't it be more helpful to your team if you were back working and not out here talking to the performers?"

My toe joints tingle like they always do when I'm nervous or about to confront something—in this case, some-one—that makes me uncomfortable. Luckily Lindsey is never uncomfortable; she seems to thrive on confrontation.

"Do we *look* like we work here?" She gestures to her outfit, a far cry from the solid black ensembles and sensible shoes the staff wears.

"Sami, they're not employees here, unless that's the world's greatest coincidence. This is my new friend Hillary, from the coffee shop, and her friend Lindsey." He sends a subtle wink my way.

My ears burn with embarrassment as she looks from my face to my clothes. "Oh. Right. I think I remember you saying you had people coming." She uncrosses her arms and snakes one behind Dalton's waist, then rests the other on his chest as she leans into his side. "Ugh, I'm so exhausted," she whines. "Can we get going, babe?"

Lindsey doesn't skip a beat. "What about your tea? I know how important it is to you."

Samantha draws Dalton closer as she yawns, and his arm is suddenly around her shoulders. "I'm just really tired all of a sudden. Honey, can we go, please?"

His eyes go cloudy, and he looks down, toeing the floor. "Sure," he tells her. Then he offers a small wave to Lindsey and me. "It was great to meet you, Lindsey. Great to see you again, Hillary. Thanks for coming."

....

"What a bitch," Lindsey says a minute later as we walk toward our station.

When we left the club, Dalton was holding open the door of a black town car for Samantha. Our eyes met as the club door closed behind us, and I hoped Samantha didn't see. Or maybe I hoped she did. Either way, my toes are tingling again, and it sends chills up my spine and down through my fingertips.

"She was something."

"Something *awful*," Lindsey says and fake gags. "Did you know they were dating?"

"I did not. It never came up." I shake my head at the thought. "But why would it?"

Lindsey stops and grabs my arm, turning me toward her. "Girl, seriously. I saw the way he looked at you."

My heart somersaults and I want to throw up a little. I'd been sure I just imagined it, but hearing Lindsey say she noticed it too makes me feel excited and a little sick, too. Like a wild roller coaster on a hot summer day.

Maybe she reads something on my face or maybe she just figures out how I'm feeling, but she pulls me in for a hug and rubs my back. "I'm sorry the world's most perfect man has the world's worst girlfriend."

When she lets go, we head back to her apartment in near silence, drowning in the sounds of sirens and traffic and tourists and subway trains. We take turns taking showers (Lindsey always says it's important to wash off the city before climbing into bed at night). When I emerge from mine, Lindsey has a bowl of fresh popcorn, a bag of chocolate chips, and an oversized cozy blanket in her arms.

Her pitying smile confirms what I already know: *Dalton Tremaine is off limits.*

So we curl up at opposite ends of the couch. I pour chocolate chips into the bowl of popcorn, its heat melting them just enough to ensure our hands will be streaked with dark chocolate within minutes, while Lindsey turns on *Die Hard*.

When I startle awake at two thirty, Lindsey is fast asleep, some of the popcorn has spilled onto the floor, my eyes burn, and my pillow and my cheek are damp.

SEVEN

Every time my phone buzzes, I scramble to see the newest notification. Every time, I'm disappointed. Then I'm frustrated with myself for being disappointed. Other than a response the morning after his show, a very simple YW. Glad you enjoyed, it's been radio silence from Dalton. Which is fine. Considering the amount of time he occupied in my first two days in New York, I really need these distraction-free days.

I spend the rest of the first week in the city exploring museums and parks, finding inspiration in the history and art and humans and settings around me. I bring my journal everywhere I go, jotting down phrases or character descriptions as they come to me.

On Sunday I wake up early. The sky is layered in thick gray clouds, so I opt for leggings instead of blue jeans and a pair of broken-in sneakers. I put on a long gray tunic and zip-up hoodie, grab my backpack, and set out to explore a quieter version of the city.

I smile and nod at a few people out walking their dogs, forgetting that interacting with strangers is very much a *not-in-New-York* thing.

I'm not sure where I planned to go when I set out this morning, but when I see the sign for Eunoia after an hour of walking and observing, I duck inside for a pick-me-up.

A group of three women lounges near the fireplace, but no one else is there. I release the breath I didn't know I was holding, relieved.

"Good morning," greets the barista. It's Shan, and she has a long blond braid draped over each shoulder. "What can I get started for you today?"

Within moments, I'm seated at the countertops that line the windows with a vanilla latte and a lemon blueberry scone. From here I can see the city's weekend crowd and get more character ideas. I pull out my journal and sip some coffee, then take a nibble of my scone.

I'm scribbling notes an hour later when my phone buzzes. I ignore it completely, the first three times. On the fourth buzz I look, see Dalton's name, and set the phone back down, facedown. I'll text him back later. Right now, I'm in the zone, soaking in the mannerisms of the people passing by on the other side of the window and accidentally eavesdropping on the trio by the fireplace, getting great plot and conflict ideas for a future story.

When I look up after writing a full paragraph, a man stands in front of me on the other side of the glass. He's got on a pair of jeans, a green tee-shirt under an open flannel, sunglasses, and navy hat. He's staring right at me, I'm sure, though I can't see his eyes. He holds up his phone and wags it. As my family's undisputed Charades Master, I decipher his clues and pick up my own phone, seeing the series of missed messages from Dalton. The most recent asks, Want to go for a walk? The timestamp is from a minute ago.

I look back up and he's smiling at me. He lowers his sunglasses, which are totally unnecessary on another overcast day, and winks.

I pack up my journal and slide my backpack straps over my arms. Then I hold up a finger to say *wait one second*, return my empty mug to the dirty dishes bin, and order two small iced black coffees (one of which I fill with plenty of milk and sugar until it's khaki-colored) to go. Then I'm outside, falling into stride with Dalton, who smiles as I hand him his drink.

"What a nice surprise," he says.

I shrug. "It's just coffee."

"Who says I was talking about the coffee?" He takes a sip and looks straight ahead as we walk, which is fine, because I have no idea which of the thirty-seven emotions I'm feeling is displayed on my face.

Instead of asking what his girlfriend would think about his comment, I ignore it and all the butterflies it awakens in my stomach. "Thanks again for the tickets the other night. We really enjoyed the show."

"Sure thing," he says. Then, playfully, "Did it inspire you?"

"What?" I look over toward him, and I can see his eyes shift my way behind his dark glasses.

"You said you came to the city to be inspired—by all types of art."

A half-smile crosses my lips, surprised he remembers, because for a moment I did not. "I did say that, didn't I?"

He nods. "You did. But you never told me about your need for inspiration."

"Who says I have to have a *need* to be inspired? Why can't I seek inspiration just for the sake of having inspiration?"

He turns his face toward me and says, "You just seem like a purposeful person. Like there's a reason for everything you do."

"Ha!" I turn sideways, grapevining down the sidewalk a few paces ahead of him, ending with a dramatic twirl.

There aren't many people on the sidewalks this morning, since it's still early and this part of the city isn't as touristy, and the few who are out and about barely acknowledge what I've just done. *God, I love this city.* "Was there a reason for that?"

"Yes," he smiles. "To try to prove that you do things without purpose."

"*Seriously,* man?"

He laughs.

"Okay, okay. Fine. I have a purpose. I'm here for a reason. But I'm also whimsical and free-spirited."

"If you have to *tell* someone that you're free-spirited, are you *really* free-spirited?" He scrunches his nose and cocks his head to the side, a playful smile creeping across his lips. Before I can protest, he adds, "Relax, Hillary, I'm just messing with you."

"You're lucky."

"I am. I can only hope I have escaped your wrath for many moons."

We've meandered west, and we're climbing the steps to the High Line when I stop and look at him. "Why are you spending time with me?"

"What do you mean?" he asks, still smiling.

"I mean, why on earth did you talk to me for hours the other day, invite me to your show, and ask me to come for a walk today instead of just passing by the coffee shop?" I almost add, *I'm nobody,* but I worry that he'll think I'm putting too much emphasis on his *somebody* status.

He stops a few steps above me and takes off his sunglasses, tucking them into the neckline of his shirt. Suddenly serious, he replies, "I think you're interesting. I don't get to spend a lot of time just talking to interesting people."

"Ha! You're surrounded by interesting people. Heck, your girlfriend seems pretty interesting."

"My girlfriend?"

"Yeah, Samantha."

He snorts. "She is *not* my girlfriend."

"Okay, *babe*. Sure seemed like it last week, *honey*." I try to walk past him, but he reaches for my elbow and stops me. It sends a chill through the right side of my body and my knee twitches. I hope he doesn't see.

"Seriously. We're just friends. We've worked together, known each other for years. She gets a little flirty sometimes, but she is way too intense for me."

"So, too much purpose? Not enough whimsy?"

"I didn't say that. Just too intense. And yes, I work with a lot of interesting people, but we don't just sit there talking. We work, then we go home." He drops his arm and continues up the stairs. I slide over behind him so a mother and child can descend, then skip a step to walk next to him again.

"Don't think I haven't noticed," he says, "that you still haven't told me why you're really here."

"It's stupid."

"I'm sure it's not."

I exhale. "I'm here to escape a little from my regular life, so I can finally focus on writing my book."

He stops and a crooked smile crosses his lips. "You're writing a book?"

"I'm trying to. And there are entirely too many distractions at home, too many people whose stories I already know. When the opportunity presented itself to come and stay with Lindsey for two months, I had to jump at it. Being in a new place, with new people, new sights and sounds and smells and experiences—it's all just—"

"Inspiring?"

"Yes," I sigh as I continue along the path. He falls into step beside me. "I know, it's dumb."

"I don't think so at all," Dalton says, turning to me. "There are so many creatives here, all lured by the siren song of the city. Heck, that's what brought me here, too."

"Do you ever regret it? Leaving West Virginia, I mean." I look up at him, squinting into the sudden streaks of sunlight.

He pauses a moment, then shakes his head. "No, I don't think so. Coming here opened the door for me to pursue my passion. Sometimes I miss it. I miss being able to see the stars. I miss the slower pace, especially at times like this, when I'm reminded of how refreshing it is to just go for a walk without having to worry about anyone crashing into you."

"So being here with me makes you wish you were back home."

His face twists, and I can't hold back my laughter.

"Relax. I'm just messing with you."

We walk side by side, enjoying the relative quiet for a few moments.

"What's your book about?"

I shrug in response. "Not sure. I haven't figured it out yet."

"So, you need more inspiration?"

I laugh and take the last swig of iced coffee before throwing both of our empty cups in a nearby trash can. "I need infinite inspiration." And the confidence to really commit to a story.

"Maybe I can help," he says, sincerity filling his words. He flits so easily between playful and pensive. He pulls over and removes his hat, just to swoop his fingers through his hair. No one is near us, and it seems to make him comfortable. He leans back against the railing and puts his hat on backwards, then crosses his arms.

"What do you mean?"

His shoulders rise and fall. "I don't know. Maybe I can check with some friends of mine, get some tickets to their shows. You said musical theater was the thing that most spoke to you."

"I did, but—"

"And I've got a friend who sometimes shows at a gallery in Brooklyn, if you wanted to check out the art," he interrupts.

"I don't—"

"I mean, that's just off the top of my head, I'm sure there's more we could—"

"Dalton, stop!" It comes out louder than I mean it to. His eyes shift left and right.

"I'm sorry. I didn't mean to sound so crazy there. It's just... *you* were sounding a little crazy and then I went a little crazy."

"*I* sounded crazy?"

I nod. "It's really nice, incredibly generous. And I appreciate it. But it's also—it's too much." I sigh, long and slow. "I am not looking for anything from you, other than—"

"Other than what?" he asks, his eyes searching with the start of a smile, or worry, or both.

Shit. I hadn't meant to say as much as I'd said.

"Nothing. I'm just not looking for anything from you."

"Hillary." He scolds me with my name, the way my mom used to, where it's dripping with disappointment. It's definitely not a smile forming on his face.

"I just—I don't know." I look up to the now blue sky, left to the path ahead of us, down to my old running shoes, then into the black abyss of the insides of my eyelids. So, pretty much, everywhere but his face. "It's your *time*. I just like spending time with you."

When I breathe and open my eyes, I'm shocked he's still in front of me. I half-expected him to run off. Apparently, words along those lines tumble into the space between us.

"Why are you surprised? I already told you I like spending time with you, too."

"I don't want to be one of those people whose motives you question." There. The whole truth—or at least the part he needs to know—is out there.

His head bobs and he smiles. "I appreciate you saying that."

"Funny. I thought you'd appreciate me *meaning* it, but if *saying* it's enough…"

"I believe you mean it, which is refreshing."

"Refreshing…like a walk in West Virginia?"

"Like a walk in West Virginia."

EIGHT

Scribbles and blank space. That's all I've got.

I've been in New York for more than five weeks and all I've managed to do is watch people, jot down notes, write a few free verse poems, gain five pounds, and develop a doozy of a one-way crush on Dalton. Even at almost thirty years old, just thinking about him has my skin about to break out with stress-acne that will rival the zits I dealt with all through ninth grade—the last time I was this boy-crazy.

The spring marches on; time's pace is relentless. I feel like I just got to the city, but I'm supposed to go back home in barely two weeks.

Lindsey and I have spent a good amount of time together when her work schedule allows. Fitness classes on Tuesday mornings. Dinner at home when schedules align and dinner out every Thursday. On Wednesdays and Saturdays we'll jog along the sidewalks early enough that the city is still asleep after its wild nights of neon lights and glitter and sexy people meeting sexy people on dance floors, music blaring, pulses racing.

She occasionally bails on the early morning runs because she has spent a late night out with friends, helping them find their own sexy people, getting lost in the excitement of rhythm and laughter and her new friends in New

York. Sometimes I run solo; a few times I've called Dalton to join me.

My Sundays always belong to him.

We start at Eunoia, talking over coffee before walking the High Line, taking a lap around Central Park, bowling, or seeing a show before dinner. We always meet early and part ways after dark. Each week seems to drag, weighted with anticipation. But Sundays—when the world fades and it's just the two of us—those fly by.

On one of the best of those days, a dreary early-April Sunday with low, gray clouds, we shop our way through Times Square before grabbing giant cookies from Hershey's, swapping halves of them on the red steps in the Square, and learning more about each other.

I think I could teach a college course on Dalton Tremaine.

"Ready for another round of Really Random Fun Facts?" I ask, letting gooey chocolate melt on my tongue from the bite of cookie I just popped in my mouth.

He shrugs and passes me the bag with a s'mores cookie half inside, which of course I need to sample. "Bring it," he says with a sexy half-smile that makes my heart thump in my chest.

At work—when I had a job—I managed our employee engagement, which typically consisted of bulletin boards hung in our break room with our staff's faces and their answers to random questions about themselves. These questions have worked equally well for getting to know coworkers and for carrying on conversation with my weird uncle at Thanksgiving dinner.

We complete one round—discussing the weirdest thing we ever ate. Alligator for me, caviar for him. I think for a moment and land on another question. "Got it. What is something you collect?"

He barely pauses before he says, "Easy. Baseball cards."

"How many do you have?"

He swallows a bite of a triple chocolate cookie before answering. "Now, about three dozen. But if I had to guess, back in the day I probably had a thousand."

"That's a lot."

"Yeah, it was a pretty good collection. I kept the ones that meant something to me and sold the rest to pay for some dance classes once I got to New York."

"That sounds responsible." Mom would love him. "So which ones did you keep?"

He counts a few off on his fingers. I don't recognize many names. "I guess I could get rid of a few more of them, but there's one I definitely cannot get rid of, and that's my favorite card." His eyes light up and he's giddy. It's adorable. "When I was ten, my parents took me to see my favorite player. We sat just above the dugout, and he autographed the card for me."

I don't have experience with baseball cards, but I know how exciting it is to get an autographed Playbill. *Cringe.* I shake off the guilt. "It's awesome that you have your favorite player's autograph."

Pink floods his cheeks, and I try not to laugh. *Try.*

"What's so funny?"

I shrug. "It's just cute, you blushing like that."

"I am not."

"You one hundred percent are. Are you embarrassed?"

Now it's his turn to shrug. "I don't know. Maybe? I don't normally fangirl over people, at least not openly. Or maybe I'm hearing how it sounds that I'm a grown man with baseball cards that sit in a display case in my childhood bedroom."

"I don't think you need to be embarrassed at all. Actually, I think it's great that you get so excited about it. If the cards you're holding on to mean something to you, why wouldn't you display them?"

He swipes a hand through his hair and smiles.

I reach for the bag of cookies, but he snatches it away from me. "Don't think you're getting off the hook so easily."

"You're withholding chocolate from me?"

"Only until you answer the question. What do you collect?"

My go-to here is a stack of Playbills, or a coffee mug from every show I see on Broadway, and each collection is growing at the same rate my bank account is shrinking. But I can't tell him about either collection because I'm afraid he'll have questions I don't want to answer. Instead, I mull over other things that I've collected by accident; things I've amassed over the years in large quantities, unintentionally.

"I have a pretty exciting collection of journals," I finally say.

"Journals? Like diaries?"

"Please don't call them diaries."

"Okay, okay," he says, pulling back, holding his hands in front of his chest. "Sorry. Journals. How many?"

"Mmm, maybe fifty?"

His eyes grow wide. "Fifty? That seems like a lot. How'd that start?"

I tell him about the first journal I ever owned—a gift given to me by my fifth-grade teacher after she grew tired of me writing limericks in the margins of my tests and quizzes. *You have a gift,* she'd written inside the front cover. *Keep writing*. And over the years, it was an easy gift from friends every birthday, in Easter baskets, in stockings on Christmas.

"So you love journals, huh?"

"I mean, I do. I love writing by hand. And one day—" I bite my lip. "Nevermind."

"Oh, no way," he laughs. "You have to finish that statement now."

"It's so dorky."

He answers only with his expression: bright eyes, goofy grin.

"Fine. What I'd love, some day—I was going to buy it for myself when—if—I publish my first book—is a fountain pen."

"A fountain pen? Like a seventeenth century poet?"

"Ha! Not a *quill*. Just a special pen, for writing the next book, or—" I cut myself off and shake my head.

"For what? Book signings?" He's guessed it.

"It's stupid."

"It's not," he says, leaning in. "I actually love that."

Color floods my neck again. "Well, some of them are ridiculously expensive, so it'll likely never happen. I passed a specialty pen store a few years ago, and ever since then I thought it would be a cool reward for finishing a project."

"Well, we'll have to make that happen. That would be a huge accomplishment, and it deserves a celebratory pen." He passes me the bag of cookies, and I start eating to avoid talking more.

When the rain falls, we buy an umbrella at a nearby newsstand and huddle under it as we walk, trying to keep our new purchases dry.

We grab a late lunch and cocktails in a restaurant that used to be a rooftop greenhouse, watching the raindrops spatter on the glass around us, and when evening rolls in and we approach the subway station, I wonder if I'm the only one who hates to say goodbye.

....

The next day, out of nowhere, Lindsey suggests a weekend getaway. "It'll just be for two nights—I'll take off Friday and we can go down in the morning until Sunday afternoon, then drive back. The drive isn't even three hours long, so you'll have plenty of time each day to write. And you'll probably be able to observe people who aren't miserable and in a rush, for a change."

Four days later, Lindsey parks in front of a sweet, pale-pink Victorian home. The stark white railing of a wrap-around porch frames its cotton candy hue.

"Ta-da!" she exclaims, apparently proud of her finding. "Home sweet home, for the next two nights. What do you think?"

I hold my hand to my forehead, trying to block out the sun. "It's got character."

"Yes, and maybe *its* character will help you develop a few of *yours*," she laughs, knowing I've made no progress on my story. When I don't echo her laughter she adds, "C'mon, Hil, how can you come to a place like this and not be inspired?"

"Who says I'm not inspired?"

She eyes me before shutting off the ignition. "This is going to be great for you. A nice break from the city, some fresh ocean air…"

"Staying in a house made of bubble gum," I finish for her with a wink. She throws her head back and laughs.

"Yes, I thought it would be a great idea for a horror story, if that's what you want to write. 'Two gorgeous, independent women escape to their coastal paradise for a sweet weekend away, only to find that their B & B has a deep, dark, bubble-gum pink secret. Will they be A-OK? Or will they wind up DOA? Find out in the best-seller from Hillary James, *Check Inn For Murder.*"

"Stop!" I shriek, both of us now surrendered to laughter. "You make that sound so easy! I would read that book!"

"Feel free to *write* that book," Lindsey says, "or any other book that comes to mind." She opens her giant straw tote, pulls out a small package wrapped in floral paper, and hands it to me. "I saw this and thought you needed to have it."

"Thanks," I say, ripping the paper off in one continuous tear. Underneath is a solid black journal with gold scripted lettering: *Future Best-Seller.*

"And so it is decreed," she smiles, "that you will write and you will publish and you will sell a bajillion copies."

"Thank you, Linds. It's really thoughtful."

"I know. Now can we please go check in? It was a long drive, and I finished a large iced latte an hour ago."

We settle into the room and play a round at the nearby mini golf course, then explore the main stretch of boutiques before grabbing dinner at an Irish pub. Lindsey, exhausted from having an actual job and adult life, decides to head back to the room to call Marco and get to bed. "We have an action-packed day tomorrow, filled with relaxation and writing. Gotta rest up," she winks.

After dropping her off at the Victory Ann Inn, I follow the sound of the crashing waves to the shoreline. White clouds linger in the sky, streaking the pink and orange sunset. The sand, pressed hard beneath my bare feet, is cold this early in the season. Risking the life sentence of having sand *everywhere*, I lower myself to the ground and pull my knees to my chest.

For, I think, the first time in months, I breathe deeply. And then my phone chirps in my bag.

Dalton's face stares back at me with his text message alert. Just got tickets to KneeSlapperz for the Up-and-Comer Comedy Show. Show's in an hour—want to join?

Ugh. I groan toward the sky. Would love to, but I can't. Lindsey has kidnapped me. At the beach for the weekend.

Once the message goes through, I add, So sorry. Was very last minute. Forgot to tell you I won't be home until sometime Sunday evening, probably.

I lay the phone on top of my bag and turn my attention back to the waves, rolling and crashing, exploding onto the sand like they're sharing stories from far-away seas.

When my phone sounds again, I jump. This time it's an invitation to a FaceTime call.

"Show me everything," Dalton says as soon as I answer.

"What?"

"Sand. Sunset. All the things. What are you looking at?"

"I was looking at the beach, but now some dude's face is in the way."

"Ha, ha," he mocks. "Seriously though, what are we working with this fine Friday evening?"

I switch the camera out of selfie mode so he can see the shore, and I scan the horizon to give him a panoramic view.

"Gorgeous," he says.

"It really is," I reply. And that's it. Minutes pass. We don't fill the silence—the waves do that for us, roaring and whooshing and retreating just to roar and whoosh again and again. When my arm gets tired, I prop the phone against my bag so Dalton can continue his view of the beach.

"Have you ever seen anything so beautiful?" I ask absent-mindedly, when the colors in the sherbet sky intensify.

"A time or two," he answers, "though it's rare to find something so perfect."

My heart leaps. I'm grateful he can't see my face.

"That's the hardest part, you know? Sunsets, quiet nights on the beach, landing your first big part or publishing your first book, first kisses, first steps, first loves, dreams coming true—these moments that last such a short time—these fleeting things that are so perfect and pure. We try so hard to hold onto them, but it's their brevity that makes them so wonderful."

My mouth goes dry at the items he lists together. "Is it? Some might argue that brevity is their worst quality."

"Think about it, Hil. First steps are great—but if we stop there, when do we run? When do we feel the breeze in our hair as we jog on a Sunday morning? When do we feel the accomplishment of not just taking a first step, but a final stride across a finish line? If we hold onto first loves, how do we open ourselves to find *true* loves? If you capture a firefly, and you put it in a jar to keep it and admire it like you'll never see another, won't it die? First the light that makes it beautiful, then the whole thing, altogether?"

Warmth courses through my veins. I'm speechless, but I think it's okay.

Silence answers silence and I'm afraid we've lost our connection, but I still see him blinking as he watches the same waves I watch, from 150 miles away.

I clear the lump that catches in my throat and ask, "Did you need to get ready for your show tonight?"

His head shakes slowly. "Skipping it," he says. "It's not the same, going by myself."

"I'm sure you could find plenty of friends who'd want to join you."

"I'm sure I could. But I don't want to be anywhere but here. With you and the waves."

"In about five minutes it'll be too dark to see them." I skip over the first part of his comment.

He shrugs. "Then we'd better enjoy these next five minutes, before the moment is a memory."

Twenty minutes pass before I realize my battery is nearly dead.

"Sorry to cut short your time of listening to distant waves," I say as I stand and wipe the sand from my legs. I gather my belongings and switch the phone back to its front-facing camera.

"You were wrong earlier," he says. His eyes look heavy; even his hair seems tired. He's so far off topic it catches me off guard.

"What?"

"You were wrong, when you said I could find plenty of friends who'd want to join me. I don't actually think that's the case."

"Oh." I wish he was watching the ocean again, that he couldn't see my face. I don't think I'm supposed to respond.

"I think you're it."

"*It?*" I ask, confused.

"I think you're my only real friend, Hillary. Like, my only go-anywhere, do-anything, always-have-time-for-you, no-ulterior-motives friend. And if I only get one, I'm glad it's you."

"Oh," I say again. "Sorry I wasn't there for you tonight."

He smiles unconvincingly. "You were." He rubs the bridge of his nose. "Okay, be safe. Text me when you're back at the inn?"

I nod and he half waves before hanging up.

I pocket the phone and trudge through the sand, back to the road. Butterflies overtake my stomach. I don't want to hinder the future. I don't want to make things awkward when I see him next. I don't want to kill the firefly. What I do want is to remember this night—the look of calm on his face as he watched the ocean, the feeling of belonging as we sat together, feeling understood and known, hearing him say I'm 'it'—for as long as possible, fleeting though it may be.

NINE

On Saturday morning Lindsey and I run along the Promenade until we spy a bakery and café, then we wind our way through the shaded side streets to the inn, pick-me-ups and pastries in hand.

Through a mouthful of jelly donut I say, "I thought the whole idea of a Bed and Breakfast was to actually eat breakfast there in the morning."

Lindsey laughs. "First and foremost, who says we can't eat breakfast there, too? And second, if you'd like to seat your sweaty self in the midst of a sea of retirees, help yourself." She takes another sip of her smoothie. "I, on the other hand, will be devouring this sticky bun and enjoying a bubble bath while you create something magical."

"Jealous."

"Um, who should be jealous of whom, here, after your romantic walk on the beach last night?"

To say that the memory of the night before comes flooding back to me is a lie, because I never stopped thinking about it. It kept me awake last night for hours after I got back, it filled my dreams, and it's had me dizzily preoccupied all morning. But hearing Lindsey mention it, my toes tingle and my palms go clammy.

"Really? No response?" she asks. I barely hear her. "Hey—Hillary." She steps in front of me and eyes me. "Are you alright?"

"Yeah, fine," I lie. Truthfully, I'm confused, which is stupid. There is nothing to be confused about. I'm falling for Dalton Tremaine, and I'm going to end up with a broken heart. No crystal ball needed.

But Lindsey knows me too well to believe it. "When you give short answers, something's wrong. You've been this way since we were thirteen."

"People change."

"Hillary." Her eyes soften. I feel her pity, her surrogate heartache.

"Okay, fine, you caught me." I inhale and shake my head. "I know how crazy it sounds."

"Oh my gosh, you love him and you're pregnant with his love-child!"

"What? No!"

"Oh, good. Then whatever you're about to say isn't all that crazy-sounding by comparison, I bet." She winks. I'm grateful for her.

"I mean, I definitely have feelings. And I'm trying to figure out why I'm letting myself have these feelings, why I'm spending days with him when I know it won't go anywhere."

"Have you ever gone for a drive? Just for the sake of driving?"

I shrug at the unrelated question. "Once upon a time. When I first started driving, probably, and gas cost a quarter what it does now."

"Yikes, don't remind me. Nothing says 'you're getting old' like reminding me of prices from our teens." She shudders and waves a hand. "But I digress. *Why* did you go for those drives?"

"When I first got my license, it was because I had the independence to do it."

64   MEGAN BECKER

She nods, slowly, and steps next to me, resuming a patient pace back to the inn. "Any other reason?"

"I don't know. I guess I'd take the long way home after band practice, just to unwind or enjoy the sunset. Or if it was a nice morning in the spring I'd just go out with the windows down to feel the breeze and enjoy the first few days of good weather. Usually with music playing, singing along. It was almost therapeutic."

"Hmm. So you would do something without purpose—driving out of the way, driving around, just because it was pretty, or because it felt good or made you happy."

"Yes."

"And you walk aimlessly around New York for the same reason sometimes?"

"There's usually a trip to a café or bookstore in there, but sure."

"I'd expect nothing less," she smiles. "So why are you so willing to do those other things because they make you feel good, but you hesitate with Dalton?"

I process her question before carefully responding. "Because driving around feels good and eventually I'm home, unharmed. With Dalton though—if I give into whatever these feelings are—all that's going to happen is I'm going to get hurt along the way."

"Maybe, maybe not. Wasn't there risk involved though, when you were just driving around? Risk you'd crash or hit a squirrel or something?"

"That's different."

She shrugs and rolls her eyes. "Okay, fine. But Hillary—even if you don't explore this, if you avoid him altogether, aren't you still going to end up hurting? Won't you wonder in the future what could have been? You miss one hundred percent of the shots you don't take."

"I appreciate what you're doing, Linds." I shovel the last bit of jelly donut into my mouth, buying time before she expects a response. "I guess I've been trying to ride the line a bit. Just trying to be friends and hide all the other feelings. Hoping for the best of both worlds, to an extent, where I protect my heart as much as I can, but still get to experience him."

"Are you happy with that?"

"It's fine."

"That's not what I asked."

We've reached the Victory Ann Inn and Lindsey swings open the gate. "Obviously, you can do whatever you want. But as your friend, I would just hate to see you give up on a windows-down, sunroof-open, Natalie Imbruglia sing-along kind of spring morning just because a squirrel might sprint into the street."

....

Lindsey's taking a long bubble bath and will join me "eventually," so I head down to the beach with a blanket and my old journal and pen. As I cross the last street toward the beach, a car turns on a yellow light and cuts me off in the crosswalk. "Watch it!" I yell to the rear bumper of an old burgundy Dodge Neon.

Back on the beach today?

The text is waiting for me when I sprawl out on the blanket I've splayed on the sand. In conjunction with the near-death experience with a certain make and model just a few minutes ago, it feels like a sign. Of what, I'm not sure. But it has a very distinct *sign* feeling.

I am. Just sat down.

Nice. How are crowds?

I look around, surveying the sand. Nonexistent.

He responds with a GIF of an old Survivor episode, a contestant sitting solo on a sandy island.

Best player of all time, I text back.

For sure. I thought I was the only one who still watched this show.

I mean, that's an expensive production for one viewer…

I guess I thought I was the only one who could eat solid food who still watched it.

I know I need to focus, but I can't shake the feeling that's been growing in me since last night that something is just off with him.

How's your day going? I ask.

I wait, watching my phone for a few minutes with no response. Finally I set the phone down and pick up my pen and journal.

Paid-off Dodge. Gina Thompson. Picks her up for date— she sees the car and says no?

An idea clicks as I gnaw on the cap of my pen.

Goes solo to date — movie theater. When leaving, sees another girl there whose date fell asleep & they strike up a friendship over the absurdity?

As the plot develops in my mind and words spill from brain to hand to paper, my phone dings. I ignore it to allow the stream of ideas to flow, but when I finally check the messages the writing seems insignificant.

Honestly, not great so far.

With one quick tap of the screen, I hear his voice.

"Hil?"

"Hey."

"Hey." He exhales, all his usual energy evaporated.

Unsure of exactly what to say, I dive in anyway. "I just wanted to—"

"I know. Thanks."

"So what's going on?" I want to know, but only if he wants to share. I don't expect him to tell me all his secrets. "If you want to talk about it. If not…"

"No, it's fine." He takes a deep breath. "You know that project I was working on?"

"The new musical? Yeah, I remember you said it was just about ready to show investors."

"It's over."

"No way. Just like that—it's done?"

"It is for me."

"I'm so sorry, Dalton." A pained lump rises in my throat. "What happened? What will you do now?"

"Not sure yet," he says. "Hopefully there's something around the city for me. But for now, for this show, I've been recast."

"That makes no sense."

He doesn't immediately respond, which is fine. While we've enjoyed walking and talking together over the last few weeks, we've also come to accept silence as another element of our friendship. It provides an opportunity to just *be*, and we don't shy away from the space to exist as we are.

"Is something else bothering you?"

He clears his throat and pauses before saying, "About last night, Hillary."

I tilt my head to pinch the phone between my shoulder and my ear and start preemptively massaging my toes.

"I'm sorry if I made things weird."

"How do you think you made things weird?" I need him to say it, to clarify his thoughts and feelings, before I even consider acting on any of my own.

I can sense him shrugging, trying to explain himself. "The stuff about the fireflies. And the thing about you being my only friend. I feel like I made no sense."

"You made perfect sense. But I'm glad to hear you don't think you've just got one friend."

"Oh. No, I meant that. You really are the one person I feel like I can trust." After a momentary pause, he continues. "I know it sounds crazy."

"No." I don't mean for it to come out, especially not so emphatically, but I've said it, and he's heard it.

"No?"

"No," I repeat. There's no choice but to get behind the wheel. To roll down the windows and go for the drive. "I mean, yes. It does sound crazy, probably, to other people. But honestly, other than Lindsey, I feel the same way."

"Oh. You do." It's part question, part statement.

"I think so."

"Huh."

I grit my teeth as he processes the information. 'Huh' could mean so many things, and I have no idea what's running through his head. There are no eyes to read, no visual cues. Just silence.

A flash of color draws my gaze and I look over to see Lindsey schlepping toward me with her beach chair and too-big tote.

"Lindsey's just about here, so I should probably get going. But did you still want to get together tomorrow, maybe for dinner if I'm back early enough?"

"I think that's a smart idea. Definitely gives us time to talk through some things." He clears his throat again and I feel a lump creep into my own. "Do you want to text me when you have an idea of when you'll be back? I can set up a reservation and pick you up."

Lindsey is within earshot and her eyes get wide when I say, like an idiot, "It's a date. I mean—sounds good."

"Great. I'll see you tomorrow, Hillary."

We hang up and Lindsey's jaw drops. I hold my hands up to stop her.

"Before you say anything," I playfully scold her, "yes, I am in the car, cruising through the back roads. You can ride along, but I'll be the one controlling the knobs and, most of all, the speed."

"Did you just plan a date with Dalton Tremaine?"

"No, I planned *dinner* with Dalton Tremaine."

"Just the two of you?"

"Yes."

"In a restaurant?"

"Yes."

"And he'll pick you up? Instead of meeting you there?"

I hesitate to answer. "Yes."

"Like a date?"

I roll my eyes at her. "Is it a date when you and I go out for dinner, just the two of us?"

She shrugs. "I mean, I always thought we had something special, but if you're saying it meant nothing to you…"

"Very funny."

"Seriously, Hil, this is awesome. Look at you, getting back out there."

"I'm not 'getting back out there,' I'm meeting a friend for dinner."

"Ah, yes, a friend. My apologies," she says, setting up her beach chair in the sand. "I just assumed that if you're yelling the guy's name out in your sleep he's beyond 'friend' level."

"I was not."

Lindsey balks, laughing. "Once last night. Once about two weeks ago."

I bury my face in my hands. I knew I'd dreamt about him more than once, and Peter had told me a few times that I talked in my sleep. "That's mortifying."

"That's normal," she coos, her sing-song voice compounding the embarrassment I feel. "Especially when the person is indisputably dreamy."

I spread my fingers and peer at her through the opening. "Did I say anything else?"

She shakes her head, twisting her lips. "Nothing that stood out to me. I mean, other than your social security number."

"Ha, ha."

She rummages through her tote and pulls out a book—"*Your new favorite contemporary romance*," claims the review scribbled across its orange cover—and flips it open to the bookmarked page.

"Listen," Lindsey says, holding her place with her index finger and lowering her sunglasses with her other hand to make direct eye contact with me, "I truly am very happy for you. You deserve this—to have someone worth dreaming about, to have dinners and walks through the park and late-night phone calls with someone who makes you feel special." There's an unspoken *unlike Peter* at the end of that sentence.

She smiles and turns back to her book, its pages fluttering in the sea breeze. I watch the waves roll in, glistening under the late morning sunlight. I snap a picture and text it to Dalton with the caption, There's a great big world out there. Remember that. The right opportunity is out there, somewhere.

I'm behind the wheel of a car. I'm unsure of the destination, but the windows are down and my hand surfs the air as decade-old pop love songs play, and for the first time in a long time, someone's in the seat next to mine.

TEN

'm awake at half past six on Sunday. Lindsey sleeps in since last night was a rough one for her. She misses Marco; his dad's condition worsens every day, and he's not ready to come back to New York. She drank most of a bottle of wine last night—after a few cocktails at dinner—and her sniffling woke me up at least once in the middle of the night.

After washing my face and brushing my teeth, I change into shorts and an oversized sherpa, grab my journal and wallet, and set out for the beach one more time. I take just a few strides in the sand and park myself on a bench overlooking the waves. I set an alarm for nine to make sure I have time to pick up coffee and get back to Lindsey at a reasonable time before our drive back to Manhattan.

I manage to scribble four mediocre pages within an hour. My phone vibrates, but when I look at the screen to turn off the alarm, I see Mom's picture come up with the inbound call.

"Hi Mom," I say, sounding as positive as I can, despite only feeling positive that the pages I've written are worthless.

"Hi, honey, how are you?"

"Good, everything's great here!" *Fingers crossed she believes that.*

"Oh, good. I hadn't heard from you in a few days and wanted to make sure you were okay. How's Lindsey doing?"

I push the image of her—eyes stained with running mascara and drinking straight from a bottle of Pinot—from my mind and pretend everything is great. "All good. Lindsey's good. How are you guys doing back home?"

"Well you know we miss you so much, but otherwise we're alright. Stacy got a promotion at work."

My sister, the wunderkind we could all only hope to be.

"I bumped into Peter the other day."

"Oh?"

"Mmhmm," she says. "Seems like he's in a better place now, like he'd be ready for a healthy relationship."

"That's good. Should save the next girl some pain."

"Hillary, you were together for so long. I don't know why you seem so opposed to the idea of giving him another chance."

I hope she can sense my eyes rolling back so far they're surveying the intricate roadmap of my brain. "I'm incredibly opposed to giving him another chance because I'm not interested in moving backward, Mom."

She goes silent. Then, hopelessly, she says, "It just feels like you're not interested in moving *back*, either."

"Mom—"

"I know you're out there to discover yourself or whatever, but New York is not your home, Hillary. Lindsey is not your family. This new friend you've made is not your family. Your family is here—Stacy, your father, Nan, Pop…*me*."

I swallow hard, choking back the lump in my throat and the tears that come with it. "I just need time. I need to do this. For *me*." It's hard to confess my selfishness, which is on full display just by me staying a few months in New York, just like it was when I left my family to move off to college.

She huffs on the other end of the line. "Just remember who you are. And who has always been there for you."

The alarm sounds on my phone and I start walking back to the inn. "I know you have been, Mom."

"I just don't want you to change, sweetheart."

How do you tell the person who has raised you to be who you are that *change* is exactly what you need?

....

My conversation with Mom distracts me on my walk back, and I completely forget to stop at the café. Luckily, light breakfast and coffee are available back at the inn, so I swipe two muffins and pour a cup of coffee with light cream and sugar for Lindsey and trek back up to our third-floor room.

"You are an angel," she says, propping herself up in bed and blowing on her coffee. "I feel like shit."

"I can imagine. How are you holding up?"

She closes her eyes, inhaling. "I'm okay."

"If you want to talk about it…"

"It's just that I miss Marco so much, and I feel like I should be there, but what can I do?"

I chew a bite of muffin and pull my legs up onto the bed, holding them to my chest. "I'm sure there's nothing you can do, but maybe just being there is enough. Maybe Marco just needs you there with him to help him through it."

A crumb falls from her lips as she responds through a mouthful of muffin. "Maybe, but I can't just abandon you in New York."

"Whoa, hang on. Why do you think that?"

She rubs the back of her hand against her forehead, pushing back the hair that falls into her eyes. "Hil, I would hate to leave you alone in the city."

My heart flutters and I weigh the pros and cons of saying what has been building in me for the last few weeks. But she needs to know it's okay to leave so I remind her, "I'm not really alone." Her chewing slows and she swallows. I can tell she's considering this as an option.

"Plus, I'll be there to watch the apartment for you."

"For how long?"

"What do you mean?"

"What if Marco needs me for like, a month? Is that too long for you to stay in the city?"

My conversation with Mom replays in my head. But this is selflessness, right? I'm staying *for Lindsey*, to help her while she helps someone she loves.

"I was already planning to stay for at least two more weeks, anyway. What's a few more on top of that, if you need me?"

"Good point," she says. "I just want to make sure you're okay with it. I know it's a huge change to live solo in the city."

My eyes roll instinctively but playfully. "I think I can handle it."

She purses her lips. "Let me think about it." She finishes the muffin and washes it down with coffee.

I sit to write more while she rests her eyes for another half hour, takes a shower, and gets dressed. Once she's ready, we pack our things and check out of the inn.

Marco calls after lunch, just as we're about to start our drive home, and I slink into a boutique so they can chat privately. I browse the clearance rack and find a hot pink T-shirt dress with lime green pockets and aqua trim on the sleeves and neckline. It's so garish it's cute and also severely discounted.

I add to my findings a lightweight off-the-shoulder khaki sweater and a straw fedora trimmed with a thick cream-colored ribbon. When I try the hat on and look in the mirror, I'm surprised at how good I look. Not, like, *come hither* good, but *at peace* good. *Happy, healthy* good. Despite not actually being in the ocean, the salty air's given my hair waves, and the time I've spent outside this weekend has given my nose and cheeks a pinkish-brown hue. Even with no makeup on I feel confident. I credit the hat and the start of a tan.

When I take my wallet from my purse to check out, I see a missed text on my cell screen. I pay for my things and head outside, phone in hand and squinting into the bright afternoon sun. Lindsey's waiting for me a few steps away.

"Anything else you wanted to see or do down here?"

I shake my head. "Everything good with you and Marco?"

"Yes. I'm going to fly out tomorrow morning, if you're sure you're okay with that."

"Of course," I assure her.

We fall into stride in the two blocks to the car. Inside, with my door closed and seatbelt buckled, I finally take a moment to read the waiting message: Thanks for the picture. Hopefully I don't need the great big world. Looking for something closer to home. Still on for tonight?

I text back, Absolutely. Will send ETA ASAP.

Then I settle in for the long drive.

ELEVEN

The scene at Lindsey's apartment is not a pretty one.

"Why didn't anyone call me?" she yells at the super.

"We attempted to call Mr. Salas but got no answer."

"*Shit.*" She looks around, surveying the damage. Everything is soggy. Chunks of ceiling and strips of insulation lay in a mangled heap in her kitchen.

"We took care of the flooding the best we could and put the fans in to try to control the moisture…"

The voices trail off as I clamber around the mound of materials that has fallen in the middle of Lindsey's living space, the result of an apparent pipe incident from the apartment above hers. In the spare room, which is a straight shot back from the kitchen, my clothes on the portable garment rack are wet and dusty from the fallen drywall and spraying water. Salvageable, but only after an extended trip to the laundromat.

When I return to the living room, the super is gone, and Lindsey is sitting on the floor by the front door. I sit next to her, and she rests her head on my shoulder.

"You okay?"

"No." She sniffs and wipes her nose and eyes on her sweatshirt sleeve. "It'll take them at least a week to get this all cleaned up."

"Okay."

"And there are no other units available for us to stay in while they do the work."

"Oh." The realization hits me a moment later. "But you're still going up to Marco's parents' place?"

"Yes, but—"

I shake my head and put on the bravest face I can. "I'll be fine, Linds. I can either stay in a hotel, or I can—"

"Don't you *dare* go back. Not yet. It's not time."

A laugh escapes, in spite of or inspired by the whole messy situation, but I'm not sure which. "I'll be fine. No matter what." But my stomach sinks. I don't have the resources to book a room in the city for a week. And Lindsey tells me she's packing a few things and heading to the airport tonight, trying to get an earlier flight to North Carolina if possible since she has nowhere else to stay.

"You can take my car, if you need to," she says. She knows I have no need for a car in the city; she's offering in case I need it for the drive to Lemming.

"This sucks," she says, resting her head on my shoulder. I rest my head on hers and agree.

A faint sound grabs my attention. At first I attribute it to the city, but it's a consistent, steady *bzz bzz bzzzz. Bzz bzz bzzzz.*

"Oh, no, no, *no!*" I jump up and run to my bag, which hangs on the edge of a bookshelf above the debris field of Lindsey's apartment floor. I swipe to answer the phone but I'm too late—the call is gone. It doesn't matter; I'm already sprinting out the door and down the stairs.

A black car waits at the curb and Dalton stands outside, wearing an emerald cashmere sweater and those perfectly-tailored pants, holding a bouquet of wildflowers wrapped in brown paper. When he sees me, disheveled and dirty, his whole expression shifts.

"I am so, so sorry." I feel the tears well in my eyes but can't place the source for them. *Disappointment? Anger? Sadness?*

His face falls. "Are you okay?"

I sniffle, my chest shuddering as I hold back the sobs that want to burst out. "No," is all I feel comfortable saying. I breathe deep—once, twice—and continue. "When we got back, we found out the whole apartment's flooded. Pipe burst or something a floor above ours."

"Oh gosh—okay. What do you need? I can help clean up." He takes a step toward the door and already has one sleeve pushed above his elbow.

I reach out, my hand landing on his forearm. "Wait, Dalton."

He stops and his eyes snap to mine. "What's wrong, Hil?" His forehead creases with worry.

It's impossible to hold the tears back now. At first they come slowly, but they intensify as I consider the circumstances of the night and what this night was supposed to mean for the future. "I ruined our d-" I catch myself. "Our dinner. And poor Lindsey—she and Marco don't need this stress right now, with everything with his dad. And we can't stay here, so she's flying out tonight. And I—"

I can't bring myself to say the words *I'm leaving.* So, next best thing: "I'm *hungry.*"

Dalton laughs, that deep, makes-you-feel-safe laugh. He wraps an arm around me and pulls me into him as I'm wiping tears off my face, so I'm awkwardly pinned against him—not that I'm complaining. He gives a quick, one-armed squeeze and I think I feel his lips graze the top of my head.

"Wait one second," he says, then retreats to his still-waiting car. He leans through the open passenger window for a few moments before the driver takes off.

"Okay, we've got a plan. Mike will be back with pizza. He can get Lindsey to the airport after dinner. Until then, point me in the right direction to help clean up."

I'm pretty sure I'm gawking. *Who is this good, kind man, and why can't there be more like him?* "Seriously?"

"Seriously."

I throw my arms around him and give him one of the hardest hugs I've ever given. His chest is firm against mine. It's very possible I hold on a half second too long but when I do let go, he's extending the flowers to me.

"I brought these for you."

I take the bouquet and bury my nose in the fragrant blooms. Uncontrollable laughter bubbles out of me, like a bottle of soda that's rolled down a flight of stairs and lost its cap.

"Um, are you okay?" he raises an eyebrow at me, half smiling.

"Yes," I grab his hand and pull him toward the door with me. "I was just thinking, I've got some water I can put these in."

TWELVE

We devour the pizza, standing in the middle of the cleared part of the living room, before it's time for Lindsey to get to the airport.

"Thank you so, so much," Lindsey says. She pulls Dalton into a hug, grateful that he not only committed his driver to getting her to the airport but also carried two giant suitcases down the stairs and outside for her.

He shrugs and looks at me, then pats her back. "No problem."

Lindsey turns and arches her eyebrows, as if to say *wowsers, he's great, huh?* and hugs me, too. "I'm so sorry, Hil. But take care of you, okay?" She raises her brows twice more and smiles. "And have fun," she whispers with a wink.

"I will. All of it," I say. *As much as I can, at home*, I think.

She drops her keys into my hand, slides into the town car, and waves goodbye as the car pulls away. Which leaves me alone with Dalton on the sidewalk, not quite ready to say goodbye but fully aware that I'll need to.

"You okay over there?" he asks.

The world is fuzzy around me. I press my hands to my eyes, and they're wet when I pull them away. "Sorry."

He shakes his head. "Nothing to be sorry for." He looks up and down the street, down at his feet, and finally, eventually, back up to me. "So. What's next."

"Next, I pack everything I can salvage."

He nods, his eyes reflecting the light from the sconces by the building's entrance. "Just let me know how I can help."

....

Surveying the damage from just inside the front door, I feel the weight of the moment in my stomach, throat, and shoulders. Dalton lingers just behind me.

"You can't stay here."

"I know." How he hears the words, I'll never know.

"Do you have another place lined up, or—"

I nod, grateful he can't see my face. "I'll find a hotel for tonight."

He pauses. My heart lurches. "And tomorrow?"

My non-answer is all the answer he needs.

My name is barely a whisper as it crosses his lips; his breath is warm on my neck, and it sends a chill down my spine.

"You can't leave."

"I can't *stay*," I correct him. "I can't afford to."

"Find a place. I'll cover the cost."

"No." I whip around to face him. "Absolutely not."

"Why not?"

"Because I'm not here for your money."

"It doesn't sound like you'll be here at all after tomorrow," he shoots back. It's the kindest scolding I've ever received.

I bite my tongue and inhale slowly, deeply. "It sucks. But I have to go home. Just for a week, until the apartment's fixed."

His brow furrows as he looks around at the damage. "Just a week?"

I follow his gaze and am skeptical of the timeline the super provided. It seems like a lot of work to complete. "That's what they said."

"Hillary."

There's something in the way he says my name, the gentleness and the firmness of it, that makes my throat catch and my stomach somersault.

"Stay with me." He doesn't ask, doesn't request it. It's not an option—it's *the* solution.

And I'm so caught off guard that I can't think. My jaw loosens. All that comes out is a very unconvincing "I can't."

"There's no good reason not to. I've got an extra room and could use the company."

In an instant, Friday night's phone call rushes into my memory, followed by yesterday morning's, and I realize he's here, in dust-covered cashmere, because we were supposed to be on a date—at least I think it was supposed to be a date, based on the cashmere and the conversations and the flowers—and it's so painfully obvious to me, but I don't know how to put it all into words. I try anyway.

"Don't you think it would be weird for me to move in for the week, considering…" Okay, I tried and failed.

"Considering… what?"

"It's just that," I begin, "we were supposed to be talking through some things tonight at dinner. The 'weird' stuff. Fireflies and…*stuff.*"

His body stiffens as he steps backward, and he runs his hands through his hair while he looks everywhere but my eyes.

"Hillary… I'm sorry if I led you to believe… I wanted to talk to you tonight to apologize."

"Oh." I feel my heart in the pit of my stomach and a heaviness in my chest.

He scans my face. "You should totally move in for the week. I'm happy to have you. I'd do it for any of my friends."

It's possible I'm projecting the emphasis on the word *friends*, but I am definitely not making up the distance that now exists between us. Not dreaming up his crossed arms or imagining his clouded eyes.

Whatever tension had existed with his heart-quickening breaths earlier is now nearly evaporated. The heat that travels through every vessel in my body when he's around—and when he's *not* around but I'm thinking about him—dissipates.

Tonight was supposed to be special—dinner at a nice restaurant, talking about being each other's *it*—but instead I've been suddenly friend-zoned. Hard.

I'm exhausted.

I'm overwhelmed.

I don't want to fight or to think.

I'm crazy enough to say yes. "At least tonight. Then I'll figure out what comes next."

I pack up a few things I need from my room while he calls for a car to pick us up. Then we carry my bags down to the car and ride wordlessly back to his apartment.

THIRTEEN

"**S**o just to be clear, you—a man who is afraid of heights—live on the fourteenth floor, and you spend a good portion of your free time on your balcony overlooking the city?"

"I think they lured me in by calling it a terrace—sounds less intimidating than balcony—but yes, that seems to be the situation."

He hands me a stemless wine glass filled with a pink Moscato and sits in the chair diagonally from mine, swigging from the mouth of a beer bottle.

At times, the mid-April breeze rushes along the Avenues, creating wind tunnels through the city. The first time I shivered, Dalton disappeared inside and extended one of his old sweatshirts to me when he returned. Now I pull my legs up to my chest and tuck them inside the oversized hoodie.

We've successfully avoided talking for most of the night since we left Lindsey's apartment, and the soundtrack of the city below serenades us as we sit and sip.

I scan the skyline, taking in the other lofty buildings around us. When my eyes get to the space above and beyond him, his head turns away from me and focuses downward.

My gaze falls and my heart sinks. After the day I've had, I just need a friend. As he made perfectly clear less than two hours ago, that's what we're supposed to be.

But he can't even look at me.

Finally he speaks, asking, "Do you have any certain time that you normally go to bed or anything?"

"No," I shake my head. "You? I don't want to screw up your schedule."

He waves off the idea. "I don't have a schedule anymore."

"Oh. Right."

"Yeah." His head droops again.

"So you never really explained what was up with the show. What happened?'

"I told you, my part's been recast." He leans forward, resting his forearms on his thighs, and picks at the label on his beer bottle.

"I can't believe it. Who in their right mind would want to replace you in their show? You're like, the best there is."

He raises an eyebrow and stops picking. "Pretty confident statement from someone who's never seen me on stage. Have you been spying on me?"

Heat floods my face. "I may have done some recon work." I hope he doesn't see through the lie of omission. "Plus, I heard you at your concert, remember?"

"I remember," he nods. "I'm just screwing with you." One corner of his lips curls upward for a moment, then he shakes his head and resumes fidgeting with the bottle. "Anyway. Can we talk about something else?"

"Sure."

But instead of choosing a new topic, he sits in silence.

"Sorry about our plans getting so messed up tonight."

He reclines back in his chair and crosses one leg over the other. "No big deal."

But it *is* a big deal, to me, and I had thought it was a big deal to him, too. After all, he's the one who planned it, who showed up with flowers. Who told me I was *it*.

I feel his eyes on me, but I can't bear to look at him. When I sense his gaze has shifted, I chug the rest of my wine. Standing and turning toward the door I tell him, "Thanks for saving the day today. For me and for Lindsey."

"Oh—" he says, rising. He strides to the door and our hands grasp the handle at the same time. We both pull back, magnets of the same polarity, pushing each other away.

The alcohol sends my head spinning, or maybe it's the electricity from his touch, causing every sensor in my brain to light up like Times Square itself.

I want to dive into his arms.

I want to yell at him for the mixed signals he's sending.

But most of all, I want to stay in New York, specifically with *him* in New York, and I can't do that if I throw away our friendship. We've built something over the course of the last month and a half, and a phone call or text or living condition won't change it. It can't. Because then I have nothing.

I breathe in, filling my lungs with the chilly evening air. And then I wait.

Dalton's chest rises and falls. Puffs of air escape his lips, which are parted ever so slightly, like he's ready to speak but unsure of what to say. His eyes convey the same thing, darting back and forth across my face.

Finally, after an eternal second, he regrips the handle and slides the door open for me. He follows me into the kitchen and takes the wine glass, setting it in the sink.

The clothing I had begun washing in his in-unit washer and dryer is early in its dry cycle, but I'm in desperate need of a distraction.

"Any chance I can borrow a towel and get a quick shower?"

"Yeah, of course." He glides from the kitchen to the bathroom and pulls a gray towel from a small linen closet inside. He hands it to me without making eye contact and says, "You're free to use anything you need. There's decent stuff in the shower already—shampoo, conditioner, body wash—" I swear his neck goes pink when he says *body.*

"Great, thanks. I never even thought to grab those things from the apartment."

When he leaves, I creep to the door and lock it behind him, then strip and turn on the water. It sprays from so many shower heads it looks like a carwash for humans.

The warm water feels great, until I consider again the date-that-wasn't and the way he came through for Lindsey, the flowers, his expression when he saw me, his breath on my neck, him telling me I was going to stay with him. When his hazel eyes and muscular arms flash through my head I turn the water temperature down.

I stand a few moments in the shower even when the water's finished streaming down, wrapped in the oversized, cozy towel. I have nothing clean to change into—I'm so used to darting in my towel four feet from the bathroom to the spare room at Lindsey's that I never thought to bring anything in here with me. Not that I could have, because it's all in the dryer between the bathroom and Dalton's room.

After a quick scan of the room—white and black marble and chrome fixtures everywhere—I come up with five reasonable solutions to the problem:

1. Put on the robe that hangs behind the door, embroidered with Dalton's initials.

2. Walk out in dirty, dusty clothes to find clean clothes in the dryer.

3. Walk out in a towel or his hoodie to get some clean clothes from the dryer.

4. Ask Dalton to bring me clothing.

5. Stay locked in the bathroom till I die.

All options seem equally appealing at this point, though I opt to slide back into his sweatshirt and my shorts, naked underneath. I sneak into the hallway, glad to hear that the dryer has stopped. I grab an armful of clean clothes and drop them off in the spare room—*my* room— then return to the bathroom for the dirty clothes I'd left behind.

As I leave, sweaty bra and today's underwear in hand, I nearly collide with Dalton.

"Sorry," he says. He holds an empty laundry hamper in front of me. "I wasn't sure if you could use this."

"Oh, um, that would be great, thank you." Hiding my underwear the best I can, I take the hamper from his outstretched hand.

He sidesteps to allow me to pass him back to my room. My ears are hot with embarrassment.

When he's safely *not* in the middle of the hallway, I finish switching my laundry around, then put on a pair of worn-in black leggings, yoga bra, and an old long-sleeve T-shirt from my senior year track team that I deconstructed when I started to outgrow it. I venture to the living room with my journal, where I find Dalton lying on the couch, scrolling on his phone.

"Hey."

He turns his attention my way but doesn't even try for a smile. "Hi."

"Is it okay if I—" I point to the armchair across the room, its back to the terrace.

"Hillary, you don't have to ask permission to do anything. You're an adult."

"I'm a guest, and you were generous enough to host me for the week. I don't want to intrude on your alone time."

He scrunches his face and sits up, discarding the phone on the seat next to him, and leans forward again. "I like spending time with you. You know that. Why are you acting weird?"

A lump catches in my throat but I force it down. "I'm sorry, I know." I wring my hands and clear my throat. "Can I tell you something really embarrassing?"

His lips twist and twitch, like he's afraid I'm going to say what I really want to say. "Yeah, if you want to."

I do the only logical, face-saving thing I can think of: I modify the truth. "It's just that I got really freaked out on Friday night when we talked, thinking you were *into* me, or something, and then yesterday I was worried that our dinner tonight was supposed to be a date or something."

"What's embarrassing about that?"

"Seriously? Thinking the amazing Dalton Tremaine—Broadway It-Boy, Rumored Beau of Samantha Darling—is romantically interested in me? I'm an idiot. Too much time spent watching TV rom-coms."

"Ha. Yeah." He sits back again, now wringing his hands.

I cringe, sure he doesn't like that I've referenced his status. "But anyway, I was overthinking and worrying over nothing. So," I fake a smile, hoping it passes as real enough, "I'll stop being weird, we'll carry on as usual, and I'll just be your new roommate."

"Hillary."

Whenever he says my full first name it carries an intensity that twists my stomach.

"Yeah?"

"Don't do that."

I swallow hard. "Do what?"

"Don't think or talk like you're not special enough. Not for a second. You're wonderful." He sighs. "It's just that—"

"I know," I save him. "And thank you."

We exchange the most pitiful smiles before I plaster on the happiest face I can. Truthfully I don't know how he was going to finish that sentence, but it doesn't matter. "Anyway—tomorrow. If I'm not cramping your style, do you want to hang out?"

"Sure," he says, and I imagine he's grateful for a change of subject. "What do you have in mind?"

I shrug. "What sounds like fun?"

He thinks for a moment, then smiles, his eyes sparkling for the first time since he arrived to pick me up at Lindsey's apartment. "I have an idea, but you'll need to rest up."

"Oh geez. What torture are you putting me through?"

He laughs his glorious laugh and says, "I'm taking you on a real tour of New York."

FOURTEEN

At seven there's a knock on my door. Not a gentle *sorry if I'm waking you* knock, but a *get the hell out of bed now* knock. I whip open the door immediately, and Dalton stumbles backward.

"Gah!" he cries, startled. "I didn't think you'd be up yet."

"Joke's on you, New Yorker. I've been up since six."

"Someone's excited for their tour."

I strike my model poses, showing off my ripped jeans and navy sweater. "I'm ready!"

"Not quite," he laughs, shaking his head. He models his own outfit—a pair of shorts, sweatshirt, hat, and running shoes.

"Noooooo," I moan. "This isn't a cute tour of museums and architecture?"

Again he treats me to his laughter. "Oh, we can see the museums. From the outside."

I throw my head back and groan. "What kind of monster makes someone run through the city at seven on a Monday morning?"

He snickers as he closes the door. "I'll wait out here."

A few moments later, he hands me a banana as we walk out the door. I've got my normal running leggings and shoes, and I've layered the sweatshirt I borrowed last night over my tank top. *Sweet, sweaty payback.*

"I know Lindsey has given you a list of her favorite spots in the city, but I want to show you mine." He tucks his phone into his pocket and opens a door.

"Um, what's this?" I ask, pointing through the doorway.

"Those are stairs, Hil. Ever see those before?"

"I know what they are. But why are we looking at them?"

"Because they're our warm-up."

I stare ahead into the staircase, then longingly at the elevator just a few feet away, then pleadingly into his eyes. "Oh man, here goes."

My heart is racing when we reach the street. "Is that it? Are we done?"

"With stairs," he winks.

Suddenly it feels like my friend is back. I smile, thankful for the normalcy.

"You okay?" he asks.

"Yeah, why?"

"No reason," he smiles back. "Are you ready to get started?"

I pop in a piece of mint gum I'd grabbed before leaving. "Yes. Show me everything."

He bumps his shoulder gently into mine. "Try to keep up."

....

At one o'clock, I'm exhausted. We've seen the Museum of Modern Art, Central Park, the Chrysler Building, and hopped on the subway to Coney Island where we take in hot dogs and a bay breeze from a bench overlooking the beach.

"It's really a shame," I say, his sweatshirt tied around my waist, as the cool air blows over the water.

"What is?"

"That the coaster's not running today." I nod my head toward the Cyclone.

He laughs. "Yeah, too bad."

We take the subway back to Manhattan and are greeted by cooler air, water, and a lush, green park just beyond the tangle of pavement in front of us. I pull the sweatshirt back on, despite the sun shining high above us.

"I promise, no more running today."

"Thank you."

"This is our last stop—then it's about a two-mile walk back to the apartment."

"That I can handle," I tell him.

I follow him to the southern end of the park, where rivers meet and Ellis Island looms ahead of us.

"This is one of my favorite places in the city."

"Mine too."

I lean against a railing, into the breeze. "Can you imagine how scary that would have been, leaving everything you've ever known, coming to a new place to start a new life, with nothing but what you could carry? No resources... no connections..."

Through my periphery I can see his eyes on me as I continue looking at the island. When I turn my attention to him, he meets my gaze and doesn't look away.

I wait for him to make the first move, to say something to justify his eyes on me, but he doesn't. Instead, I add, "Plus, in the early eighteen hundreds they hanged pirates here."

He laughs at my non sequitur.

"You're just full of surprises." He stands and brushes his hands on the back of his shorts. "But now it's my turn. Follow me."

We cut across a grassy patch onto the main pathway. Ahead of us sits a rounded building, its roof twisting in two layers to its peak. The glass walls reflect the sunlight and the greenery around us.

"Have you ever been here before?"

"To the park? A few times."

"No, I mean *here*, here." He motions with his head to the building.

"Never. I don't even know what *here* is."

His smile widens and he readjusts his hat. "You're going to love it."

We enter the building and see the most beautiful, iridescent, larger-than-life fish. "What is this?"

"This is the SeaGlass Carousel."

"It's stunning," I say, looking at the fish.

"It is," he says, looking at me.

I catch him and smile. He smiles back, eyes flickering in the soft light. When it's our turn to ride, I choose a modest angelfish seat and he takes the elaborate fish with spikes on top, next to mine.

"What kind of fish is that?"

He shrugs. "Lionfish, maybe?"

"Fitting," I say. "You both have great hair."

The joke earns his laugh once more, and when the ride starts I sink back into my seat, enjoying the serene, perfect ride.

....

I buy us coffee on the way back to the apartment.

"I owe you a dinner," he says, dropping his keys onto the pristine kitchen counter.

"You've more than made up for it," I motion to the apartment.

Dalton shrugs. "Okay, fine, I *want* to take you to dinner. The last stop on our tour."

Last night I would have blushed when he said he wanted to take me to dinner, but today I'm thrilled to be back to normal. *Our* normal. Friends, and nothing more.

We take turns showering. I go first, and this time I take a change of clothes into the bathroom with me. In the excitement of the day, I never stopped to pick up my own shampoo, conditioner, and body wash, so I lather up in his products again, drenched in his scent.

I dry off, twist my hair up in a towel, and throw on the sweater from the beach with some distressed skinny jeans. I leave a trail of watery footprints down the hardwood hallway and blow my hair dry while he's in the shower.

I'm halfway through my makeup ritual/dance party when the water stops. A few minutes later, when the bathroom door opens, I set down my mascara.

"I should've asked earlier, but how fancy—" I stop, just outside my bedroom door. Dalton's like a deer in the headlights, his lower half wrapped in a towel, his chest still damp and glistening from the shower, his hair dripping in haphazard spikes. "Sorry!" I turn sideways and bring my hands to my face, shielding my eyes from the view I really want to see.

You're just friends, dummy, my head says. Everything else urges me to get another peek. *Hubba, hubba.*

"Fancy is not necessary," he says. "What you're wearing is fine. What I'm wearing is not."

"Great…thanks. Sorry." I retreat back into my room and hear him close the door behind him in his.

I finish my hair and slowly reemerge in the hallway.

"Hey," comes his voice from his bedroom doorway, right

next to mine. "I'm clothed now, so you don't have to sneak around, trying to avoid me."

My face goes hot, and I laugh. "I'm so sorry."

"Oh yes, your laughter definitely carries remorse."

I bite my lip but can't control my nervous laugh. "I *am* sorry—I just—I can't believe—"

He playfully shoves my arm. "It's fine. I'm just messing with you. I appreciate you not selling pictures to the gossip mags or calling the paparazzi."

"Do the paparazzi really follow you?"

He feigns offense. "Ouch. Am I not famous enough for the paps?"

I shrug. "I don't know. I'm not sure what their qualifications are. But I don't think you're dramatic enough for them."

"Again… ouch."

"No!" I protest. "It's a good thing, I think. You're so normal, so down-to-earth."

He crosses his arms; his upper body's shaking.

"You're screwing with me again, aren't you?"

"Yes. Most definitely."

I shove him back, hard, laughing. "Jerk."

• •

The restaurant is a dream come true. It's dark and moody, with old Tiffany lamps and a lounge area downstairs with plush seating and a fireplace. In the lounge, creatives of all ages sit solo with journals and songbooks and classic novels, drinking cocktails named after famous authors. From upstairs, we can see it all through the railing next to us. We've got an old mahogany table and two deep booth seats, and most of the tables around us are empty, giving us a quiet setting to people-watch and talk.

The menu in front of me reads *Nom Nom de Plume*, and I laugh at the name. "Very cutesy for such a moody place."

"I love it here," he says. "Name and all. A perfectly bohemian hideout."

We order cocktails to start: a Bloody Mary Shelley for him, and a Long Island Agatha Chris-Tea for me.

"Do you come here often?"

He shakes his head, sipping water. "I used to, back in the day. I found it refreshing to be surrounded by so many people like me."

"And now?"

He shrugs. "Now I'm old and grumpy and just want to be by myself."

"Cool." I bite the inside of my cheek to keep myself from smiling.

"Present company excluded, of course," he says, reading my reaction.

"Of course."

Our server arrives to take our order and a moment later delivers the drinks, which Dalton happily gulps, a welcome distraction.

"Anyway…I wanted to introduce you to this place, in case you want to come here and write sometime. It's no beach, but it's inspiring in its own way. I know a few playwrights who've written entire works sitting down there. They've got a coffee bar and a *bar* bar down there, all day, every day."

I find myself nodding. "That sounds pretty perfect, actually."

Instead of returning my smile, he takes another drink.

"So what does tomorrow hold for you?" I ask.

"I've got a call with my agent, for sure, but beyond that, who knows." He turns his drink, his fingers leaving clear voids in the beads of sweat that cling to the glass. "How about you?"

"Well, coffee, to start. Then maybe some time spent here. We'll see where I end up."

"That sounds nice. You're allowed to hang out at the apartment, too, Hil. If you want to sit on the terrace and write, or just hang out and read, go for it."

We make small talk while we wait for our food and even after it arrives. I share half of my Shrimp Poe-Boy with him, and he transfers part of his Shakesbeer-Battered Fish and Chips to my plate. The food is deliciously indulgent after such an active, busy day.

He pays and carries our bag of desserts—two Fleming Brûlées—back home. It's only five blocks to the apartment, but my feet are killing me and my legs are sore, so it's a slow walk. Plus I'm distracted by the window displays of stores along the way.

"Where do people even wear this stuff?" I ask, stopping in front of a storefront with a feathered red gown in the window.

"Museum openings, yacht parties, weddings, brunch…" he lists.

The next window has more of a grunge aesthetic, with shredded black jeans and red and black plaid skirts, cropped vintage rock T-shirts, and fishnet shirts layered underneath. "And this?" I ask.

"Fashion week, clubs, work, brunch…" he quips, and I roll my eyes before shoving my shoulder into his arm.

The next few storefronts display sneakers, then baked goods, and then I stop in my tracks. "Wow."

The gorgeous gold gown in front of me has a high halter neck and a mermaid silhouette with structured beadwork that reminds me of the Manhattan high-rises. The beads catch the light from the streetlights around us and twinkle teasingly.

"I don't think you could wear that to brunch," Dalton says.

"I don't think I could wear that to anywhere I would ever go."

I gawk a moment longer, then continue to the apartment, slip into my pajamas, and curl up opposite Dalton on the couch where I fall asleep to an action movie while he absentmindedly rubs my foot.

FIFTEEN

D alton Tremaine snores.

First quietly, then with the intensity of a hundred bowling balls rolling down the alley all at once.

It wakes me before six, which is too early to be awake but too late to go back to sleep. So I do the most reasonable thing and put on the clearance dress from the beach with a jean jacket and slip-on shoes, and I walk myself and my journal to Eunoia.

I'm there for maybe an hour when he texts me. Where did you go?

Either the lack of sleep or the creative juices from writing this morning—or a dangerous combination of both—compels me to respond in riddle form.

Out the door and down the street
Gotta move those morning feet
I came to where the coffee brews
If given options, the place you'd choose

I set the phone down and go back to writing, gulping coffee as I go. Gina Thompson is really developing as a character, and although she's a total bitch, there's something almost likable about her.

"Very clever, Ms. James."

Dalton's standing over me, smirking.

"You found me!"

"I did." He drops into the seat across from me.

I've inherited a nervous and uncontrollable laugh from my mom's family. Dad's nose. Dad's eyes. Dad's propensity to grow white hairs around the age of thirty. Mom's nervous laugh. And it comes out in full force now.

"I'm sorry. I know it was really stupid." It was stupid, and now it's stupid that I can't stop laughing over something so stupid, and my nostrils flare even as I cover my face and I pray that I won't snort.

"Geez, Hil." Dalton says, leaning back, an amused expression landing on his face.

It's early enough that there are very few people in Eunoia and those that are here are grabbing coffee on their way to work, their faces buried in their cell phones and earbuds firmly planted in their ears, so he's not concerned about the volume and drawing attention our way.

Finally the laughter dies down and I reveal my stilled nostrils and wipe the tears away from my cheeks.

"That was new. Does that happen often?"

"More than you might imagine." I'm still drying my eyes, on the verge of more laughter.

"Well," he says, smiling wide, "I look forward to the encore." He turns, scoping out the line. "I'm going to grab a drink and let you get back to your day, Madame Poet."

I pantomime a dramatic bow from my seat. "Good day to you, sir."

Once he leaves, I return to writing, lose track of time, and only stop when my stomach rumbles. I buy a scone, pack up my journal, and wander the streets of New York.

Lindsey calls.

"I am so sorry I didn't check in yesterday. How are you?"

"I'm fine," I promise.

"Does Lemming still suck? Do you hate me?"

"Actually," I begin, just as an ambulance passes, siren wailing.

"Wait—are you still in the city?"

"I am."

"You managed to find a reasonable hotel?"

"Actually, it's the weirdest thing. I ended up not needing one." I feel a stupid smile spread on my face and I'm certain I look like a goofy idiot on the sidewalk.

"Well I know you're not at the apartment, which I also wanted to talk to you about. But hold on… where are you staying?"

I bite my bottom lip, afraid of her reaction. "A friend offered to let me stay with them…"

"*Shut up.* Are you serious?" she asks, reading between the lines.

"Mmhmm. He suggested it on Sunday after you left."

"And you said yes?"

"Of course I said yes. I had no other options."

"Did you guys ever talk? About your feelings for each other or whatever?"

I think back to Sunday night and push the memory from my mind. "Yes, we talked, and we realized there was nothing to talk about. He doesn't have feelings for me like that. He just said some things he didn't mean."

"Things he didn't *mean*, or things he didn't mean *to say*? Because there's a difference."

"Didn't mean at all. And it's fine. I'm fine. We're great."

She pauses. "If you're sure."

"Totally. Yes." I'm pretty sure I believe it and hope she

does, too. Things are good at Dalton's place, and I don't want those feelings reemerging, screwing it up.

"If you're sure you're good, then good. Because I have some updates."

....

"Another *month?*" The disbelief is scribbled across his face, in his hairline-high eyebrows and his wide eyes. "How is that even possible?"

"Lindsey said the super found a lot of mold when they went to replace the water-damaged drywall, then electrical problems that snaked through multiple apartments. Because both official tenants are out of town, their apartment's not the top priority, and they're already having a hard time finding a contractor who can do the repairs at a decent price in a reasonable timeline for people who are here in the city."

He lets out a low whistle. "That sucks."

"It does," I confirm. "And listen, I hate to ask this, but—"

"So help me, Hillary James—if you even ask if you can stay another month."

It's the answer I feared. "Understood," I say, rising from a stool at his kitchen island.

"Whoa, whoa, whoa." He reaches across the island to grab my arm. "What I mean is, you don't even have to ask. Of course you can stay."

"Really? You're sure?"

He nods, his lips twitching, hinting at a smile. "Of course. The last forty hours haven't sucked."

I rush around the countertop and throw my arms around his neck. "Thank you, Dalton. You have no idea how much I appreciate it."

"Not a problem," he says, returning the hug briefly before sliding from my grip.

"Okay, so the apartment situation is handled, but that's not even the biggest news of the day!"

"Oh, really? I'm nervous. That's how my dad told my mom that he bought a classic Bel Air, and she did not react well."

"Okay, one, relax, this is all good. Two, does he really have a Bel Air?"

He nods. "Mid-life crisis."

"Hm." I have questions, but I power on, shaking them from my mind. "No. Next, I'm going to tell you that I got a job!" I strike an end-of-company-dance-number pose with jazz hands as I make my big announcement.

"A job? In the city?"

"It would be weird to ask you if I could stay here a little longer if the job was in Podunk, Missouri."

He rolls his eyes and steps backward to lean against the fridge. "So, what's the new gig?"

"You know that little bookstore I love up on Seventeenth?"

His forehead creases. "I know it well."

"So, I was just browsing today—retail therapy, after Lindsey told me about the apartment—and I got talking with one of the owners. I said I was probably going to have to leave the city since I couldn't afford to stay, and she offered me a job on the spot."

His lips part as if he's about to speak, but I cut him off before he gets the chance. "I told her it would depend on my living situation, of course. I didn't want to make any assumptions."

"Ah. Well, that's exciting."

"Yes, your voice exudes excitement."

He rubs a hand along the countertop and shrugs. "Will you have time to write?"

"Mmhmm, sure will. I'm going to sign on part-time, maybe twenty hours a week. I just want to be able to keep covering my expenses here." Before he can mention it, I let him know, "I can start paying rent, too. It won't be much, but it's something, at least."

Dalton holds up a hand to stop me. "You'll do no such thing. You're not paying rent."

"Agree to disagree."

"I mean it, Hillary. Please don't even try." Then he throws my own words back at me. "I'm not here for your money."

I can feel my face burning and I know he sees it, too. My spine straightens. "Okay." It's barely a squeak.

He abruptly and graciously changes the subject. "By the way, it is not lost on me that you have avoided the topic of your book every single time we've talked about your writing."

It's true. "To be fair, I literally only developed an idea within the last four days. So there really wouldn't have been much to tell prior to that."

"Ah, so there's at least an idea now," he taunts. "Do tell. What's it about?"

Shaking my head, I answer, "Can't tell ya. I'd have to kill you."

"Doesn't seem like a reasonable response."

"It's top-secret information. It's the *only* response."

He raises his hands in surrender. "Fair enough."

When our staring contest ends, I say, "So tell me more about this Bel Air."

....

It's a mild evening so we order salads and sandwiches from

the deli down the street and have dinner outside on the terrace. Though we've talked about family before, tonight we develop a full character profile on many members.

First up: Dalton's dad, Thomas, who has a 1957 Bel Air convertible, painted Tropical Turquoise. Never misses an opportunity to play a round of golf when his son comes home for a visit. Owned a hardware store in Greentree, West Virginia, and after working six days a week for more than a quarter century he sold the store three years ago so he could retire early and enjoy life with his car and his wife. He gets bored, though, and still works part-time at the store.

Olivia Tremaine taught third grade for thirty-three years. She volunteers to help with adult literacy programs and enjoys gardening. She has run three marathons since she turned forty and has also taken up painting. According to Dalton, Olivia believes it is never too late to learn something new. She also loves taking her husband's Bel Air out for a spin when he is distracted by a game of golf. Clearly she is my new favorite Tremaine.

His brother, Jordan, is an adventure tour guide back in West Virginia, leading hiking and rafting excursions for visitors looking for a thrill. He's three years older than Dalton, on his second marriage, and afraid of nothing.

"Not heights?"

"Nope. He loves climbing anything. Always has."

"Snakes?"

He makes a face. "He'd be the world's worst adventure guide if he was afraid of either of those things."

"Touché."

"How about you? I remember you saying before that you had a pretty big family."

"Yeah. I mean, mostly it's Stacy, me, Mom, and Dad. And Stacy's husband and kids. But growing up the whole gang was always together, like twenty cousins playing outside on holidays, camping trips together, picking blueberries in the summer before running barefoot and fully clothed into the stream to cool down…"

"That sounds amazing."

I nod. "It really was. But now…" I sigh. I set the empty salad dish aside and take a sip of wine, buying time before revealing this piece of myself. His eyes are kind but prying; he wants to know more, not for the sake of just knowing, but for the sake of knowing *me*. Like when some people drive by a car wreck and want to look to see how bad it is because they're nosey—he's the Good Samaritan who looks to make sure everyone's okay. *He wants to make sure I'm okay.*

"Now everything is a competition. You can't just sit and talk with Grandma about your life, because Grandma brings everyone else into it. 'Kelsey has two kids and she's three years younger than you are,' or 'I wish I could see you more often. Lucas comes to visit every Tuesday and takes me to breakfast,' but Lucas is jobless and bored and invites Grandma to go out for breakfast because he knows she ends up paying every single time."

I catch myself ranting, and I catch a glimpse of his understanding expression. "Anyway. All that to say, it was easier when we were kids. Even if there was competition between our parents about our soccer teams or report cards or whatever, we were oblivious. Just playing in the lawn, laughing together."

"The way it should be."

"Right?"

Sighing, I add the final piece to this puzzle. "And when I was doing well—when things were going right and I had my life together, it was fine. But now everything is so screwed up."

"And that's why you ran away?" he asks, a gentle accusation.

"I didn't run away," I shoot back.

"But you don't want to go back. That's why you're here, right? With me?"

"I'm here with you because—" *I want to be*, or *because you make me feel free*, I want to say, but I catch myself and feel my toes tingle.

His eyes brighten and his chest expands and he inhales deeply. "Because, why, Hillary?"

Clearing my throat, I respond, as matter-of-factly as I can. "I'm here with you because Lindsey's apartment flooded and you forced me to move in. Temporarily, of course."

"Of course," he says, so quiet I almost don't hear it. The green fades from his eyes and they turn cloudy brown. A moment passes.

He picks up his finished dishes from dinner and wordlessly walks inside.

SIXTEEN

"Good morning, dear," says Mrs. Charles, co-owner of Books Off Broadway, as she hangs the Open sign in the window. "Come in, come in!"

"Thanks! I really appreciate you giving me this job, Mrs. Charles."

"Mrs. Charles?" she scoffs. "Please, dear, call me Sue. And we are so very grateful for your help." She smiles warmly and motions me into the store.

I rifle through my bag, withdraw the paperwork she needs. "I brought everything you asked for to make it official," I say, turning over the documents.

"Thank you, Hillary. I'll get these pesky forms filled out right away. Make yourself at home while I do."

She disappears into the back room, and I venture to the corner of the store, a plush sitting area surrounded by sky-high bookcases. I walk the length of the shelves, my fingers grazing each crisp paperback spine, taking in the titles and textures. At the end of the row, I check out yesterday's new releases and judge each by its cover. I want them all.

Sue returns minutes later. "All clear, darling. Welcome to the team!"

"Great!" I take back the papers she no longer needs.

"Let's start training," Sue says, and when I roll up my sleeves she laughs. "Let's start with the basics." She lowers herself into a chair and motions for me to do the same.

"Steve and I opened Books Off Broadway thirty-five years ago. We were young, newly married, entrepreneurial go-getters who couldn't wait to get off work on Fridays and dive into a good book all weekend long. When corporate America ate away at our souls—which didn't take long, mind you," she says, rolling her eyes, "—we opened the store. We've run it mostly by ourselves ever since."

"That's incredible. I can't imagine how much work that takes."

Her lips curl upward, with effort. "Yes, it's been a labor of love. But to see so many faces come through, to meet so many people, to help children develop a love of reading and watch so many of them grow up with us and with our own daughter, it's all been worth it."

I feel myself nodding along to the cadence of her words. "Does your daughter work here, too?"

"She used to work here after school and on summer breaks, yes. Not so much anymore; she's busy with her own work. She's about your age."

I wonder what it would be like to have Sue and Steve as parents. Steve is bookish, a tall, slender man with thick, black-framed glasses. Sue is an artist at heart, which is evident in her assortment of handmade jewelry. I've seen her wear matching sets made entirely of forks. Her clothes are all soft and flowy and her gray hair is cropped in a stylish pixie cut. I bet they're the kind of parents who put artwork on refrigerators and taught their daughter about her metamorphosis from caterpillar to butterfly with her beautiful, changing body.

In our house, straight-A report cards made the refrigerator door and all conversations about "becoming women" were avoided.

"It must have been wonderful to spend time together here at the store."

"Mmm. It was. We always thought she'd take over the business, but her passion led her in a different direction." She waves the thought away. "Anyway, dear, it is so wonderful to have you join our little family. I don't know how long you're planning to be in the area, but we can certainly use your help, however long you're willing to give it.

"Now, when you're just starting out, of course, Steve or I will be with you always. If you start feeling comfortable we can give you a few hours here and there on your own."

"Of course. I'm happy to help, however I can."

"We're closed on Mondays, and we've got a healthy book club that meets on Wednesdays. We feature up-and-coming authors, typically," she says with a wink. I've been in the shop enough times, struck up enough conversations, for her to know about my ambition.

"Good to know," I laugh. "If I happen to come across any I'll be sure to let them know."

Sue smiles and pats my hands. "I believe in you dear. You've got heart, that's for sure. And that's the first ingredient in the recipe for success."

She guides me through the rest of the store, the stockroom, helping customers as they come in. I've worked retail long enough to feel comfortable with customer interactions, and she teaches me how to process a transaction, place an order, and handle a return.

After six hours and a mini late-afternoon rush, she readjusts her open cardigan and gives me a high five. "You were excellent, dear. Why don't you get back to your life for tonight, and we'll see you tomorrow. Around nine, maybe?"

"Nine sounds great. Thanks for everything today!" I grab my tote bag and give a final wave as I walk out the door and head back to whatever awaits me at Dalton's apartment.

....

I've been here for three hours, during which I poured a glass of wine, sat on the terrace to write, and came inside to read with a fresh glass of wine when the rain started. All before Dalton walks in the door a little after seven.

"Hey."

He returns my greeting with a grunt.

I close the book and twist to get a better view of him from the couch. "How was your day?"

In the kitchen, he rummages through a cabinet and pulls out another wine glass, then fills it nearly to the top with a dry red he's been working through.

"That good, huh?"

With three gulps, he's downed half the glass. "Just great."

"Want to talk about it?"

He rubs the glass with his thumb and pushes back his hair with his free hand. "No."

I watch him a moment longer, waiting for the Dalton I know to make an appearance, but this moody clone avoids my gaze.

A year ago—hell, a month ago—I would have indulged him his temper tantrum. But part of my growth so far is learning that I don't have to just put up with other people's nonsense to make them feel better.

He can have his pity party, but I refuse to attend.

Instead, I change into running clothes and go out to clear my head.

SEVENTEEN

When I'm dressed and ready to head to the bookstore, a latte and a banana wait for me, set atop a note that reads,

Hillary—

Sorry for being a jerk last night. Rough day.
Hope you had a nice run + have a good day at work.
Dinner tonight, maybe?

—D

The shower's running and I need to be at work in twenty minutes. I scribble back,

Sorry your day sucked
Hope this one is heaven
Dinner sounds lovely
Can we plan for seven?
Thanks a latte!

—HJ

PS: In all seriousness, I hope today is better than yesterday for you.

By the time I reach the bookstore, I have a text from Dalton. *Thanks for the note. Good luck today. See you tonight.*

Today Steve greets me, just as warmly as Sue did yesterday. "Good morning, Hillary. Great to see you."

"You too."

"Sue says you had a busy first day."

I nod. "Yes—we saw a little bit of everything, I think. I learned a lot."

"Ah. That's good." He finishes shelving the stack of books in his arms and waves me over to the register. "If you want to tuck your things behind here, you can, or in the stockroom, whichever is most convenient for you."

"Thanks." I assume my position behind the register.

Only a few customers trickle in at first, but around lunchtime the number of shoppers picks up. I handle most transactions on my own, only needing to call Steve for help twice.

"I really appreciate your help today," he says when things slow down again around two. He takes a break from the display he's assembling and rests his forearms on the counter. "Sue was so excited to have the opportunity to take a day off and have lunch with our girl."

"Happy to help, however I can." I mean it. It's good to have purpose, to feel like a valuable member of a team. I've spent too much time wandering the city alone, getting lost in other people's lives and missions; it's time to focus on my own.

"You don't happen to have a degree in book displays, do you?" Steve wipes a bead of sweat from his forehead with the back of his hand. "I'm trying to surprise Sue with a Mother's Day display, but anything aesthetic was always her wheelhouse."

Craning my neck, I can see the small wooden table in the middle of the room, just past a rotating greeting card rack. There are a few books with pink or floral covers, but nothing to really grab anyone's interest.

"Would you like me to give it a try?"

"I thought you'd never ask." He winks and hands me a cookbook.

"Anything in particular you're looking for?"

"Anything you can think of, Hillary. Work your magic."

An hour and a half later he stands behind me, nodding and smiling. "This looks great."

Warmth rushes to my cheeks. I'm always a sucker for a compliment.

The table holds an assortment of books, including titles for moms-to-be and working moms, some mommy-and-me craft books, cooking and baking books, cozy mysteries, and contemporary romance novels. I've also added in some books by or about famous first ladies and notable women in history. Mingling between titles are some mugs and candles, along the front sits a small display of bookmarks, and in the center is a bouquet of fresh peonies in various shades of pink that I picked up from the florist two blocks away.

When she handed me the flowers, wrapped in familiar brown paper and tied with twine, my heart ached.

"She's going to love it," Steve says confidently. "How'd you get to be so good at this?"

I shrug. "In a past life I did a lot with weddings and banquets. A different kind of table setting, but still all about making things look nice."

"Well, young lady, you may have just lost a register job. I think I'm going to need to put you in charge of the sales floor moving forward." He beams and claps me on the shoulder before pulling out his cell phone and taking a photo of the display.

He shakes his head, smiling, as he returns to the register area. I tidy up the books I pulled but didn't use for the display, straightening up other shelves along the way. The city noise swells as the door opens and I can hear Sue and Steve greeting each other.

"Hillary? Where'd you get to?" He calls for me, then to Sue he says, "She's a miracle worker. Look at this."

When I rise from my knees I see them taking in the new display. Sue's hands are clasped in front of her mouth, her wide smile extending far up her cheeks.

"Darling, it's so beautiful!" she exclaims. Then she and her lightweight poncho wrap me in a hug. "What a treat it is to have you here."

"Um, Mom?"

Sue turns, creating a clear path to Samantha Darling.

"*Mom*?" I repeat, not meaning to. All three of them look at me now, and I try to shrink into myself.

"You? It's… Hailey, right?"

"Hillary." I don't believe she needed the correction.

"Wait—" Sue's eyes ping-pong between us. "You two know each other?"

"We've met," Samantha and I say at the same time. Neither of us says it kindly.

"What are you doing here?" Samantha asks. She crosses her arms and juts her hip to the side.

"Honey, Hillary is our new employee. She's here to help out for however long she wants to, just to give us some relief and time off. Actually, her being here today is the whole reason I was able to escape and join you for lunch!"

Steve chimes in. "How exactly do you two know each other?"

"A mutual friend," I tell them.

"Not sure I'd say *friend*," Samantha argues. "She knows Dalton."

Sue flinches. "Oh."

Everything changes. It's subtle, but it's there. Sue's smile fades and Steve's eyes flit between me and Samantha. I decide that "knowing Dalton" is dangerous enough information and revealing any details about our current arrangement would definitely not work in my favor.

Sue says to Steve, "Sweetheart, Sami was telling me at lunch that Dalton is finally ready to go public with their relationship. Isn't that wonderful?"

Steve turns squarely to Samantha. "It is. No more hiding? No more sneaking around, going on dates in private?"

She shakes her head theatrically (why would I expect otherwise?). "Nope. We're planning a reveal with our social teams, so mum's the word until it's actually out there. But tomorrow the world will know that Dalton Tremaine and I are Broadway's newest power couple."

....

As soon as the door closes, I curse. Loud. I don't mean to, but *shit*. Dalton and Samantha, actually a couple.

I sink to the floor, back against the door, and feel hot tears sting my eyes.

"Rough day at work?" Dalton peeks out from behind the pantry door, then eases it closed.

I swipe at my eyes, drying my face. "Work was fine."

"Rough walk home?" His lips curl up into a tentative smile, trying to help, as he squats down to my level.

"You lied to me." I scramble to my feet and his smile vanishes.

"What do you mean?"

"You said you and Samantha were just friends. Sometimes coworkers."

"Right…"

"That you weren't dating."

"I'm not hearing a lie anywhere here."

"It's not even that you *are* dating." *Okay, it is a little.* "I mean, you made it abundantly clear to me that you and I are just…anyway." I point my finger into his chest and force my words past the lump in my throat. "I just hate that you felt like you needed to lie to me. I thought we were supposed to be honest with each other."

"What on earth are you talking about, Hillary?"

"I'm talking about your little 'announcement' with Samantha Darling tomorrow."

He winces, the words stinging as I had hoped they would.

"Hil," he says in a voice so soft and uncertain I think I imagine it.

My chest and shoulders rise and fall with my anger. I clench my jaw tight, trapping the sobs that long to escape and hope that my eyes look angry and not just utterly devastated. My heart is shattered into a million little pieces, not just because I want to be with him, but because, even though I can't be, he deserves so, so much better than Samantha Darling.

All I need is to hear him say that I'm wrong, that I'm confused, or she's confused, or *something*.

But instead, what I get is, "Let me explain."

I swallow hard, turn my head, and retreat to my room. He trails behind me, repeating my name. "Hillary, please." And, "Hillary, can we just talk?" And finally, when I'm sobbing freely behind the closed door, I hear a soft thud on the other side, and, "Hillary, you can't keep running away."

He's right.

I've run away from home. I've run away from my feelings for him. I literally *ran* away last night, and now here I stand, locked in my room, avoiding the difficult conversation I know we need to have.

When I slowly open the door, his forehead is pressed against it.

"Oh, Hil." This time his voice oozes what feels like pity.

"I wanted to tell you tonight, at dinner." Maybe he thinks he's helping his case, but he most definitely is not.

"So you *are* seeing her?"

"No—I—." He pauses and sighs. "Come with me."

I follow him to the living room, and we sit at opposite ends of the couch. "Sam and I are not dating."

"Does she know that?"

"As much as she ever did, yes."

"Then why did she tell Sue and Steve—"

He massages his temples. "I knew this was a bad idea," he groans. He closes his eyes and exhales, then says, "Sam and I are telling the press that we're dating. Tomorrow. But we're not. Ever."

"Why would you—"

"Publicity."

Before I can react, he explains, "Sami is at the top of her game. She's popular with the Broadway crowd but also has a huge following with some of her movies, too. I don't have that, especially now, with leaving the show. We've known each other for years, and there's always been speculation, so when I met with my agent yesterday, she thought it would be a good move to 'share in Samantha Darling's success.'"

"Famous by association?"

"Exactly. And Gretchen got Sami's agent on board."

"And Samantha won't turn down the opportunity."

He shakes his head.

"Shit."

"Shit is right." He drags his hands over his face. "Look, I am really sorry that you found out this way. I wasn't trying to hide it from you, and I definitely did not lie to you. I had planned to tell you tonight. I even ordered this big fancy dinner for us, which should be here in about half an hour."

"It's fine," I say, actually meaning it. "But why did you think it was such a big deal to tell me?"

He hesitates. "Because it changes things. It has to."

The reality of his words hits me. If the public thinks he's dating Samantha Darling, then he can't be seen with a woman who is definitely *not* Samantha Darling.

"Oh. Right."

"And don't worry—I'm not asking you to move out or anything. We just have to be careful about coming and going together, or being seen alone together."

"No more walks on the High Line? Dinners out?"

When he shakes his head, I sense disappointment. "Sorry."

"It's fine. Luckily I'm keeping pretty busy with work, so that gives us less time to get caught together."

"Work. I can't imagine how awkward that was, when she showed up there today."

"I think Sue nearly had a heart attack when Samantha said I was your 'friend.'"

"Oh, man. I'm sorry. I think she gets so weird because you scare her."

My jaw drops at the same rate my eyebrows arch. "Excuse me?"

He laughs. "You don't see it?"

I throw a pillow across the couch at him and laugh in return. "Uh, no, I definitely do *not* see it. Because there is *no way* she's scared of me."

Dalton nods. "I promise you. Since day one, after the concert, she's been intimidated by you. Sami's not really used to competition. She gets what she wants from everyone she knows—her parents, her agent, directors, castmates…"

"I am zero competition for her."

He rolls his eyes. "Okay, sure. I'm sure her parents just loathe having you around the store."

"Fine, I'll give you that one. But what about the last month? Why has she hated me since the concert, like you said?"

"Okay, first, she doesn't hate you. And second—" He shrugs but doesn't drop his shoulders. "I think she just wanted me to be available whenever she was bored. But then there you were, so friendly it absolutely intimidated her, and then…nevermind."

I scold him with a wag of my finger. "No, no 'nevermind' around here, sir. Spill it. What were you going to say?"

"Look, Sami and I are friends, we've hung out, but I think she knew that if given the choice between a wild night out with her or a coffee date with you, you'd win every time."

The knock on the door saves us the embarrassment of unpacking words like *date,* or his matter-of-fact tone when he says I'd win. He jumps up and answers the door as I sink down into the far corner of the couch. But it's just the doorman, delivering the buffet that Dalton's ordered for us tonight, since he doesn't want to go out for dinner with this announcement coming tomorrow.

"Are you ready for all the attention coming your way?" I ask between bites of loaded tater tots and shrimp tacos.

"I'm ready to get some opportunities to work in the city, and if this is what it takes…" He trails off, eating a sweet potato fry. He's such a private person that I can't imagine him really being on board with a plan that will get his personal life—even a fake personal life—in gossip magazines and viral social media posts once word gets out.

I don't even have to fake sincerity when I say, "As long as you're happy."

When he answers, his eyes meet mine and his Adam's apple dips. "Someday I will be."

EIGHTEEN

The first week is easy. I'm busy with work and writing, finally finding my flow. Dalton and Samantha are out and about frequently, and I often have the apartment to myself.

I do my best to keep things with Mr. and Mrs. Charles light, like before they thought I was trying to make a move on their daughter's man. Things are better than ever when I make up a new man (who may or may not be, but totally is, based on Peter and the good times we shared) that I've got my eye on and talk about him *constantly*. I only want to vomit a little when I talk about him.

But in the apartment, sometimes I hear parts of conversations I shouldn't, like when Dalton takes a call on the terrace or disappears to his room with his cellphone.

"She doesn't know that I'm here, does she?"

I ask the question after a particularly intense argument between the two of them. She wants to come spend the weekend with him so they can be photographed at brunch and strolling hand-in-hand on the streets of New York. He tells her he doesn't want to lead people right to his front door.

To me, he shakes his head. "No. I never told her. Didn't think she needed to know."

I feel like a dirty secret, something to hide and be ashamed of.

I ask Mr. and Mrs. Charles at work, "Why did Samantha change her name? Where does the 'Darling' come from?" They exchange glances and smile, like a fond memory has passed between them.

Steve says, "Well, you've heard Sue talk."

"Sure."

Sue sits and straightens her necklaces. "When Samantha was little, I would always say 'Come, Sami Darling' or 'Time to eat, Sami Darling.' When she wanted to make it in theater, she was afraid Samantha Charles was too pedestrian, and she wanted to set herself apart a bit. Plus, she wanted to use a different name for privacy purposes. She picked Darling, so she could make it clear to us she wasn't distancing herself from us."

I'm annoyed by how thoughtful the tribute is, but I just smile and say, "That's really sweet. I love that story."

We're in the living room reading—him, a script for a guest part on a show filming in the city and me, a book I picked up at the end of my shift today—when there's a rapid knocking at the door. He bolts upright on the couch while I stare at him from the floor where I've sprawled out.

"Who do you think that is?" I whisper.

He shrugs in return, then creeps quickly to the door and looks through the peephole. "Holy shit."

The door swings open and on the other side I see the same faces I've seen staring back at me in at least three framed photos throughout the apartment.

"Mom! Dad!" He holds his arms open and both parents step into his hug.

I'm seated on the living room floor, wondering if holding my copy of Beck Strehle's *Edge of Destruction* in front of my face will make me invisible. The title feels a little too on-the-nose.

His dad notices me first.

"Hello there," he says, breaking free from the group hug reunion at the door and approaching me like I'm caged in a *who-is-the-strange-woman-in-my-son's-apartment* zoo.

"Hi," I say, forcing a smile as I stand.

Olivia joins Thomas at the kitchen's edge.

"Mom, Dad, this is my friend, Hillary James." He gulps as they turn their attention to him. "She's visiting from out of state and through a very strange turn of events, came to be living here. Temporarily, of course."

"Of course," I repeat. A smile eases onto his lips at the inside joke.

"It's nice to meet you." I extend a hand to Thomas, then to Olivia. "I've heard so much about you both."

It's clear neither can say the same about me.

Instead, Olivia releases my hand and lowers herself onto the couch. "So you're visiting New York?"

"Mmhmm. I moved up here a few months ago to stay with my friend Lindsey."

She squints her eyes and tilts her head.

"Her apartment flooded, and—"

"And I offered to let her stay here," Dalton adds, stepping into the living room next to his dad.

"Temporarily, of course," I note.

He winks and mouths so only I can see, *of course.*

"Clearly there is more to the story than that, but that's the short version." He takes a seat next to Olivia and says, "I didn't realize you were coming to the city."

"We thought we'd surprise you," Olivia responds.

"Well, you definitely did that. How long are you in town?" Thomas answers, "Three nights. We have tickets to a matinee tomorrow and a show Sunday night. Then we head back on Monday."

"And we thought we'd take you and your new girlfriend out for dinner."

He turns to his mom, who has a playful look on her face. "You've talked about her for weeks now, but you never told us you were officially dating. Imagine, sitting down to read the paper with your morning coffee and learning through a newspaper that your son is settling down."

The tops of his ears turn crimson. It's easy to miss because he manages to keep the color from flushing his cheeks, but I see it.

"I'm not 'settling down' with Samantha. There is nothing to settle. I'm not out here living a Hollywood bachelor kind of life."

With a blink, Olivia's eyes flick to me, then back to her son, who definitely did not see what I saw. For that, I'm thankful.

"Anyway, I'm not sure Samantha would be available for dinner. I think she has plans with her parents this weekend. Isn't that what you heard, Hil?"

His parents' faces both turn slowly toward me. There's an urgency in his eyes and I want to help him, but I don't want to be part of the series of lies he's been telling.

"Actually, Steve is out of town this weekend."

His eyes widen, pleading for help.

"But I think Sue's mom was coming in tomorrow to try to spend some time with Samantha and see her on stage. And of course, she's got four shows between now and Sunday night."

"See? I just don't think it'll work." He sounds relieved.

"Think she'd be available for dinner before or a glass of wine after tonight's show?" Thomas asks.

Dalton swallows hard, the pink snaking from the tops of his ears down to his lobes. "I can find out."

....

"Good luck tonight."

He adjusts the clasp on his titanium watch and smooths his button-down over his torso. "I definitely need it."

"You'll be fine." I close the book around my index finger and sit up, dropping my legs from the couch to the floor. "Why are you freaking out about this?"

"Have you met Samantha?" he asks. Frustration fills his voice. "I'm afraid she's going to say something insane, like we're trying to have a baby or looking at houses upstate or some other crazy shit, that is going to make my mom freak out and suggest we get married or something."

"She wouldn't do that."

"I assure you, that exact conversation is a possibility."

"Yikes."

"Yeah. And what are the chances that my parents make it through the night without asking something stupid like, 'Do you know that pretty girl that lives with Dalton? What do you think of her?'"

I know he's acting like his parents, but his insertion of the word 'pretty' mobilizes the butterflies in my ribcage.

"Have you considered telling them the truth?"

He carries his shoes to the armchair across the room and sits to put them on. Tying the laces, he answers, "I would get such a lecture from my mom about lying, messing with Samantha's life, yada yada."

"I'm sure Samantha is just devastated that you're pretending to be the boyfriend she always wanted you to be."

"She doesn't seem to mind so far."

"Why would she? I don't know her all that well, but I would guess, based on what I *do* know, that she is certain you will fall head-over-heels, madly in love with her throughout the next few weeks...months...however long this all lasts, and propose to her in some glorious fashion by year's end."

He laughs and his eyes indicate he means it. "If this turns into a *Misery* situation—"

"Should we microchip you now so we can send in a rescue team if needed in the future?"

"That might not be a bad idea."

"Or—hear me out—maybe you will actually fall for her. I mean, the rest of the world loves her. Maybe you will too, if you really dive in."

His face turns immediately stony. "I guarantee you, I will not fall in love with Samantha Darling."

I dip my head, relieved.

"Anyway, I should head out. I have to pick up my parents from their hotel and lay the ground rules for tonight."

"Okay. Try to have fun. You're spending time with your parents. Samantha is just along for the ride."

He nods, grabbing his keys and wallet from the kitchen counter.

"Oh hey—" I call, craning my neck to see him. When

our eyes meet I ask, "Any chance your dad brought that Bel Air to the city and wants to let me take a drive?"

Smiling, he rolls his eyes and leaves.

NINETEEN

When the noises wake me, it takes a moment for me to register where I am: sprawled on the couch in the living room. Light filters inside from the surrounding buildings, but the sky is still mostly dark.

I lie still, afraid to move, wondering if Mom was right about New York and if tonight will be the night I'm violently murdered.

It's quiet for a moment, then through the wall next to me I hear the sounds again. Slowly, I reach for my phone on the floor and check the screen for the time. It's 4:32 a.m.

The toilet flushes and the bathroom door opens. Dalton shuffles from the bathroom to the kitchen, filling a glass half-full with water. His hand shakes and he sets the glass down after two sips, bracing himself against the counter.

"Are you okay?"

His head snaps up and a hand rushes to his forehead. "Ow."

"Sorry," I whisper, cringing. "It's just me. Are you okay?"

"I have never felt this close to death in all my life. And I've ridden the Cyclone."

"What happened?"

"I either drank way too much, or I ate something bad at dinner. Either way...ugh."

"Yikes."

"Yeah." He drops his head. His hair is matted and sweaty, and his face is pale.

"Can I help?" I actually don't handle sickness well, but I hate seeing him like this and want to help.

He shakes his head and reaches for his glass. He misses; instead of grabbing it, he bumps it and pushes it dangerously close to the sink.

I hurry to him and move the glass out of the way. "Okay, let's get you back to bed." I wrap an arm around his waist, and he drapes an arm over my shoulder. His hands are clammy, and he reeks of whiskey and wine. His shirt is drenched in sweat.

In his room, I help him sit on the edge of his bed, and his top half falls sideways onto the pillow. I find the bathroom trash can, empty it into the kitchen trash, and line it with a plastic bag. When I return it to him, he's seated on the bed, shirtless.

"Oh, I—sorry," I say, turning my face. "I just brought you this, in case you need it tonight."

"Thanks."

"Do you want me to bring you anything else?"

"I feel like shit."

"I can tell."

"Not that." He motions to himself. "Not this." He grabs my arm as I set down the trash can next to the bed. Our eyes meet and his are crystal clear, boring into me. Begging me to understand him.

"It's Samantha. You. This whole lie. All of it."

Through my nerves I force out a smile. "It's fine, Dalton."

"It's not fine, Hillary. You deserve so much better than this. Than me."

I don't have you.

I gently lift his fingers from my wrist. "I'm going to get you some water and saltines. Then you should rest, okay?" He's already asleep when I bring him the crackers and water. I wrap myself in a blanket, grab my journal and pen, and venture out to the balcony, hoping the early morning air will give some relief from the fire he's lit within me.

·······················

My alarm goes off at seven, and I'm sure I look half-crazed in yesterday's clothes and a messy ponytail. I've been writing on the terrace since helping Dalton hours ago and only took one break to finally take in my first New York City sunrise. I stand and stretch, pack up my journal and head in through the sliding glass door.

Dalton is still asleep, snoring and shirtless, in his room. I watch longer than I should.

I skip the shower in case he gets sick again but change quickly and brush my teeth before heading out for coffee.

Instead of heading straight to Eunoia, I lap three blocks to clear my head. The sun warms what the early air chills, and the vacant sidewalks are perfect for thinking.

Thinking about how much these quiet morning walks remind me of home.

Thinking about how lucky I am to still be in the city, considering the catastrophe with Lindsey's apartment.

Thinking about how grateful I am that Dalton came to the rescue.

About his swoopy hair and deep hazel eyes and his abs, sweaty on display in the middle of the night.

About the words he said to me…

I shake it all from my mind as I open the door to Eunoia.

Jolie sees me and starts making my order before I can even ask for it.

••••••••••••••••••••••••

Dalton is, I would say, *reluctantly* awake when I get back to the apartment at half past nine.

"Good morning."

"Hiiii," he growls in return.

"Feeling better, huh?"

He looks at me, expressionless, and goes back to rummaging through the refrigerator. "I can't decide if I need to eat something or if I never want to think of food for the rest of my life."

I extend the white paper bag and cup of iced coffee to him. "If you think this will help…"

He snatches the coffee from my hand and drinks a few sips. "What's in the bag?"

"A bagel. Jolie sent me back with some goodies for you."

"That was nice." He squints, taking the bag.

I agree, then lower the shades on his wall of windows to the outside world. They darken the kitchen and living room substantially.

"God, that's so much better."

"Good. Looked like you were really in pain there."

He nods, then says, "Hey, thanks for helping me out last night."

"Oh. Sure." I swallow past the lump that rises in my throat. "You, uh—you remember last night?"

He laughs and seems to regret it, reaching for his head. "Hell no. I just figured you helped because of the trash can next to my bed. That, and the shirt I wore last night was actually in the washing machine this morning."

I freeze. *Please don't think I ripped your clothes off. Please don't think I ripped your clothes off.*

"Anyway. Thank you for taking care of me."

"Sure thing."

He groans when his phone rings. "Ugh—why isn't it on silent? It's always on silent. Who actually uses the ringer?" he says, disappearing back to his room.

He comes back, squeezing the bridge of his nose. "I'm not sure, Mom. I feel like crap, too. I thought I drank too much but maybe we both ate something bad." He rests his elbows on the counter and runs a free hand through his hair, stopping at the nape of his neck.

"Is she okay?" I whisper during a pause on his side of the conversation. He meets my eyes.

"Actually, Mom, hang on a second."

He places a hand over the mouthpiece of his cell phone and asks, "Do you have plans today?"

I shake my head.

"Do you want some?" He winks, then winces.

I shrug. "Sure?"

"Great. Pick out something nice to wear—you've got a date with my mother."

······················

"I'm sorry to hear that Thomas isn't feeling well," I tell Olivia when I meet her outside her hotel.

"It's unfortunate. He was really looking forward to seeing this play." She tucks her hair behind her ear and squints into the sunlight. "And poor Dalton is no better, it seems."

"It sounded like he had a rough night."

"Mmm. Thank goodness you were there to take care of him." Her displeasure is not well-disguised. "So tell me, how did you come to be his house guest?"

"It's a long story."

"It's a long walk."

I sigh. "Well, we met very randomly one day, quite literally over coffee."

"Oh?"

"Yes. I was visiting a coffee shop nearby, and when I was leaving, we collided and coffee went everywhere."

She turns and looks at me. "It seems like he does that a lot."

"It does?" I risk a sideways glance at her.

She nods. "Yes. Apparently a similar run-in is how he came to meet Samantha, as well."

We stop at an intersection as a crowd congregates at the corner, waiting for the light to change so we can cross the street and continue on our way.

"I had always thought they met at work. Anyway, we just started talking, then went our separate ways. I had left my backpack behind by accident, and he found it and arranged to meet. We bumped into each other again, randomly, a few days after that and found ourselves talking, like two very old friends. And that just kind of started this friendship." Aware of how it sounds to literally everyone else, I add, "this very *platonic* friendship."

"And you said there was some kind of flood?"

"Oh, yes. My friend from back home, Lindsey. I'd been staying with her and then a pipe burst and flooded her place. She took some time to stay with her boyfriend, whose father has been sick, and when I told Dalton I was going to be heading back home, he insisted I stay in the spare room.

"It was just supposed to be a week, but then they found mold, and it's a whole thing." I feel myself shudder, wondering how long the mold had been there before the pipe incident. "Best estimate was it'll take a month to fix it."

"Wow. That sounds like quite the set of circumstances."

I nod. "It was pretty crazy. It all happened so fast. But Dalton was there, saving the day."

She's quiet for a moment. "I think I heard about that night. He skipped a date, right? To help you?"

It's a sucker punch to the gut, to hear the word 'date' be tied to that night. "It definitely was *not* a date. We were supposed to just have dinner that night. Sundays are our day to hang out and explore the city; he's shown me a lot of really great places over the weeks. But that night when he came to pick me up, I'd just gotten home from a weekend away, and that's when all he-" I stop myself from swearing mid-word, "-eck broke loose."

The longer she looks at me, the redder my face grows. Her eyes narrow, like she's running through the story in her head, making sure I'm not a snake in the grass, ready to strike and ruin her son's relationship with Samantha Darling.

"How long ago did you say you two met?"

I shrug. I feel trapped. If I am a snake, and if I do strike, it'll be in self-defense. "Feels like forever and like a day, all at the same time. I guess it's been about two months?"

"Interesting."

Maybe I said the wrong thing, but I wasn't given a script for this. I can only tell the truth. Even when she asks me about Samantha, I avoid lying and do my best to change the subject altogether.

"I actually haven't known Samantha very long. I met her shortly after I got to New York—actually, at Dalton's show uptown—and recently I started working at her parents' bookstore."

"Do they seem happy together?"

I weigh my options, but the safest response seems to be, "I haven't spent enough time around them to see for myself." Not a lie. For good measure I add, "But he talks about her all the time."

Also not a lie. He's usually telling me stories about how miserable she is to be around now that they're fake dating. I don't mind those stories and usually feed into them because she makes me miserable, too.

"Do you know my biggest hope as a mom?" Her demeanor's changed. She seems relaxed, her guard down, willing to share her deepest secrets. I can see where Dalton gets it. "My biggest hope as a mom is for him to be happy. He's got a great career, temperamental though it may be, and a family that loves him. And I know that he has been happy with that for years."

We've reached the theater. As we wait to enter, Olivia pushes her sunglasses up into her hair and looks at me once more. "I would love for him to know the joy of a happy relationship, with a partner who loves him and with whom he can share the highs and lows of life. And I think he's finally found that."

My throat goes dry, and I force a smile. I hold it together the best that I can until we're safely inside the theater, and then I excuse myself, lock myself in a bathroom stall, and cry.

· ·

"The show was excellent," Olivia raves when we're back at Dalton's apartment. He and Thomas are feeling better, so we've picked up a pizza to share on the terrace.

"Did you like it, Hillary?" Thomas asks, and I nod.

The Tremaines carry on conversation, with an update on Jordan's life in West Virginia and stories about outlandish customers at the hardware store.

When Olivia touches my shoulder I jump. All three of them are looking at me, and Dalton's head is tilted, inquisitive.

"Sorry. What was the question?" I assume they are all waiting on an answer.

Thomas laughs. "The car. Dalton said you showed an interest in the Bel Air. Are you a fan of classic cars?

I shake my head. "No. I actually don't know much about cars in general. But I saw an old Bel Air in a calendar once in our garage and have been a little obsessed with them ever since."

The response launches Thomas into a dissertation about classic cars, which I tune out as soon as I hear the word *carburetor.* Olivia hangs on his every word.

When I look up, Dalton's eyes are locked on mine. He mouths, *you okay?*

I shiver and excuse myself to go inside. Dalton follows close behind me. He slides the door closed and nearly whispers as he crosses the living room to me.

"Hey," he says, reaching for me.

I'm mid-stride so his hand grazes my arm but catches my fingers. He closes his hand around mine.

"Hil, what is going on?"

It takes a moment before I can turn and face him. But I plaster on the smile I know I'm supposed to wear and say, "Nothing, just getting a jacket."

His thumb smooths over the back of my hand. I swear he pulls me an inch closer. The worry in his eyes is by far the sexiest thing I've ever seen, once I place the emotion.

Peter never looked at me like that. *That's all it is, Hillary Joy. You were wrapped up in a dysfunctional relationship for so long you lost track of how normal people are supposed to care about each other.*

"You two alright?" Olivia asks. I didn't hear her open the door.

I pull my hand from Dalton's and feel the weight of both sets of their eyes on me, both concerned, I think, but with different reasons.

"All good here," I say, passing Dalton and returning to the terrace.

Thomas smiles politely when I sit down again but otherwise avoids eye contact. I feel like the snake, sure they saw the awkward hand-holding. And let's be real, that's *not* normal. I've never stood like that with Lindsey. Could Olivia be right? Does he really love Samantha? And if so, what in the actual hell is he doing, reaching for me like that? And not just physically, but actually *caring* about what I do and how I am, looking at me the way he does?

The door reopens and Olivia walks out and takes her seat. Dalton is a few steps behind her.

"Here," he says, offering me the oversized cardigan I often wear around the apartment. He takes his seat again across from me and leans forward in his chair, forearms on thighs, watching the ground. Occasionally his gaze rises to meet mine, and though I try I can't look away.

"Honey," Olivia says, and both men turn. "Don't you think it would be lovely for Hillary to join us in West Virginia in two weeks? For the party?"

I wrap the sweater around me and ask, "Party?"

Dalton's head snaps up and he stiffens in his seat. "I don't think Hillary would want to travel all that way—"

Thomas seems confused and maybe a little nervous.

Olivia's smile widens as she focuses her attention on me. "It's our fortieth anniversary party. Dalton and his brother have been planning it for months."

"Mom—"

"And it'll mostly be us old people."

"Mom, I really—"

She holds up a hand without turning to acknowledge him. "I think it would be great for Dalton to have someone his own age to spend time with. Especially since Samantha is unable to attend." She turns to him, lowering her hand, almost inviting him to try to argue.

He scowls at her. "Sami has shows all weekend long. You know she can't just drop them to drive all the way out to West Virginia."

"And I wouldn't expect her to, dear. Unless you were really serious. In that case I might think it would be worth it."

"I wouldn't want to impose." I do my best to insert myself and get him off the hook.

"You're not imposing if you're invited," Olivia smiles.

He glowers at me, his eyes moody and miserable. *Please, say no*, they seem to say.

I come up with a foolproof excuse, phrased like a "possibly" RSVP, though I never intend to follow up on it: "I'll have to see if I can get off work."

TWENTY

We're picking up a rental car in New Jersey. I appreciate that, when Olivia asked the Charleses if I could have off for the party, she didn't tell them who she was; I'm pretty sure they would have fired me on the spot if they knew Samantha's boyfriend's parents were recruiting me to travel across state lines for multiple nights to attend a soiree with him.

So now we're getting ready to spend seven hours in the car together. I don't think this is what Lindsey had in mind when she came up with that car analogy on the beach.

"It's no Bel Air," he says about the sensible sedan they've given us.

"Do you think your dad will let me drive it?" I hope the excitement in my voice is enough for him to petition for me if necessary.

"Highly doubtful."

"Bummer."

"But, if you're really nice, I bet you could talk him into taking you for a drive."

"Well if our first meeting is any indication I'm pretty sure your dad hates me and that'll be a no-go."

"You got one of my parents to love you. I bet it's not much longer till you get the other, too."

We catch each other's gaze as we finish loading our bags

into the hatchback.

He clears his throat. "You never did tell me what made my mom so weird."

"I can't tell you what I don't know. What I *do* know is, she was not my biggest fan before our day together, but that night she was not taking *no* for an answer about this party."

He closes the hatch and lifts his hat to run his fingers through his hair. "And nothing strange happened?"

I shake my head. "She asked how we met, why I'm shacking up with you, and then said she was glad that you were so happy with Samantha."

His head jerks back, like a scared goose, right before it chases a helpless bicyclist down a trail. "Really? I didn't get the impression she liked Sami all that much."

"Maybe it doesn't matter if she likes Samantha or not," I shrug. "She said that her greatest hope is basically that you are happy like she and your dad are happy, and she thought that you finally were. Maybe that's enough."

....

We drive through Greentree, past the school where Dalton's mom worked and the hardware store his dad used to own.

"It's beautiful," I say as we travel along the main road, a divided street with pink and purple flowers sprouting in the grassy median.

"It's a run-down old town," he counters. "But the further west we get, the more I like this place."

Dalton's parents are waiting for us at his childhood home—a rancher set on four acres in the hills. They usher us in and waste no time in helping me get settled into Jordan's old room.

Dinner is served at six o'clock, and Jordan Tremaine makes his grand entrance via motorcycle with one minute to spare. He's got a thick reddish-brown beard, and dimples appear when he greets us.

"Sorry Caroline and the kids can't join tonight. She's gotta shuttle Emmy to dance and then Connor to basketball."

Olivia wraps him in a hug, her delight evident. "We'll see them on Friday night for dinner. I'm just so glad you could make it home to see your brother before the weekend craziness begins." She steps aside, clearing the path to Dalton.

"Hey Jordan," Dalton says, extending a hand.

Jordan laughs—a chortle if ever I heard one—and his dark eyes dance as he swats Dalton's arm away and substitutes a bearhug in place of a handshake. "Hey, little brother."

Dalton gasps when he's released, and Jordan turns to me. "And you must be the apple of my brother's eye. You're just as pretty as he described you."

My mouth opens, but words don't come out. My face feels hot, and I'm grateful when Thomas says, "This is your brother's friend, Hillary."

Jordan gives me the same bearhug treatment he gave Dalton. I'm pretty sure he bruises my ribs.

We enjoy Thomas's homemade lasagna on the back patio. Conversation and laughter roar around me, and I savor it all. The Tremaines are all storytellers, and hearing them—no, *watching* them—tell their stories with exaggerated gestures and facial expressions is the best way I could have hoped to spend the night.

And they don't exclude me, which I love. We talk about roller coasters and favorite foods and camping trips and s'mores recipes and how funny Dalton looks in the photo from his senior prom, which Jordan has inexplicably set as the background image on his phone.

"It's a good thing Samantha's not here to see that," Thomas laughs from the head of the table. The mood shifts, at least for a moment, at Dalton and Olivia's seats.

"When do I get to meet this new lady, brother?" Jordan leans back and crosses his arms over his broad chest.

"I don't know," comes the response, a manufactured energy propelling it out of him.

"Well, I can't wait. I remember getting that text from you, then one from Mom, so excited. 'It's finally happening, Jordy. Your brother thinks he's found the one.'"

My face has to be as red as the tomato sauce my eyes are now glued to.

Dalton shifts next to me. "Seriously, Mom?"

I hear the smile in Olivia's voice. "Of course! I'm thrilled for you, dear. You deserve to be happy."

"I *am* happy. I've been happy for years."

"I never said you weren't. But you have to admit, there's something different about you these last few months."

"We've only been dating for three weeks."

Olivia breezes by the response and pulls me into this conversation. "Hillary, you spend a lot of time with him. Don't you think he's different?"

"We really don't need to have this conversation," Dalton mutters under his breath.

I raise my glass for a drink of water. "I haven't noticed anything different, honestly." I want to be far, far away from here.

Dalton must want to be far, far away as well, because he pushes back from the table and stands, dropping his napkin on the chair before walking away. "I can't do this right now."

Olivia rises and calls after him, "You can't tell me you've met 'the one'—how'd you say it? 'She's *it*, Mom'—and expect me to not get excited."

Dalton stiffens and stops at the door.

I choke on the water, coughing, sputtering. Olivia, Thomas, and Jordan all turn at the sound. I wheeze out "I'm fine" and when I've convinced them I'm not in danger of dying all eyes turn back toward Dalton.

Rather, all eyes turn back toward the spot where Dalton just stood.

....

"I'm so sorry for how things happened at dinner." Olivia and I clear the table while Thomas and Jordan wash dishes inside. She has really warmed up to me since that first meeting in New York.

"It's not your fault." I shake my head. "He gets really weird when we talk about Samantha."

"So I see. It seems like he also gets weird when we *don't* talk about—" she pauses and emphasizes, "*Samantha.*"

Inside, my stomach lurches. Outside, I'm still stacking plates and silverware, trying to keep my hands from shaking and my jaw from hitting the floor. I muster, "I'm sorry?" and avoid eye contact at all costs.

"Hillary." Olivia stops and sets her stack of cups on the table. She turns to me with a hand on her hip. "We don't need to play this game."

My face goes hot in an instant. "What game?"

"How long have you and my son been dating? And what is this hoax with Samantha?"

"Dalton and I are definitely not dating." It's the one response I can think of that is fully truthful.

"That's a shame."

I meet her gaze. "What?"

She rolls her eyes and smiles. "Sweetheart, the two of you would be great together."

My heart pounds in my chest. It's entirely possible she can hear it. "No, we—we're not—" I stammer. Sighing, I say, "We're just friends. And besides, in New York you said—"

"In New York I realized after spending the day with you that *you* make him happy. Not that awful Samantha *Darling*."

She draws me in for a motherly hug. "He needs time to come to his senses. I hope it's not too much to ask you to give him the opportunity." When she releases me she cups my face in her hands and uses her thumbs to wipe the fresh tears off my cheeks.

"I know I'm biased," she says, "but I really think he's worth the wait."

I agree.

TWENTY-ONE

I slept about 2.8 minutes last night. Between the wind and subsequent thunderstorm that rolled in and the taxidermied zoo watching me from the walls of Jordan's childhood bedroom, I couldn't relax enough to fall asleep.

I imagine most of the issue was actually attributed to dinner. What Olivia said to Dalton, what Olivia said to me—the words cycled through my head, and I tossed and turned for hours.

And just as I was drifting off to sleep, as the sky lightened from midnight blue to navy, *knock knock knock*.

Willing it to stop doesn't work, so I throw back the covers and pull on a sweatshirt before answering the door. Dalton is on the other side.

"Can we talk?"

"Right now?"

Somehow, he looks wide awake, even though I don't think he's slept either. He's got a five o'clock shadow and is dressed in blue jeans and a white T-shirt. His eyes are alive, intense. Yes, he means right now.

I pull the door further open but he shakes his head. "How soon can you be dressed and ready to go?"

Yawning, I answer, "I dunno, ten minutes, maybe?"

"Great," he nods. "Meet me out front when you're ready."

I have no idea what we're doing or where we're going, so I brush my teeth in the bathroom down the hall and tiptoe back to Jordan's old room. I figure a pair of faded jeans, a tank top, and a zip-up hoodie are appropriate, given Dalton's attire, and once I'm dressed I slide on a pair of sneakers and head outside.

A thick layer of mist has settled into the hills, and between their peaks the rising sun has turned the sky gold.

"Wow."

"I know."

I expected him to be in the rental car, but he's sitting on a gliding swing on the front porch, a mug in his hands and another on a small table next to him.

"It's no latte, but I made this for you," he says, handing me the second mug. "I was thinking of driving into town, but it's so nice right here. Want to sit?"

I take the mug and lower myself into the space next to him, letting the hot ceramic warm my hands, offsetting the chill in the air.

"What do you want to talk about?" Last night, when Dalton got back from wherever he stormed off to, I could hear him talking to Olivia in impassioned whispers.

"I actually think I want to talk about nothing in particular. Just...talk. Like we used to."

"You woke me up at five thirty to just talk?"

He turns his face to mine, worry creasing his eyes. "Yeah. Sorry, it was stupid."

"No." I shake my head. "I like it."

A smile turns up one side of his mouth. "Wonderful."

He turns back to the mist, the mountains, and the sunrise. We enjoy the silence here like we do during a morning run through Central Park, or an evening at The Battery, where the water ripples as the East River and the Hudson greet one another. Nature is a conversation of her own, and we listen to her stories.

"What's your dream?" I ask the question with little thought first. I don't regret it.

"My dream?"

"Yes." I ignore his examination of my face. I want to leave the question open-ended. I want to hear it all and not guide him to any specific genre.

He leans forward like he always does when he's thinking, forearms on thighs, thumbs tracing the rim of his coffee mug. "I want to be happy."

"Don't we all?" I ask, dryly.

"Do we?" he counters and turns toward me. When I don't meet his gaze, he sighs and returns his gaze to the hills. "I want to make it on Broadway."

"And?"

"What do you mean, *and*? That's it. That's the dream."

I shake my head, rejecting his answer. "No, I want to know it all. Your perfect life—what's it look like?"

After a moment, he says, "I want to make it on Broadway. I want to have a role that everyone knows about—even people who don't follow theater. I'd love the recognition, an award, just to validate the time and the energy I've been putting in the last fourteen years, and, I'm sure, the next fourteen, too.

"But more than that—more than fame, more than money, more than the dream job—I guess I just want someone next to me to do life with."

"Is that it?"

"I think that's enough." Without hesitation he asks me the same question.

"My perfect life is taking my laptop or journal somewhere new and beautiful every morning and writing whatever I can. Publish a book a year, have a home to call my own, and travel the world."

"Sounds exciting."

"I think so."

"It also sounds lonely."

If he's waiting for a response, he'll be waiting for a while.

"Seriously, Hillary."

"I just don't think you need to get married to have a dream life."

"And I never said you did." He sips his coffee and furrows his brow. "It could really be anyone—a parent, a sibling, a friend..."

"Then it's settled. Lindsey and I will just have to grow old together."

"She is *definitely* who I had in mind," he rolls his eyes.

Eventually he asks, "Do you think you'll ever get married? Even if it's not part of the dream life?"

I inhale the aroma of the coffee and take a slow sip, thinking. "I'm honestly not sure. I know I'm *supposed* to. But I just don't know if I *want* to. Not anymore."

"Ahh, so there was a time when you wanted to?"

I turn my body on the swing and curl a leg up under me. "Once upon a time, yes. I loved looking at wedding dresses online or when I'd go with friends who were shopping for their gowns. I envisioned bouquets of pink and purple peonies and a three-tier lemon-raspberry cake."

"That sounds amazing."

I close my eyes and see it all. The long banquet tables lining the dance floor, flowers and twinkling lights hanging from the ceiling, organza and tulle billowing behind me as we stand at the altar outside and dance the night away with friends and family. But that was before. *Now* is very different.

His fingertips rest on my knee. "You okay?"

When my eyes open at his touch, he's leaning in, eyes wide. "You disappeared there for a second."

I clear my throat and turn back to the mountains. The sun is now fully awake and floating above the distant trees. "I'm fine."

"Where did you go?"

My fingernails scratch the base of my mug. "Back to Lemming." With a sigh, I add, "To Peter."

"Peter? You've never mentioned him before," he says, turning away from me, watching the sun.

I talk about Peter as little as possible. I've made an effort to keep the past out of my present, so I've never brought him up in conversation with Dalton. There's an unspoken rule between us: no question is off-limits. If one of us broaches a subject, any follow-up or conversation around it is fair game.

"Do you want to tell me about him?"

I look sideways at his face, his strong jawline and the poof of unkempt, morning-in-the-mountains hair that falls over his forehead. "Do you want to hear about him?"

His eyes meet mine, his face etched with something like concern. He scans my face before his gaze drops to his feet. "I want to hear everything you're willing to share. You know that."

I swallow hard and calm my nerves. I want him to know all of it, but I don't want to cry when I tell him. "Peter and I dated for three years. We broke up about a month before I moved in with Lindsey." *Breathe.* "It absolutely destroyed me. I didn't even know who I was without him. Still trying to figure it out."

"You seem to be doing well."

A snicker escapes my lips. "I fake it pretty well, I guess."

"I mean it," he says, bringing his eyes back to mine. "From the day I met you I've noticed this confidence to be your own person. To explore the city, write your story, laugh at stupid things, smile about little things. Like you're not trying to impress people, and you're just doing everything that makes you happy."

Not *everything*.

"There's a difference between being quirky and being confident."

He smirks.

"Anyway. Things were great for a while. We had an incredibly boring life together. Every night that we'd hang out, it was just watching TV reruns or playing cards and eating takeout."

"Ugh, that sounds amazing."

"Right? And it was, sometimes. But that was all he wanted to do. Video games. Watching sports. He interacted more with the TV than he did with me."

"That makes no sense."

"*Thank you.* And whenever we went somewhere, he just complained the whole time. 'This place is too crowded,' or 'It's too hot,' or 'It's too cold,' or 'It's raining! You know I hate the rain, *Hillary*,' like I controlled the weather."

Maybe it's the sleep deprivation that makes me share more than I want to.

"He even suggested we get married."

Dalton's jaw drops. "He proposed?"

"Ha! No, he didn't. Just said, 'maybe we should get married' like that was some big romantic gesture. There was never a ring, just a comment. But I think the whole town expected it would happen, eventually, because that's what you do. You settle down and start a family. The earlier, the better, as far as they're concerned."

"Did you consider doing that?"

My head shakes all on its own. "Not really. I knew it wasn't right. That doesn't mean it wasn't hard to end it, though."

"No?"

My stomach knots and I keep my gaze locked on the mug of coffee in my hands. "No. I mean, there was a lot of other stuff going on in my life at the time, and on top of everything else I was basically going to be a spinster who broke Peter's heart because of my selfishness. Everyone's so embedded in the community, and they don't understand why anyone would want to leave."

"So what made you end things? The non-proposal?"

"He adopted a kitten."

"Is that a bad thing?"

"Okay I realize how that sounds," I say. "Adopting an animal is great. But he knows I am severely allergic to cats."

"Wow. That's a dick move."

"Yeah. In all of our time together I never really saw him get passionate about anything. Not about birthdays or anniversaries or anything. And then he gets this damn cat, and he's all in."

"So what happened? Did you lay down the law? Say 'not in my house' and tell him to get rid of it?"

My eyes snap toward him, and I snort. "Well, it wasn't *my* house. He could do whatever he wanted."

"Wait, you guys were together for three years and you weren't living together?"

I can feel my cheeks reddening. "No."

"Oh. I just figured—" he says, biting his lip.

I shake my head and repeat, "No." Then, to ease the tension, "What, you think I'm just out there moving in with any guy who'll let me?" I nudge his shoulder with mine and he smiles.

"Anyway," I sit up straight again, "I let him know I was angry. Actually, more hurt than anything. That if he was serious about us, he needed to lose the cat. Then the next night that I went over it was still there. And the next night. And the one after that."

"Ouch."

"Yeah. I think he figured it was empty words, that I'd just somehow get over my allergies." I roll my eyes. "And that I'd continue to put up with his bullshit. But then I stopped."

"Good for you."

"Thanks."

He watches the mountains and the mist. "Did you love him?"

"I did. Without him, I was just on my own. We'd spent so much of our time together, so I didn't really have many friends outside of our relationship. I loved having a person to do nothing with."

He nods and turns to me. "But did you love *him*?"

I've wondered that often and convinced myself that I did. Maybe a part of me has wanted to feel the heartache, to be a victim. To have someone to be angry with. But maybe I just loved the idea of a relationship and being part of something so I didn't feel so alone. Maybe I wanted to be able to blame someone else for my life being messy, so I didn't have to blame myself.

"Honestly, I don't know. I don't really have anything to compare it to. I don't know how love is supposed to feel."

His Adam's apple bobs as he swallows. His lips part and close again and he shifts his focus to the sky.

I lean my head against his shoulder. "Sorry to dump that on you."

His body, initially tense, relaxes. "Don't ever apologize for sharing who you are."

Suddenly it's like we're back in Eunoia or on the High Line, absorbing each other's lives and stories, learning about and appreciating one another—all the dinged-up, bruised, broken parts.

But instead of being in a noisy city, filled with strangers at every turn, we're alone on a perfectly peaceful morning, sitting on a swing, drinking our coffee like his parents must have done so many mornings in their forty-year marriage. My head on his shoulder. His hand crawling, a centimeter here, an inch there, across the seat toward me.

Peter flashes into my mind and I replay our three years together in hyperspeed. The initial butterflies, the first few dates to baseball games or parties his friends threw. The video games. The reruns. The hatred of coffee shops and farmers markets and bookstores. Even when we sat to watch TV, we had our own separate chairs. If we sat together on the couch, he was suddenly not content with just sitting and watching TV.

Everything was what Peter wanted, what Peter liked. And that never included just *being* with one another, talking and learning and appreciating. Never like this.

Never this chest-heaving, breath-quickening, *just-touch-me-already* feeling, like I have sitting here watching Dalton Tremaine inch closer to me.

I know I *should* sit up. I know I *should* go inside, shower, and prepare for the day. I know I *should* remind him about Samantha and their arrangement.

But what I *do* is casually drop my hand from the mug in my lap to an empty space on the seat cushion, between my leg and his hand, so that in two more movements he'll graze my fingers with his.

And when it happens, fire erupts through my body. I clench my jaw and try to regulate my breathing. Part of me hopes he can't sense what this does to me. Part of me hopes he can. All of me hopes he feels the same way I do.

His pinky interlocks with mine, then inches further toward me again as I turn my palm upward to him. His fingers weave into mine and his face turns against my head.

And suddenly it's over. He pulls his hand from mine and stands, coffee splashing from his mug as he rises. "Hi, Dad," he says.

My face burns, embarrassed, sure I look like some homewrecker to Thomas Tremaine, who is standing in the doorway three feet to my left and, as far as I can tell, still thinks his son is dating a starlet.

Thomas clears his throat. "I could use your help in the basement. If you're free." He disappears back into the house.

Dalton stands a moment longer, his eyes fixed on the door, as a vein throbs in his forehead. I've seen it before when he's stressed. Finally he looks at me and hooks a thumb toward the house. "I gotta—" he says, and he clears his throat.

"Yeah, sure. Of course," I answer.

He lingers a moment longer and takes off after his dad.

....

"Oh, hello dear," Olivia greets me in the kitchen when I wash my mug. "Have you had a good morning so far?" I swear she winks.

I nod. "The mountains were beautiful this morning."

She smiles warmly and rests a hand on my wrist. "The mountains are *always* beautiful." She draws a smile from me as I dry the mug, then takes it from my hands and returns it to the proper cabinet.

"Did you enjoy the sunrise?"

"Yes, very much."

"Good. Thomas and I have enjoyed many sunrises on that swing, too."

For what seems like the millionth time already this morning, I feel myself blush. Thankfully, she moves on.

"Would you like to come along for a drive with me today? I've got to pick up my dress for this party."

I'd really like to do nothing today except be with Dalton, but she sweetens the deal. "We can take the Bel Air."

"Sold!" I laugh.

I shower and let my hair air-dry while I rub a little creme shadow onto my eyelids, swipe waterproof mascara over my lashes, and glide on a berry lip gloss. I pull on a smocked sundress with straps that tie into fluttery bows.

Dalton and his dad have taken off in Thomas's pickup, heading to the hardware store for a few odds and ends, so I leave a note for him, just in case.

Shopping with your mom
Picking up her dress
Thanks for putting up with me
Even when I'm a mess

—HJ

I never said the note was *good*.

The mid-morning sun warrants a top-down ride through the hills of Greentree, and Olivia blasts early nineties pop music through the CD player Thomas installed shortly after he bought the car. When we arrive at our destination, neither of us cares that our hair is windblown and knotted. We're all smiles as we walk into the bridal shop.

I browse the racks of gowns as Olivia changes, and when the fitting room curtain opens, she's beaming in a floor-length gown. The A-line skirt is a deep burgundy, and the black bodice has a square neckline and elbow-length sleeves. The two colors meet at the waist with a dramatic, asymmetrical bow.

"Wow," I whisper.

"What do you think?"

"It's beautiful."

"I think so, too!" She turns to the shop's owner, who is also the seamstress. "Rhonda here has been so great, creating this from scratch for me."

My jaw has to be on the floor. "You *made* this?" I ask, and Rhonda blushes. "It's absolutely stunning."

"Thank you," she says.

Olivia faces a mirror and squeals, and I catch myself, severely underdressed, in the reflection. "I didn't realize the party was so formal."

"Oh, yes. It's black tie. I'm shocked Dalton didn't tell you—he and Jordan have just been going on and on about this black-tie thing, which I didn't even want at first, but now…" she smooths the bodice of her gown, watching her reflection in the mirror.

"How is that Dalton, by the way?" Rhonda asks. "I saw

on the internet he was dating that nice young lady from New York."

"Samantha *Darling*," Olivia says. "Yes, I think my son is absolutely smitten." But she's looking at me, her eyes twinkling.

"He always was such a good kid," Rhonda says, tidying a display of clutch purses. "You know him too?" she asks me.

I smile and nod. "Yes, we've met." It feels like the safest answer I can give.

Thankfully Olivia chimes in. "Much as I hate to take this off, Rhonda, I think I probably should. What do I owe for the final alterations?"

The women disappear into the fitting room and, overwhelmed by the sea of wedding dresses, I explore the bridesmaids section. Though I should be looking for a dress for Saturday night, my eyes land instead on a pair of shoes: sky-high gold-heeled stilettos with beaded straps across the toes and around the ankle. It's possible I drool at the sight of them. It's possible I drool even more when I try them on and they fit. I can't even say what happens when I see the price tag.

I packed a plain black cocktail dress for this trip; it's not exactly black tie, but I can dress that up with these shoes and call it a day.

"I'm so glad someone is finally taking those shoes off my hands," Rhonda says when we all meet at the register.

"Are you kidding? They're fabulous!"

"You don't have to tell me—I'm the one who ordered them! But they're maybe too flashy for this area."

"They're gorgeous," Olivia smiles.

I happily turn over my credit card for the $14.99 she's charging for them.

Olivia pays for her dress and carries the garment bag to the car as I follow behind, still clutching the shoebox.

The Bel Air winds along the hillside roads back to their rancher. We're back by lunchtime. "Thanks so much for coming along with me," she says, resting a hand on my shoulder. "You're good people."

I return the smile and thank her for the trip, then follow her inside. I put the shoes with the rest of my things and find Dalton in the kitchen.

"Hi," he says from behind the island. He's got a bowl of grapes in his hand and various foods all around him.

"Hi," I smile. I hope it looks natural. I hope he can't see my nerves.

"I have a little afternoon adventure planned for us."

"Is that so?"

"Yes. And you're going to want to change. Can you be ready in ten minutes?"

I nod. "I guess. What are we doing? What do I need to wear?"

"It's a surprise," he shares. "But wear something comfortable that can get a little dirty."

TWENTY-TWO

"That'll work," he says when I model my leggings, sneakers, tank top, and hoodie for him.

Outside, his dad's truck is loaded with two kayaks on its roof, and Dalton's got a cooler in the back. "Time for an adventure," he winks.

On the drive to wherever we're going, I toy with the idea of laying my hand in the seat next to me, or resting my elbow on the armrest to see if his hand will come searching for mine again. I end up keeping my hands clasped in my lap, and his hands stay at ten and two the whole trip, other than to adjust the volume when a good song comes on the speakers.

"I never took you for a country music fan."

He stops singing long enough to say, "I love all types of music."

I arch an eyebrow at his story. "I just think that if you actually liked country, it would've come up by now. That's a bombshell secret you can't just keep from the people in your life."

He laughs. "I enjoy it when I'm here. It just fits."

He parks the car in a gravel lot with a stack of kayaks and canoes and an old port-a-potty off to the side. A few other cars are here already, but there's no one visible on the small pond next to us. Tall weeds line the perimeter, and a narrow concrete dock slants down into the water.

"Have you ever kayaked before?" he asks, and I nod.

"Once. About two years ago."

"Need a refresher?" he asks.

"No, I've got it. Can't guarantee I'll go in a straight line, but I can paddle."

The words draw a laugh from him. "Straight lines are no fun anyway."

Once the kayaks are on the ground, our life vests are on, and snacks are stowed away in his kayak's storage compartment, he hands me a water bottle and locks the truck door.

"You ready?"

"As I'll ever be."

He helps me push off from the shore first, then nearly falls into his kayak as it wobbles during his boarding. His laugh fills the air and mine responds. Soon we're both paddling, and I'm relearning the art of moving forward and not just in 180-degree arcs.

Trees surround the pond, and we're content to sit quietly at times to hear the distant woodpeckers or the *purdy purdy purdy* call of the cardinals that flit from tree to tree. At some point we decide to race to the far end of the pond, except the far end isn't an end at all.

Initially hidden from view, to our left there's now an opening to a much larger lake, with a sandy, stony shoreline on its left and cozy cottages on its right bank.

"Wow."

"Isn't it great?" he asks.

"It is."

I paddle along, following just behind him, letting him guide me through the larger body of water. He points out a few houses on the right that belong—or did, at one point—

to friends of his from high school.

"That blue house there, with the dock on the water. That's where I fell in when I was fishing."

"You're kidding."

"Caught a tire. I was eight. It reeled *me* in."

I throw my head back and laugh, loving hearing his stories, loving the sunlight on my face for a fleeting moment before it disappears again behind a heavy cloud.

We're gliding slowly, and he dips a paddle in the water to turn, and my kayak skims his. He reaches out with his paddle and pulls my kayak alongside his, then tethers them together. "Let's have lunch."

So we sit side by side, on a perfect day in early May, eating grapes, bananas, and sandwiches, floating on the water in a picture-perfect place.

"I loved coming out here when I was growing up."

Through a half-chewed bite of sandwich I ask, "Have you always kayaked here? Or mostly just fished?"

"Anything. Everything. I loved being on the water. And that, over there—" he points to the shoreline behind us and to our left, "—that was our beach growing up."

"Seriously?"

"Yeah. We'd come down here every weekend and swim over there, set up lawn chairs in the sand. That little building on the right, that's the snack hut. My first job was there, dipping ice cream cones."

I feel a smile spread on my lips as I think of him as a teenager, serving sundaes to beach-goers and paddling around in a kayak when his shift was over, maybe over to a friend's house across the lake to fish.

"You're making a face," he says.

"I'm smiling."

He eyes me and pops a grape into his mouth. "You're judging."

I shake my head, smiling wider. "I'm imagining. I'm learning. I'm loving this."

"I bet," he winks.

"Hey—I enjoy learning more about you. Where you come from, who you were as a kid—it's all pieces of the puzzle."

"As long as you don't ask my mom for my baby album."

"That is actually a *great* idea. Gives me some plans for the evening."

He dips his hand in the lake and flicks his fingers at me, splattering me with fishy water. "Hey!" I shout, returning the favor.

A strong breeze rolls in, rocking the kayaks, and the clouds grow thicker.

"We should head back," he says, though I don't think either of us wants to leave.

He packs up the last of the fruit and stows it in the dry compartment, then untethers us just as thunder rolls in the distance and a flash of light streaks across the sky.

"Follow me."

With the wind pushing against us, it might be a fifteen-minute trip back to the shore where we parked. With rain already falling in steady sheets, he leads me on the five-minute trip to the beach. He steps out of his kayak into a foot of water and steadies my boat.

Thunder growls as I clamber from my cockpit and join him on the sand. We pull the kayaks completely out of the water, and he grabs my hand, leading me as he darts to the shelter of a small pavilion that houses a trio of wooden picnic tables.

Rain blows in behind us.

He runs his hands halfway through his hair, then shakes them vigorously, releasing water droplets like a dog who shakes after a bath. "This is nuts!" he yells over the rain that pounds off the roof above.

"It really is! It came out of nowhere!"

"Do you still love thunderstorms?"

I nod. "You?"

He turns serious and squints one eye as water drips from his hair to his eyelashes and nose and then past his lips. "More than ever."

Suddenly a phone rings, and he pats each of his pockets to find it. It's buried in a zippered compartment in his cargo shorts. "Mom?" he asks into the receiver. "Mom, can you hear me?" And he's using the same trick I used that day when we first met, squishing the tragus over the ear canal to block out the sound of the rain that pounds the roof and ground.

"We're fine, Mom. We're okay!" He argues with the phone a bit more, then hangs up and starts typing out a text message.

"Everything alright?"

"Yeah, just my mom making sure we're okay. This storm came out of nowhere and she was worried."

"It's nice that she still worries about you."

He pauses and raises an eyebrow. "I'm a thirty-four-year-old man whose mother still checks in when it rains."

"Well, when you say it like that…"

"She's probably just making sure *you're* okay. You two seem very buddy-buddy today."

"I really like her. She took me with her to pick up her dress for the party. Which is apparently black tie?"

"Yeah, you didn't know?"

"How would I have known?" He shrugs and returns to his text message. "Anyway, it's fine. I think I have something I can wear, and I got a great new pair of shoes today."

"Nice," he says, without really paying attention. When he finishes his message he pockets his phone.

I step out from the pavilion, stretching my arm into the rain, welcoming the droplets on my skin. "It's slowing down, a little."

"That's good."

"If there was no lightning and I was on an open road, I'd be running in this right now."

"I'm sure you'd get quite a workout. That sweatshirt's got to be adding, what, eight pounds?"

"It's like a weighted vest. But squishy."

"You know," he says, standing and looking up at the sky from the pavilion's edge, "I haven't seen lightning in a while."

"And the thunder doesn't sound as close anymore."

He pulls out his phone again and opens a weather app. "Radar shows the storm is past us. Just rain now, for at least an hour."

"Mmm. Probably not the best kayaking conditions."

"Probably not. You up for a hike instead?"

And so we set out into the trees that tower overhead. He turns on a playlist that he promises will "keep the snakes away." I turn up the volume as loud as it will go. The rain trickles down, filtered through layers of leaves, and the ground is spongy beneath our feet.

A toppled tree blocks our path, and he takes my hand as I climb over it.

"Probably not today, but if you're really quiet here on a spring evening, right at dusk, you might see deer, or maybe a fox."

"That sounds amazing."

"It is. There's a clearing up here, and if you're lucky you might catch five or six of 'em, just grazing there."

"Do you hike back here often?" I crave his stories; I yearn to know every detail that has led to him becoming the man he is. "Did you, I mean?"

"All the time. I'd dip the ice cream, go for a hike. Kayak around the lake, go for a hike. And right up there—in that clearing—we'd get together on Friday nights in the fall to build a campfire and make s'mores and tell ghost stories."

"Quintessential teenagers."

"It gets better," he says, winking. "I had my first kiss up here."

"Really."

He nods. "Sure did. Mary Carver, sixth grade."

"Wait—" I stop, grabbing his arm. "I'm sorry, you mean to tell me you had your first kiss when you were in sixth grade? What were you, eleven?"

His eyes dance. "Twelve, actually, and I never said it was a good one. I came up here with my friends and their older siblings, and someone dared Mary to do it. She was in eighth grade and had never kissed anyone."

"I have so many questions I don't dare ask." I laugh loudly, and he does too. It echoes over the sound of the rain around us.

We reach the clearing and I step out hesitantly. The rain has ramped back up to a torrential downpour, but I'm soaked anyway, so I step out further. A different song comes on—one that was popular about twenty years ago. "Is this what you were listening to when you and Mary were sucking face up here?"

I know the song well and start dancing along in the clearing, filling in the gaps from memory when I lose the lyrics and the beat in the rain.

He smiles from the tree line and leans against a sturdy trunk. "You're crazy!"

He denies every one of my requests for him to join me in my impromptu dance party, choosing instead to lean against a tree with his arms crossed and a goofy grin on his face. When the song is over, he says, "I want to show you one more thing," and leads me down one more path. The rain has slowed again, and the sun works diligently to make an appearance.

Ahead, the ground takes a sharp incline on the left. Someone has built a rock garden in a smaller clearing to our right, and in the cliff next to us there is an opening, forming a small alcove. It's shallow, but tall enough for us to stand in without bumping our heads.

"Last thing, and then we can go back."

"Okay." I don't want to go back at all.

"When I was in high school, I'd come up here on really cold days, or rainy days like today when no one in their right mind would be here, and I'd just sing into the woods."

"You would?"

He nods. We're shoulder to shoulder in the alcove, looking out over the rocky audience and the towering trees. "I wanted a place all to myself, where I could practice for my college auditions or my school musicals, or just for fun, and not have Jordan or my parents around. And then I tried coming up here to write songs, and that didn't go well at all."

"No? Why not?"

He shrugs. "Not sure. Just didn't have that gift, I guess. Or not inspired enough."

The rain has turned to mist, but drops still ricochet down from rich green leaf to rich green leaf.

He sighs. "He's an idiot, you know."

I turn to him, looking for clues, but his eyes are fixed on the woods. "What?"

"Peter. He's an idiot. I hope it's okay that I say that."

My heart beats faster and my breaths are shorter. "I mean, I say it all the time."

Normally he would laugh. Normally he would say that was funny or fill the air with his deep, hearty chuckle, but not right now. Instead, he says, "It's not too rainy. There's no such thing as too rainy. And there's no such thing as too hot or too cold—not with you. Because with you, everything is perfect. Every moment. Every day. It's exactly how it should be."

If I'm supposed to respond, my brain doesn't get the script. My response is physiological; every part of my body reacts, save for the vocal cords.

His fingers, hanging beside mine, search the space between us until our hands are entwined together again, and he turns to me. His free hand cups my chin and he raises his other hand to do the same. When he lets go of my hand, my fingers fall to his wrist, then follow the curve of the muscles in his forearm.

I hadn't looked until now, but his T-shirt is soaked through, clinging to his muscles. But I can't look at that for long, because his eyes are on mine. They move to my lips, then scan my face for any instructions they can find.

I know he's read me clearly when he tilts my chin upward and leans toward me, two magnets drawn together. He hovers inches from my face, his eyes alive and green, his lips parted. Warm breath that smells of banana and hazelnut touches my skin and his eyes close as he places his mouth gently on mine.

It doesn't last long—it's a trial of sorts, to read my reaction, which is a silent begging, pleading for more.

He knows me. He's learned so much about me, can interpret every sign, that he pulls us together again. His left hand slides up my neck and into my hair, his fingers splayed through the wet strands. His right hand holds my waist, drawing me in for a deeper kiss. Then his tongue finds mine. Soon both hands are on the sweatshirt zipper, sliding it down, pushing the heavy fabric from my shoulders. The sun has reemerged, and its rays warm my skin.

Everything is warm regardless, because Dalton is against me and heat courses through every vein in my body. His hands, finding bare spots of skin where my tank top lifts in our embrace, ignite me. The mostly-smooth rocks are damp and cool on my back, and Dalton's chest and abs are firm against mine. I'm quite literally between a rock and a hard place.

My nails dig into his back through the barrier of his dripping shirt, but when his mouth moves to my jaw, then my neck, I push against his chest.

He pulls back, surprised. "Are you okay? Is this okay?"

Yes, it's so fucking good.

"I just think—"

Shut up, brain! Shut up, mouth!, my body scolds. Clearly logical thought has taken over, and my heart is quite displeased. As is literally every part of me.

I avoid his eyes, because I know that if I see them, I will lose myself in them and give in to every desire I have. "I just think maybe it would be a good idea to get back, just in case another storm comes in."

If he's upset, he doesn't show it. Instead he pauses and nods, then releases me from his hands and runs them through his hair. "Yeah. That makes sense."

When he steps out ahead of me, I exhale. My heart is still pounding. My knees are weak. I want all of him wrapped around me, warming me, holding me. But instead I've got a water-logged sweatshirt and an ache in my chest.

....

We glide across the lake as the remnants of the storm make the water around us dance. At times, he stops paddling and takes in the shoreline on either side. I wriggle myself lower in my seat and recline to open myself to the sun, which warms the sticky air and beats through my still-damp leggings.

"I know I told you I don't regret leaving," he says, "but coming back here—this is the one place I miss more than anywhere else."

"Because of the memory of your first kiss?"

"Ha! No. It was an awful kiss, by the way." He shakes his head, and the silliness seems to disappear. He surveys the pond, the trees, the hills; he says, "This is my favorite place."

"Really? This lake?"

"Mmhmm. At least, it was my favorite place as a child."

"What about now? Still your favorite?"

He shrugs and looks into my eyes. "Depends. I think my favorite place changes pretty frequently and is somehow always the same."

"That makes no sense."

His eyes dance like the water, and his lips curl upward. Then he returns his attention to the shore and says, "Race ya back. Loser buys winner a drink."

His toned arms expertly move his paddle, alternating sides of his kayak, gliding in a near-perfect line. He doesn't appear to be in a hurry. I, on the other hand, flail and overexert myself moving my whole body with each choppy stroke, but I muscle past him—a surprise to both of us. As Dalton pulls up to the dock ten feet behind me he's doubled over, mocking my competitive spirit or my form or—more likely—both with a deep laugh roaring from his lungs.

I'm panting and laughing, and I smear the happy wind-induced tears that have welled in my lower lids across my face. "That—that was amazing." A fresh round of giggles erupts before the old round has a chance to fade.

"You're pretty pleased with yourself, aren't you?" His chest still bobs with laughter.

"Oh, I am *very* pleased with myself. Do you know how good you are at going in a straight line? How fast you are?"

He grins and one loud chuckle bursts out of him. "I thought I did."

We manage to tie the kayaks back into the truck, though random bursts of laughter delay the process a few times. He opens my door for me, and I climb ungracefully into my seat.

He takes a minor detour on the way back to his parents' house, stopping at a gas station with a self-serve coffee station. I wait in the truck, and he emerges with a toasted marshmallow flavored cappuccino.

"What do you think?" he asks as I take the first sip.

"It's not terrible," I answer. "Thank you."

"So we're even then."

Realizing what he's done, I turn sideways in my seat and

see the smirk forming on his face. "Um, no. Not even. This does *not* count as the drink you owe me."

"Really?"

"Really."

"So, I need to take you out somewhere?"

"Those are the rules."

"To a bar, or a restaurant?"

"Yup. Either."

He cocks his head to the side as he maneuvers a winding section of road. "So you want to go out? Like on a date? Is that what you're saying?"

I watch his expression transition from fake confused to downright mischievous. "Clever trick, Tremaine."

"So that's a yes, then?"

I roll my eyes at him, though he can't see it. "We've gone out to dinner plenty of times before."

"That's different," he protests.

"How so?" I ask, pivoting toward him and planting my elbow on the armrest between us, resting my chin in my hand. We make the turn onto his parents' road.

"Because before, we were friends."

I want him to put words to what happened, or what we are, or help me make sense of everything that has happened this afternoon. "And we're not friends anymore?"

"You know what I mean," he says, pulling my hand from under my chin and clasping it in his. "We were *just* friends before."

My heart races, but I try to keep my voice even as I ask, "And what are we now?"

We're three houses from his parents' home, and he leans in to kiss my hand. "I don't know exactly, but I think I'll enjoy finding out."

A shiver rolls through me as I consider his lips on mine again, him discovering more of me, and learning who we can be together. "I think I'd like that, too."

He holds my hand on the armrest as we pull into the driveway and drops it when he sees who is sitting on the porch swing.

"What the hell?"

Never one to miss her cue, Samantha Darling comes bounding across the lawn.

TWENTY-THREE

At least three times in the last twenty minutes, Samantha has complained about the slow cell service.

We're trying to play Clue, and all she wants is to post a picture of her and Dalton and their "quiet night in with his parents" to Instagram. "My fans would love to see this," she'd said as she handed me her phone. She then proceeded to delete the photo I took for her before posting a selfie of herself practically sitting on Dalton's lap.

The rest of us have avoided cell phones since Dalton and I arrived yesterday, instead enjoying our time together at dinner and breakfast, on the swing, or—and I nearly blush thinking about it—walking through the woods.

"It's your turn, Sami," he urges.

Thomas finishes refilling wine glasses and passing out fresh bottles of beer. Dalton takes a swig of his as I lift my glass to my lips across the table. He mouths *are we even?* behind Samantha's back and winks.

She rolls the dice and says, "I just really think my followers love to see pictures of us together. They want to see me happy. They also want to see our future babies."

Dalton nearly spits out his drink but somehow manages to swallow it all down. "I'm sorry, what?" he asks.

Olivia frowns.

"Oh, yeah. Don't you agree that our babies would be gorgeous?" she asks, kissing his forehead and leaving behind a faded red lip-shaped stain.

Olivia eyes Samantha, then Dalton, and saves her son. "So, Samantha, tell me again about this change of plans. I thought you weren't going to be able to be here this weekend."

She passes the dice along to me. "I was supposed to be working, but I told them I had a little tickle in my throat and knew I couldn't give the quality performance the audience deserved, and here I am!"

"Wonderful," Thomas chimes in. "The more the merrier."

She smiles at him and turns her attention to Dalton, fingering his still-damp hair. "So babe, what on earth possessed you to go for a hike in the pouring rain earlier?"

"In our defense, it was not pouring when we started the hike."

"That's a lie," I say, regretting it immediately. His eyes snap up to me and the others look, too. "It wasn't pouring when we started our *kayaking*. But it was coming down hard when we went for the hike."

"But still," Samantha shrugs. "Why go out at all with the weather so gross?"

Dalton says, "I wanted to explore a little," with a look my way that he tries—and fails—to hide. Goosebumps flood my skin.

Olivia adds defensively, "It was his favorite spot growing up."

There's worry or FOMO in her eyes when Samantha looks at me. "I want to see it, too."

Dalton's eyes shift between us, locking on mine for a moment, just before he responds. "That's okay. You don't have to go. I know you don't love all that outdoorsy kind of stuff."

If she can read the signs, the silent conversation between us, she'll be pissed. She has to be, at the very least, suspicious, and she presses again.

"Babe, if it's important to you, I want to see it. And I love being outside. Just last week I was at a party at the new rooftop bar off Sixth."

He glances my way again. I want to tell him, *you don't need my permission to take your fake girlfriend to your special happy place*, and I want to scream, *please don't take your fake girlfriend to your special happy place*. To avoid saying either I raise my glass of wine to my lips and down the last few gulps.

"Yeah, sure," he tells her. "If we have time this weekend, we can definitely go."

When the game ends, Thomas and Dalton take a tray of steaks out to the grill and start making dinner. Samantha asks if it's alright to take a quick shower. Her expensive-looking overnight bag sits just inside the front door.

"Would you mind showing me to my room, Olivia?"

Olivia bites her lip and furrows her brow. We both know every room in the house is spoken for.

"You can have Jordan's room."

Both women turn to look at me, and Olivia asks, "Where will you sleep?"

I shrug. "I can spend the night on the couch, an air mattress somewhere…"

"I hate to displace you, Hillary. I could just stay in Dalton's—"

"Absolutely not." Olivia doesn't let her fully finish her sentence. *Note to self: thank her later.*

Samantha, freshly scolded, has sad puppy eyes. "I'm sorry, I didn't mean to—"

"No, I'm sorry," Olivia interrupts. "I shouldn't have raised my voice. It's just that I'm not really comfortable with him sharing his room—like that—here."

"Respectfully, your son is thirty-five years old. He's an adult who can make his own choices."

"*Respectfully*, my son is thirty-*four* years old. And he is free to do whatever he pleases and whomever he chooses in his own space. But in *my* house, and for the comfort of all who are staying here, there are rules in place."

It's very likely that Samantha wants to argue more, but Olivia doesn't give her the opportunity. She turns on her heels and walks outside, leaving me alone with Samantha.

"I'll grab my things out of Jordan's room." I duck my head as I walk past her and lead her to the room two doors down from Dalton's. All I've got are a shoebox, oversized tote, and a basic black dress hanging in the closet, so hopefully I can escape quickly.

"Is she always this…intense?"

I'd never use that word to describe Olivia. "I think she's just doing what she thinks is best."

"Repressing his sexual energy?" she spits.

Would Olivia hate me if she knew the thoughts I had about Dalton or if she knew that his tongue had been in my mouth?

"Maybe she just wants to make sure nothing exciting happens. It's a big weekend, it's a small house, and everyone needs their sleep."

"Whatever," she says, sitting on the edge of the bed and sliding off her shoes. "Doesn't matter. We'll be back in New York in no time and then we can get back to being a normal couple. Without these *rules*."

"Sure. Anyway," I say, gathering the last of my things in my arms, "I'll get out of your hair. Enjoy the room. Bathroom's right next door."

....

"I had no idea you could cook like this," I gush, wiping my mouth with a paper napkin after finishing as much as I can eat of the steak.

Dalton's smile grows as Thomas corrects me: "It's not *cooking*, it's *grilling*."

"Well whatever it is, it's incredible. Ten outta ten."

"He's a great cook, too," Samantha adds, which we all know is not true.

"I am?" he asks, and Thomas laughs.

"Yeah," she says. "Remember the night you said you wanted to take our relationship to the next level, you made me that salmon and those really good, cheesy Brussels sprouts?"

Dalton meets my gaze. "Oh, right. That."

"Was that the hickory maple glaze salmon you had told me about?" I ask, hiding my smirk behind my glass of water.

"I believe it was, yes," he answers, raising a glass.

I had made the meal weeks ago, when we were tired of ordering takeout. So when Samantha insisted he come to her apartment to celebrate their relationship going public (so she could post their photo for her followers), I prepped the meal again and sent him over with ready-to-heat salmon and sprouts.

"It was honestly so, so good," she says, leaning her head against his shoulder. She stretches her right arm across her body and rests her hand on his forearm.

I pull my gaze from Dalton and see that Olivia is watching Samantha, her face wrinkled, swirling her wine in her glass so much it nearly spills over the edge. *She does not like this woman.* When my eyes travel to Samantha, she slides her left arm around his right and hugs it. Everything about her "relationship" with him is so performative, and it drives me crazy. I wonder if that's what has kept them from actually being in a relationship: Dalton's real, save for this whole arrangement, and Samantha is decidedly not.

Except when she looks at him. That expression—that yearning, that desire—that is real. And I am certain she's always wanted to be with him and doesn't know how to win him over.

It's nearly eight o'clock and Thomas decides we should watch their wedding video. "You're here to celebrate us, aren't you?" he asks, popping the old video tape into the VCR.

"Dad, we paid for that to be turned into a DVD years ago. Why are you still watching it on a fuzzy old VHS?"

"Because, son, you don't mess with the classics."

He reclines in an old La-Z-Boy. Dalton and Samantha take the couch, Olivia lowers herself onto a puffy ottoman, and I sit cross-legged on the floor next to her.

"So help me if any of you mock the fashion..." she says, and I answer with a laugh.

There's a fair amount of footage of them getting ready with their bridal party: makeup, pinning on boutonnieres, and lots of hairspray.

Then there's the ceremony. Olivia at the back of an old church sanctuary, floating down the aisle to a cello and piano duet of Pachelbel's Canon. On the video, Olivia beams, on the verge of laughter as Thomas wipes his eyes with the back of his hand. When she makes it to him, it's easy to read his lips: *You look beautiful.* And her response: *Thanks. You do, too.* And then their shoulders shake under the laughter they try to hide, standing in front of their friends and family, sharing a carefree moment during one of the most important moments of their lives.

Family members and friends read scripture passages I've known by heart since I was little: verses from Corinthians and Ephesians. Thomas's mom says a prayer. Olivia's college classmate reads an original poem.

When she finishes, I turn and rest my hand on Olivia's. "That was beautiful," I whisper. "And so incredibly special."

"Thank you. It's one of my favorite moments of the day, and one of the most meaningful things anyone has ever done for me."

I catch Dalton's eyes when I turn back toward the TV. Samantha is curled up into him and his arm is draped over her as she nuzzles into his shoulder. He looks so serious, so glum. I want to know everything he's thinking, but Samantha stirs and I panic, afraid she'll catch us in this phenomenon together, where every extended gaze is an intimate moment.

For the remainder of the video, I glue my eyes to the TV—even when it's hard to watch, like when her bridesmaids in ruby-red, drop-waist satin dresses with puffy sleeves scramble to catch her bouquet.

When reception highlights are over, there's a final portrait of Thomas and Olivia displayed on the screen. Her wide sweetheart neckline frames a heart-shaped ruby.

She sighs behind me. "I still can't believe I lost that necklace," she says. "I would have loved to have worn it this weekend, to the party."

Thomas and Dalton shift in their seats and exchange a look.

"Well," Thomas drawls, standing. "I was going to save this for when it was just the two of us, but now feels like as good a time as any."

He retreats to the kitchen and returns with a package that he'd kept hidden on top of the cabinets, where Olivia would never look and could never reach.

"Sweetheart, you've had my heart for more than forty years, and I want you to know you'll have it forever." He extends the gift-wrapped box to her.

When she unwraps it, she opens the velvet jewelry box to reveal a large, heart-shaped ruby pendant, surrounded by swirling gold and tiny diamonds. She gasps. "Oh, honey, I love it."

"I was hoping you would," Thomas says, his cheeks turning pink. Olivia climbs to her feet and he fastens the clasp behind her neck.

She pulls him close and kisses his cheek. "Thank you, my dear. I love you so much."

Samantha is on her feet, begging to see it. "It's so, so beautiful," she says. She tugs on Dalton's arm. "I've always thought a ruby engagement ring would be so special. Wouldn't that look gorgeous?"

He bites his lip and Olivia's smile withers. Not much, but I notice it.

I touch her arm and she turns to me. "It'll look perfect with your gown for the party."

Her smile brightens again. "I think so, too."

"And how fitting that the official 'gift' for the fortieth anniversary is a ruby."

"It really is," she says.

Samantha yawns, eliciting a matching response from Thomas.

"It's getting late, kiddos. I think I'm going to hit the sack. G'night," he waves, padding to the edge of the living room to wait as Olivia says her final goodnights, too.

Samantha disappears to unpack a bit more, and then it's just Dalton and me.

"You should take my room—I can sleep out here."

I wave off the suggestion. "No way. Your baseball cards have been waiting for this reunion."

I want to taste the smile that spreads across his lips.

"Anyway, I'm fine on the couch here, if that's okay."

He shrugs. "Yeah, if you want to. I'll grab a pillow and some blankets."

"Thanks."

When he returns and hands me the stack of bedding, his fingers graze mine. Neither of us moves, like our fingers are connected to a circuit we don't want to break.

"Your parents' wedding video was pretty fun to watch, huh?"

"Fun? I guess you could say that." His fingers slide away from mine, and he thrusts his hands into his pockets. "We grew up watching that video every year on their anniversary."

"So you've got the whole thing memorized?"

"Basically. And we're recreating bits and pieces for Saturday."

"Seriously? They'll love that."

He nods and cranes his neck to look down the hall toward his parents' room. "Yeah. There's just one issue."

I lower the blankets and pillows onto the couch. "What's wrong?"

A floorboard creaks down the hall and muffled voices seep through walls. "I can't ask you in here," he whispers, taking me by the hand and sneaking me to the back patio. With a hushed voice, he says, "We tried to get Wendy, Mom's college friend, to come read one of her poems again."

"What? She would *love* that!"

"Agreed, she would. But when we tried to find her, we couldn't. I mean, we could, but..." he shakes his head. "She passed away last year."

"That's terrible."

"It is." He bites his lip and paces the length of the patio, running his fingers all the way through his hair and then rubbing his neck. "I hate to ask you this, but is there any chance—I mean, would you be interested in—"

"Do you want me to read the poem Wendy wrote for their wedding? Is that what you're asking? Because I'm happy to help however I can."

"Would you write something yourself?"

I'm flattered, but I don't think I am the best fit for his parents' anniversary party. His parents, who have only known me for a month. His parents, who know of me as their son's random friend and temporary, secret roommate. His parents, who think Samantha Darling is his girlfriend. His parents, who would be as utterly confused as I am as to why I would be writing a poem for something as intimate as their anniversary party. But when I tell him this he waves off the concern.

"If you haven't noticed, my mom adores you. Dad does too, but he's on Team Samantha as long as he thinks we're actually dating. I promise you, they would be absolutely honored." He closes the gap between us and gently grips my forearms. "Please, Hillary."

God, his eyes. His freaking jawline, that bobbing, pleading Adam's apple, those lips parted just enough I feel his hot, steak- and stout-scented breath across my face. I can't resist him. But I do.

Then his jaw clenches and he swallows hard. "Please."

"I can't do this for you, Dalton. I can't just whip up something in thirty-six hours on my own. But maybe we can work together on it?"

"What do you mean, together? I'd be no help to you."

I nod. "You really would be. You've got their whole history to work off of. That's what I'm missing."

His eyes scan mine. "Okay. Just tell me what you need."

What I need is another ~~glass~~ half bottle of wine and a psychological evaluation. What have I just agreed to do?

I check my watch. It's already eleven. "I just need to know the whole story. How it started. Big steps along the way. But it's getting late—let's just talk tomorrow, okay?"

"Oh," he says, releasing my elbows. "Yeah, I mean, if you're tired. It's been a long day."

"It has been. But a pretty great one, too." *Watch it, Hillary. That's dangerously close to flirting.* The bulbs strung over the patio bathe us in warm yellow light, but even without them, the moon glows bright and stars litter the clear sky.

"Walk with me."

When I turn away from the stars and the moon his eyes are on me, urgent and warm. "Right now?" he asks, and I realize I'm the one who suggested the walk.

Shrugging, smiling, I reply, "I guess so."

His lips curl upward, and a chunk of hair falls over his forehead. He says, "Let me grab a few things" and I need to do that too: shoes, a journal and pen, sweater, my self-control…

We have the road to ourselves. Nothing in Greentree is open this late, apart from a bar across town. Still, we stick close to the shoulder, our own shoulders rubbing until we're far enough away from the house that his fingers entwine with mine.

"What do you want to know?" he asks, gazing at the moon.

I can't write anything down when his hand is occupying one of mine, so I'll save my questions about his parents for a little later. Instead, I try, "What drew you to music? To New York?" I've asked this question a hundred times (as have fans and various interviewers) and I've gotten the same answer every time: the love of music, being able to bring it to life for an audience, the excitement of the city, blah blah blah.

Dalton Tremaine—honest, authentic Dalton Tremaine— is most authentic here, at home, surrounded by people who love and support him and who need and want nothing from him. And here, nearing midnight on a Thursday night under the glow of a near-full moon, Dalton Tremaine is raw and perfect and poetic.

"I truly can't explain it. Music has always been a part of who I am, this thing that I am drawn to, *always.*" He pauses for an objection but there is none, and he continues. "I picked up songs quickly my whole life, loved everything that came on the radio. Music makes me *feel*, in a way that no other artform or facet of life does. The crescendos, the building of the orchestra or voices or—" he tosses the idea aside, "—whatever, they all speak to me. Draw this emotion out of me. Send chills down my spine."

"That's beautiful."

He looks straight ahead. "Thanks. It just feels like something I'm supposed to do, like I'm denying who I am if I'm not making music."

"Why don't you tell people *that* answer, when they ask?" He shoves me a little with his right shoulder. "Did you hear how crazy all that was, Hil? I can't tell people that."

It doesn't sound crazy at all, I want to tell him. I always thought people loved music as much as I did, until I met Peter. I always thought we all had this universal emotional reaction to music. But Peter was indifferent to it, immune to its power. He'd complain if I turned on music when we were cooking dinner together, never wanted to go to a concert with me, and even though I made a special playlist for his commute to work he turned off the volume and rode in silence each way.

But all of that is behind me. There's a long road ahead, and at least for now I'm walking that road with someone by my side who shows an interest in the things I like, in my thoughts and opinions and even my *feelings.* There's safety here, wrapped in my sweater, my hand held by his. And finally I am at a place where I can say the things I want to say.

"It doesn't sound the least bit crazy. It sounds magical. And I feel the same way."

He tightens his fingers around mine. "You do?"

"Everything you said about the crescendos, the building, the ebbing and flowing, plus the dissonance to resonance and rich, deep harmonies that just invade your veins and make you feel—"

He stops suddenly, pulling me into him, bodies touching under a sea of stars. The perfect moon lights his face, and I can see the idea to kiss me flash through his eyes.

When it happens, it's deep and warm, a continuation of the afternoon. No hesitation, no introduction.

My free hand slides upward to his neck, fingers mixing with hair, pulling his mouth more firmly into mine. My journal-holding hand finds the small of his back and I wrap tightly around him. I want to keep his body against mine as long as I can. I want to feel safe in his arms forever. And while my hands are pulling and holding and unwilling to surrender him, his hands are searching, and I dare to let myself believe he's enjoying feeling my body.

This can't be real life. Dalton Tremaine is groping me. But, like, in a super-hot way.

He's got a hand tangled in my hair, which he uses to tilt my face skyward to make my neck more accessible for his mouth. His other hand has cozied up inside my sweater, firm and flat, like he wants to feel as much of my skin as possible. He kisses my neck in warm circles until both hands meet at the top of my jeans.

He teases me. Fingers find my skin below the layer of denim, begging for a response. Daring me to nod or utter a breathy "yes" into his ear to give him the permission he craves to go further.

And as badly as I want to do that, just as my hands have reached the hem of his shirt, mustering the courage to find his waistband and dive into something new and absolutely insane, I don't get the chance.

Dalton, his hair disheveled, his forehead creased, pulls his hands off of me so forcefully that he stumbles backward.

I struggle to catch my breath. *What just happened?*

He shakes his head. "I didn't mean to—I don't have—" and then he groans and drops onto the grassy hill along the roadway.

I run three times a week, and it's still not enough to prepare me for the chest-heaving, cardio adventure that is making out with Dalton Tremaine. I'm still trying to calm myself. "What are you talking about?" I ask, lowering myself a few feet away.

He looks at me, his eyes glowing and cloudy all at once. When he looks away he says, "Not here. It can't be here."

"*What* can't be here?"

He glances back at me, wordlessly, but it speaks volumes.

"Oh." Hopefully the midnight light doesn't show that my cheeks are red as a Baywatch swimsuit.

"Should we talk about that? I mean I don't even know if you want—I mean, do you? Are you interested in that? With me, I mean?" When I don't immediately answer he says, "Forget it. It's stupid."

I scoot closer, but not so close that I can smell his shampoo or that he can hear my heart racing in my chest. Just close enough to touch his arm and pull back. "It's not stupid. It's just confusing." *Sigh.* "I mean, it's *not* confusing, but there are certainly some…circumstances…that might make things weird."

Please don't say her name. Please don't say her name.

Thankfully, he just nods. "Point taken."

"And for the record," I tell him, diving into the safe feeling, the *I-can-tell-him-anything* trust we've built, "I would really hope you can tell that I am interested."

He stretches his torso across the grass and brings my face to his, kissing me again. Somehow, him being basically horizontal makes this kiss feel even more salacious than the last. He feels it too. "I think I need a cold shower," he breathes.

I nibble his lip and laugh. "Want me to help calm you down a little?"

"I don't think that's possible."

I laugh, turning and picking up my notebook and pen. "Tell me about your parents' relationship."

TWENTY-FOUR

Sizzling grease and hushed whispers wake me. My journal's open, upside down across my stomach, an uncapped pen on the floor in front of the couch next to an empty beer bottle and half-full wine glass.

I rub the sleep from my eyes and the drool from my face, then finger-comb my hair before sitting up. Olivia and Thomas are making breakfast just behind me in the kitchen, and they greet me with warm smiles.

"Ah! She lives!" Thomas laughs, and Olivia echoes him.

"Barely," I say, stretching while I yawn.

Olivia holds a *World's Best Mom* mug to her lips. "Did you have a late night last night?"

"I must have." I don't even remember what time we got back.

"It's weird," Thomas says. "I got up at one point, probably just after midnight, and came out for a cup of water. Didn't see you though."

"Oh. I'd gone out for a walk. The moon was too bright to resist. I don't get much of that in New York."

They exchange a sideways glance, and Olivia takes a bite from a crispy strip of bacon. "Dalton's always been the same way. Never could resist the draw of a starry night out there." Her eyes move to the glass and bottle next to the couch and twinkle with suspicion, but not displeasure.

"Speaking of—is he around somewhere? I had a question about the party."

Thomas shakes his head. "He left about half an hour ago, heading out with Samantha to show her his happy place."

My heart sinks. I know she begged to see it, but I hate that he's sharing it with her. I know it was special to him long before he ever knew me, but I was hoping it was more special now. Too special to take Samantha there.

"But Jordan should be here in about an hour, and he's been very hands-on with the party-planning too, so he may be able to help you out."

"Great. Thank you, Thomas."

They offer me breakfast, but I decline, opting instead for a shower and some time sitting on the swing out front to review what I've written so far and figure out the rest of the poem for tomorrow's party.

Jordan arrives around nine thirty. He's brought a pickup today, a big noisy one with wide wheel wells, and an electric guitar solo blasts through his open windows. "Oh, hey Hil," he says after killing the engine. "Dalton around?"

I shake my head. "He's out with Samantha."

"Poor guy."

I stifle a laugh and close my journal. "So what's up?"

"I've been trying to reach him all morning. Apparently there's an issue with the party and they want us to come settle some things. Not my kind of scene though—I figured if one of us is in a position to judge formal crap it'd be him."

"He left his phone here this morning." Try as I may, I cannot fight the urge to volunteer my opinion on all things party-related. "Could I try to help?"

His eyes narrow as he considers the offer. "You sure you want to get involved? Hate to put you to work on your vacation."

Party-planning and procrastination are two of my favorite hobbies. "Not a problem at all, if you're okay with it."

"Yes, please." He gestures with his head to the truck. "Hop in. I'll give ya a ride."

When he starts the truck, Olivia appears on the porch.

"Hey! You come over here and don't even say hi?"

"Sorry, Ma," Jordan calls over the roar of the engine. "We've got some major party-planning to do." Olivia glides over the front walk and rests her forearms in the opening where Jordan's window should be. "I'll be back in a few hours," he tells her.

She tousles his hair and winks. "Do what you need to do, but next time, say hello first."

"You got it. Love you, Ma."

Olivia steps back so Jordan can reverse out of the driveway. It's about a thirty-minute drive to the venue, so I use the time as wisely as I can and interrogate the older Tremaine brother about his family.

"This for the poem?" he asks, after I ask him about his favorite aspect of his parents' marriage. (For the record, his answer is, "They had me.")

"Mmhmm. Dalton gave me some good content last night, but I want to make sure you're both represented in there."

He shakes his head. "I don't know how you do it. Never could get into any of that artsy stuff."

"I feel the same about what you do. I don't think I have much adventure in me."

He snickers and adjusts the rearview. "You live in a concrete jungle. There's got to be some adventure there."

"Have you been to the city recently? Seen Dalton in any of his shows?"

Jordan shakes his head. "Saw him on tour around here when he first started out, but it's tough to get the whole crew to the city and to take the time off work. Just staying in town for the party this weekend is tough enough. People tend to be free on the weekends, so that's when I'm busiest."

"Ah, the life of service industry employees."

"You know it well?"

"Very," I tell him. "Back home, I always worked in some sort of customer service. Not quite *Adventure Guide* service but restaurants, retail, then hospitality. That kind of thing."

He cranes his neck to look for oncoming traffic at a blind intersection. "Did you enjoy that kind of work?"

I nod, though he can't see me. "I didn't *hate* it. I actually enjoyed helping people most of the time."

"But you left."

"Mmhmm." I swallow hard and force the sound from my throat. "Not by choice, necessarily."

"Ooooh," he sings. "That sounds like a fun story."

I retell an abbreviated version of the story: dating Peter, his unwillingness or inability to care about anyone else's needs, the breakup, the way it wrecked me for a month.

The fact that I was working a wedding on what should have been our three-year anniversary and the bride got wasted before lunch and started telling her hair stylist about her fling with the best man before flirting with her photographer.

"You tell one groom to abort mission and suddenly you're not cut out to be an assistant to the event planner of a boutique hotel in the middle of nowhere."

"Ouch."

"Which part?" I chuff.

He pulls into a parking lot and turns to me, lowering the volume on the stereo. "It all sounds like it sucks." He reaches into the backseat and hands me a box of tissues.

I finally feel the tears he saw welling in my eyes.

"Do you make a habit of telling people when they're with someone who's no good for them?"

Laughing, I reply, "I was not commissioned to write an epic break-up poem for your parents, if that's what you mean."

He shakes his head, suddenly serious. "He'll listen to you, you know."

"What?"

"My brother. He'll listen to you. If you have another urge to tell someone when they're about to make the biggest mistake of their life."

Jordan shuts off the car and unbuckles his seatbelt, and I follow him into the venue.

....

Graystone Manor is a gorgeous estate set on two hundred acres, with a stable and horses at the far end of the property and an arched stone bridge over a stream that runs through one of their most-requested ceremony sites.

The resident event planner greets us before we're out of the truck. "Jordan, hi."

"Hey, Luce." He pulls her in for a quick hug. "Lucy, this is Hillary, Dalton's friend. Hil, Lucy, the one who's hopefully going to save the day."

"With your help," she says, motioning for us to follow her. Along the walk we hear all about how the dining configuration doesn't allow room for the dance floor. Lucy leads us into the sunroom, a huge room with arched windows to a patio outside. I count ten round tables set up for dinner, six chairs at each.

She walks to the center of the room and gestures to the various walls. "Bar's over here," she says, sweeping her arm to one corner of the room. She continues on about the layout and how there just isn't room for the bar, dessert station, dance floor, and photo booth Dalton wants to set up.

I wander the room, fingering the white wooden chairs and squinting into the sunlight that streams through the eight-foot windows. The patio outside is nearly as large as the sunroom itself, and fields and mountains complete the view beyond. I check the forecast for tomorrow night, and clear skies and comfortable temperatures are predicted again.

"Hey, Lucy?" I ask, interrupting their conversation.

"Yes?"

"What if the bar moved outside?"

She furrows her brows. "I don't think the bar is the problem; it's got its own little area, tucked back in the corner."

"Right, but for anyone to be able to access it, you're losing space with your seating in that general area, since you have to have room open for people to stand in line and socialize."

"Okay," she thinks out loud. "So if we move the bar outside—which I have to see if Scotty can even do— how else do we free up space for things?"

Hm. I need to play with the space, figure out what can go where. "How many people on the guest list?"

"Fifty-seven," Lucy and Jordan say in unison.

"Well, fifty-eight, I guess, if Samantha's coming," Jordan adds.

"Does that include your parents?" When he nods, I continue. "Okay, and they're at this sweetheart table. So fifty-six guests, and we have ten tables. Do you have a seating chart?"

Hesitantly, Jordan nods. "I would *not* recommend touching it. Dalton has been very protective of it for weeks."

"Yes, but he also said the dance floor was non-negotiable," Lucy counters.

"You don't think he'd be open to changing it to make room for his beloved dance floor?"

Jordan's eyes smile. "You gonna be the one to ask him?"

He'll listen to you, you know. "Sure. Unless you think he'll murder me. Then I'm out."

He laughs and raises a fist in the air. "For the dance floor! Huzzah!"

"Huzzah!" I repeat, echoing the movement. There's one problem solved. Well, solved-*ish*.

"Okay, what about this," I ask, thinking out loud. I explain my thoughts: reduce to eight tables instead of ten, move the bar outside ("Scotty will find a way," Lucy assures us), reroute guests from the side entrance off the parking lot to the patio, eliminating the need for an open area at the opposite end of the room. Now there's more usable square footage and fewer tables, which allows space for the dance floor to be centered in the room. Thomas and Olivia's table will sit just to one side, next to a small platform for the band Jordan's hired, which will fit nicely on the now-widened dance floor.

"All of this sounds great," Lucy says, "but what about the dead space over here?" She turns and ponders an alcove around the corner.

"Oooh the dessert station," Jordan chimes in.

"Yes, right," she confirms. "And the photo booth?"

Jordan and I exchange glances. "What exactly did he have in mind for this photo booth?"

Two minutes later we're in Lucy's office, reviewing the plan for the party. Linens, decor, menu, and a box of props

Dalton had shipped to the Manor a week earlier. They're black-tie themed photo props, like little black bow tie cut-outs or champagne flute-shaped pieces, all attached to sticks.

"Did he know what he was ordering?" I think aloud.

"These look like they're meant for a dorky, pimpled kid's thirteenth birthday."

"Jordan!" Lucy screeches.

"What?" he responds to the scolding. "You already know I'm a terrible person. That's why we split up, remember? You wanted to be married to someone '*decent*.'"

He rolls his eyes and they both laugh for an instant before she elbows him and turns serious again.

She clears her throat. "I don't really know what to do with these."

"Won't people be wearing real bow ties? Or carrying real champagne flutes?"

"Or beer bottles," Jordan adds.

The three of us exchange looks and decide, wordlessly, to misplace the box and its contents in the trash can.

"So, what about the photos?" Lucy asks. "What are we going to use for props?"

I refold a white napkin on her desk. White napkins, black tablecloths, white candles, white chairs... Something is missing from the decor.

"What if there are no props?" Meeting their gaze, I smile, excited for the idea to pull Olivia's favorite color into the event. "Imagine a photo backdrop, made of some greenery and red roses. It could go over by the dessert station, or, better yet, out on the patio. And maybe we could string some lights out there."

"That layout would help alleviate the crowding inside, too." Lucy approves and suggests putting out some white rockers to make it more comfortable outside.

Jordan chimes in, agreeing with all the proposed changes. "Looks like all that's left to do is to tell Dalton we're changing all the details of his party."

"And acquire a giant backdrop. I'll check with the florist," Lucy adds.

It's after noon. Jordan and I head back to the house with a to-do list in mind.

....

Dalton and Samantha get back from their hike after two o'clock. Dalton's on board with the changes and helps to recreate the seating chart. He's sure to keep separate all the people who cannot get along. "Small town. Big gossip. Have to be careful who's near who," he explains.

Lucy communicates throughout the afternoon about the progress of the flower wall. It's going to cost nearly a thousand dollars to get the flowers needed for the wall backdrop, which Jordan agrees to. (That's one change Dalton will just have to be surprised by tomorrow.) She'll have the flowers delivered tomorrow morning, which will give us a few hours to create the wall.

In addition to being a popular event venue, Graystone Manor also has accommodations in their carriage house. Dalton has reserved all four rooms for us for both tonight and tomorrow, and at four o'clock we pack up everything we'll need for the party and drive half an hour south to the property. Jordan heads home to pick up his family on the way, Dalton and Samantha drive their rentals separately, and I ride along with Thomas and Olivia in the back seat of the Bel Air.

Thomas checks the rear-view and asks, "Are you enjoying your visit so far, Hillary?"

"Very much so." Spending time with the family has been wonderful. The way they interact and laugh together is everything I love about family and miss about my own. "Thanks so much for hosting me this week and for the invite to the party."

Olivia turns and smiles, her eyes hidden behind a pair of dark, tortoise-shell sunglasses. "I'm so glad you agreed to come."

I return her smile and sink back into the leather seat.

The property's manager shows us to our rooms on the second floor. Thomas and Olivia have a junior suite at the end of the hall, with Jordan's family in a room across from theirs. The last two rooms, side-by-side at the opposite end of the hallway, were meant for Dalton and me, but now that Samantha's here, we're one room short.

By some divine intervention, Olivia reemerges after stowing her luggage and suggests that Dalton take the sofa bed in their suite so Samantha and I can have our own rooms. Of course Samantha is not thrilled with this idea, but I breathe a sigh of relief and volunteer to take the smaller room at the top of the stairs to give her the more spacious option.

Jordan's family arrives by five and checks in, and most of us help them carry their things up to their room. While they unpack and unwind, Dalton asks to see the revamped sunroom.

The tables and chairs have all been set up; a folded pile of linens lies on each table. I gesture to the location of the bar and entrance so he can picture the full experience and he nods. "It all looks great. I just have two questions."

"Sure. What's up?"

"First, where are my photo props?"

I pause, my mouth agape, then bite my lip. "Um, that's a great question…"

"Relax, Hil," he says, resting a hand on my arm. His touch is always electric. "I heard they were awful and got vetoed."

"Oh, good. I mean, good that you know. I was afraid you'd be upset."

He rolls his eyes, feigning offense. "Yes, I'm devastated that my twelve-dollar purchase was a bust."

"The alternative will be significantly better, don't worry."

"So I've heard," he says, smiling. "Any hints on specifics?"

I shake my head. "You'll just have to be surprised like everyone else."

"Fair enough."

"You had a second question?"

He nods. "Do you think this dance floor is big enough?"

Looking around, I really believe it will be, and I tell him as much as he takes his phone from his pocket and touches the screen.

"I guess there's only one way to find out for sure."

Music streams from the phone, a hollow sound in the large sunroom. He extends his hand to me, but I shake my head. "I don't think we should."

He steps closer and smiles. "Please? Just to make sure?" And when that doesn't work, "For my parents?"

Olivia and Thomas have become my weak spot. "Fine," I groan. "For your parents."

I take his hand and let him lead me to the center of the floor. He's turned on a pop ballad and hums the melody as he spins me around and pulls me in close to him. But mostly he holds me close, swaying gently, my hand in his, his other hand on the small of my back. For someone who wanted to make sure the dance floor was big enough, he's used startlingly little of it.

When the song ends and the next begins, we don't drift apart. Instead he says, "You're remarkable. Do you know that?"

He tilts his head downward and presses his forehead to mine. Our eyes lock and I swallow hard. I will him to blink, to step away and free me from the trance that always captures me when he's around, but he doesn't.

As badly as I want him to kiss me, I know it's a terrible idea with his entire family, the staff, and Samantha so close by. And truth be told, it's this moment of anticipation, when his lips are parted and his breath is hot and hurried and slow all at once, that sends the tingling feeling directly to my toes. The *thought* of him kissing me is maybe sexier than him actually doing it. Which is not to say that his kisses don't impress me, because another truth be told, I long to have his mouth taste every inch of my skin.

He blinks for a moment and pulls away. Still he watches me, and a half-smile he doesn't believe in crosses his lips. "We should go."

....

Dalton gives Jordan an approving slap on the shoulder when we return to the carriage house. "The room looks great. Thanks for handling that today."

"Sure thing. Though Hillary gets the credit. She nailed it." He directs a smile my way.

"Noted. But I will commend you for making it through the day without finally convincing Lucy to kill you."

"It was a close call." Lucy appears in the foyer and beams at Dalton. "Hey, you. So good to see you again!"

"You too!" he says, wrapping her in a tight hug. "How've you been?"

She shrugs, once freed. "Can't complain. Not the last fifteen years, anyway," she adds, shoving Jordan's shoulder.

Dalton drapes an arm around Jordan and fills in the gaps for me. "Lucy was Jordan's first wife."

"First wife, first victim. To-*may*-to, to-*mah*-to." Lucy grins at her own joke and the snort it pulls out of Jordan. "Anyway," she says to me, "I've known these guys for forever, basically."

"You grew up together?"

She nods. "You could definitely say that. I think we go back to diapers, pretty much." She redirects her attention to Dalton. "Anyway, I have just a few things I need to run by you, if you have a second."

"Sure," he says, excusing himself.

....

I'm unpacked, sprawled on my stomach on the plush queen-size bed, elbows propped below me while I work on my poem (which is nowhere nearer completion than it was when I woke up this morning since my efforts have been redirected all day long), when Dalton pokes his head into my doorway.

"Hey."

"Hi," I smile, dropping my pen into the crease of the open journal.

"We were going to head out for dinner soon. Think you could be ready in ten?" He's wearing the same sweater he wore the night he rescued me from the flooded apartment, dress shoes, and a pair of fitted chinos.

I'm sweat-sticky from running around the sunroom moving tables this morning, and there's no way I'll be presentable enough for a nice family dinner in ten minutes.

"I'm actually good," I lie. I hope he can't hear my stomach, which gurgles its plea to go out for dinner.

"You sure? You've had a busy day."

"Mmhmm. I'm fine. Maybe bring back something for me?"

"Sure," he says. "I can do that." And he can, because we order in so frequently, or cook together, and he knows basically everything I will and will not eat. No mustard, no mayonnaise, mozzarella sticks are always welcome, and the cardinal rule: I don't care how pretty its name sounds in French; if it sounds gross in English, don't even think of giving it to me.

A door creaks open and Dalton whips his head to the right and straightens. "Hi, Sami."

"Hey. Did I hear you are going out for dinner?"

"Yeah," he says. "Most of us are, anyway. Hillary's going to stay behind, but I was just coming to see if you were ready."

"I'm just really exhausted, after all the hiking today. Do you think you could bring something back for me, too? Like a salad with grilled chicken, or salmon or something?"

"If that's what you really want." He doesn't fight her decision to stay behind.

"Thanks babe." His agreement apparently warrants a kiss on the cheek, and she throws her arms around his neck to show her appreciation. "Oh, hi Hil," she says, arms still around him.

Then, as quickly as she acknowledged me she loses interest, turning back to Dalton and dragging a hand across his chest. "This color looks amazing on you. Don't you think it looks amazing on him, Hil?"

His eyes meet mine as he tries to pry her hands off of him. I bite my lip, though I can't tell if I'm trying to keep myself from laughing or crying. I hate seeing her hands all over him like that.

"It's a great color," I agree.

"Okay, I need to get going." He's finally loosened her grip on him. "I think everyone's waiting on me. I'll bring back something for each of you."

"Thanks," I say.

"Thanks, babe," sings Samantha. "You're the best." Then she turns his face to hers and pulls him roughly to her to kiss him firmly on the lips.

She walks away, leaving a lipstick-stained Dalton in my doorway. *Sorry*, he mouths, and my chest tightens wondering how many times that has happened before, in restaurants and on sidewalks and at friends' apartments, in the woods...

I wave it off. "Thanks again for grabbing dinner."

He nods. "Anytime. I'll see ya." He disappears, old wooden floorboards creaking under his weight as he retreats to his room.

....

My stomach is absolutely *livid* that I opted out of the family dinner. It's growling and demanding food that I am unable to feed it. Somehow, it's holding my brain hostage, waiting on the ransom drop of (hopefully!) mozzarella sticks before it frees my brain to write again.

So basically, here I am, useless and miserable.

Maybe a change of scenery will help, like it sometimes does back in New York. The carriage house has a small parlor off the foyer, and I slip on a pair of flip flops, grab my journal and pen, and head down there to finish my poem and wait for dinner. When I walk in, Samantha is already there.

"Oh, hi. I didn't realize you were down here." I consider walking back upstairs, but she talks to me, and I stay.

"It's alright." She smiles, and it's not warm like how she smiles at her parents or Dalton, or cold like how she smiles at me, but rather altogether very sad and very lukewarm, like milk that's been sitting out for an hour and won't sour for some time but is also unpleasant to consume.

"You okay, Samantha?"

She nods and smooths her sweater. "I'm fine."

I hesitate to enter, but she waves me in. "Please, sit down. Don't let me scare you away."

"You're not scaring me away," I tell her, and she raises her eyebrows at me, challenging that statement. "Okay, you're not scaring me away *right now*."

"Ha! That is very fair," she laughs. She gestures with her head to my journal. "What are you working on?"

My fingers curl tighter around the book's spine. "Just some writing."

"Well I figured that," she says, her smile fading. "If you don't want to talk about it, just say that."

How do you tell someone that her fake boyfriend asked you to write a poem for his parents' very important anniversary party, when you're supposed to be such a small part of their lives? And do you leave out the parts about you fantasizing about her fake boyfriend ravishing you in the rain in the middle of the woods? I shake the idea (and vivid imagery) from my head.

I land on the truth, or some abbreviated version of it: "I have a poem I've been working on all week. Needed a change of scenery to see if that would help clear some writer's block."

"Ah." She crosses and uncrosses her legs. "Do you find it easier to write out here than in the city?"

My head shakes *no*. "I wouldn't say *easier*. It's just different. But right now I'm more stuck than I've been in a long time."

It's weird, revealing anything about myself to Samantha Darling. Maybe it's weirder that she's encouraging me to reveal it.

"Sorry. I bet that's frustrating."

I nod and very much wish to not talk about myself anymore. "So what are you up to?"

She shrugs and takes a sip from a teacup that's been sitting on the coffee table between us. "Just came down here to think."

Instead of filling the silence, I wait. I have no idea what to say to Samantha—what I can say, what I should say. Does she know that I know that she and Dalton aren't a real couple? What if I say something I shouldn't? It's safest to stay silent.

"Hillary, have you ever been in love before?"

What is the obsession with this question? It's barely been thirty-six hours since Dalton asked me basically the same thing. And the answer is no clearer now than it was then.

Actually, it might be a little clearer, but it's still infuriatingly complicated.

"I think so," I answer, as truthfully as I can. "Though I don't know that he was in love with me." That seems to sum up my relationship with Peter quite well, actually. *Yep. Peter. Sure.*

"Mmm. That sucks," she says. She traces the rim of her teacup with a perfectly manicured finger.

My throat goes dry just thinking of asking her more, but I have to know, so I stumble through the question: "What about you?" *What about now?*

Her eyes dart to mine before she lowers them back to her tea. "That's a great question. Maybe the same as what you said?"

"Oh. Are things not great with Dalton?"

"They're fine. I mean, there's nothing bad, necessarily." She shrugs and looks out the bay window, past the covered wraparound porch, toward the mountains in the distance. "I am not cut out for this life."

"For what life?"

"For—" she motions to the window, "—*this*. This slow-paced, dirt-road, great-outdoors, takes-an-hour-to-get-anywhere-worthwhile life."

"Do you think you need to be?"

Her head turns so fast I'm afraid she'll have whiplash. "What's that supposed to mean?"

"Well, I just—I mean—were you thinking of moving out here?"

Shaking her head, she says, "Not yet. But what if he wants to, someday? What if he wants to raise his kids out here?"

I choke on my own spit. "You're already thinking about having kids?"

She smiles again. "Hillary, I'm thirty-two. I'm always thinking about having kids."

I get it. Sometimes all I hear is the ticking of that stupid 'biological clock.' I feel like Captain Hook being chased by that damn crocodile, except my crocodile shape-shifts. Some days it's a photo of my niece that my sister texts me. Some days it's the silence as I lie awake in bed thinking about how messy my life has gotten. Some days it's Dalton's eyes or smile, when I imagine how amazing he would be as a dad.

"Hillary?"

"Hmm?" I shake myself out of the fog. "Sorry. Was just thinking about—my family."

"Oh. Anyway," she continues. "I just can't imagine being happy out here. In the woods. With the bugs and the snakes and the snow in the winter."

"New York gets snow in the winter, too."

"Yeah, but it's different. It's *New York.*" She sips her tea and changes course.

"When Dalton and I first got together, it was intense. Like, super hot. Like lightning or solar flares or the inside of a Hot Pocket when you take it out of a microwave."

"I'm sorry, you eat Hot Pockets?"

The least Samantha-like sound I've ever heard escapes her lips. A *guffaw.* "*That's* your takeaway?"

My laughter answers hers. "Just pieces of the puzzle that is Samantha Darling."

"Charles. Please. Samantha *Charles,* when I'm not working."

"Charles. Got it."

She smiles, much more warmly than earlier, and resumes the story I'm not entirely sure I want to hear. "Like I was saying—*hot.* You couldn't keep us apart. But we were both so busy with work, so it kind of fizzled. When we actually had time together, it was—" her cheeks turn pink and her hand dances in the air. "You get the idea. But we never saw each other. We were each doing eight shows a week, and so between that and…*that*…there was never a good foundation built. We never just talked, got to know each other.

"So we decided just to be friends. No benefits." She rolls her eyes and chuckles. "But of course, just because we said something five years ago, it doesn't mean that'll last forever. And now, we're spending all this time together again, and I'm just worried that there's still no foundation."

My stomach churns. It could be the excessive hunger, but it could be the idea that Samantha and Dalton have been spending so much time together, apparently *not* talking. *Has he been lying to me this whole time?*

Samantha's still talking but I only catch every other word. My mind is racing. Did Dalton tell me he was fake-dating her just because I confronted him? Did he make up an elaborate story to cover for himself? And the most important question: *Have I been making out with another woman's boyfriend?*

Headlights from two cars tear through the parlor.

Samantha smiles. "Looks like they're home." Then, a line of worry I am sure she will pay far too much money to have erased snakes across her forehead. "Hey, please don't repeat anything I told you, okay?"

"Not a problem." I stand abruptly, bumping the high-back chair I'd been seated in and sending it skidding backward a few inches. I grab my pen and journal and turn to exit the room, just as the Tremaines ease out of their cars, laughing hard enough we can hear them through the window.

"Where are you going?" Samantha asks. "Aren't you going to wait for your dinner?"

I shake my head. "Suddenly I don't feel very hungry."

I take the stairs two at a time, closing and locking my door just as I hear the carriage house's front door swing open.

TWENTY-FIVE

*A*re you guys married yet or what?

My phone buzzes to life at 5:00 a.m. with Lindsey's text message, a response to a selfie I'd sent her Thursday night after (apparently more than one glass of) wine and poetry writing time. I definitely don't remember sending it, though I don't remember taking it either. With the caption, Cheers, from Dalton Tremaine's childhood home, I'm holding my wine glass and sitting on the couch in the Tremaines' living room. Dalton photo-bombs me, drawing laughter that we both immediately *shush*.

I remember the laughing, the noisy whispers that could've been full volume for all I know, trying not to wake up anyone else. The photo beautifully captures the freedom of the moment: the silliness he rarely gets to show, and a smile I forgot how to wear for far too long.

Sorry I didn't respond right away. Been crazy here.

I sit up and respond, No worries. You OK?

It's just... a lot.

I never know what to say in moments like this. Texting feels too impersonal for serious updates about Marco's dad, but it also doesn't seem like she really wants to talk about it (or like she has the time to sit and gab about it, if she's responding at 5:00 a.m. to a day-old text message).

I land on a bland but hopeful response. Sorry you're going through so much. We'll have to catch up when you're back in the city. Apartment should be done soon!

The screen displays a "...", and then it disappears. This repeats at least three times, and then, after a minutes-long pause, I receive Lindsey's message: Yes, we'll have to catch up soon.

I flop backwards and watch the ceiling fan whirl above me in steady, rhythmic circles. The idea of drifting back to sleep sounds so tempting, but I know I have too much to do today. Instead I watch the blades spin, wondering how Olivia and Thomas knew when they were nineteen and twenty-two that they had what it took to make it to forty years, still going strong.

Maybe they didn't know. Maybe no one does. Maybe they were just so infatuated with one another then that they dove into marriage, not knowing if it would work out in the end.

Maybe they're just as impressed that they reached forty years as I am.

I roll over to my journal, which is almost always in bed with me because I never know where inspiration will strike, and turn to the page marked with the ribbon bookmark.

The mostly finished poem stares back at me, just like the takeout container from last night does from the nightstand. Like Dalton did yesterday afternoon when he danced with me. Like Dalton did last night when I wouldn't even open my door far enough for him to pass my dinner through to me, and he had to turn it sideways to hand it over.

If I want to finish this poem, I need to clear my head.

Dressed in yesterday's leggings and an old T-shirt, I slide my running shoes onto my feet and pull the laces tight. I slip out of my room and down the stairs, avoiding the steps that I know will creak and groan based on my experience with them last night.

Fog hangs low over the valley, dense and sticky, when I take off running around the property of Graystone Manor. I've been wanting to see the full property since Jordan and I arrived yesterday, but considering today's activities include making a flower wall and attending a party, this might be my only chance.

There's a paved walking trail for guests, and I follow it past the main residence where the party will be later, along the creek, through the vast lawn to their outdoor ceremony site, then past the barn and horse pasture into the wooded area that surrounds everything else. It's the thick border of trees that really sets Graystone Manor apart, physically, keeping it separate from its neighbors. That separation also creates an oasis, lush and green, so that the outside world can disappear.

Unless the outside world, with all its pain, caravans in with you, of course.

A late-spring breeze rustles the budding leaves around me, and the fog from the pasture and the fields has lifted. Now the *splat* of fat raindrops on green leaves fills the air, and for a moment I let myself smile.

No. Not for a moment. I love the rain, damn it, and I refuse to let this craziness with Dalton and Samantha affect this thing that I love and the memories attached to it.

He asked me, under an umbrella on maybe our third walk on the High Line, "What is it about *books?*" But he didn't say it like he hated books or reading, just that he didn't understand what it was that drew someone to want to write one.

I just laughed and told him the same story I'd told everyone else who'd ever asked. "I had a teacher once who was a real free spirit. And one day she asked our class, 'Did you ever read a book so good, so *special*, that when you finished it, you just had to touch it?' And she sat there, the whole class in a circle around the room, while she rested her hands on this book's cover, then held it like she couldn't bear to let it go. And that was kind of this moment for me, when I realized I wanted to write a touchable book." Since then, he has asked regularly if my book is "touchable" yet.

There's so much more to the story, of course, of what drew me to writing, but that answer has satisfied him for weeks and I'm in no hurry to relive some of the more painful plot points of my own life. Even if he is an amazing listener. Even if he lets me vent and yell and cry when I recount those things. I struggle to share the worst memories with just anyone, and it'll be a long time until I trust Dalton Tremaine again if everything that Samantha said last night is even remotely, possibly true.

I pinch the bridge of my nose and feel the tension fade away. This is, after all, not his day. It's not mine, either, and that's why I have to get back to the carriage house—to make this day perfect for Olivia and Thomas.

So I run through the glorious, healing rain, half a mile back. I'm a dripping mess when I return and greet the elder Tremaines on the front porch, seated in side-by-side Adirondacks, sipping coffee.

Thomas smiles. "Nice morning, huh?"

"Look at you," Olivia says, laughing. "Did you fall into the stream?"

I can't stop the smile. For once in recent history I can't— I *won't*—bottle it inside me. "Perfect morning for a run. I love the rain."

They exchange a look, and he winks at her.

"Do you know how many mornings we have spent sitting side-by-side on our porch thinking the exact same thing? Or how many days we were thankful the rain got in the way of the boys' baseball tournaments or outdoor swim meets so we could just be at home?" She's so calm, like she's remembering the unexpectedly peaceful Saturdays they were awarded due to Mother Nature's timing.

"Those were the best days, really," Thomas adds. "Building forts when they were little, impromptu movie nights or game nights when they were older."

Olivia rests a head on his shoulder and drapes an arm around his neck. "And now they're grown and we're doing those things with grandkids."

"Forty years have flown by, that's for sure."

I feel like an intruder, though not unwelcome, hearing their private memories, seeing them cuddle together while watching the rain. As they gaze off into the incoming sunlight, Olivia tracing the seam at the shoulder of Thomas's quarter-zip sweater, I shuffle along into the house to change.

Inspired by what they said outside and refreshed by the rain, I edit parts of the poem, finishing it by nine. On a clean sheet of paper I rewrite everything without scribbles, then take a photo and text it to Dalton for his thoughts.

After a shower, I pull my wet hair into a messy bun and slip into a maxi dress to meet Lucy and work on the flower wall. She's waiting with buckets of red roses when I reach the sunroom.

Halfway through, we take a break for a glass of water and a snack of carrots, pretzels, and hummus. It's the perfect treat for my grumbly, post-run hunger.

"This looks so cool," Lucy says, crunching a pretzel.

"It does." I crunch a carrot and cover my mouth as I chew while talking. "Thanks so much for making this happen and for being here today. I bet you'll be happy when this party's over."

"Ha! I'll be happy to have Dalton lose my number for another decade. He goes a little crazy over these parties." Her eyes twinkle when she smiles. "He's always been that way though, so detail-oriented, such a perfectionist. I know he wants it to be just right, but come on, man. Let me do my job." She shakes her fist at the sky and laughs. Then, "I'm totally joking, just so you know. And I appreciate you helping yesterday with that layout snafu."

"Sure thing. I thought he was going to keel over when we asked him to redo the seating chart."

"Good thing he didn't. I'd hate to be the one who has to plan his funeral someday. I would imagine if they use the wrong flowers or read the wrong passage, he'll haunt them for all eternity."

I return the laugh and cough as I nearly choke on the carrot. "It seems like Jordan is the more easy-going brother."

Lucy snorts and rolls her eyes. "Jordan's easy-going, alright. Easy going from one woman to the next. One thing to the next. Whatever makes him happy in the moment is what he does."

"Yikes."

"Nah, he's fine. Finally settled down with the right person." She waves off the topic and motions to the flower wall. "Anyway, shall we finish?"

I have two hours to re-shower and get ready for the party by the time we finish the flower wall. It looks awesome, and Lucy brought in a white neon sign that says "Love" that she has used for weddings and bridal brunches before. Her set-up team will affix it to the wall when it's taken outside just before the party begins. Now when guests are getting drinks they'll be able to stop by the wall for photos.

When I cross the lawn to the carriage house, I check my phone for updates to see if Dalton texted me back about the poem. Instead of approval from him, I have a notification that my picture failed to send. *The joys of being in the middle of nowhere, disconnected.* I head straight to my room and grab the journal from my bed, then knock on the second door from the end of the hall—the parlor of the Tremaines' suite, where Dalton is staying.

There's no answer, so I knock again. This time the door opens, and Samantha greets me with a fresh-faced smile. "Hi, Hillary."

"Oh." *Very smooth, dumbass.* "Hi, Samantha."

"What's up?"

Right, idiot. She would very much like to know what you're doing at her boyfriend's bedroom. "Oh, right. Um, is Dalton around?"

"Yeah—just a sec, I'll get him." She turns and disappears inside, her pink satin robe billowing behind her, motioning for me to follow her into the room to wait. Then she hollers through a doorway, "Babe, Hillary's here to talk to you! I'm going to start getting ready, but come on over then!"

Samantha waves to me and leaves the room, leaving the door cracked open behind her. *Good defense.*

Just as I lower myself onto the oversized ottoman, the other doorway opens. Dalton's hair drips perfect circles on the old tasseled rug that stretches the width of the room. "Hey, Hil."

If he says anything after that I don't notice. Who can focus on words when his strong, round shoulders roll forward and backward as he writhes into a white T-shirt that stretches over his pecs and abs and comes to rest at the waistband of a pair of khaki cargo shorts that sit an inch lower than they probably *should*, but I'm absolutely not complaining.

"Hey," he says again.

"Hi, sorry." I force my eyes to rise to meet his. "I tried to send this to you earlier, but it didn't go through." Wagging the journal, I add, "The poem, if you want to read it."

"Oh, great," he says, reaching for the book. His fingers graze mine, but he doesn't take the journal from me. "I missed seeing you last night, after dinner." One of his fingers rubs one of mine and his eyes glow gorgeous green.

"Right. Sorry. I just—I wasn't feeling well."

"Oh. I'm sorry. Samantha said you had a nice time talking?"

Samantha. Samantha, who said things between them were hot and foundationless because all they do is make perfect, beautiful, passionate love (I'm paraphrasing). Samantha, who just left a freshly-showered Dalton's room in a robe.

"We did. But I felt a little sick, so I went up early." I stand and shove the journal into his hands, pulling mine back. "Anyway, the page is bookmarked, if you want to read it."

He examines the journal. "Is there an option to be surprised?"

"Yep," I nod. "You can be surprised when you open the book and read the poem."

A maddening grin crosses his perfect lips, and he steps closer to me. "What, no private reading?"

I shake my head and back away, right into the corner of the desk. The *thud* and my wince occur simultaneously. "Ouch."

"Oooh, you okay?" he asks, contorting himself to bring his face under mine.

"Yes. Fine." I can feel the bruise forming on my butt already. "Anyway."

"I'll read it."

"Thank you."

Avoiding his gaze, I leave the journal with him and retreat to my room. Once inside, I shake out my fingers and tingly toes and arms and legs and head. It's been a long day already, and soon I'm going to endure an evening of watching him dance with his crazy-gorgeous girlfriend while I'm a wallflower in front of a flower wall.

I throw my head back and roll my neck side to side, easing out the tension that's accumulated there. Less than two hours till party time, so much to do.

First things first, I need a shower after sitting on the floor and working on the flower wall. Just as I strip out of my dress, there's a knock at the door.

"Hillary?"

"Yeah?" I wrap a towel around me and rush to the door to make sure it's locked.

"Can I come in?"

Shit. Probably should've verified the timeline of him reading through the poem. "Sorry, just about to step into the shower." *And some of us shower alone.*

"Okay. I can bring this back—"

I unlock and unlatch the door just wide enough for my hand to fit through the opening, grasp the book, and pull it inside with me.

"I can't wait to hear you read this."

"Soon enough."

"Soon enough. And Hillary?"

Goosebumps appear on my arms despite the heat bursting in every direction from my chest. I swallow against the lump in my throat. "Yeah?"

"Thank you."

. . . .

There's a white box on the bed that I didn't notice before my shower. The door is latched and locked, so it must've been put there earlier today. Maybe I just missed it against the backdrop of white linens.

The note attached has my name on it, and the card inside reads,

Hillary,

I wanted you to have something special because you are so incredibly special to me. Thanks for shining a light into my life.
You could do it in sweatpants, but I thought you might like this better.

—D

P.S. Am I doing this right?...

Here is something shiny gold
It is new, it is not old
I hope you have an excellent time
Poem, poem, rhyme, & rhyme.

P.S. Again—This probably would not work for brunch.

I lift the lid off the box, and inside is the gold beaded dress from the windows we passed on our way home from Nom Nom de Plume.

TWENTY-SIX

At quarter till four I hear a faint knock and a near-immediate squeal. Must be Samantha, right next door, getting picked up for the party.

I finish my gold smokey eyes with black waterproof mascara and swipe on a pale gloss. My hair is curled and pinned back on the left with a geometric gold pin.

Now, for the moment of truth.

The truth is, I'm a little afraid to put the dress on.

The high neckline is contrasted by the dangerously low back; two thick straps snake up the sides of the dress, from my waist to the neckline, where they fasten with two diamond-esque buttons that do not want to be buttoned. I check to see if Caroline is in her room, and luckily she's there, threading an earring through her ear.

Her auburn hair is braided into a headband, then swept up into a curly updo. Her dress is black and breezy, with sheer ruffles that drape across the bust and arms of the off-the-shoulder neckline. "Get a look at *you*," she says, while I admire her effortlessly cool look.

"You look beautiful, Caroline."

"Thanks. You know the best thing about this dress?" she asks.

"Pockets?"

"*Yes*," she says. "You get it. Anyway, what's up?"

She buttons the dress quickly when I ask, and we walk over to the party with Emmy and Connor. A fresh copy of the poem is safely folded and tucked into the evening bag I carry along, and as I descend the stairs I lift the front hem of the dress to avoid tripping and tumbling down.

Jordan greets us on the patio. "Gorgeous," he says to his wife, giving her a soft kiss on her cheek to avoid smearing the candy apple red lipstick she's applied. He pulls his kids in—the only tweens or kids invited to the party—and gives each a simultaneous side-hug. "You clean up decent, Hillary," he says with a wink. Caroline smacks his chest with the back of her hand.

"Be nice," she scolds with a smile.

I step out of their circle and pull my cell phone from my bag. "Here—get together in front of the wall and I'll get a family photo for you."

They squish together, a perfect, happy family, and I snap a few pictures. Each one is perfect, but Jordan pinches Caroline's butt in the first one and she's laughing, eyes closed, red lips sharing her joy with the rest of the patio. After that one they're all perfect smiles, elegant and fun against a formal wall of red roses, the "Love" sign making the cut just over Jordan's shoulder in the one zoomed-out photo I took.

It's absolutely the right word to describe their family.

"Excuse me? Ma'am?"

It takes me a moment to realize that someone is talking to me. I turn when a woman gently taps my shoulder. "Oh. Hi."

"Hi!" She beams from below a mountain of black curls. Her hot pink, strapless dress with its gathered skirt reminds me of something I wore to prom more than a decade ago. She extends a cell phone to me and hooks a thumb toward the flower wall. "Would you mind?"

"Oh! Sure," I say, and I take a photo of her with her date. "Mind if I get one on mine, too, to share with the Tremaines?"

She shakes her head and I grab a quick shot of the two of them. A line has formed, and for the next thirty minutes I am mingling on the patio and taking pictures for guests and for Olivia and Thomas.

"Looks like you could use a break." Dalton steps next to me and offers a mixed drink, loaded with ice, in a sweating glass.

"If you do this again for their fiftieth, I'd spring for a photographer."

"Noted. Though I wouldn't need one if we didn't have such a nifty backdrop." He raises his glass and I raise mine, too. *Clink.* I sip the fruity, rummy drink through its short black straw.

"Seriously, Hil. It's perfect. My mom's been talking about it since the party started."

"I'm glad she likes it. I wanted to add in a pop of red for her."

"Thank you for this. For all of it, really." He gestures to the bar and the lights overhead. "This is great out here. I love making the patio a part of it."

I shake my head. "It's no problem. It was fun for me. And anyway—I should be thanking you."

"Me?" he takes a swig of whiskey. "What for?"

For the weekend away, time with your family, friendship... take your pick. "For being okay with the changes. For trusting me. And, obviously, *thank you*," I say, motioning to the dress.

His cheeks redden and he drops his gaze, scanning the patio discreetly. He raises his glass back to his lips and says under his breath, "You look beautiful, Hillary."

The "thank you" comes out so quietly it's barely a whisper. "And you—" *You look dressed, at least.*

"Thanks." He's always been able to read me well so it's not like I even have to finish what I was going to say, but tonight he's jumpy, not even giving me the chance to get the sentence out. And it hits me that we're not alone. That we can't say the things we might say if we weren't surrounded by people who think he's dating Samantha Darling.

And so tonight, friends dressed like James Bond and Ginger from Gilligan's Island, we're all we were ever meant to be.

My mind reels at the thought, mourns the loss of this magical, romantic evening spent dancing in his arms, or resting my head on his shoulder as his parents share a kiss, or laughing over family memories told by aunts and uncles, my hand hooked in his elbow under strung lights and stars. If Samantha hadn't come, it would be different—or at least, it *could* be different. But she's here, and I have no rights to magical moments with him, and especially not with an audience around.

Because alcohol is *always* the best choice when your head is already spinning, I down the drink. "I am going to go inside and mingle a little bit."

"Oh, okay." He takes my empty glass and sets it on a nearby tray. "I can introduce you—"

"No," I interrupt. "*I* am going to go inside and mingle. *You* should find your date and talk to her." *Build a foundation.*

He recoils but nods. "Right. Sure." But when I walk inside, I feel his eyes on me.

· · · · · · · · · · · · · · · · · · · ·

I make it through dinner, sandwiched between Caroline

and Samantha, listening to them trading stories about the brothers, Caroline gushing over Samantha's made-for-TV movies.

I'm surrounded by wonderful people, but the secrets of those private, stolen kisses with Dalton make me feel so alone.

He avoids making eye contact, which doesn't help. So I do my best to interact with Caroline and Samantha, Connor and Emmy, and Olivia, Thomas, and Jordan.

When dinner is over, the band's lead singer asks Olivia and Thomas out to the dance floor to start off the party. Midway through the song, he asks all the other couples in attendance to join them.

Jordan chugs some of his beer. "Liquid courage!" he says, taking Caroline by the hand and pulling her onto the wooden floor next to our table.

Samantha rises and waits for Dalton, whose forehead creases and whose gaze stays level. "Ready to dance?" she asks, a gentle prodding.

I excuse myself back to the bar, hopefully making the decision to get up and dance easier for him. The music spills out onto the patio, and I wait in a line three people deep to get another cocktail. When I open my bag to tip the bartender, my phone's screen shows missed calls from Lindsey.

Weird. She knows I have the party tonight, and we just talked, sort of, this morning. I ignore the calls and shoot a quick text her way.

Hey, sorry. Can't talk right now... maybe tomorrow?

Then, a quick selfie in front of the now abandoned wall of roses.

I drop the phone back in my bag and sip my drink, looking everywhere but the dance floor.

The band wraps up its song and everyone inside applauds. Next comes something up-tempo, and Jordan appears on the patio.

"Hey Hil, you're not in there dancing?"

I shrug. "No partner to dance with."

His smile fades. "Ah, right. Well this one, you don't need a partner. And I'm calling next on slow dances; Caroline will just have to deal."

"I'm fine, it's fine," I say, but the idea of not repeating a slow dance-less senior prom actually sounds great. He gets his drink, and we walk together back into the sunroom.

The thing I really, truly miss about my previous life is seeing the joy on people's faces when you plan a kick-ass event and everyone has the time of their lives. Tonight that excitement comes flooding back, despite the fact I didn't plan this party. But the patio's a hit and guests are having a great time dancing, and I'm proud of Dalton and happy for him that the event is such a success. His parents haven't stopped smiling all night.

Caroline sets my drink and bag on the table and pulls me to her on the dance floor, and we dance to the Macarena like it's still 1996. Then it's a cover of a Rascal Flatts song. Then Sinatra, where I cash in on that slow dance with Jordan.

"Thank God," Caroline says. "My feet are killing me. I needed an excuse to sit down."

As the song wraps up, Dalton speaks to me for the first time since before dinner. "Are you ready to read?"

Jordan releases my hand and the three of us return to the table.

"The band is going to take a break after this next song, and dessert's going out soon, but they want us to do our stuff first."

I nod. "Sure thing." But the idea of reading this poem—the smiling, laughing, dancing people stopping their fun and staring at me while I, a nobody to them, read a poem that may not even be any good—it's terrifying, and I feel very *un*sure.

But then it's time, and Jordan adjusts the mic stand in front of me while Dalton introduces me as his "very good friend" and an "up and coming author," and I smooth the wrinkles of the page in my sweaty, shaking hands.

At the mic, I turn to Olivia and Thomas, seated at the table just to the right of the platform. "Before I begin, I just want to say that it has been a joy to get to know the two of you. To see this amazing, beautiful thing you've built over forty years—it's just...*wow*."

A singular *whoop* and a smattering of applause from one or two people pop up in the far corner of the room. Olivia's warm smile and the sight of Thomas's loving hand on her shoulder help to calm me, and I begin:

> We're not meant to walk this world alone
> as solitary creatures, no heart to call home

I should have asked Dalton or Samantha for their advice, as professionals, on how to recite all of this, but in the moment I let the words and the emotion behind them move me.

Before the final few couplets I look up and take a breath, and my eyes catch Dalton as they sweep toward Olivia's comforting presence. His elbows are propped on the table and a stray finger curls over his upper lip. Something like sadness fills his eyes. Disappointment, maybe? But I can't think about it, because there is a poem to get through, and this is not about him.

And in the sunshine or storm, day or night
we weather it together, with a love so right.

"Congratulations, Thomas and Olivia," I add to the end, and
Jordan raises his glass of champagne to toast them.

"Cheers!" he calls from his seat, his full and husky voice
reverberating around the sunroom.

As he steps onto the platform, Dalton hands me a glass
of champagne and bypasses me, taking the mic. Olivia
wraps me in a hug when I return to the table.

"Thank you, dear. That was beautiful."

Dalton runs a hand through his hair, clears his throat,
and snickers. "That's a tough act to follow—I'm not sure
why I scheduled myself to follow it." His carefree humor
draws light laughter from the rest of the crowd.

"In all seriousness, though, thank you, Hillary, for sharing that with us." He claps in my direction and others join
in. My face flushes and Caroline smiles, dipping her head
down to my shoulder.

"So, no pressure after that, but a few of us have prepared
a little something as well." Jordan and Thomas rise and
join Dalton behind the microphones, and Lucy shuffles in,
handing a guitar to Jordan.

"Our parents raised us in a home filled with joy, love, and
music, so when we were planning everything for tonight, we
knew we wanted to dedicate a special song to our parents.
Then, of course, Dad had to be involved. So I guess this
one's for you, Mom."

The friends and family throughout the room laugh again
as Jordan begins strumming a gentle chord progression. Then
Dalton begins the first verse, and the world stops. His voice
ebbs and flows with the lyrics, a song about finding love in

friendship. The staff has even stopped milling about, setting up dessert, to watch and listen as this seasoned performer tells a story through song. And though his eyes scan the room while he sings (ever the professional) they linger longer here. And it drives me crazy in the best way possible, until Samantha sniffles from the seat next to mine and I remember that *they* have been friends for years, and their relationship is *hot* and she needs *foundation*.

Then Thomas adds lines of harmony and any thoughts or questions I might have about Dalton and Samantha and this song's ties to his personal life disappear, because the only thing I can focus on is that Thomas is a *terrible* singer.

But Olivia is absolutely loving it, her smile stretching wide across her face, tears glistening on her cheeks. I can only imagine the pride she must feel, to see her boys performing like that, and the love she must feel, knowing that they put this all together for her.

I reach into my bag and pull out a pocket-sized pack of tissues, passing them along to Samantha and Olivia. Samantha sniffles again, but there's something off about her expression. She takes a tissue and dabs at her eyes.

When they finish their song, Olivia starts a standing ovation, which doesn't really catch on. But the band comes back to the stage and announces that dessert is served, which creates a similar effect of people rising at the same time. Hugs and compliments swirl around us as guests meander to the bar or the dessert table or dance floor.

After entertaining Dalton's cousin, Gregory, whose hands are clammy and cold and, shall we say, exploratory on my back, I look for Dalton with no luck. I tuck the tissues back into my bag and when my phone screen illuminates, I see a series of missed texts from Lindsey.

The most recent says, I'm so sorry. I know you're busy and this is the worst possible way to tell you this, but I needed you to know.

Concerned, I unlock my phone and open our messages, scrolling up to her first text after I sent the selfie to her.

Things with Marco's dad are worse than we thought. When the time comes—and the doctor says we have maybe a month—Marco wants to stay here with his mom to help.
And I want to stay with him.
My lease on the apartment is up in two weeks. I've got to let it go.
I'm going up next weekend to pack up and move out—hopefully I'll see you?
I'm so sorry. I know you're busy and this is the worst possible way to tell you this, but I needed you to know.

"Hillary?"

"Mmm?" startled, I drop the phone back into my bag and turn toward the sound of my name.

"Did you want dessert?" asks Caroline, and I plaster on the best smile I can and follow her to the dessert station. Full of ganache and mousse, I find myself back at the bar, ordering a large glass of wine.

"Sure you can't fit the whole bottle in there?" I ask the bartender, only half-joking. I drop a five-dollar bill in the tip jar and turn with my glass. Dalton's there, solo, and he waits for me to join him in the middle of the patio. By now the lights are useful above us, not just for decoration, and crickets chirp in the field beyond us. I look around, trying to find Samantha.

He reads my mind. "She's not here."

"Oh. Everything okay?"

He shrugs and dips his face toward mine. "I told her everything."

I nearly spit out my wine. *Everything?* "What do you mean?"

He looks around the patio and the party, its crowd thinning slightly as some friends and family head home, but he says nothing.

"Dalton?" I mean to touch his arm lightly, get his attention. Instead, I'm sure I've dug in hard, like a pterodactyl flying around Isla Nublar with an unsuspecting tourist. "What do you mean, you told her everything?"

He turns, a glimmer in his eye, a crooked half-smile rising on his lips, and gestures with his head toward the growing darkness in the formal gardens beyond the patio that wrap around to the other side of the mansion and sunroom. "Walk with me."

I swallow two more gulps of wine and then discard the still half-full glass on a tray at the edge of the patio, wondering if I want to be blissfully tipsy or stone-cold sober for what comes next.

I fall into stride beside him as we round the corner, heels scuffling along the brick walkway, and wait for him to speak. My question has been asked; I wait now for his answer.

Alone, save for the roses and lavender, he inhales deeply and shoves his hands in his pockets. "I owe you an apology."

Not the words I expected to hear. "An apology for what?"

"Everything. This whole stupid thing with Sami." He stops and turns to me. "I'm sorry, Hillary."

I shake my head, biting the inside of my cheek. "You don't have to apologize to me. I—"

"I do." He pulls his hands from his pockets and his fingers coil around, then weave into, mine. But he says nothing, just looks as his thumbs rub the backs of my hands.

Then his chest rises and falls. He exhales, long and slow, but he continues to avoid my eyes. "I don't know where to start."

"I mean, if you're apologizing for something, you could start by saying what you're apologizing for." I shake my hands, the motion traveling up to his shoulders, and try to get him to just look at me. Somehow, when we look at each other, words come more easily. Or maybe they don't come more easily—maybe they don't need to come at all, because we can read each other that well.

"This whole plan was stupid. I knew it was stupid, but I was selfish and went along with it anyway. It wasn't fair to her, or to me, or to you."

It *was* a stupid plan, this fake dating thing. And it wasn't fair, but we're all adults, and *fair* left my vocabulary in the ninth grade when Katie Carmine showed up on the first day of school with boobs and highlights in her already perfect hair and I was still stick-straight and had a face covered in acne and home-cut blunt bangs.

"The fact is, Hillary, I decided years ago that getting off the ground in New York was my top priority and everything else could wait. And when I met you, that thought—those priorities—changed. And it was scary as hell."

He inhales through his nose and scans me. "You're cold."

Here I was thinking I could really go for a spare stick of deodorant right about now, and he's noticed my goosebumps. I'm hot and cold all at once, my insides on fire and my spine tingling with anticipation. He slides out of his jacket and drapes it over my shoulders.

"It really goes with the dress, I think." Because of course I can't just let the moment exist without making a dumb joke.

He bites his lip and hides a smile. "I'm sorry I couldn't—didn't—say it earlier. I should have. But you look absolutely stunning tonight."

A fresh shiver runs through me, but I'm definitely not cold.

"And your poem for my parents. I'm blown away. I was not expecting that."

"You read it earlier."

He smirks and tucks a curl behind my ear.

"Wait—but you said—"

"I said I couldn't wait to hear you read it. And I meant it. And it was beautiful and poignant, and I should have told you that, but I couldn't with everyone there, watching. And honestly—" he sighs and shrugs. "I wanted to tell you so many things tonight, but I felt like I couldn't because people thought—"

Neither of us wants to say her name, so I nod. "I get it."

"And that's what made me tell her. I didn't want to pretend anymore. I want to live my life and not some manufactured version of it."

"But earlier—before the party, she was in your room, and—"

He waves off the concern. "She was bringing me a hair dryer because mine was broken."

I don't mean to laugh, but it comes out anyway, loud and snorty and cackling. "I'm sorry," I manage to get out, and I cover my nose and mouth with my hands, hiding my flaring nostrils.

His smile grows, and he brushes a few stray, wind-blown hairs from my face. Then he takes my hands in his and pulls them from my face.

His kiss is intoxicating, which has nothing to do with the whiskey on his breath but everything to do with his tongue's gentle movement inside my mouth. His hand curls around the back of my neck and a thumb traces my jawline to my chin, then down to the base of my neck. The other arm wraps around me, pulling me close to him, which is completely unnecessary because I've snaked my arms around his waist, desperate to never let him go.

But all good things must come to an end, and he pulls his mouth away but rests his forehead against mine. I bite my bottom lip, tasting only him, and I'm dizzy and so very glad I didn't finish that glass of wine. I want to be present for all of this. No liquid courage needed.

"We should probably go back into the party," he says, his breath warm and rich on my face. "Unless you don't want to."

I don't. I can think of a few other places I'd rather be right now. But we've got a long drive back to New York tomorrow afternoon and those hours can be filled with talking and hand-holding and kissing at traffic lights and rest stops. "We should go back in."

He straightens and presses his lips firmly against my forehead, tasting some concoction of sweat and foundation.

I hook my hand into the crook of his elbow and walk with him back through the gardens and the patio to the party, where most of the remaining guests are mingling with one another or saying their final goodbyes of the night to Olivia and Thomas. Even the band seems about finished; their lead vocalist stands off to the side drinking water while her bandmates shine on guitar and keyboards.

Caroline's seated at our table, massaging her feet while the kids play games on their cell phones. "There you are," she smiles as we walk in. "I was afraid you left us here with—" she looks around and whispers loudly, "the old people."

We laugh in response and Dalton excuses himself, then approaches the singer.

"We would never abandon you guys."

"'We,' huh?" she asks, her eyebrow raised. "I couldn't help but notice a certain starlet is missing this last half hour." Her eyes twinkle and she leans in toward me. "Did you guys bury a body somewhere, or—?"

"What do you think makes the garden grow so nicely?" I wink.

Caroline laughs out loud, drawing a few looks from guests as they leave. She waves to them, since she has their attention. "That was funny. But seriously..."

I shrug, and I can feel the goofy grin growing on my face, but I don't care. I'm happy.

Her jaw drops. "No way. Are you guys official now or something? I have so many questions."

"Honestly? Me too."

There are about twenty of us now, and the band finishes their song before Dalton takes the mic one more time. "I just want to thank those of you who are still here for joining us this evening to celebrate my parents. It's been so great to celebrate their love story and their example, and we're glad you were able to come out with us tonight. We've got just a few songs left, so if you're so willing, please join us on the dance floor."

His invitation has an effect opposite its intention— the remaining guests take their coats and give a hurried goodbye to the Tremaines as one more up-tempo dance song comes on. No one wants to be caught on a sparsely-populated dance floor.

The Tremaines do. All of them, from tweens to Thomas. And it's so amazing to be a part of it and to be included in their revelry.

I reach into my bag and draw out my phone to take a few photos and videos, seeing one more text notification from Lindsey.

Text me back when you can. And please don't hate me, Hil.

I'd forgotten, in the whirlwind of the night, all about the apartment. I swipe away the notification and record the fun unfolding before me before dropping the phone back on the table and joining in myself.

Then the band slows it down one last time, and Dalton draws me to him. He grasps one of my hands in his, and his other hand, sweaty and warm, plants firmly on my lower back. The feel of his skin against mine is something I may never get used to, and my heart races.

His years of dance classes show, and he takes the lead, twirling me out and back, away from and closer to him. At the end of the song he dips me, and when he pulls me up again I'm pressed tight against his chest. His smile is wider than I've seen in the last two weeks, and his hazel eyes glitter green.

I only remember we're not alone when the lead singer says, "Thank you, and congratulations to Thomas and Olivia," into the mic. Dalton releases me with his hands but not his eyes and joins his family in their applause. I hold his gaze and clap as well, giving a well-deserved *whoop!* to the band. His grin grows.

Lucy reemerges to oversee the cleanup process and Olivia bounds to her. "Lucy, you've done it again. Thank you for hosting us. This was amazing."

Lucy smiles graciously. "It was a pleasure, Olivia. And wonderful to see you both again." With a nod toward Dalton and Jordan she adds, "Your family really knows how to plan a party."

"That they do," Thomas laughs, and with one final goodbye we all gather our things and traipse, exhausted, back to the carriage house.

A final tray of champagne-filled flutes for the evening awaits us in the parlor downstairs. Jordan and Caroline send the kids upstairs to get ready for bed and the rest of us relax in the velvety armchairs just talking about the party.

"Whatever happened to Samantha?" Thomas asks after nearly half an hour. Olivia cranes her neck to check the room and must also realize that she's missing.

"About that," Dalton says. "We talked. She and I really work better as friends."

"Oh thank *God*," Olivia says, immediately covering her mouth. When the round of laughter subsides, she drops her hands and reveals her flushed cheeks. "I'm sorry, dear. She is lovely, but she's not the one for you."

"No, she's not."

He says it with such certainty that my heart celebrates until my brain shuts the party down. *That doesn't mean* you are *the one for him.* It's the head and the heart bickering all over again.

As if he knows my internal dialogue, Dalton shifts his position in the armchair next to mine and glances sideways at me; his eyes sparkle with something magic and his lips pucker into a blink-and-you'll-miss-it smile.

One by one everyone heads up to bed. Dalton assures his parents he'll be up eventually but wants to have another glass of champagne. At her suggestion I climb the steps with Caroline, and one last, longing look over my shoulder reveals a brooding Dalton, champagne in hand, eyes locked on mine.

Jordan sits opposite him and gestures as he speaks, but I can't hear a word he says over the questions ricocheting through my brain:

What could he be thinking right now?

What exactly are we?

What the hell comes next?

Ten minutes later I'm sprawled like a starfish on the bed, too exhausted to take off the dress or wash my face. But definitely not too exhausted to remove my shoes because they are equally as painful as they are sexy.

The knock on the door is so gentle I don't really notice it until the doorknob itself jiggles. I scoot off the bed, rush to the door, and throw it open. And finally here he is, his bow tie untied and haphazard under his unbuttoned collar, his hair damp from dancing in the late spring humidity, and his eyes a bit of everything.

Playful.

Pleading.

Hopeful.

Happy.

"Can I—" he whispers, and I slide out of the way to let him enter. He checks the hallway to make sure no one is there, then steps into my room and closes the door behind him.

TWENTY-SEVEN

The *ca-clink* of the chain sliding into place sends butterflies scattering into every possible part of me. My fingers and toes tingle in anticipation, and there's a nervous lump in my throat I can't swallow past.

When he kisses me, my insides warm; I melt at just the thought of his lips. But when he touches me, my body recoils, unsure how to react to being touched with such delicate passion. Not just the first time, but the second, and the third…

He pulls back, hands sliding off my skin. "Sorry."

I shake my head and draw another kiss from his perfect mouth. "Don't be." My fingers curl into his hair and his head tilts backward. I kiss his neck and my hands snake into the collar of his jacket, sliding it down his shoulders. He lets it fall to the floor.

His fingers dig into my back, and his lips move from my mouth to my jaw to my ear. This buildup to experiencing the full effect of his attraction pulls a soft moan from my mouth. He's unlocked this piece of myself that I've kept hidden away from the few guys that came before him—this fortress of raw, unashamed pleasure, where I don't hold back.

He kisses me again and rests his forehead on mine, connecting us even when our mouths part. I bite my lip and run my palms along his chest. *Holy hotness.* I take a deep breath and begin unbuttoning his white dress shirt. *He looks like a Chippendales dancer.* I'm giddy with excitement, and something laugh-like comes out as I take in the look and feel of his pecs and abs.

He follows my eyes and that crooked, amazing smile spreads across his face again. "Hillary James, are you objectifying me?"

"Yes," I whisper, biting my lip again. "I totally am."

I fumble with the last few buttons, then run my nails up his back on either side of his spine.

He groans and presses his mouth harder against mine.

We're connected at the hips, and he feels like literally the most perfect thing *ever*, pressed against my thigh, pulsing with every kiss and undulation as our bodies move like waves on the shore against one another, crashing and breaking and receding just to crash and break and recede again.

"Are you sure this is what you want?" he asks, his eyes gleaming.

I shake my head against his. "More."

He kisses me again before stepping forward to guide me toward the bed. I happily let him.

When the mattress hits the backs of my knees, I lower myself, holding the end of his tie, pulling him closer to me as I lie down across the middle of the bed. He props himself on his elbow next to me, and his hand travels from my jaw to my hip, grazing my breast as he goes, then not-quite-tenderly traces my hips and digs his fingers into my skin as I fumble one-handed with his belt.

I'm clumsy. Always have been, always will be. And apparently that trait does not simply go away because I'm rounding first base to second with a man who makes me forget that I am clumsy and awkward and so much less than perfect.

I shove his shoulder backward so I can straddle him. He readjusts the pillows behind him, propping himself up as I keep working at his belt. He slides his hands under the hem of the dress, roams from ankles to thighs, then rolls us over and hovers over me; his fingers glide along my legs, and his mouth follows the same path with gentle, sensual kisses.

Every nerve is sensitive to him; the lighter his touch, the more lightning strikes that spot. Which is why, once again, I squirm with every breath exhaled onto my leg, every connection from fingertips to skin.

"We don't have to do this."

"I want to, though. It's just—" I bite my lip. *It's just embarrassing.* "It's just that I'm not used to this level of interest. Or effort."

He slides my leg over his hips, tracing it again, his mouth on mine. "I am very, very interested, Hillary." He nibbles at my lip and asks, smiling, "You're not going to, like, secretly grade me or anything, are you?"

"Only if you want me to."

I feel him grin as his lips meet mine.

"That's a lie," I breathe. "Like it or not, there'll be an evaluation at the end, but I think you're already working for extra credit at this point."

He laughs his big, hearty laugh, and it launches me into a fit of giggles. I try to push it down, but every time he kisses me or touches me, the laughter returns.

Dalton backs himself off the bed and takes my hands to pull me up with him. He turns me so my back's to him and snakes his fingers into the sides of my dress so they graze my waist, then the side of each breast, and suddenly the giggles are gone.

His shirt's wide open and his pants are unzipped and he's struggling to unbutton my dress. I know that when he finally gets it...

Dalton pulls his hands off of me, and when I try to ask why, he holds a finger to his lips and gestures toward the door.

Shadows dance in the light that creeps in beneath the door, and with them, hushed voices. They're stationed right outside my room. One shadow disappears, and then the knocking starts.

We move together, my footfalls covering his as I approach the door and he rushes to hide in the bathroom. When he's hidden I catch a quick glimpse of myself in the mirror, lipstick smeared, cheeks pink, and I panic. On an open shelf next to the door is an extra blanket, and I envelop myself in it. Its plush filling helps to hide the lower part of my face when I pull it tightly around myself. I feel like a burrito. *A very horny burrito.*

I open the door to see Samantha Darling.

"Are you okay in here?" she asks. Her eyes are puffy and tired.

"Oh, Samantha," I manage a hopefully realistic-looking yawn. "Yeah, everything's fine. What's up?"

She cranes her neck to peek into the room and I side-step to block her view, with the help of my trusty, plush comforter. "I thought I heard voices, that's all."

I shrug, not that she could see my shoulders shift. "Maybe it's someone else down the hall? Or maybe I was talking in my sleep. Could be either, really." *There's a reason I am not an actress. I'm terrible at this.*

"Mmm." She peers around me again, and this time I step too far to the right. "Is that Dalton's jacket?"

"What?" *So this is what a heart attack feels like.*

"There, on the floor." She tries to enter but I block her way.

"Oh, yeah. He let me borrow it earlier when I got cold, walking back from the party."

She rolls her eyes. "Figures." She turns to leave but stops and spins back to face me. "It's you, isn't it? The girl he wants to be with?"

I'm not sure what to say. Eventually she'll know the truth anyway, especially if she and Dalton remain friends, or if her parents ever let me work another shift and I happen to mention something. But I don't want to get into all of it now.

It doesn't matter; she cuts me off. "I should've known. Everything was going great, and then he drops out of the show, saying he wants to stay in the city? And wasn't that just a month after meeting you? Crazy timing, huh?" She shakes her head and repeats, "I should've known." Samantha sighs. "He's the greatest, Hillary. And he must really like you, to throw it all away. So be good to him, okay?"

Tears I refuse to let her see burn hot behind my eyes. "I will."

"And Hillary?"

"Yeah?"

"Do you always sleep in evening gowns?"

My cheeks flush brighter red than before. "I—um—"

She laughs and turns on her heels. "Good night, Hillary." Then, slightly louder, "Good night, Dalton."

I close and lock the door again, shell-shocked from the knowledge bomb Samantha just dropped. Dalton creeps out of the bathroom, his eyes dark brown, his hair disheveled, his smile vanished. He looks like I feel. I tell him, "I think we need to talk."

TWENTY-EIGHT

"**W**hat was Samantha talking about?"

"Hillary..."

I step back when he reaches for me, and I hold my arms up as a barrier. "What did she mean, about you dropping out of the show? I thought you were recast."

He nods. "I was. When I dropped out."

"Dalton."

"Hillary."

Silence fills the space between us, and we wait to see who will end the standoff first.

He rolls his eyes and sinks onto the foot of the bed, propping his elbows on his thighs and resting his head in his hands. "This is not how I saw this night going."

"What, being called out on a lie?" It comes out harsher than I mean, but the damage is done and there's no going back.

His head snaps up and he cops an attitude right back. "And you've never lied to me?"

Only since the day we met. But that was more of a deception, a lie of omission. "No."

He exhales a sigh, and his expression loses its edge.

"All I'm saying is, you shouldn't make yourself smaller for me. You can't."

"I would never."

"But you did. It already happened."

"Hillary, I wanted to stay in New York. Yes, because you're in New York, but also because I want to be there. It's not you, it's me."

"Ha!" I've never heard that expression used positively before.

He turns sideways, curling a leg in front of him, and takes my hand in his. "Honestly, I left the show for me, but because of you, if that makes sense."

"Not even a little bit."

He scratches the back of his neck, pulling his half-buttoned shirt open with the movement of his arm. "This job—the city, the line of work—it's all so transient. People come and go, and you make these connections that are really intense but also really brief. And half the time, everyone's competing with everyone else. Most of the time it doesn't really feel like you belong to something. I feel lonely a *lot*. And then I met you, and there was no competition. No coming and going. Just you, being there, every Sunday at the very least. And I didn't feel alone anymore."

"But the plan was only ever for me to be in the city for a few months. What about when I move back home?"

Gold flecks glow in his hazel eyes, and a smile hides in the corner of his mouth. "C'mon, Hil, you're a perfect fit for the city. Do you really think you'll leave?"

Shit. Lindsey's texts. "Actually—"

The word has power over him, and the magic that danced in his expression a moment ago disappears. "What? What's happening?"

"I was going to tell you tomorrow." I bite the inside of my cheek, keeping my lips from turning downward. Once they pass a certain point, tears automatically flow, and I refuse to cry right now. "Lindsey texted me earlier tonight. Her lease is up in a few weeks, so she's going to give up the apartment to stay with Marco."

Then, the part that threatens to break me most of all, for so many reasons: "I'm moving back home, Dalton."

"Oh." He drops his gaze, and his thumbs stroke the backs of my hands.

"Which is why you need to get out there—tour, or do the out-of-town run, or whatever the options are—"

"I can't imagine spending a year without you."

A *year*? Is that how long we'd be apart? I smile and clear my throat and double down. "It'll be rough, but we'll still talk."

"I know we'll *talk*," he says, and my ears prickle with heat even after he changes the subject. "Do you even *want* to go home?"

"Of course not," I admit. I guess it wouldn't be the worst thing, and I've realized that I miss small-town life since spending the last few days in Greentree. But there's a difference between small towns, which I love, and *my* small town, which makes me want to don a meat dress a la Lady Gaga and climb into the lion exhibit at the Bronx Zoo.

"You could always stay at my place, you know. Whether I'm there or not. You're always welcome."

His jaw tenses as he swallows, and its rigid line reminds me of all the hard lines of his body. I yearn for him, this missing puzzle piece that makes me complete. And I just encouraged him to leave.

But it's for the best, and it's what we both need. Especially with the weekend's developments—there's no way I'd be able to focus on anything with him just inches away, pulling me in like a magnet and tasting each other's lips whenever we want.

He said in our walk through the gardens earlier that his priorities have changed, but shifting the order doesn't change the fact that having a successful career is *still* a priority. Just like my writing is still a priority for me. A thousand kisses may feel great and fulfilling in the weeks it takes to earn them, but if they cost me this life-long dream of publishing, is it worth it? And is it worth him missing out on being part of a show that could propel his career forward, especially when it doesn't work out, in the end?

Because it never works out. Or it never has, I guess, is the more accurate way to phrase that, but still.

But I look into his eyes, green and brown and gold-flecked and warm and deep and understanding and I melt, and I want to tell him *screw everything I just said and stay with me forever*, but I can't.

"Of course," I say instead, delayed and heavy, and I wonder if he has any idea of the internal dialogue I've just talked through to reach those two vague words.

A smile creeps into one side of his mouth, but the rest of his face doesn't get the memo. The creases and lines that tell so many stories are noticeably absent. This is a surface-level smile.

"So, what comes next?" I ask, and he shrugs.

"Next I see if they'll take me back. And if not, I look for other opportunities."

I nod along and realize I wasn't actually asking about what happens next, when we get home. The question escapes, throaty and desperate. "And now?"

His fingers wind into mine, strong and warm, and I'm taken to the day we met when he saved me from the bike messenger. Hope lurches in my heart.

"I don't want to leave," he tells me.

"Then don't."

He fumbles again with the buttons, finally freeing them from their too-tight loops, and his hands skim my neck and back as he says, "Okay, you're good to go."

"Thanks." I close the bathroom door behind me and shimmy out of the long gold gown and into my favorite pajamas: worn-in capri leggings, a bralette, and one of Dalton's old T-shirts that I rescued from a throw-away pile three weeks ago. His scent is woven into the fabric.

I pull the clip from my hair and remove my contacts before slipping my glasses onto my nose. After brushing my teeth, I open the bathroom door and hang the dress in the closet while Dalton gets ready to go to sleep, too.

"So beautiful," he says, and I thumb the beadwork on the long skirt.

"It is. Thank you, again."

"Not the dress."

I can feel my neck and cheeks and ears flush with crimson. "Why do you do that?"

"Do what?"

"Why do you say things like that?" I release the dress and turn toward him.

He shrugs and gives a final fluff to one of the feather pillows. "'Cause it's true."

"Dalton." I display the T-shirt, which has developed a hole in the armpit that helps me prove my argument, and nearly threadbare leggings. "Seriously."

"Seriously. It's not about your clothes, Hillary."

I snort out a laugh. "Clearly not."

"Do you want me to tell you what it is?"

My heart pounds in my chest, because *no*, since I don't

take compliments well, but also *yes*, because I want to know what he sees in me so I make sure he sees it always. Since I don't know what to say, I say nothing, and our eyes are locked again on each other's. He raises his eyebrows and grins.

"Okay, okay, you don't have to beg!"

He meets me in the middle of the room, wearing the black pajama pants and heathered gray T-shirt he snuck out of his parents' suite when I was changing, and proves that you can be sexy regardless of what you're wearing.

"First," he says, "your eyes. They're always so big, so full of excitement."

"I think that's fear, mostly. I'm a very scared person."

"Don't do that."

"Hmm?"

He shakes his head. "The self-deprecating humor. Take the damn compliment. Let me just tell you what I love about you."

I almost throw up, in a really good way. I mean, the timing would be *terrible*, but this feeling that captures my stomach and chest and throat is something. It's hope, happiness, or something like it. And I know he didn't say he *loves me*, just that there are things that he loves *about* me, and it's different. But right now it feels the same, especially when his neck turns red as he realizes what he said.

"What else?" I whisper, because I don't want him to freak out and stop. "What else do you like about me?"

Dalton clears his throat. "I, um… Your shoulders."

Warmth radiates from his fingers through the T-shirt as he draws small circles on my shoulders.

"My…*shoulders*?"

"Mmhmm." He nods, biting back a smile. "I don't know if you know this, but they're always moving. Always dancing to some music only you can hear. You could be cooking or writing or cleaning, and there they are, shimmying or swaying."

I never noticed I did that.

His fingers follow my arms to my hands. "And these— they make magic, every time you sit down and start typing. They *help* people. They saved this party, with a little help from your beautiful brain."

"They're a good team, I guess."

He smiles. "A very good team." He kisses my forehead and winds a hand behind my neck to tilt my face toward his, whispering kisses on my lips next. "And these—" He interrupts himself to kiss me more, and his fingers are stuck in thick, hair-sprayed curls, and my toes tingle. I grope the air blindly for him, finally finding his waist, and I wrap my fingers in his T-shirt so that I don't grab something else.

He breathes into me in an unfinished kiss. "*Mmm. I've wanted to do that for so long.*"

My answering laughter reverberates in his mouth. "You've done it a few times this weekend already. Am I really that forgettable?"

"You're not even remotely forgettable." He rests his forehead against mine. "But those other kisses were different."

"How so?"

He readjusts his fingers in my hair, tucking pieces behind my ear, and gives a sincere smile. "We had to be more careful then. More secret."

I twist his T-shirt tighter, holding on for the answer to my new question. "And now?"

When he swallows, I can feel the muscles in his forehead contract. But he doesn't say anything right away, and I'm worried that asking him to define it crossed a line I don't see. "Hillary," he says, finally. "I want to be yours. And I don't care who knows it."

I wrap my arms tight around his waist and bury my face into his shoulder. He smells like Old Spice and comfort. "Are you sure you're okay to stay tonight?"

"There is literally nowhere on earth I'd rather be than exactly where you are."

When we climb into bed, the room drenched in moonlight, he snakes one arm through the crook of my neck and drapes the other over me. Within seconds I'm entirely too hot and starting to sweat but I don't dare say anything, because who knows how much longer we'll be exactly where the other is.

....

I forgot that Dalton Tremaine snores. So at five o'clock I'm awake, feeling surprisingly well-rested considering I was also awake at 1:35 and 2:47.

I stretch my arms overhead and glance over at him. He's thrown the covers off and lays on his back, arms and legs twisted in a way that might tempt someone to make a chalk outline of his body. His chest rises and falls in a steady rhythm, and I could stay and watch him all morning. Instead I slide out of bed, brush my teeth, and sneak out of the room with my journal.

The parlor is, understandably, deserted. I tiptoe across the creaky floorboards and find a chair in the corner where I can see everyone as they come and go later in the morning. Then I crack open the journal and start to write.

Olivia is the first to come down to the parlor, just a little after seven. She smiles, but her eyes are tired, worried.

"Everything okay?" I ask.

"I think so." she says. "Just worried about Dalton. He wasn't in the suite this morning."

"Oh." Shame latches into the hairs on my neck and my ears go hot. She was so adamant about him having his own room. I clear my throat, the discomfort tangible there. "I'm sure he's fine."

She looks at me over her shoulder as she dunks a bag of oolong into her teacup. "Have you seen him, Hillary?" When I clear my throat again and open my dry mouth, unable to respond, she winks. "Ahh. Then I'm certain he's doing better than 'fine.'"

"What's this, now? Who's fine?" Jordan rubs the sleep from his eyes as he shuffles into the parlor.

Olivia's eyes sparkle from the corner of the room with the tea setup, and she says, "Your brother went missing last night. But it seems he just got lost and turned left at the top of the stairs. Right, Hillary?"

"No shit," Jordan says, his eyes suddenly awake. "It's about time, you guys."

I open my mouth to object, but Olivia waves her hand to quiet me. "We don't need details. We're just glad he finally realized he needed to get his act together."

"What do you mean?" I ask, still flushed with embarrassment.

Jordan rolls his eyes and plops into a chair across the room, not bothering to cover a yawn. "Mom told me all those texts were about you. All the mushy, gooey things."

"Yes," Olivia adds, blowing across her cup as she crosses to the seat next to Jordan's. She taps his knee as she passes, and he sits up a little and scratches at his beard. "I realized it in New York, the day you and I went to see that play."

She takes a sip and crosses her legs. "Jordan, do you remember those messages?"

"Remember?" snorts Jordan. "I have them in our group texts." He reaches into his hoodie pocket and pulls out his phone, then starts scrolling.

"Okay, March sixth, from Dalton: 'Sorry for the late reply. Got caught up talking to the most amazing girl today. Totally collided with her—had to replace her coffee, didn't want to leave.'"

I set the journal aside. I'm torn between wanting to hear every word and feeling like I'm not meant to hear any of them.

"Blah blah blah," Jordan says, scrolling to the next message from his brother. "Okay, here, Mom asks when she can expect grandchildren…"

"I did not," Olivia laughs, rolling her eyes. Then she clears her throat and flicks her gaze to me for the shortest second before looking away. My mouth goes dry.

"Oh, right," Jordan says. "Okay next up, April twelfth. 'Wish me luck—big date tonight. It's normal to be crazy nervous before these, right?' I asked if he wanted me to send an escape text ten minutes in, but he said he'd hunt me down if I disturbed him at all."

Olivia, who hasn't stopped watching me while Jordan reads, asks, "Remember, in New York? I asked about him skipping a date to help with the flood situation. And you said—"

"I said it wasn't a date. We just had dinner planned, like every Sunday." I remember it well, and how Olivia's demeanor changed when I said it. She must have realized then that he was never talking about Samantha.

"I have some more, just between the two of us," Jordan says. "But yeah, at that dinner the other night it was pretty clear he's obsessed with you and all these texts are about you and not—"

"Samantha!" Olivia cries as I see movement just beyond the parlor. "Hello!"

Samantha's blond head pokes into the parlor. "Oh, hi. Good morning." She gives a small wave to the three of us and adjusts the sunglasses on top of her head. "Olivia, thank you for allowing me to join you all for the party. It was great to see you again."

"Are you heading out?" Olivia asks, rising, and Samantha nods.

"Did you want any breakfast first? Coffee for the drive?" I'd know that voice and that helpful urge anywhere.

Samantha shakes her head. "I'm fine, thank you."

"It was nice to meet you, Jordan. And Hil—remember what I said, okay?"

When she says my name, Dalton shifts in the hallway and appears in the entryway behind her. "Morning, everyone," he says, but his eyes don't move from mine.

"I will," I nod to Samantha, and I return the smile she shoots my way.

"Great. Safe travels. Thanks again, Tremaine family!" She holds the front door open as Dalton lugs her suitcase and garment bag outside. Jordan and Olivia's gazes follow them outside then slowly turn to me.

"Does she know?" Jordan asks, wide-eyed, at the same time Olivia says, "She's taking this well."

Luckily, before I can answer, Dalton is back inside, and the attention has turned to him. "What? What'd I miss?"

"Did you have a good night last night, little brother?"

Though he doesn't move his head, his eyes dart to mine, and that's all Jordan needs.

"Yeah, thought so," he winks. "Mom, should we get out of here? Let them have some privacy?"

"Shut up, Jordan," Dalton says, rolling his eyes. But he's smiling, and suddenly he's in a chair next to mine. He angles himself toward me and lowers his voice. "Good morning."

The most basic greeting sounds suddenly sensual. Maybe it's his gravelly morning voice. Maybe it's the memory of last night. "Hi."

"Hi," Jordan says, waving to get his attention from across the room. Dalton turns toward his family.

"Late night, dear?"

"The latest," he answers. "I must've rewatched that video of Jordan dancing at least eighty times. Then I went through all the photos Hillary took to find some good candidates for our Christmas card this year."

I love the way he deflects from the intimate details of what happened between us last night to something so trivial, and his family takes the bait.

"Two words: Prom Picture," Jordan retorts.

Olivia shakes her head. "Hillary, do you see what I deal with on a regular basis?"

I nod and Dalton turns to me again, smiling. And suddenly everything's right. Being here with his family, sinking into their banter like it's an old La-Z-Boy. He takes my hand in his.

Brunch is served at eleven on the patio where the bar was set up last night, and at one o'clock Dalton and I head inside to finish packing so we can start the drive back to the city.

Alone for the first time today, he pulls me into him and drapes his arms over my shoulders. "How bad was it this morning?"

"Um, super awkward, considering your mom's rule about having your own room."

"Mmm. Can I fill you in on a secret?" When I nod, he continues, "that's not really her rule. She just made it up for Samantha."

"Are you kidding?"

He shakes his head and grins. "I'm dead serious. She knew I didn't really want to share a room with Samantha. I think she's been Team Hillary all along."

"No, she's Team *Dalton*. She just wants you to be happy."

He shrugs. "Like I said. Team Hillary."

His fingers follow my hairline from the center of my forehead down to my ears, then he cradles my neck as he leans in to kiss me.

"You ready to get home?"

I nod, but *no*. I'm not ready. Because as soon as we're back in New York he'll be trying to get himself into another show that could take him out of the city. For a year, maybe. And I'm terrified of losing him.

TWENTY-NINE

The knocking on my bedroom door frame wakes me around eight o'clock. I was so tired when we got home late last night that I autopiloted into my room and collapsed into bed.

"Morning," I say, stifling a yawn.

"Morning," he smiles, holding two to-go cups from Eunoia. "First day back after a crazy weekend. Figured you could use some of this."

"Yesss, thank you." I sit cross-legged and extend my arms. He lowers himself onto the far corner of the bed and passes a cup to me. I close my eyes and breathe in its warmth, feeling his gaze on me.

"I'm surprised you were able to sleep so late, considering you slept for a good bit of the car ride yesterday."

I sip the coffee. "To be fair, I had gotten very little sleep the night before."

He cocks his head and blinks.

"I'm just not used to the snoring."

"Yikes. Am I that bad?"

"I think it would be quieter at a Miami bar during Spring Break."

He winces. "Ouch. Sorry." Then, "Is that why you slept in here last night?"

It's a strange sensation, when someone makes you feel

wanted. No, *desired*. I felt it at first with Peter, but then we settled into a rhythm, and he stopped caring, stopped desiring. He stopped pursuing me because he thought he had me, but he took no steps to keep me.

This *thing* with Dalton feels different in every way, like there will always be coffee and walks to nowhere in particular, questions about what I want and how I feel. And like how I feel will always matter.

"I slept in here because my zombie legs carried me in here last night about half a second before I passed out. But also—" I shift and thumb the cup sleeve. "We didn't really talk about—"

"Our living arrangement?" He cuts me off, and I nod. "Mi casa es su casa, Hillary. You can be anywhere you want to be. And no pressure to go anywhere you don't want to go. Full stop."

Peter had asked me to move in with him twice in three years, once in the beginning when he thought we'd be having sex every night, and once a year later, when I had gotten really into cooking and organizing, and he thought that me moving in meant I was going to be a 1950s housewife.

I lean forward, coffee still in hand, and kiss him once. Then a second time, a breath longer than the first.

Before I can sink back on my heels, his hand strokes my jaw and cheek and he kisses me again. His teeth graze my lip when he pulls away, and he holds his face close to mine.

"What was that for?"

"Just—" I clench my jaw and swallow. "Thank you. For being you."

"Of course." He drops his hands and I sit back, taking another drink. "I know we've always had this thing where we can talk really openly about things, and I'm so glad we do. Because there's something important I really need to ask you."

Everything tightens and tenses and I brace myself to have to answer questions I don't have answers to. "Okay. Anything." *That is the rule, after all.*

He sits back, brows furrowed, and motions with his head toward the spot next to me. "What is that?"

I glance to my right and then turn back to Dalton, whose eyes crease with the birth of a smile. I hold up the stuffed animal in question and feel zero shame. "This is Eunice the Unicorn." And before Dalton can say anything, I explain more. "Peter and I had an argument once at a festival near us. I wanted to play games, he thought they were a waste of money. I don't necessarily disagree, but I also know I'm a great Skee-Ball player."

"I'd expect nothing less, and I'll challenge your skills any day."

"You're on," I smile, appreciating his frequent humor. "Anyway, he stormed off to get a snack or whatever, and I sunk a few quarters into Skee-Ball. After two games I had enough tickets to cash in for this unicorn."

He looks at the pastel toy, then back to me. "So you keep a unicorn from date night with your ex because…"

I shake my head and correct him. "I keep this unicorn from the time I did what I wanted and proved that I'm capable. It reminds me that I shouldn't let others dictate to me what I can or should do. Also," I pull it close for an over-the-top hug, "it's very fluffy."

"I love it," he says, reaching out to feel its plush.

"And, full disclosure, it's really nice to have something to snuggle with. It makes me feel less alone."

The gold flecks in his eyes glimmer and I know he holds

back from saying what we both know—I don't have to sleep alone anymore.

At least, not for now.

Instead he asks about my schedule for the day, which includes a shift at Books Off Broadway, as long as I haven't been fired. But I'm only supposed to be there from ten till four, so my evening is free.

"Great," he smiles. "Because I owe you a drink."

Despite the fact that the store is closed today, we've got a lot of work to do, getting ready for a big sale. The city noise disrupts the quiet when I walk in, and if either Charles is upset with me they don't show it. Sue greets me from behind the register with a wide grin.

"Good morning! Welcome back!"

"Hi! Thanks."

The city is busy this morning, a shock to the system after the relaxed pace of West Virginia, but time slows again inside the bookstore with its familiar smells and friendly faces. There's a sense of belonging here, always, in the books and in the people.

"Did you have an amazing weekend?" she asks as I drop my bag behind the counter.

Steve glances over from a stack of used books he's sorting through. "Hiya, Hillary."

I wave to him and answer Sue. "I did—thanks for asking. It was really nice to get away for a bit."

"I'm sure it was. Bring back any souvenirs, particularly of the tall and talented variety?"

My heart stops, but her smile breaks into laughter.

"I'm just messing with you, dear. Sami told us a bit about

their *deal.*" She gives air-quotes to the word. "She said the two of you seem to be a great match, though."

Relief washes in a wave over me. "That was really nice of her to say. I thought for sure she'd be beyond mad."

Steve shakes his head. "No one said she wasn't. But she's probably mostly embarrassed. It'll pass."

"Steven Eugene Charles!" Sue scolds him for sharing that secret about their daughter, and his ears flush.

It hadn't occurred to me that of all the possible emotions she could be feeling, Samantha was embarrassed. It was clear from our conversation that she had feelings for Dalton that never really went away from years ago when they first started spending time together. *Like Hot Pockets.*

But then Sue waves it all aside. "Anyway, none of that matters. It's good to have you back."

And the day continues like nothing's changed until four o'clock when it's time for me to clock out and head back to the apartment.

....

Dalton texts me at five thirty to apologize for running late for the drink he owes me, then returns home at seven thirty with pizza and a bottle of wine.

"For the record," I tell him, raising my glass over a paper plate full of three-meat pizza, "this doesn't count."

He raises his glass in return, his hair falling lazily across his forehead, his eyes mischievous. "Good."

....

I spend Tuesday at the bookstore again; new release days are always busy. When I get back to the apartment around seven Dalton is noticeably absent, but there's a note on the kitchen counter:

Still kind of early. Not at all late.
Tonight let's cash in on that date.
I'll pick you up right at eight.
(Sorry these rhymes aren't so great.)

−D

I blast some music and notice, while I'm touching up my makeup, that my shoulders are shimmying even while applying mascara. The thought of Dalton's fingertips on my skin—talking about how much he *loves* my shoulders, my eyes, my hands—makes my spine tingle with heat that radiates through every attached nerve.

With hair and makeup done I grab a sleeveless button-up dress with a square neckline in a hue of lavender that reminds me of that cotton candy sunset at the beach weeks ago. The night he told me I was "it." The night he told his family I was "it," too.

A few minutes before eight I'm ready to go, and I grab my phone and open my door. The hallway to the kitchen is lined in votives and pink rose petals. "Whoa."

"Hey," says a startled Dalton, peeking his head out of his bedroom next door. "You're early."

"I—I didn't realize I was supposed to wait in here. Sorry."

"No, you're fine," he smiles. He disappears another moment and reemerges with a bouquet of wildflowers wrapped in brown paper. His favorite sweater's sleeves are shoved halfway up his forearms. "These are for you."

I take the wildflowers and breathe in their aroma. "Thank you. They're just as beautiful as the bouquet from April."

The words ignite something in him, and his face lights up. "You remember."

"Of course I remember. That sweater, the flowers. The license plate on the car that took Lindsey to the airport."

When he laughs, every one of my muscles relaxes. I'm giddy every time I see him, like every moment with him is a once in a lifetime opportunity. And then he smiles or laughs or looks at me with eyes that tell me I'm *it* and the giddiness fades—no, *melts*—into something stronger and calmer and filling, like warm honey.

"You don't remember the license plate."

I smile into his laughter. "J-L-Z-two-zero-zero-eight."

He studies me, a vein appearing in his forehead when he swallows. "You know I could actually check that, right?"

"Are you going to?" I challenge.

He shakes his head and lowers his gaze to my lips. "No. I have more important things to focus on."

I tilt my head upward, inviting his kiss. It's gentle and warm and perfect.

Dalton leads me to the kitchen, puts the flowers in water on the island, and pours two glasses of White Zin. He gestures to the sliding door, and in the glow of the white lights he's strung around the terrace I can see he's also set up a table and chairs outside.

"I know I told you I'd take you out somewhere for a drink, but—"

"This counts. This definitely counts."

"Fire hazard," he says after blowing out the votives in the hallway. Then he braids his fingers into mine and leads me to the loveseat outside. "Dinner should be here soon."

I'd completely forgotten that I haven't eaten today, but now my stomach flips and I hope he doesn't hear it growl.

Until dinner arrives, I curl my legs up behind me and rest my head against his shoulder. With his arm around me, we take in the sky's surrender to the sunset. Then he gets a text that draws him inside and he returns minutes later with two plates filled with chicken cordon bleu, roasted carrots, and Brussels sprouts gratin.

"Where did you get this?" I ask, lowering myself into a seat he pulls out for me.

He shrugs. "I made it."

"You did not."

"I did. I used Art's kitchen next door earlier. Prepped everything, had it in his oven, and he just took it out when the timer went off."

"This looks amazing. Nicely done."

He shrugs again. "We haven't tasted it yet, so—"

But then the first bite of chicken is tender and delicious, the carrots are cooked to perfection, and he's mastered my Brussels sprouts recipe. And we spend dinner talking and laughing like we've done for months, but now when our feet brush against each other we don't pull away embarrassed or apologetic. "Assuming that is the correct license plate," he says, "why the hell did you memorize it?"

"I wanted to commit the whole night to memory. The good, the bad. Every second with you. I thought—" The second glass of wine rushes to my head and my body goes numb and my face turns red. "I thought I was leaving. I thought I'd never see you again. And even before then, before we knew about the flood I was thinking about every-thing, ready to memorize everything because I thought it was a—"

"A date." He leans back in his chair, chewing a bite of chicken.

"I'd thought so, yes. But then, obviously, it wasn't. Or was never supposed to be." I remember him apologizing for that all-important firefly conversation.

His lips curl up, then down. "Imagine how different it would've been if I'd been honest with you."

I set the wine glass down and fold my hands in my lap. "What do you mean?"

"I mean—if I would have told you that night how I felt. If I would've explained myself, instead of..." He bites the inside of his lip and shakes his head, running his hands down his face. "I didn't want you to leave."

"I didn't want to leave either."

"Would you have moved in with me if I'd owned everything from that weekend? If I told you how I honestly felt?"

The soft white lights around the terrace suddenly feel more like interrogation lamps than romantic mood lighting. Deep brown eyes reflecting orbs of white, boring into me, waiting for an answer. "I guess it depends on what you would have told me."

His jaw clenches and a vein grows in his neck as he swallows past his nerves. His eyes don't leave mine. Finally he says, "I would have told you that I'm crazy about you. That I can't imagine not having you near me."

My heart catches in my throat when he says it, and every part of me goes tingly and warm and nervous.

"I would have told you that the reason I was recast is because I told the team I wasn't able to leave New York. Truthfully, I wasn't ready to leave you. So when you said you were leaving—"

"You were scared."

He shakes his head thoughtfully. "No. I was... devastated. Heartbroken. I couldn't let you leave, but you seemed so intent on it, because you thought it would be weird to live together if we had feelings for each other." He runs a hand through his hair, then leans forward, resting his elbows on the table. "Tell me—and be honest, Hillary—it's the only reason you stayed, isn't it? Because I told you that the whole phone call was meaningless."

He's absolutely right. I was ready to walk out the door and move back home until he said he'd host any of his *friends* who were going through what I was going through. When I felt his breath on my neck and the closeness of his body that night, and when I thought of the help he provided to both Lindsey and me with the cleanup and the pizza, and when I thought of the wildflowers and the dressed-up Dalton who arrived in the black town car to pick me up for what I knew was a date, it all felt overwhelming and terrifying. "Dalton—"

"I don't regret it, Hillary." He sinks back in his chair.

"I just—it felt like so much, so fast."

He finishes a sip of wine and holds it in his mouth before asking, "What did?"

What I love about Dalton is that we can tell each other the hard things, the honest things. I trust him with every part of my head and my heart, every secret and story and embarrassing moment that pulls laughter from his chest and a sympathetic *I'm so sorry* from his lips.

"I knew how I felt about you, and then you told me that I was *it*, and then you were asking me to stay at your place. So yes, if you would have told me that you were—"

"Crazy about you," he nods, filling in the words that I struggle to say despite everything that's happened in the last week.

"Yes—that. You're right. I would have gone home. I would have hated it, but I would have gone home."

I close my eyes and inhale the evening air. It's fresher up here than the sticky, stale air at the street level, but it's no West Virginia. When I exhale and open my eyes, Dalton's reaching for me. "Come sit with me," he says, and we ditch the table for the loveseat.

Curled up in the corner, his hand woven into mine, I tell him everything.

"You scare me. *This* scares me."

His forehead creases when he has questions, and right now there is a very big, very deep crease.

"I mean, obviously *you* don't scare me. But these feelings I have for you—the feelings I thought you had for me that night—they're scary. But they're also amazing. Honestly, I've never felt this way before. Ever. And that uncharted territory is terrifying."

His fingers tighten around mine, and he smiles.

"I know that I know you, Dalton, but I also know that I don't know *all* of you. I don't know your past with women, though I can imagine…"

"Wait—" he says, his grin gone, when I trail off. "Are you asking how many women I've slept with?"

"No. I don't think so. I just— I don't want to disappoint you."

"You could never," he says, his voice firm, like he's stating an obvious fact. "And as for the other thing… it's not a lot, if you want to know."

I *do* want to know, though I also do *not* want to know. Maybe what scares me isn't the quantity as much as it is the quality—stars like Samantha Darling, or dancers in some of his other shows, all toned and flexible and ready for endless cardio, with interesting lives and limitless potential. "I was afraid that, whatever the number was, I wouldn't be able to compete."

"Hillary."

When I was younger, my mom always burned candles that came in glass jars. She hated blowing them out because the smoke lingered thick and black in the air, and the aroma of the candle was lost in that haze. Instead, she'd put the glass lid back over the still-flickering fire, robbing it of the oxygen it needed to live, and watch it calm itself into stillness before it disappeared altogether.

The way Dalton says my name—he's the lid, all my discomfort the flame.

"You have no competition. Not for me." When I dare glance into his eyes, the golden flecks are bright in the twilight. "I mean it, Hil."

I lean in to kiss his cheek, then curl up into his side. "For as much as I think I understand you, I really don't understand you."

He snickers. "Welcome to the club." Then he kisses the top of my head and asks, "What can I help you understand?"

The question has been a muted addition to every kiss, every conversation of the last few days, certainly. But it also goes back months at this point, to the day we met. I've choked it down with every sip of coffee we drank together, gulped it back with wine through so many dinners. All along I knew I could ask it, and all along I was afraid of the response. But I'm not afraid anymore.

"Why me?"

He doesn't reply right away. Instead, he strokes my hair and tucks loose, wind-blown strands behind my ear. He rests his cheek against the top of my head, and I can feel his muscles tighten as he swallows.

"I just have never understood why you even took the time, that very first day, to sit with me. And I don't understand how you have your dream job waiting for you, and how you have all these options, and you still choose me."

"That very first day," he breathes, hoarse and dry. He clears his throat and continues. "That very first day, I was so in awe of how you handled the coffee incident. You didn't yell, you didn't complain. You *laughed*. And you were *nice* about it. And I was immediately intrigued."

He brushes my hair behind my neck and runs a finger along the skin from my ear to the top of my shoulder. "Then you danced in the rain in the middle of a New York City sidewalk. You listened—you always listen. You're beautiful. Your heart is *good*. My mom loves you as much as I do, and *no one* is good enough for me in her eyes. You're honest. You're generous. Want me to keep going?"

Yes.

No. I sit up, detaching myself from his body.

"What did you say?"

He snorts. "You want me to repeat the whole monologue? I didn't rehearse it, but I could try to go from the list of reasons swirling around up here," he says, tapping his head with two fingers.

I shake my head. "No, not the whole list. Just the one part—about your mom."

He pauses, thinking back to everything he just shared, and his cheeks burn red. "Oh. That."

"Yeah. Did you need a do-over on that part, or are we keeping that in there?" *Ah, yes, terribly timed humor. Very on-brand.*

He exhales. "No do-overs. No edits. No notes." It comes out as naturally as a breath when he says, "I have loved you since the day we met."

His mouth opens, ready to say more, and I don't mean to interrupt, but the words come out anyway. "That's crazy."

He closes his mouth and smiles. "Maybe it would be more accurate to say, I knew I was going to love you since the day we met. When we started our walk-and-talks, spending every Sunday together—I loved you for your friendship. And then, little by little and all at once, I knew I *loved* you, loved you." He closes his eyes and shakes his head, then beams his hazel eyes right into mine. "I *love* you."

My throat stings with a mixture of nerves and tears and probably snot from all the ways I want to cry, happy and relieved, and most of all, madly, deeply in love. Before I can speak, he's already taking the pressure away.

"I don't expect you to say anything. I mean, I wasn't trying to—"

I throw my arms around him, pressing my lips against his. "Of course I love you."

His arms coil around me and I slide into his lap, bending to kiss his lips, which feel warm and pillowy, like marshmallows barely touched by a campfire.

He kisses my chin, then my neck, as his hands glide down my back and land at the base of my spine. My chest tightens and warm goosebumps spread across my arms.

A siren wails below us and my hand tightens in his hair, startled. I pull away and release my grip. His eyes meet mine, crystal clear, intense green. Curious.

"I'm sorry. I just—should we go inside, maybe?"

The corners of his lips turn upward. "Hillary James, are you trying to seduce me?"

I nod and laugh when I kiss him again. "Is it working?"

"One hundred percent," he answers.

I take in the dinner dishes and set them in the sink. Dalton's right behind me with our empty wine glasses.

"Did you want a refill?" he asks. I bite my lip and shake my head no. Maybe I should, but I want to remember every bit of what's coming.

He sets the glasses on the counter and looks at me—eyes to lips to chest to legs to bare feet and back—and he sighs. "God, you're beautiful."

"I promise you, I am very average."

"No," he says, shaking his head. "You're perfect." He takes my hand and pulls me to him, and I feel his solid chest against mine when he kisses me again.

At first my hands grab at his sweater, but as his tongue flicks at mine and his hands find the buttons on the bodice of my dress, my fingers grope for his belt and hook into the leather, pulling his hips against my own.

When he's unbuttoned the top three buttons and brushed the dress straps off my shoulders, his fingertips dig into my back and his mouth kisses any skin it can find. His teeth graze my collarbone and I moan his name.

"Are you okay?" he asks, planting warm kisses along the side of my neck.

"Mmhmm."

A kiss on my throat. One on the other side of my neck. His thumb stroking my jaw. "Is this okay?"

"Mmhmm."

My knees buckle when he undoes the next button and rests his forehead against mine. "Do you want to—"

"Mmhmm," I moan, more enthusiastically. "Yes, please."

I half expect him to laugh, because it's absurd, really, that here we are, all because he spilled coffee on me three months ago. And it's absurd that we're professing that we love one another, all because we happened to be in the same place at the same time. In a city of millions, we were lucky enough to bump into each other.

But he doesn't laugh. He swallows and draws me in with his eyes while he backs up through the kitchen and down the hallway to his room, me in tow.

His hands cradle my neck as his mouth and tongue greet mine.

My hands find his belt again, unfastening it first, then moving on to the button on his pants.

Soon his fingers sneak under the layer of peeled-back lavender linen, sliding over my bra, warm against my midsection.

I find his waist, and when his teeth graze my ear, I steady myself in fistfuls of cashmere. I pull up, exposing his abs, then his chest, until he grabs hold of the hem and peels off his sweater. *He looks so good.*

I giggle. One barely audible giggle, and of course he hears it.

"Something amusing to you?" he asks, repressing a smile as he pulls back.

Another bit of laughter comes out as my hands skim over his toned torso and trace the grid of his abs. "Just thinking about how much fun this is going to be."

He laughs in return, and his chest rises and falls with the sound. "You have no idea," he promises, and he tugs on the dress to pull me back against him.

We topple onto the bed, kissing in a burst of laughter, and he kicks his shoes onto the floor before rolling me onto my back and kneeling over me. His eyes are fire; they evaporate my laughter and melt my smile. This is suddenly serious: I feel it, and the glowing amber in his eyes tells me that he feels it, too.

He draws in a breath and his thumb grazes my cheek. When his mouth is on mine again, I'm ablaze inside; he fans the flames with every touch of his lips on my jaw, my sternum, my stomach, as he unbuttons the rest of my dress.

He sits back, drawing lines up my leg from ankle to thigh with electric fingertips, then curls his hand around my hip. I gasp, and his eyes dart from his hand to my face.

"Sorry. Please don't stop."

But he does stop, just long enough to stand and shove his jeans down his legs while I shimmy out of my dress altogether and discard it on the ever-growing pile of clothing on his floor. He kisses me again and promises to be right back. I appreciate the way his boxer briefs hug his perfect body as he leaves the room—and as he walks back in a few moments later. *This will be worth the wait.*

He's carrying a bag from the bodega down the street and unpacks two items: the first, a box that he lays on the nightstand, and the second, a nightlight that he plugs in, casting the room in a soft golden glow.

He lowers himself into bed next to me and twists his fingers into my hair. Then we're both mouths and hands, all over each other, slow and savoring every connection our bodies make.

His hands wrap around my back, and he pulls me, somehow, more tightly to him. He locks his eyes on mine. "Are you sure you're ready to do this?"

When he pulled me out of the bike lane three months ago, my heart pounded in my chest, pressed up against his, and I wished then that his would do the same. Tonight, we both react to this closeness and anticipation with the same *thump-thump*ing, and I've never been more ready for anything in my life.

He twists away, grabs the box from the nightstand and takes out a little plastic square, then kisses me. My mouth is on his, with a quick field trip to his neck and shoulder, while I slide my underwear down my legs. When he's ready, he rolls on top of me, and he bites his lip as he watches our bodies finally come together. Finding a rhythm comes as easily as every conversation we've ever had—this give and take, asking and answering, has always been natural to us.

Then he wedges an arm under my back, fighting with the clasp of my bra. I arch toward him, giving him more space to work, and once he has it unhooked, he eases the straps off my shoulders before dropping the black lace balconette onto Mount Clothing.

"Happy now?"

"Very," he says.

I laugh and his forehead creases.

"*Wow*, that feels good."

I'm giddy, seeing the pleasure my body brings him. It makes me want to laugh more.

He skims a hand along my side; his thumb reaches inward and grazes my breast. He bends and puts his lips against it, too, planting long, slow kisses across my chest.

I've got one hand gripping the sheets, channeling my pleading desperation through my grasp; the other slides into his hair like he's a marionette and each strand is a string. When I want to kiss his neck, pull back. When I want his mouth on my skin, pull in.

When his hand journeys *there* and everything intensifies and I lose complete control over myself, I just pull. *Hard*. He grunts in pain, which matches my surprised yelp, as far as embarrassing sex noises go. But then he smiles, and his eyes dance, and he presses his mouth to mine and there are no frills—just perfection as our bodies move like rolling waves.

When it's over, he lays next to me, our fingers entwined, and kisses my shoulder. We just let ourselves be, sweaty and heaving and smiling and smitten and unashamed and madly, magically, somehow in love.

THIRTY

On Wednesday afternoon, when I have a day off from the bookstore, Dalton comes home from a meeting and leans over my shoulder to kiss my neck while I write at the kitchen table.

I crane my neck backward and kiss him upside down, like in that superhero movie. Then he's kneeling next to me, holding my waist. "You busy?" he smiles.

"I'm about to be."

I abandon my journal on the table as he pulls my legs around his waist and carries me back to his room. We kiss through our laughter when he loses balance and crashes sideways into the wall just outside his bedroom. Then we fall into bed and pull each other's clothes off.

In the daylight, I'm more aware of the beads of sweat that form around his hairline, the way his eyelids flutter with moments of pleasure, the rolling muscles in his shoulders, forearms, and chest. I hope if there's anything new that he notices about me in the daylight, that he regards it with the same appreciation I have for him.

He smooths back my hair, interlocks his fingers with mine, and presses his lips against my skin. I'm a mess of contradictions when he's inside me: clear-headed, yet my mind is racing; goosebumps cover my skin, yet warmth radiates through me; breathless, yet full of life.

"Are you okay?" he asks, his voice sending my thoughts scattering.

My eyes meet his as he hovers over me. My arms are hooked under his, and my fingers dance across his shoulder blades. "I'm great."

"You seem like your mind is elsewhere." The worry disappears from his face when I laugh; his eyes close and creases form around his lips. "Maybe I should be worried that you laugh during sex, but it feels so damn good."

I laugh again, which makes him laugh as he bites his lip. "My mind is right here, thinking about how much I love this. How much I love you."

"You'd better," he answers, kissing me.

"Well *that,* and also thinking how ridiculously hot your body is." I slide my fingertips along his arm, giddiness surely evident on my face.

He reaches a hand up toward my face and I intercept it, catching his wrist, kissing his palm, and guiding it down to my chest as I lean into his lips.

....

"I could stay in bed with you like this all day," he says when we've finished.

I shrug. "Then do it."

I wonder if he thinks the same things I do—that he could be gone in a month, on tour somewhere, or doing an out of town run of a show—and that's why he wants to be just like this as much as possible. This vulnerable, this connected. This free.

He shimmies closer to me, and I lay again next to him, lifting my head just enough for him to slide an arm around my shoulder.

"Can we just lay like this?" he asks, his hand in my hair, his eyes scanning my face.

I pull the sheet up and snuggle my head into his shoulder. "For as long as you want."

And so we lay together, his arm around me, his fingers skimming my arm in long strokes. I draw circles on his chest and inhale the scent of Old Spice.

A hushed hum fills my throat.

"What is it?" he asks, kissing the top of my head.

"Just—you even *smell* good."

"Thanks?"

I kiss his chest and twist to look up at him. "I was just thinking back to my first night here—showering after cleaning up Lindsey's apartment, having to use your body wash and shampoo. And I remember liking it because it made me feel like you were close to me."

"Almost like I was right next door?"

"You know what I mean." He kisses my forehead when I roll my eyes at him. "It was comforting."

He nods and strokes my hair again, and once I'm re-snuggled he asks, "Of all the scents in the world, which is your favorite?"

I know immediately what the answer is, but I stall. "That's a weird question."

"We've asked each other lots of weird questions."

He's not wrong. "You first."

"Sure, okay." He pauses a few moments before responding. "Pizza."

I sit up, the sheet pinched between my arms and torso. "I'm sorry. What?"

A smile dances across his lips. "You heard me. Pizza. It's my favorite smell."

I laugh and shake my head. "Sorry, but I'm going to need more information."

"Point one," he begins, "pizza just smells great. It doesn't need an explanation. But because you asked I'll tell you more. Point two, and this is the kicker, it's tied to the best memories. Birthday parties from basically every year of my childhood. Family game nights. The cast party after my first musical in high school where I played spin the bottle with Gina Thompson but got stuck kissing Missy Donovan. Dollar slices when I was new to the city and broke and needed cheap dinners, but at least I was *here*, in the city."

"Valid argument," I nod, approving of his list. "No additional explanation needed."

"Thanks," he says. "Now yours."

I bite the inside of my cheek, thinking. "I don't know that I have just one."

"You have to choose."

While the answer formulates in my head, I lower myself back down and rest my head against his shoulder, draping my hand across his torso. "Worms."

He repeats the word, and it sounds like a thought more than a question. A moment passes, then another, before he asks me to explain.

"I smile whenever I smell them. And I know the smell is *awful*."

"It really is. And yet—"

"Yet it's my favorite." I shrug. "You know how it is, every time a storm rolls in, at least back home, you get that earthworm smell. And I love rainy days, so it just fits."

He's nodding, slowly. "Interesting."

"But really, it makes me think of my grandfather."

That seems more reasonable. "How so?"

"He was just the best. Did everything for everyone. Had a great sense of humor. Was always out fishing."

"So he smelled like earthworms?"

"Sometimes," I nod. "But really, my favorite moments growing up were the summer days my sister and I would spend at my grandparents' house while my parents were at work. We'd pick blueberries or play in the yard or play some old-school computer games. But when the rain came and cooled off the air, Grandpa and I would read outside on the covered porch. No matter how hard it rained, we just read on, noses buried in books while the roof protected us from the worst of it. Sometimes he'd smoke his pipe, which was the one smell that masked the scent of the worms. But usually it was new book smell and earthworms."

Dalton's free hand finds mine, and our fingers twist together.

"He's the reason I fell in love with books."

"Oh?" he asks, and I brace myself against the coming grief in his fingers.

"Whenever we got good report cards, we went to the discount bookstore a few miles away, and he'd buy us a new book as a reward."

"You must've been the prettiest nerd at your school," he says, and the tenderness in his voice makes me smile, despite the sadness.

"I was Nerd Queen."

"Of course you were." Then his hand clenches mine more tightly. "And now?"

"He passed away about two years ago. When I was ambitious and dating and too busy to be there with him because the rest of life seemed too important to spend time sitting on a porch, reading."

He kisses the top of my head again, long and slow. "It's not your fault, you know. That he's gone."

I swipe at the tears threatening to drip onto his bare chest. "It is, though," I confess. "He had asked if I could drop off some groceries for him so he could make dinner for Grandma that night. He'd had some health issues, and he wasn't supposed to drive. I got caught up at work and was running really late, and he called me, saying it was a beautiful day so he'd just walk. It was less than a half mile down the street, and he'd done it a million times before. But I guess there was a driver who was yelling at her kids in the backseat or something, and her car drifted to the shoulder where he was walking—"

I don't even try to stop the tears when they fall onto his skin now. They burn my eyes as they stream across my face and onto his chest. And I love that he lets them fall, that he lets me be exactly who I am in all these messy, exposed ways.

His body is warm against mine at all the places we connect, and I feel safe at his side.

"Everyone hates me, back home."

"Why would they hate you?"

I sigh. "Because it's my fault. If I had been there—"

"Wait," he slides his arm out from under me and turns sideways, propping himself up on his elbow. "You think the town hates you because someone else made a terrible, tragic choice?"

"Yes. He did so much good in the community, knew everybody. And they all know that if I would've been there for him—"

"You can't do this to yourself, Hillary." And he offers what words he can to tell me I shouldn't beat myself up, despite me and everyone else in Lemming knowing that I should.

"Is that why you really left?" he asks.

I shrug again. "Yes and no. It was Peter, it was the job. It was this, all mixed together. I knew I needed to distance myself from my past, to get away and go somewhere to figure out who I am and what I want out of life."

I close my eyes and inhale to calm my nerves, to quiet my thumping heart. When my eyes reopen, his are still on me, soft and warm and golden and hazel and caring. "It's hard to discover who you are when you're surrounded by people who have already defined you."

"I can imagine."

Of course he can, because he's lived it too. The name in town that everyone knows. The glances from people on the street. The assumption he's changed into some arrogant star, that he thinks he's too good for them these days. They define him by their standards every day.

"Why didn't you tell me any of this before?"

I prop my head on my elbow and avoid his gaze. "Because I don't want to keep reliving all the hard things. You're an escape from my past life."

"Hillary—I don't want to be an *escape* from your life. I want to be *part* of it. Part of your story. I know we've only known each other a few months, but—"

My toes tingle and my heart lurches, and I kiss him fiercely. "You *are* a part of it. The best chapters."

He kisses me back, all passion and tenderness, and he strokes my hair as we lay there together until my stomach rumbles. I ignore it at first, but when it happens the third time Dalton checks his watch. "Have you eaten anything today?"

I shake my head. "Just a banana at breakfast."

"We should get some dinner."

I nod in agreement. "We should." I grab my phone and place the online order for delivery, then drape a naked leg over him and curl up in his arms until I get the text that dinner has arrived.

They drop the box on the doorstep as requested, and I retrieve it wrapped only in a robe. I pad back the hall to Dalton's room for dinner in bed, and he laughs when he sees the large pizza box in my hands. I crawl onto the bed next to him as he takes the box from me, but he sets it aside and unties my robe, kissing my neck and my collarbone. He pulls me on top of him and kisses the space between my breasts before looking up and twisting his fingers into my hair, delight dancing in the grin on his face. "See what I mean? It's tied to all the best memories."

THIRTY-ONE

Wednesday night we sleep in my bed while his now pizza-scented sheets are in the laundry.

Thursday I spend the day at Books Off Broadway and come home to Dalton putting spaghetti on the table. "It's not much," he says, "but it beats takeout. Again."

Friday he's up early for two auditions. On my way out the door to the bookstore, I see a note on the counter.

Hillary—

Wish me luck. We'll see how it goes.
I'd love to be cast in one of these shows.

—D

P.S. I think I'm getting better at these? Also, check the fridge.

When I look in the refrigerator there is a cup of cold brew waiting for me in a Eunoia-stickered cup. I send him a quick thank you text, then see a notification of unread messages in the group exchange with my mom and sister.

Most recently, Mom asks, Did you see this?, including a screenshot of a headline about Samantha and Dalton's split. She's been a fan of Samantha's made-for-TV-movies for years.

Stacy writes, Does it say why they broke up?

An excited shiver tingles my spine as I contemplate exactly how to tell them about what's happened this week. Before I get the chance, Mom's sent another message:

Sounds like he dumped her for some other woman. She must be so proud of herself for breaking up such a great couple.☹

I look up the article online and skim through. Finally I find quotes from Samantha:

We are better as friends, and *I wish Dalton all the best, always.*

The writer has added speculation, wondering, *Could Broadway's Dalton Tremaine have a new leading lady?*

"Shit," I say to the empty apartment.

I fill my travel cup with ice, then pour the cold brew over it to get ready to walk down to Books Off Broadway. I text back, Interesting, then pocket my phone and move on. I've participated, barely, but it's enough for now.

Dalton's in good spirits when I get home, feeling confident after his auditions. We spend most of the evening on the outdoor loveseat, his arm wrapped around me as we watch the city from our perch, then he lifts my chin with his finger so his lips can meet mine, and we're tangled up in each other again, all hands and lips and laughter and love.

....

I grab two lattes and a black coffee and head to Lindsey's apartment at nine o'clock Saturday morning. It's hard to believe that this is it—this is goodbye, for now, again. It's harder to believe that the apartment is no longer a back-up option like it has been the last few weeks that I've been staying with Dalton, because now it doesn't feel like I'm just *staying* with Dalton, but actually *living* with him—unofficially—and it feels substantially more serious and scary and *I love him* but it's still a big step that I've never taken before, let alone with a certified celebrity and someone who loves me and *what the hell comes next?*

My mind races until I knock on the door and Lindsey answers, with Marco at her side. They drove in last night so they could spend one more night in the apartment, which they worked so hard to afford for the last few years. Lindsey practically salivates as she takes the cup carrier from my hands.

"It's nice to finally meet you," I tell Marco, throwing my arms around his neck, "though I wish it was under different circumstances."

"You and me both," he smiles, patting my back. "I've heard so many great things, Hillary."

"You and me both," I smile back, winking.

Then Lindsey hugs me, long and hard, and her tired eyes are already misty.

"We have all day, friend." I wipe the start of a tear from her eye and try to look happy.

Then we dive into work, packing up dishes and movies, planters and books, and all the knick-knacks that have made this space their home for so long.

When they move into their bedroom, I retreat to the one I used for a few short weeks that feel like a lifetime ago. I start packing up what few things I have left there, like the blue dress I never got to wear, my shampoo and conditioner. Everything I touch is a memory tied to Dalton.

At one o'clock pizza arrives, delivered by Dalton himself. We take a break to eat, finding whatever space we can to sit in the living room. It feels nice to be still, taking a break from working in the sticky early-summer heat that's crept into the apartment.

"Seems like you're taking good care of my buddy here," Lindsey says, hiding a mouthful of veggie thin-crust.

The tips of Dalton's ears turn pink as his eyes flit to mine. "She doesn't need anyone to take care of her." Then his lips curl upward, and he adds, "But I am very much enjoying every moment together."

"Who'da thunk," Lindsey says, "that your little run-in would turn into a bona fide friendship."

He opens his mouth, then closes it without a word. He looks at me instead.

"It's pretty great," I say, smiling at Dalton. "Though it's harder to borrow his clothes than it was to borrow yours."

"Yes, but I'm sure his are all much fancier than mine," Lindsey laughs, drawing smiles from Marco and Dalton.

We eat in relative silence for a few moments before Dalton sets his pizza down and turns to Marco. "How's your dad doing?"

Marco swipes a napkin across his lips and shrugs. "He's holding on, longer than the doctors thought."

"Well that's good. I'm sorry you and your family are going through so much right now."

"Thanks, man," Marco replies, and Lindsey reaches over to squeeze his hand.

There's not much left to do in the apartment. A few pieces of furniture will need to be carried down to the car, and all the boxes, too, but nearly everything is already packed.

When lunch is over, Dalton offers to help carry the larger pieces down to the pickup and small trailer that Marco somehow navigated into the city last night. They take down the couch and two mattresses while Lindsey and I disassemble the bed frames and bag up all the loose bolts and hardware.

"He seems really great," Lindsey says, setting the bag on the kitchen counter, near the door.

I nod. "He is. The best."

"Good. I felt so bad when I left, like I was abandoning you. But I think you really got an upgrade on your '*I want to find myself in New York*' experience."

"I wouldn't say *upgrade*. I was lucky enough to have two awesome roommates. No favorites." I take a sip of water from a bottle sitting next to the fridge. "Do you have gum?"

"Yeah," she says. "In my bag." She gestures to the black tote on the floor of her bedroom. "And as far as *favorites* are concerned, I assure you, I will never have the abs I imagine that man has."

"You have no idea," I say, rummaging through the bag's infinite pockets for a stick of peppermint gum.

"What was that?" she calls from the kitchen.

"Nothing," I yell back.

"And as much as I love you, my friend, I can't guarantee I'll ever look at you the way he does." She laughs at her own joke but stops when I come out of her room, the gum forgotten, a black velvet box in my hand.

"What is this?"

Her smile flickers, disappearing and bouncing back in bursts of joy. "Snoop much?" she asks, biting her upturned lips.

"Lindsey."

She rolls her eyes and laughs, then takes the box from me and opens it, showing off the shimmering solitaire diamond ring inside.

"*No way!*"

She smiles and nods. "Yep! Last night. He said he wanted to propose in the place where we made so many memories—to make one more awesome memory, just the two of us." She giggles and slips it onto her finger, modeling, trying to catch whatever light she can to show its sparkle.

I jump to hug her. "Congratulations! I'm so happy for you!"

"Thanks," she says, sliding the ring off her finger to replace it in the box. "I think part of it, too, is so he can tell his dad he finally did it, so his dad will be at peace, or something, and know that he has someone."

She breezes past me to drop the box back in her tote, then reemerges with a stick of gum. "Don't tell Marco that you know, though. Our families don't know yet, and he wants them to be the first to find out."

I mimic zipping my lips closed and throwing away the key. "Your secret is safe with me," I say, lips still closed, and she laughs at my mumbling.

Then the front door opens, and we try to make it look like we've been busy and working hard this whole time. The guys are red-faced from their repeated journey up and down three flights of stairs in the hottest part of the day, so I grab a bottle of water from the fridge and hand it to Dalton.

"Thanks," he says, and I absently touch his arm.

"Oh gross," I laugh. "You're so sweaty!"

His eyes crease as he lets out a deep laugh. "That never bothered you before."

My face burns at the innuendo and Lindsey arches an eyebrow at me. I clear my throat and cross my arms as Dalton drinks the water, taking the hint.

"Hil, why don't you help me with the last few boxes in the bedroom?" she asks, and I hang my head as I follow her. I grab one of the two remaining boxes there, but she corners me. "Am I missing something here, Hil? What's going on with you two?"

Not that the color had previously faded from my face, but I feel it redden again and my mouth goes dry, despite the gum. "We—um—"

How do I say, *We made out in the rain and almost got frisky in a field and then were interrupted a different time when his still-kinda-but-also-fake girlfriend knocked on the door but don't worry because we had crazy good first-time-together sex three nights later and also good-as-pizza sex the afternoon after that* in a way that *doesn't* make me sound totally nuts.

"Hillary?"

Lindsey's voice snaps me out of the litany of *almost*s and *how do I say*s that swirl in my head. "Sorry."

The concern in her face manifests in her voice, too. "You okay? You're like, super red."

I nod, sweating. "Yeah, I'm fine. Just not used to the heat yet, I guess."

She opens her mouth like she's going to say something, but thankfully Dalton appears in the doorway. "You two alright in here?"

"Sure thing," I say, thankful for the interruption that I use as an opportunity to rush out the door to take the box to Marco.

Once all their belongings have been loaded into the trailer, Dalton and I wait with the truck while Lindsey and Marco say goodbye to the apartment that saw them through the beginning of their relationship, their first and only fight, promotions at work, his father's diagnosis, and now a proposal.

"Was this their first place together?" Dalton asks, arms crossed, leaning back against the side of the trailer.

"First and only," I confirm, watching the door, pacing the sidewalk.

As if he's reading my mind, he says, "Lots of memories there, I bet. Lots of firsts."

"Mmhmm." I bite the inside of my cheek and check my watch.

"Kind of like our place."

The words catch me off guard, though maybe they shouldn't. "*Our* place?"

"Well, yeah. Of course. We both live there, don't we?"

"*Temporarily,*" I remind him.

"But what if it wasn't? Temporary, I mean."

I spin around to face him. "What are you saying?"

His eyes sparkle at me, green and gold. "I'm saying, I think we should make it more official. Redecorate. Have a guest room."

"You're crazy." *Isn't he?* "Already?"

He nods and the corners of his lips twitch, torn between a smile and seriousness, like he's also a little nervous but I'm not sure if he's nervous because he asked or because I haven't actually answered yet. His hands run the length of my goose-bump covered arms and he rests his forehead against mine. His breath smells like pepperoni and onion and I love it, because it's his, and he's close, and my heart is goo in my chest.

"Say yes, Hil. Move all your stuff in with me. I want to share a home with you."

My gooey heart catches in my throat and the word "No" escapes my lips.

He pulls his head back and steps backward. "No?" He looks disappointed.

"No," I repeat, and I can't help but smile. "My stuff is far inferior to yours—it wouldn't match your aesthetic. But I *will* pick up extra shifts at the bookstore to afford a little shopping spree with you to buy some new stuff for *our* home."

He takes my face in both of his hands, radiating excitement from his eyes and lips. "Seriously?"

"Seriously." I get out half the word before his lips are on mine, again and again, lips, forehead, nose, and cheeks.

And then a throat clears behind me, and Lindsey's jaw is basically on the sidewalk.

"Holy shit," she says.

"Surpriiiiiise," I say, giving terrible jazz hands and a scared grin.

She and Marco have a long drive home, so they give their final goodbye hugs. Through tears and laughter, she points a finger at me and says, "Don't think we're not talking about this."

"I would never," I promise, hugging her as tightly as I can. I whisper "Congratulations" in her ear, then out loud say, "Good luck. With everything." Then, with a final squeeze, "Thank you, Lindsey."

"Of course," she smiles, not trying to mask the tears this time. "Good luck to you, too."

Dalton extends an arm to shake her hand, but she pulls him in for a hug. "I know she doesn't need it, but take care of her anyway, okay? She deserves all the best."

"I know," Dalton says. "I will."

Marco and Dalton shake hands, Marco and I hug, and Lindsey hugs me one more time before Marco pulls her away. "We need to go, love," he says, and she's still yelling to me out the window as they drive down the street.

"You're awesome, Hillary! You got this! Be good to each otherrrrr!" And then she's drowned out by the sounds of the city, sirens and subways, traffic and trains. My own beating heart and Dalton's voice in my ear as he wraps his arms around my waist and sets his chin on my shoulder.

"Let's go home."

THIRTY-TWO

I wake up on the couch on Saturday morning, a new throw pillow under my head, a new blanket covering me, my journal and pen fallen on the floor. I stretch and soak in the homey touches we've added since making our living arrangement more official a week ago, including the fresh hydrangeas in a stoneware vase on the table.

"Did you sleep well?" Dalton asks, pulling headphones from his ears in the kitchen. Sweat follows the curve of his biceps. "I tried to wake you last night, but you were out."

"I slept great. Just not enough." I yawn and sit up, dropping my hands in the linen blanket. "You go for a run already?"

He nods and chugs a glass of water from the tap. "Yep. Wanted to get out before it's too hot." He swipes the back of his hand across his forehead. "You have plans today?"

"Just some more writing. I'm getting close to the end of this first draft."

"Already? That's great!"

"Maybe," I shrug. "It could all be garbage. Hard to say."

He tilts his head and purses his lips. "What makes you say that?"

"That it's garbage?" I shrug again and bite the inside of my lip. "I just assume most of what I write is garbage with moments of brilliance, until someone tells me otherwise."

"So you need validation?"

"Like everything else in my life."

He shakes his head and his brow creases. "I wish you could see you the way I see you."

"And how's that?" I ask.

"Beautiful. Fun. Quirky. Want me to continue?"

When he looks at me like this, when he says these things to me, everything warms from the inside out, from my chest to my toes, and my head spins. I slip the blanket off my legs and swing my feet to the floor. "Yes, please." It comes out dry and breathy.

He smirks. "Okay. I've got a list." He sidesteps the island in the kitchen and rattles off his string of compliments, and I float toward him—though it's probably more like shuffling but it *feels* like floating, led by some imaginary string tethering my heart to his words. The more he speaks, the further reeled in I am, until suddenly our arms are around each other, morning breath and sweat mingling between us.

"I don't deserve you."

"You deserve so much better. Or did you just skip my TED talk on your awesomeness?"

"I'm serious. Thank you."

And he turns serious, too, and rests his chin on my head, his arms tightening around me. "Always, Hillary."

Then he showers and we're hand-in-hand, picking up coffee and walking the High Line again. Sometimes we stop, just to look into each other's eyes, just to kiss, just to take in the view, just because.

"When I was younger, for about ten years, I thought I'd grow up to be an architect." He stops and leans against the railing, taking in the skyline. "My parents took us to Pittsburgh for a football game, and when we drove through I just kind of fell in love with all these buildings reflecting the sunlight, mirrored in the rivers. Then I started looking online for pictures of cool buildings, and I fell in love with New York."

I sit in front of him on a bench and watch his face as he gushes over the city. There's magic in his eyes, the way there is when you think of something you adore, when you talk about something you treasure.

"What made you change your mind?"

He shrugs. "For Jordan's sixteenth, he wanted to come to New York to see the Yankees play. My parents threw in a trip to see The Lion King, and I was done. I just knew I wanted to pursue acting, and even though it wasn't practical or smart, I went for it. I trusted my talent, my work ethic, my drive."

"And you're incredible."

He smiles and drops his gaze. "Well, I'm good. Confident enough to say so, not so arrogant to say any better."

"Then I'll say it for you. Over and over, every day. Incredible. Genius. Perfection on stage."

"You've seen one concert, Hil," he protests, but the red rushing into his cheeks says he appreciates the compliment.

I clear my throat. "Actually," I say, and everything inside me screams at me to stop, to not give away the secret, to not ruin everything. But I have to tell him, because he's been honest with me. Because he told me he loves me, because we live together, and because we don't hide things from one another. "I'm actually very familiar with your career."

Confusion flickers across his eyes and he runs a hand through his too-long hair. "Do you know that I was once in the ensemble of West Side Story?"

I nod.

"And you know that I was the alternate for Raoul in Phantom?"

I nod again, my heart catching in my throat. I still have the autographed Playbill in my bedroom at home from an impromptu trip to the city when we found out he'd be on for a week to cover the lead's vacation.

"What about when I was Dax Dupree in Remarkable Normalcy?"

I crinkle my nose and squint into the sun, looking up at him. "Never heard of that one."

"You will." He shoves his hands deep into his pockets and bites his lip, but it barely dampens his smile.

"Wait…what? Did you get the part?"

He nods, unable to hide the joy anymore.

I jump from my seat and throw my arms around his neck. "Dalton, that's amazing! Congratulations!" My hands twist into his hair, and I pull his lips to mine.

His hands hold my hips against his and questions sprint through my head as my heart pounds in my chest, an answer to his, doing the same.

A man in a suit passes by, talking on his cell phone. "*Get a room*," he mutters before disappearing further along the path, dropping profanities in his conversation.

"Do you think he's jealous?" Dalton asks, pulling back, grinning.

"Oh, absolutely. I mean, who wouldn't want to kiss *the* Dalton Tremaine, star of the next big Broadway musical, Remarkable Normalcy?" I let go of his neck and we laugh, my cheeks warm with embarrassment and maybe a little sunburn from a day spent outside.

His laughter fades and he rubs the back of his neck. "I mean, that's the hope, to get an investor who believes in us, wants to take us straight to Broadway."

And suddenly it hits me, that good news is sometimes the disguise that bad news wears; sometimes winning the lottery isn't winning the Mega Millions, but the Shirley Jackson kind of lottery that beats you and batters you until the very bloody end.

"What's your timeline?"

He shrugs, looking everywhere but at me. "We start rehearsals in a week, just workshopping. Then, who knows."

Who knows. *Who knows* where he'll go. *Who knows* how long he'll be gone. *Who knows* how gorgeous the women cast next to him will be. *Who knows* if there are kissing scenes, or—

"Hil?"

"Yeah?"

"It's all going to be fine. No matter what."

Then his fingers are laced with mine and we continue on our walk, ending up at an outdoor lounge at a nearby hotel, toasting to his new role. I drink more than I should because it keeps me from talking too much, from telling him how much it physically aches, this hole already in my chest, knowing in my gut he'll be leaving soon.

"I know I'm no expert," he says as we walk back to the apartment, "and I'm not sure that I'm your target audience, but would you like an opinion?"

"What do you mean?" I ask, falling behind him for a step to make room for a man with a pack of dogs on the sidewalk.

"I mean, do you want me to read what you've written so far? If you need some sort of validation, I'd be happy to read and give an opinion. Though I'm sure it's great."

"You already sound biased," I laugh, because everything is funny when you're tipsy and nervous and with the man you love.

"Well, the offer stands, if you want me to."

By the time we get back to the apartment my head is spinning from the heat and the four cocktails I drank in two hours and the near-total lack of food I've consumed today. We heat up leftovers and have a 3:00 p.m. lunch in the living room, watching a movie. Then it's online shopping for new furniture for our apartment—though who knows how long we'll actually physically share it—before we dress up and head out to see a show that we just bought tickets for on a whim while browsing end tables and lamps.

The theater was always my happy place, always a place of make believe with happy endings and box steps and jazz hands. But tonight, with Dalton, it's a reminder of his one true love, his lifelong passion. He and I are a whirlwind romance, whipped up in thunderstorms and heat, but his love affair with the stage is a hurricane: massive, powerful, devastating.

So tonight I watch the jazz hands, ball changes, and happy endings with the worst kind of tears, clenching Dalton's hand on the armrest the entire show.

THIRTY-THREE

Nothing changes, and everything changes, all at once. Dalton's workshopped the show all summer, propelling us toward an inevitable and obvious separation. I've stopped by for a few rehearsals, delivering coffee and dinner to a few members of the team who get in early or stick around late or both, working through solos and choreography.

I FaceTime Mom and Stacy twice a week, and they know I've got a job and a roommate *and* that I'm seeing someone, but they don't need to know all the details, like names, or the fact that the boyfriend they've never met is also the roommate.

I've worked thirty hours a week at Books Off Broadway, balancing my time there with writing and taking care of the apartment, the cooking, the laundry, squeezing in dates with Dalton. So, basically, no writing has happened.

We're in this holding pattern, doing the same things every day, knowing there's an expiration date coming.

September first.

Tickets are already on sale for a two-week run in Chicago. After that it's Dallas. Then Seattle. Then… still not New York.

How are you holding up? Lindsey texts.

I'm a wreck, but I can't say that. I'll be fine. How about you?

Marco's dad passed away in late June, and it's been hard for them both to adapt to a new place and the added pressure of supporting his family through their grief. It's no New York. Then, a moment later, I miss you. I smile and text back, I miss you too, because I do, and I could really use a friend. Anytime you want to visit... She responds with a heart emoji, and I pocket my phone to get back to work.

The Charleses have asked me to make a back-to-school display, so I assemble a collection featuring banned and challenged books.

"Looks great," Mrs. Charles affirms.

With a shrug I say, "If they can't find these books in their school libraries, I want them to be able to find them easily here."

Sue's eyes twinkle behind her oversized tortoiseshell glasses. "When we opened this store years ago, we wanted to make sure we were starting something that would let readers explore new worlds, discover the great big universe out there, outside of their own backgrounds and beliefs."

"Do you think you've done that?"

She smiles. "I think if you carry the assortment of books that we carry, celebrate the authors we celebrate, love people like we love our community, there's no other possible outcome."

Sue's optimism, her love of people, her sense of duty to her neighborhood and humankind—they all make her such a joy to know.

"I agree with you. You should be proud of this," I say, looking around the two-story shelves that line the walls.

She nods. "Very. I'm so proud of all that we've built." With a wink and a longing look at Mr. Charles across the sales floor she squeezes my hand. "How about you, dear? How's your book coming?"

I groan. "Not well."

"But you were so close months ago," she says, waving for me to follow her back to the register, where she pulls out two double-chocolate muffins. She inches one across the counter to me. "What happened?"

Shrugging, I answer, "I just got too busy. There's so much going on, with Dalton getting ready to leave, running errands, picking up extra hours—"

"Sweetheart," Sue chides, "you did not need to pick up extra hours here. We're fine!"

My face flushes. "I didn't mean it like that. I know you two could run this place blindfolded with one hand tied behind your back."

"Yes, but you should see the mess we made when we tried."

We both laugh at her joke. "Take some time off. We've got more than enough help until the school year starts after Labor Day. Go write. Go build your life."

I chew the muffin slowly, considering her words. "Are you sure?"

"Positive," she chirps.

"Okay. I guess I can be back in two weeks, if that's okay."

Sue smiles. "Of course. Take all the time you need."

So I spend the next two weeks while Dalton's at costume fittings and rehearsals writing or sleeping, recovering from late-night, post-date sessions when I write into that magical time of night in New York City when the streets quiet and it's both too late and too early to be out doing anything. Those are my moments to sit on the terrace, soaking in the inspiration this city and this life can offer, sticky with late-summer humidity even in the middle of the night.

We know the end is close. Not *the* end, of course, (*hopefully?*) but the end of the *kiss-me-goodnight-and-look-into-my-eyes-and-tell-me-you-love-me* dreamworld we've been living in since May. The end of perfection. Of joy. Of bliss. The night before his last in the city, I help him pack his bags. Tomorrow is a day for zero work, just fun, so all the laundry and dishes and tidying that can be done has been done. He goes to bed at ten and I stay up late writing to get ahead of schedule, because our last day is a day just for each other, but I don't want to fall behind.

I park myself in his seat on the couch, his scent lingering in the fabric. I decide I'll replace Febreze with his body spray so the apartment reeks so much of him I swear he's there.

I've got a perfectly curated playlist of angsty ballads that accompany the creative process, so I hit *play* on my phone and slide it across the floor so I don't get tempted to scroll and distract myself from writing. Then I click my Acroball pen and open my journal.

I've been keeping a list of ideas on page one, expanded and reorganized, each item checked off when used, for inspiration when I have none. Of course, the car incident is on the list, and time with Dalton has led to more and more ideas, like kayaking and hiking and making out in the bed of a pickup truck, or driving down dirt roads, arms hanging out the windows, wind in your hair, or dancing in the rain.

I've finished two journals by hand already since I got to New York and am on my third now, a new fuchsia hardcover book with an *H* surrounded by colorful flowers printed on the front. Sue had set it aside for me when it came into Books Off Broadway, gifting it to me as a thank you for my help with their displays.

With an acoustic guitar strumming in the background, I put pen to paper and keep telling the story of the small-town heartthrob who bounced back after heartache to become a successful big-city businessman. So far, he's already run into Trina Thomas, rescuing her in his Bentley when he finds her outside their old haunt when he goes back home to visit his parents. Trina's ready to rekindle their would-be romance, but Darren is not on board, remembering how shallow Trina was all through their school years, ready for something more.

Instead he's inexplicably drawn to the town's newest face, a heart-of-gold librarian who helps with resume-writing and hosts kids' story hours and tutors high schoolers in the evenings. He tries to woo her, but she is not impressed by his flashy car or expensive watch and pines instead for the man she met decades ago—the one who drove her home from the movies after her date fell asleep.

It's coming together, and most importantly, it's good. I lay the journal upside down on the floor and stretch to reach my phone, then set an alarm and get lost in the abyss of junk mail that's been flooding my inbox for the last four days.

THIRTY-FOUR

've gotten maybe four hours of sleep, but when I hear the alarm I bolt upright, ditching the blanket to be cleaned up later and heading into the bathroom to brush my teeth. Dalton emerges into the hallway as I leave the bathroom.

"Good morning!" I infuse my voice with as much energy as I can, despite being exhausted and tired and ready to go back to bed. This day is ours, and I refuse to spend it sleeping.

"Morning," he answers, raking a hand through his hair. "Happy Us Day."

"Did we land on that name?" he asks, his mouth curling into a smile as he closed-mouth kisses me.

"We did. It's cheesy as hell and I love it."

We shuffle past each other in the hall so he can use the bathroom and I can change for our day of, well, *us*. We've each planned one must-do activity before wrapping up the day with dinner at one of our favorite places.

I'm dressed in my running capris and a tank when he leaves the bathroom.

"Oooh no," he says when he sees me. "It's, like, a million degrees out there."

"Correction, it's seventy-four, and warming every minute. The longer you take, the hotter it gets."

He groans and laughs. "I'll be ready in five."

I pass him a banana and a glass of water when he's dressed and ready. "Alright, here's the deal. It's not a long run—only about four total miles. Two miles out, two back, with a stop in the middle."

"Seems manageable," he says, biting into his banana.

"Very manageable," I confirm. I have a credit card stashed in the side pocket of my leggings and a running playlist ready to go on my phone. (*Always with the playlists,* my mom would say if she was here. *You never met a song you didn't like.*)

He leans in to kiss me, but I dodge it and open the front door instead. Now is not the end, and I don't want to start all the mushy stuff so early. I want today to be about fun and living an adventure together, making memories. A simple kiss will break me, because I know I can't stop there, not when I miss him already.

We run south and look out over New York Harbor, the air sticky and thick. We buy two bottles of water from a nearby cart and gratefully down every sip as we sit on a bench and watch the ferries for twenty minutes.

He checks his watch. "Time to head back?"

"Not quite." We drop the bottles in a recycling bin, and I buy us two tickets for the SeaGlass Carousel.

"Nice." A smile spreads across his face. We walk hand in hand into the carousel and aim for the same fish as last time: Angelfish for me, Lionfish for him. A few families filter in around us, and through the ride cycle I watch his face as he takes it all in: the kids enjoying their experience, the colorful fish around him. Then he looks at me with the same wonder in his eyes and I feel myself blush. Despite the frequent *I love you*s and kisses and more over the last few months, I still go giddy when he looks at me that way.

But my brain gets involved, and I remember how he interacted with his niece and nephew in West Virginia, and now to see how he beams at the excited expressions of the kids around us—

A conversation with Samantha comes back to me, and I wonder if he feels it too, that incessant ticking and pressure to settle down and have kids. We haven't talked about it, obviously. It's way too soon for that now, but is that the next step when the tour is over? Is it on his radar? Is it what he wants?

A knot forms in my stomach as the ride ends but I try to smile through it.

"You okay?" he asks.

"Mmhmm. Great," I answer, and his face shows he doesn't believe me.

"My stomach just hurts a little." It's not a lie.

"Do you just want to walk back to the apartment, then?"

I nudge him with my shoulder and squint against the sunlight. "Anything to get out of running, huh?"

He laughs, and I love his laugh, but now I imagine it stemming from him as toddlers crawl over him, like he's a mountain they want to conquer.

I shake the thought from my head.

"I'm happy to run, if you're up for it."

I consider it but decide walking is enough, and we hold hands along the way. We duck into Eunoia and pick up iced coffees.

"This humidity is crazy," he says on the walk home.

"Mmhmm. It's got to break, eventually. We're due for a storm."

Talking about the weather is a good distraction from the whole *How many kids do you want? Do you even want kids? Do you want kids with me?* craziness that plays out in my head.

If the clock is ticking for him, and if he's with me, does that mean he's expecting that from me? Do *I* want kids? No, these questions are not questions for today.

"Hillary?"

"Hmm?" The sound of my name snaps me out of the never-ending loop of what-ifs.

He stops on the sidewalk just outside our building. "You seem distracted today."

That's an understatement.

"Are you sure you're alright?"

I nod and force a smile. "Yes, I'm sure. Sorry."

He pulls the door open for me. "No need to apologize," he says, following me inside. "I just want to make sure you're okay."

We stand in opposite corners of the elevator and talk as we ride up to the apartment. "What do you have planned for the afternoon?" I ask.

"We're going out to lunch," he answers coyly. "And we're *not* running to get there."

We both shower quickly, and I pull on a pair of gauzy shorts and a T-shirt, because he assures me that where we're going is casual. He's wearing cargo shorts and a T-shirt with a baseball cap.

"Okay, what do you have up your sleeve?"

He smiles and we leave again, climbing into the waiting car downstairs for a long drive through the city and over a bridge.

"Where are we going?" I ask, craning my neck, trying to figure out where we've been and where we could possibly be headed.

He winks. "You'll see."

Forty-five minutes after leaving the apartment, the car pulls into a lot. "We'll take the train home," Dalton tells the driver. "Thanks so much!"

Outside, the air is filled with laughter and screams of delight, lapping water, and the smell of hot dogs.

"I promised you lunch," he says, gesturing toward the stretch of boardwalk ahead of us.

"Is that all?"

He wrinkles his forehead, thinking. "What else did you have in mind?" And then there's the moment of realization, when his eyes grow and he protests. "Nooo, no, no, no."

I nod, annoyingly, incessantly. "Please?" I ask and continue to ask as we're walking, hand in hand, toward the boardwalk.

The line isn't terribly long, and he agrees, albeit reluctantly. "I can't believe I'm doing this."

Once we've paid and boarded the coaster, his hand grips mine tighter. "This is nuts," he says, and he seems genuinely freaked out.

"I'm right here," I tell him, my heart racing because I love roller coasters, but they still scare me. Basically, roller coasters and Dalton are the same: scary, butterfly-inducing, fun, leaves me smiling.

A ride operator points to his hat, so he slides it off his head and sits on it.

"It *is* him," I hear a girl whisper on the ride platform, and my throat goes dry as I see her from the corner of my eye waving, her friend pulling out her phone.

Dalton's facing straight ahead, his jaw set, and I ask him, "Do you want me to let go?"

He turns, his forehead wrinkled. "Never, Hil." Then he pulls our hands above the lap bar and rests them there. He turns a smile on for the fans on the platform as the train pulls away. He flicks a wave in their direction as we roll out, and then we're climbing higher and higher before a steep fall pulls a squeal from my throat and a guttural yell from him. When we return to the station, his eyes are closed and he's trying to catch his breath, and I'm reduced to howling laughter. "That was amazing."

"That—that was something," he says.

He climbs out first then takes my hand as I clamber out, and we're off toward our lunch.

We split a chili cheese dog and a cheesesteak dog and cozy up on a bench, watching families play in the sand with the late-summer sun beating down, enjoying one last hoorah before back-to-school and sweater-weather seasons ambush them.

Water laps the shoreline, a change from the normal cacophony of traffic that we hear in Manhattan, and when the hot dogs are gone, I rest my head on his shoulder as he drapes an arm over me.

I want to say *I could get used to this*, but I can't get used to it, because he leaves tomorrow. Instead, I inhale his scent, now mingled with salt water and hot dog and onion, and somehow I love it even more than usual.

"Want to head back soon?" he asks.

I don't, but I say "sure" anyway.

Back means time is passing.

Back means the day will end.

Back takes us home, *our* home until the morning.

Because he leaves tomorrow.

After an uneventful subway ride back to the apartment, we've got some time to relax before dinner, which is good because my mom has called and texted me three times in the last half hour.

"Give her a call," Dalton says, handing me a glass of water. "We've got time."

Time is the one thing we do *not* have, but I place the call anyway, just to get kicked to voicemail. I've got a FaceTime request from Mom before I can finish leaving my message, so I retreat down the hall, close the door, and sink down onto our bed.

"Hey, Mom," I say, but she holds up a finger and before I know it, Stacy has joined the call, too. "Hey guys. What's up?"

"Where are you?" Mom asks, forgoing a greeting and diving right in.

"I'm in my apartment."

"Who's there with you?" she asks, in a way that makes it seem she already knows the answer, but there's no way she could.

"Why are you asking?" I reserve the right to not incriminate myself until I know where her questions are leading.

Luckily, or maybe not, Stacy interjects. "How's it going, Sis?"

"It's going fine, thanks. You?"

"Good," she says, and we both see Mom's nervous smile cross her face. That damn, hereditary, nervous smile.

"What's going on with you two?" I repeat, and Stacy shrugs.

"We were just talking to Gram at breakfast, and we

realized something. We totally forgot the name of your boyfriend. What was it again?"

I know I'm walking into a trap. "I never told you his name."

"Mmm," Mom answers. "That explains why we couldn't remember, Stacy. What's his name, Hillary?"

I roll my eyes and laugh. "You guys are ridiculous. Why the sudden interest?"

"I wouldn't say it's sudden," Stacy snorts. "Mom's been searching your social media all summer, looking for clues. She even had me text Lindsey."

"*Mother!*" I know she hates being addressed that way, so it's basically the equivalent of her yelling at us with our first and middle names all through our childhood.

She shrugs. "You could choose to look at this as me taking an interest in you and your well-being."

"In a super intrusive way, Mom," Stacy shoots, smiling. Then she directs her serious face at me. "But really, Hil, you've told us nothing. Are you guys still even together? 'Cause you post literally nothing about him."

"Yes, we're still together," I say, though my heart sinks as I do. "And that's not true. I posted a few pictures."

"Yeah, of some wildflowers and his hand, three weeks ago."

"Geez, Stace, if the accounting thing doesn't work out, I'm sure the FBI would love to have you."

Mom breaks in, always one to end an argument before it really begins, sounding just as exasperated as she did fifteen years ago when we were arguing over whose turn it was to ride shotgun to the mall. "Hillary, would you just tell us the truth already? Are you dating that actor or not?"

My shoulders stiffen and I catch my jaw before it falls

into my lap. "What?" I ask, hoarse and woozy.

"We saw a picture online today. Well, Mrs. Travis had seen it, and you know how word gets around. But it was Dalton Tremaine at Coney Island, and it really looks like it's you there with him." Stacy's voice is steady, like she's reciting a modest account balance and not a bombshell revelation.

I utter a string of *no*s and *shit*s as I open my browser and search, and sure enough, there's Dalton sitting in the Cyclone, holding my hand, though it's hard to make me out clearly because my head is thrown back, laughing.

"So that's a yes?" Mom asks, something like joy rising in her voice.

"How did that get out so fast?" I wonder aloud, a frantic whisper.

"Hillary!" Stacy shrieks, and I lower the volume on my phone as I *shush* her. "Why didn't you tell us?"

"How long has this been going on?" Mom asks.

I sit cross-legged on the bed and drop the phone in my lap, burying my face in my hands. "This is crazy."

"Hil? You okay?"

I press my fingers to my lips and squeeze my eyes shut, shaking my head toward the ceiling. "I'm sorry, Stace. I'm just—I mean, this shouldn't be—"

"Honey?" Mom asks, her voice an old sweater, wrapping me in comfort and warmth. "Let's talk tomorrow."

I clear my throat and answer, "Yeah, that sounds good." I'll have all the time in the world, because he leaves tomorrow. "I can tell you everything then. Thanks, Mom."

I hang up, cutting off both of their goodbyes, and fall backward onto the mattress, palms pressed to my eyes. I don't even know if Dalton knows that the photo was posted, or if he knows that I'm being described as his "mystery woman," or if that's how he prefers I be described.

I shuffle down the hall, my head and heart still pounding. "Dalton?"

He's sitting at the dining room table, reading. "Yeah?"

"Did you know that a photo from the Cyclone was posted today? A photo of us?"

He pauses for a moment and looks up at me. "Interesting," he says, his voice sharp.

"Yeah. My mom and sister saw it. So, they know now."

"Huh."

"Yeah."

He doesn't explicitly seem to hate the idea, but he doesn't seem to be on board, either.

"Does that freak you out, a little? That it's out there for the world to see?" I ask.

His eyes are back on his book, and he shakes his head. "No. No more than this, anyway."

I close the distance between us by a few paces, and he's focused on a series of handwritten pages.

"Hillary," he says, pinching a finger between the pages as he closes the book and holds the familiar cover up for me to see, "what is this?"

My mouth goes dry. "Why do you have that?"

"You left it open next to the couch. I was cleaning up." He looks at the cover, thumbing the corners, then shakes his head and thrusts it at me again. "Is this what you've been working on all summer?"

If I don't reach for it, maybe I won't have to own it.

If I don't speak, maybe I won't have to confess.

I look at it, then at him, and I know he can read the guilt in my eyes.

"Hillary."

I swallow, all lumps and bile, and nod once.

"*Shit.*" He slams the journal on the counter, the loud *slap* making me jump, and scratches his head. "Is this why you're here? To write my life's stories down, slap your name on it, and sell my secrets?"

"Dalton—"

"Is this what you meant by '*inspiration,*' Hillary? Just taking all the things I told you, some of which I've *only* told *you,* and putting it out there for everyone to read?"

"It's not some salacious biography, Dalton. Yes, there are some elements, but—"

"*Some* elements, Hillary? On page *one* you have a bulleted list—" he grabs the journal and opens the front cover, his finger stabbing the page as he points at each item listed. "Gina Thompson. Future architect. Campfire sing-alongs. Mountains. Scared of heights. Favorite Place—clearing in the woods." He closes the book again and waves it at me. "Those things are private. Those memories—those moments—I don't share them with just anyone, and I certainly don't want the world to read about them."

"Private enough to share with your fake girlfriend." I don't mean to say it, but I've been thinking it for months, and it just bursts out as I grab the journal from him.

"What are you even talking about?" he spits.

"You can preach about how special all of those things are to you, but you didn't hesitate to take Sami to that clearing, the day after we had our first kiss there. I thought that would have made it more special, more private."

"That's rich, Hillary. You've just been holding that in for months, waiting to use it against me?"

Yes. "No."

"For your information, I *didn't* take Sami to that clearing.

I took her to the opposite end of the lake, showed her where Jordan and his friends would go drinking on weekends. You can put *that* in your book."

Oof. There goes that argument. "Half of those memories are mine, too, Dalton. You don't get a monopoly on life experiences."

His eyes burn, brown and gold, fiery fierce, but he lowers his voice. "You can't use this, Hillary."

I can feel angry tears burning behind my nose, and my stomach sinks in sadness. "So what, I'm supposed to scrap everything? Waste months of work?" Does he really expect me to throw it all away?

"Yes."

I can't believe what I'm hearing. "Wow, Dalton. That's not fair."

"It sucks. I know. I know you've spent a lot of time on this, but it's not fair to just put my life in print, either."

"It's fiction."

"It's not fiction to *me,* Hil!" he yells, recoiling at the sound of his own frustration. "And besides," he says, softening his tone. His shoulders slump forward, and he looks exhausted. "You came to New York for inspiration. You had to have found some, somewhere other than me. The museums, the shows, the views, the history…"

His voice trails off and he stares at me, speechless, breathless.

"You're right."

He sighs. "Thank you."

"No—you're right that I came to New York for inspiration, but I also came here to figure out who I am. And thank you, for reminding me about the museums and everything I've done here. Because it's all tied back to you, isn't it?"

He straightens his shoulders and clenches his jaw.

I bite the inside of my lip, steeling myself against the tsunami of emotions I feel—anger littered with sadness, self-pity tainted with realization.

"It's probably a good thing that you leave tomorrow, Dalton, so I can do what I came to do. Because every single experience I have here has your fingerprint all over it. I didn't figure out who I am, I didn't define myself here—I just wrote a story for myself that has you scribbled all over every page."

"Jesus, Hillary. What are you talking about?"

I'm equally exasperated. "Think about it. Day one—it's me and you, for hours. Day two, you hold my backpack hostage and invite me to your show. Then we bump into each other again. Then it's every Sunday. Then the talks when I'm at the beach.

"I was so looking forward to having Lindsey's apartment to myself for a while, to really experience life solo in the city for a while, but you swooped in."

"To *keep you here*, Hillary. So you wouldn't have to leave."

"Yes! And then you bankrolled my experiences, played tour guide around the city, 'made things happen' with your connections."

"Is that so terrible?" he shouts back, his voice cracking. "How incredibly awful of me, to want you to be here, to accomplish your goals and live your dream."

My voice catches in my throat. "*My* dream? My dream of falling head-over-heels for someone, just to have him leave me for who-knows-how-long?

"You told me—"

"Dalton." I close my eyes and inhale, exhale. "I'm not mad that you're going. I'm mad at myself for not having the independent experience I swore I'd have, for making you central to my entire identity in New York."

"Well lucky you, then, that starting tomorrow you get to go it alone."

The words hang between us, above us, all around us, like a thick gray cloud, ready to burst and drown us in a flash flood of anger and resentment and the most profound longing and loneliness. So we stare at each other, knee-deep in those waters already, waiting for the worst.

He hangs his head, shaking it, toeing the floor. "Damn it, Hillary. This is not how this night was supposed to go."

I have never seen him look so defeated, and I feel it too. "No. It's not."

"So, what do we do now?"

What comes next, when you're drowning?

You need air.

"I'm going for a walk."

He doesn't move. Even as I put my shoes on, he's just there, pitiful and maddening. He doesn't object as I walk out the door.

I wait for the elevator, expecting that maybe he'll run into the hallway, barefoot and breathless, begging me to stay. But he doesn't, and I ride down with Mrs. Simpson and her poodle instead.

I hit the pavement, and the end-of-August heat is oppressive and thick. Opaque clouds blanket the sky above me, but I walk anyway, needing to be anywhere but here, and I hold back the tears that sting my eyes.

With no set destination in mind, my legs move in auto-pilot, and I'm climbing a familiar set of stairs.

So many memories were created right here—or at least somewhere along this nearly mile-and-a-half long stretch of park. Memories that are mine, just as much as they are his.

How did everything get so messy? Why am I here, alone, instead of in his arms the night before he leaves? Is it my fault?

Does it matter?

When I'm out of self-pity I wander, thinking of those Sundays when we just needed to get off the main streets and see something to remind us of home, some greenery in our concrete jungle.

Unpacking traumas and joys, laughter and fears.

The occasions when my heart would leap as our hands brushed against each other, when my face would go red and I'd think I'd caught a smile crossing his face.

The night I wanted to tell him I loved him. Five nights after the flood, when we walked the length of the park, and he draped his jacket over me, and I was certain I loved him. For everything he did to keep me here, for giving me a place to stay, for giving me stability and hope when everything in my life had been upended again. When I felt alone, again.

If it thundered before I didn't hear it, but now it grumbles from the south as droplets spatter the ground. Soon the city will smell like wet garbage.

I make my way back to street level and take off jogging down the sidewalk toward the coming storm, dodging café chairs and pedestrians as the grumbles grow to growls and booms and as rain pelts my face and soaks my hair and clothes.

The elevator ride feels like forever, and I'm jittery and shivering, freezing, dripping wet in the air-conditioned box.

I imagine that every time I walk in the door for at least a week I will feel like this: hopeless and lonely and awful.

His luggage is stacked next to the front door, the lights

are off, and Dalton is nowhere. The terrace is also empty, as expected. Self-pity floods me again, but maybe I deserve to feel nothing but the misery of standing in the soaking rain alone, and worse: lonely. I steel myself against the rain, now falling in heavy sheets, and close my eyes. I tilt my head upward, letting it wash over me.

"Hillary?" He shouts my name against the storm. "What are you doing out here?"

Dalton's standing in the doorway; water splatters onto the hardwood just inside.

"Hey!" I holler back.

"Come inside!" he calls, but I shake my head. He rolls his eyes and pulls his jacket over his head like a canopy, then joins me outside.

"What are you doing out here?" he asks again, no shouting needed, because he's inches away. He tries to cover both of us with his jacket, but we're already drenched.

"I came out here looking for you. I couldn't find you."

"I'm here now. Can we go inside?"

I shake my head. "I have to tell you something."

"Right here?" he says, and I nod.

"Here's the thing, Dalton. Here's what I realized tonight. These memories—they're equal parts you and me. You're a huge part of my New York chapter, and that's not a bad thing. But I've also worked at the bookstore, I've volunteered, I've spent time writing, exploring pockets and corners of this city that you've never seen in order to do it, and I've lived almost three decades of my life before you. I *can* be a person without you. I've done it already and starting tomorrow I'll do it again. But right now, I don't have to be a person without you. And I don't want to be."

"Hillary—"

"This is the spot where you first told me you loved me."

"I remember," he says, his voice warm honey.

"But you showed me that you loved me so many times, in so many ways, over the last few months. And I don't need you to be the main character in my books. I don't need a fictional version of you to share with the world, because your name is repeated over and over in all the highlights of my life story, and that's all I need."

"What are you saying, Hillary?"

"I'm saying—" and then thunder rolls overhead and I have to shout, "I'm saying I'm sorry!"

"I'm sorry, too!" he shouts back over the rain. "I shouldn't have freaked out earlier." He leans in and kisses my nose. "Now can we please go inside?"

I nod and kiss his lips before we scurry back to the door and inside the air-conditioned apartment, dripping and laughing.

"I'll get us some towels," he says as I slip out of my sneakers just inside the patio door, not wanting to track wet shoe prints all over the floors. My socks are soaked too, so I wrestle them off and dash, on tiptoes, to the washing machine, throwing them inside. Dalton passes me a towel and I try to absorb some of the water dripping from my hair before wrapping the towel around me.

His hair is flattened, hanging into his eyes, dripping down his face, and he has a towel draped over his shoulders like a cape. He rubs my arms. "You're a little damp, Hil," he laughs.

Still shivering, teeth chattering, I muss his hair, sending droplets flying around us. "You're one to talk."

"Well, I was relatively dry," he says, pulling me closer, "but my girlfriend wanted to talk to me in the rain, for some crazy reason."

"Well *maybe* your girlfriend had some really *good* reasons that you just haven't asked about."

His crooked smile widens, his imperfect but impossibly white teeth showing. "Any thoughts on what those reasons could be?"

"Mmhmm," I nod. "Maybe she was remembering where you first told her you love her. Maybe she was thinking back to your first kiss."

"Okay, those are actually decent reasons."

"I know." I kiss his smile. "Anyway," I say, trying to turn away from him. "I'm going to take a shower and warm up."

But he holds my arm and grabs my waist as I turn, pulling me back into him. His lips are warm and wet on mine as water drips from his hair down my cheeks and chest. When the kiss ends his hands let me go, but I can't move.

I don't want to move. I want to be right here, his urgent eyes boring into mine, his breath hot and sweet on my face. My hands reach for his waist, across his wet T-shirt and hardened torso, and inch toward his back, my nails anchored in his skin as I pull our bodies together.

I kiss his neck, catch his ear in my teeth, dig my nails deeper into him, feel him pressed against my thigh.

Then he kisses me and my heart melts, and his hands move slowly through my hair and down my chest to my waist, peeling off my T-shirt, discarding it in a pile on the floor.

"The washing machine is literally right there," I say when his lips come off mine.

His husky voice is a contrast to my joking tone. "I don't care." He kisses my jaw, my neck, and then lower; his lips caress my chest as he unties my shorts.

The anticipation and the remnants of rain send chills

through me, and I pull his shirt over his head.

He wriggles his arms out of the sleeves, and I make a show of tossing it into the washing machine next to us. I'll call it a smile, the expression that flashes across his face, and then it's gone, replaced with longing and passion and needing.

He shuffles toward our bedroom and I follow his lead, backward, lifting my face as he kisses my neck, fumbling blindly with the waistband of his shorts as my own loosen and threaten to fall around my ankles, until his hands are on mine, halting all progress.

"Can I have five minutes?" His lips hover a kiss away from mine.

"Seriously?" I ask.

"Seriously," he whispers.

"Um, sure."

"Mind waiting in your old room?"

I nod, confused.

A smile plays at his lips. "It's okay. It'll be worth it. Promise."

I swear the man's tearing up floors or taking a sledge-hammer to the walls, the amount of noise he makes. I wrap a dry T-shirt around my still-dripping hair, trying to soak up whatever I can so I look less like a wet dog. Maybe this intermission is a good thing. I peel off the rest of my wet clothes and slip into sleep shorts and Dalton's old varsity sweatshirt, which I totally stole from his parents' house months ago.

When he knocks on my door I inhale, slow and deep, before turning the handle. The hallway is lined again with votives, just like our first official date night—a beautiful bookend to our New York chapter.

Unlike that first night, he's wearing just black lounge

pants. "I actually had picked out a tux," he says, catching me staring at his muscular torso, "but I felt like it would be a little much to put it on now."

I swallow and try to clear the lump in my throat. "No, this is… this is nice."

He smiles and takes my hand, pushing up the too-long sweatshirt sleeve to kiss my wrist. My fingers brush his cheek when he does. "You look beautiful," he says. "Though I may need that sweatshirt back."

I shake my head. "Never."

"Fair enough." He pulls me to him and kisses me once, more tender than even our first kiss, that first preview of his lips. I follow him to the living room like Christine follows the Phantom, and the thought of it knots my stomach.

Framed in the windows is the picture-perfect skyline we've gazed over for months, and the trail of votives leads us to Dalton's mattress, which he's dragged out to the living room floor.

"I wanted this city to be part of our last—for now—night together. I don't want to hide back in our room. I want to fall asleep to this view and wake up to the sun, with you in my arms."

"That's beautiful."

"Sure is," he answers, and when I look over at him, his eyes are on me.

I can't tell if I grip his fingers more tightly or if he's the one to strengthen his grasp, but I'm holding on for dear life, not wanting to let go.

I lean into him, resting my head on his shoulder. "Tomorrow's going to suck."

He kisses my hair. "I know."

"But I'm excited for you."

"I know." His thumb brushes the back of my hand. "I love you."

I force a smile that he can't even see, just to mask the misery in my voice. "I know."

"And you're going to do great things, too. And I'm only a phone call away."

I nod, and the lump in my throat returns. "But tonight you're here. And I don't want to think about tomorrow right now."

"Agreed." He gives my hand a quick squeeze and motions to the mattress. "Get comfortable. I'm going to blow out these candles so we don't end up setting off the sprinklers." He runs a hand through my hair, still damp, and laughs. "Not that it would faze us if we did."

With a quick kiss, he disappears down the hall, and I slip into the bed, propped against the front of the couch, sitting with my legs under the gray microfiber sheet. I see my reflection in the window, superimposed on the skyline.

I'm part of this city, and it's comforting to know that.

"Why are you smiling?" he asks, smiling himself, as he passes me a glass of champagne.

I shrug, because I can't put it into words, except to say, "I think I'm going to be okay."

"Are you kidding?" he asks, his eyes dancing. "You're going to be great, Hil." He sinks down next to me and wraps an arm around my shoulders.

He raises his glass. "To all our tomorrows—may they be filled with promise and adventure and love, always. And to tonight—to you and me. To memories and plans and hopes and dreams."

"To new chapters, in a love story I don't ever want to put down."

"Perfect," he says, tilting his glass into mine, kissing me without tasting his champagne. And he keeps kissing me, soft and slow.

"I think it's bad luck to make a toast and not actually take a drink," I whisper into him.

Wordlessly he pulls back and downs his glass while I take one sip. Then he slides his glass onto the floor and sets mine next to it. "Better?" he asks after his mouth is already on me again, and I nod as my fingers snake into his hair.

Everything is better. Terrifying. Full of uncertainty. And perfect.

This rush of his body against mine is nothing new, but tonight it carries a specialness to it, a neediness, a blink-and-you'll-miss-it urgency.

Tonight we've got the city shining in on us, ambient light filled with neon and incandescence, and I memorize the curve of his arms, his shoulders, his chest, as I map them with my fingers. It's a multi-sensory experience.

"You're magnificent." It's barely a whisper.

His lips finish their kiss behind my ear and brush my jaw on their path to my lips. His fingers are woven into my hair. If he heard what I said, he ignores it, and I'm at least partially thankful, because *who says 'magnificent'?* Then he pulls me on top of him, and my legs are wrapped around his waist, and his hands are in my shirt. Okay, *his* shirt.

I wrap my arms around his neck and kiss him while his hands explore me, tracing my spine in touches that send sparks of heat shooting through me. I feel the moment he realizes I'm not wearing a bra, and his palms glide up each breast to my neck before he pulls the sweatshirt over my head.

Then he's eye level with my chest, and I'm trying to catch

my breath as my heart races from his touch.

He kisses my sternum. "You're hellbent on making this hard, aren't you?" Then, "The goodbye, I mean."

I laugh, shaking everything from gut to grin, and he laughs too.

"Seriously." He grips my waist and holds me at arms' length, but his eyes are focused on mine. "You're the magnificent one, Hillary."

"You heard that, huh?" I roll my eyes.

He nods, biting his lip. "Sure did."

Then his hands slide across my back, and I bend to his lips, and for an hour, maybe more, we're twisted together in the sheets, tongues tangled, hands roaming, breath hot and champagne-sweet, naked, together, bodies in perfect unison, drenched with pleasure.

We hold on tighter than we ever have, and I feel his fear of letting go, too.

So we don't. We hold each other until we've finished and while we lay there after, our foreheads and noses touching as we catch our breath. We're still holding on as we fall asleep with our city in the background, a giant nightlight to calm our fears.

THIRTY-FIVE

They say all good things must come to an end, and to some extent this feels very much like an end, this last-time-waking-up-next-to-him-for-who-knows-how-long thing.

But Dalton calls it a beginning—a new chapter, a plot twist—where we can find out who we are together, even though we're apart.

He was already out of the shower when I woke up this morning, and he cleaned up everything from last night while I was getting showered and dressed.

"It's time, I guess." He's dressed in shorts and a T-shirt with a zip-up hoodie and ballcap, ready for a day of travel with his castmates.

"I guess." I want to go with him to see him off, but there's no point. A car waits downstairs already; it's time to say goodbye.

"I got this for you yesterday. I wanted to give it to you last night, but—" he trails off and hands me a brown teddy bear wearing a T-shirt with *I ♥ NY* printed across the front. "I don't know if you can bear to part with your unicorn, but I thought maybe this would feel like I'm with you, even when I'm not."

I turn the bear over in my hands. "I love it."

Then I help wheel his bags to the elevator and through

the lobby. Once they're loaded in the trunk of the car, he turns to me one more time.

"I'll miss you."

"I'll miss you, too. But it's going to be fine, right? We'll talk a lot."

"Every day." He takes my face in his hands and uses his thumbs to dry the patches of tears that remain even after I wiped my face with his sweatshirt sleeves. "I love you, Hillary James."

He kisses my forehead and I wrap my arms around his waist. "I love you, Dalton Tremaine."

Then he lifts my face and kisses my mouth, and I taste the mint of our toothpaste and the salt of our tears, even after he climbs in the car and waves out the window as he drives away.

⋯⋯⋯⋯⋯⋯

Alone, the apartment feels far too big.

File that under the list of things I never thought I'd say about New York City apartments.

⋯⋯⋯⋯⋯⋯

I busy myself with writing—I scrap the near-finished book with its references to Dalton's life, and I have a million ideas that I scribble down and try to flesh out with varying degrees of success instead.

I pick up shifts at Books Off Broadway, working full time hours and some overtime to help the Charleses and bring in extra income.

Dalton calls every day, just like he said he would, for the first two weeks. Then he misses a day, and suddenly we're falling into a comfortable pattern of FaceTiming every other day, with frequent text exchanges peppered in between.

Look what came in the mail today, I text him, after his first week in Chicago. I include a picture of the red panda plush he's sent, a souvenir from the cast's outing to the zoo. You remembered it's my favorite.

I send a similar text during their stop in Dallas when another package arrives, this one a teddy bear wearing a cowboy hat and boots. A notecard that comes with it reads:

Hillary—

Being gone really sucks
I really, really miss you
Can't wait until I see you again
So I can hold you and can kiss you

—D

I text a selfie of me and the bear, adding my own poem.

I miss you too, it's un-bear-able
But we're both getting through
Though I can't wait until the night
When I'm not holding this, but you

My phone dings two hours later when I'm microwaving some leftover chicken sausage and broccoli for dinner; a heart emoji response to my poem.

After dinner I text my mom and sister, just checking in to see what's new, and then Stacy starts the group FaceTime.

"How are you holding up?" Mom asks after the usual updates.

"I'm fine, mostly," I say.

"Are you alright? Did something happen?"

Her worst fear has come true: I'm alone in New York.

"No, everything's fine. I just miss him, that's all."

Stacy chimes in. "It looks like the show's getting great reviews!"

I nod; Dalton sends reviews my way, not that he needs to, because I'm constantly looking them up, watching the show's social media pages for mentions of him and his performance. As expected, people rave about him.

"Do you have an idea of when he'll be back?" Mom asks, but I don't.

"Not sure, unfortunately. They're on the road at least through mid-January."

"Well hopefully that'll be it. Hopefully they come back soon."

"Hopefully. But enough about that, what else is new at home?"

They both shift their eyes, almost as though looking to the other, but neither speaks.

"Guys? Hello? What's going on?"

Mom shakes her head, but Stacy says, "Well... there have been some—shall we say—advancements, as far as some couples around here are concerned."

I roll my eyes. Small town gossip will always find me. "Okay, I'll bite. Who? What?"

"We weren't sure if you'd heard or not," Mom interjects.

"Probably not, I only really talk to you guys."

Stacy tells me, "Peter's engaged, Hil."

"Peter? *My* Peter?" Ew. I hate calling him *my* Peter, because he's not, and I don't know that he ever really was.

"Yes, honey."

"To whom?"

Stacy shrugs. "Do you remember Katie Carmine?"

Of course I remember Katie Carmine. She drove an Audi to school, and everyone loved her—all the boys in school, and the teachers, too, even though she almost never did her homework and her contributions to class discussions were mostly just asking *Why?*, which our philosophy and English teachers thought proved her genius. And, of course, she had boobs before any of the rest of us, which just extra sucked.

"Yes, I remember. But really? Her and Peter? I can't believe that she'd go for him, and that he'd actually propose. And that quickly." After all, we only broke up seven months ago.

"Well, that's what happens when you knock up the well-to-do princess of Lemming."

"Mother!" Stacy hisses at her.

My mouth goes dry, but I force out my question. "Really? They're—they're pregnant?"

Stacy nods, her face sullen. "Sorry, Sis. Didn't want you to hear it quite like that."

"Sorry!" Mom interjects. "But the nerve of that boy, to string you along like that for so long, and then just act like three years is nothing,"

"It's fine, Mom." And it is, because I don't love Peter, and I don't think I ever did, now that I'm in love with Dalton Tremaine and know what it actually feels like.

We talk a bit more, then I get back to writing. I've been developing characters based on customers at the bookstore, or people I watch from my chair at Eunoia, one-sided cell phone conversations I hear on the sidewalk, or, better yet, full conversations I hear from the psychos who use speaker phone to air their dirty laundry while browsing the aisles at the grocery store.

Since I have off tomorrow, I stay up late to write, though now all I can think of is the cluster that is my ex and my high school nemesis mating and marrying.

Just after midnight, I text Dalton. Hope you had a great show tonight!

He calls me five minutes later. "Hey. You're still up?"

"I am. It's so good to hear your voice."

"Yours too. And your timing's great—I just walked into my hotel room."

"Weird. It's almost like I'm keeping track of your schedule and accounting for the difference in time zones."

Laughter flavors his voice. "Well, I for one am ready to be in the same time zone again."

"You and me, both." I close my journal and move from the kitchen back to our bedroom. I set the new teddy bear on the pillow and sit cross-legged on the bed. "I don't think it's fair, by the way, that you know how to reach me, and I can only call or text."

"Did you have something else in mind?" he asks, and I shrug even though he can't see it.

"I don't know. I just thought I could send you a care package or something. Treats from New York, for when you miss it here."

"That's daily, so treats would probably not be the best idea."

"It's exciting though, getting to see so much of the country, right?"

"It is. And it's not really New York that I miss."

I blush. "I miss you too." Then I clear my throat and add, "Hey, if you ever want me to FaceTime you so you can see the city, like that night I was at the beach and you watched the waves—"

"I promise you, when we FaceTime, the city is at the bottom of the list of things I want to look at."

Goosebumps rush down my arms and my heart races. All our calls have been standard, basic, innocent calls, but the way he says this, I wonder if he wants more. But I have a different idea. "Just tell me where I can reach you, okay? Every city. Deal?"

"Deal," he says, yawning.

"You must be exhausted. I can let you go."

"Thanks. These two-a-days are rough. I'm not as young as I used to be, I guess." He sighs. "Hey, Hil?"

"Yeah?"

"I miss you. I love you."

"Same. Both things. So much."

We hang up, and when I fall asleep curled up in his sheets, I'm holding two teddy bears and thinking about the next time I'll see Dalton.

THIRTY-SIX

I hate flying.

I hate literally everything about it, from parking at the airport to sitting next to strangers and turbulence and lay-overs and the toddler who kicks your seat while his mom ignores it.

What I love about it, though, is that I can get halfway across the country in four hours.

I've got two days off work in a row, which gives me just enough time to leave bright and early on Sunday to fly to Dallas, see the show, spend the night with Dalton, and fly home Monday afternoon. And the best part is, he has no idea I'm here.

I bought a single ticket, center orchestra, and from my seat I get to watch him absolutely shine on stage. He's got one quirky dance number, which has the audience cracking up, and a ballad that brings tears to my eyes. There's more, of course, but those are the hit songs that the critics have been raving about.

During curtain call—and a well-deserved standing ovation—I cheer extra loudly when he takes his bow. His eyes dart left and right and grow with his smile when they meet mine. Then, ever the professional, he rejoins the line of his castmates and acknowledges the orchestra and lighting crew.

I'm slow to leave my seat while the rest of the audience filters out of the theater. I've texted Dalton, but there's no response yet.

A man wearing all black and a headset approaches me. "Excuse me, are you Hillary?"

I nod.

"Wonderful. Could you come with me, please?" I follow him to the corner of the stage, through a doorway and up a flight of stairs. Dalton's at the top, a smile spread wide across his face.

"Holy shit, Hil!"

I take his outstretched hand and follow him until we reach his dressing room, the world a blur; the only clear and real things are his arms tight around me, his fingers in my hair, his breath warm and rapid on my neck.

"I can't believe you're here."

"I can't either. But I'm so glad I am."

"Me too," he says. He kisses me, and I never want him to stop. "I just need a few minutes to clean up, then we can head back to the hotel."

"Sure." I stand in the corner, trying not to be in the way as he dashes in and out, saying goodbyes, laughing with castmates as he straightens up for their next show.

He introduces me to a few of the ensemble members, then everyone is heading out to get a post-show drink since they have off tomorrow, but he declines and takes my hand instead. "Have a good night, guys," he hollers after them.

The hotel is only a five-minute walk from the theater, and our fingers are laced together the whole way back.

"Did you get a room here, too?" Dalton asks, nodding toward the entrance of the extended-stay hotel.

I stop on the sidewalk, stunned. "I—um—"

His lips curl upward, and his eyes reflect the streetlights as he pulls me to him by our still-tethered hands. "Relax, I'm just joking. I've got a sofa-bed in my suite." He winks with the last part.

Dalton tips the bellman who brings me my bag, and I follow him to the elevator. His hand tightens around mine and loosens, pulsing this way the whole ride, like he's torn between being content standing side by side like this and pinning me against the wood-paneled walls and hiking up my dress.

I think we show great restraint by making it back to his room before we kiss again. Actually, we don't kiss again until I've unpacked my toiletry bag and outfit for tomorrow, and it's all very *normal* feeling, like we're back in our apartment tidying up and talking.

Suddenly, as I sit next to him on the couch to unbuckle my sandals, his arm slides around my waist and he kisses my temple. I melt into his embrace, one sandal still fastened and the other on the floor, as his lips fall on mine.

"I'm so glad you're here." He tucks my hair behind my ear and his fingers run the length of my neck, causing my toes to curl and my skin to shiver and warm.

Already the trip is well worth the extra hours I picked up at Books Off Broadway to buy my plane ticket.

When we try to move to the bed I trip over my sandals and stumble, laughing, and he kisses my teeth before a low laughter rumbles in his chest. He stops and looks at me, beaming, and says, "That was incredibly sexy."

"Yeah, right, okay," I say, rolling my eyes.

"I'm dead serious." And it looks like he might be, his eyes all passion and tenderness, his smile smaller, warmer. "I've always loved that about you, Hillary. Your random moments of klutziness, the way you react to them, like you just laugh it off or joke about it instead of getting embarrassed and worked up."

"I have much practice," I laugh, and he kisses me again.

"And the way you joke, even when we're about to—"

"Now *that* I have less practice with," I interrupt.

"See?" He kisses my jaw, my neck, my clavicle, and as he bends, his hands slide from my knees to my thighs under the floral fabric of my dress. "It's very sexy."

"Well then I think you'll find me irresistible in eight seconds."

"Too late, but why?"

"Because," I whisper, "I think we should wait."

He stops, pulls away, and smiles. "Like, a few minutes? Or a few months?"

"Oh, it's still happening tonight, for sure. I just—can we order a pizza? And can you tell me literally everything about your life these last six weeks?"

"Of course," he answers. "Only if you do the same."

Before and after the pizza arrives, we're curled up at opposite ends of the couch, and I tell him all the stories I forgot to bring up before, or that didn't matter when our talk time was limited, and he tells me about the cities he's seen along his travels, fan encounters, the waitress who dished up the world's best apple pie (on the house!) when they waited out a tornado watch at a random roadside diner at midnight.

"And so of course we had to show our appreciation."

"In four-part harmony?"

"Six, but who's counting."

Finished with pizza, he reclines back and rubs the top of my foot, and I catch him staring at me as I take a sip of water.

"What?"

He shrugs. "I didn't say anything."

"But what are you thinking?"

He shrugs again and shakes his head. "I still can't believe you're here."

I match his smile and set down the water bottle. "Is it crazy? Is this too much?"

"Not even a little. I mean, crazy, maybe, but so perfect."

He sits up and kisses my forehead, telling me he loves me, looking another moment into my eyes.

The way he does it, this making me feel beautiful and wanted and seen, it inebriates me. I'm drunk on the attention—the love—that I never felt before. The feeling of feeling *valued*. Of feeling *desired*.

My hands are on his waist and suddenly we're in bed, my smocked floral dress buried in the shapeless pile of clothing discarded on the floor, and we indulge in our own personal brand of intimacy, which includes sensuality and silliness, giggles and guilty pleasure.

Lots of pleasure.

We fill the night with the best parts of our relationship—talking, listening, laughing, tenderness, cuddling, and really good sex—and it's 4:00 a.m. until we finish all those things and allow ourselves to fall asleep.

....

The sun sneaks through a crack in the drapes and shines a white stripe across the blanket, cutting right across our legs. I watch how it shifts and dances as I move my ankles and bend my knees, and then Dalton's in on the dance with me, rolling onto his side, pulling me closer to him.

"Good morning."

"Morning." His voice sounds like mountain air, crisp yet hazy.

I roll onto my stomach and cross my arms in front of me, propping my chin on my hands. "How did you sleep?"

"I have never woken up better in this bed than I did this morning." He laughs as he kisses my forehead, then snakes a hand down my back. "Did you have big plans on the agenda for the day?"

"Just an eight o'clock flight. I thought maybe you could show me a few sights around the city." I yawn and add, "Though staying right here all day sounds great, too."

"It does. But do you know what would make it even more satisfying?"

I catch the twinkle in his eye, the mischief in his smile, and feel my grin grow. "What's that?"

"French toast. There's a great place a few blocks away if you want to go."

I sit up and wrap the blanket around me in one movement. "Carbs are my love language. Let's go."

....

The day is ours, as much as it can be when it also belongs to a ticking clock.

We sit next to each other in a booth at breakfast, his arm wrapped around me at some moments, his fingers interlocked with mine at others.

We hail a ride to the nearby botanical gardens—his favorite spot so far, he says—and stroll through well over fifty acres of flowers and fountains and statues.

We sip cocktails to cool down at an outdoor café because it's still eighty degrees outside, which I simultaneously love and loathe.

We play mini golf because I've had a little too much to drink and get overly excited when I see a course along our walk; he kisses me when I get a hole in one, but I think it's just to shut me up because I'm loudest when I'm excited. His lips sober me immediately.

We wind up back at the hotel around three thirty—plenty of time to be at the airport by six, so I pack my bag and I love him again, and then we lay together, talking about everything and about nothing. He rides with me to the airport and envelops me in arms more muscular than I remember them being back when we were in New York.

"Thank you," he says as he loosens his hold on me. "This was the best surprise."

"Thanks for an amazing twenty-four hours. And Dalton?"

"Hmm?"

"You were spectacular, up on stage. I'm so glad I got to see you up there again."

He kisses my forehead. "Again?"

I smile, hopefully hiding that I am stumbling through an excuse for the slip-up. "Yeah, again. First the concert a few months ago, then last night."

"Right," he says, and the driver shouts for him to hurry up.

"I should probably get in there."

"Probably," he repeats. "I'll miss you."

"I know. I'll miss you too. But this was good."

"It was." He lowers his lips to mine and kisses me good-bye, and we say *I love you* in unison, and I watch him disappear into the car and ride off into the sunset.

THIRTY-SEVEN

The show's run in Dallas was a hit.

Seattle loved it, too.

Boston's up next, for five weeks in November and December.

My collection of teddy bears grows.

We still text or call nearly every day. I'm optimistic that we can at least spend Thanksgiving together, but his parents drive from West Virginia to Massachusetts to be with him for the holiday, and I've committed time to my family, so we're apart for our first major holiday. Which is okay, because we're still new to this couple thing—still working out the things couples work out and throwing a national tour into the mix, too.

I promise to help the Charleses with the Black Friday sale at the bookstore. We set up a table with Christmas romances on display, another with holiday cookbooks, another with wintery cozy mysteries. We've partnered with a local bakery to sell some of their flavored hot chocolate powders and other treats, peppering those goodies throughout our displays. And we decorate—lights everywhere, artificial trees dripping with themed ornaments throughout the store, displays of finished kids' coloring pages along the register counter.

It's a busy day, with our summertime staff coming back

to help with the volume, and even Samantha coming by for an hour to check on her parents, bringing lunch for the whole staff with her.

When my shift's over, I'm on a late train out of Penn Station, bound for Lemming. Stacy picks me up just before eleven and drives me to Mom and Dad's house. I guess I could say Stacy drives me *home*, because technically this is still my official address.

"Mom? Dad?" Stacy calls as she closes the door behind her. I've told her a million times she didn't have to pick me up; she's got her life together and should be home with her family. But she insisted, and here we are, breaking and entering at our childhood home at 11:20 p.m.

I follow her toward the siren song of the eleven o'clock news aglow on the living room TV, and Mom turns from her perch on the couch when she sees our movement.

"Goodness, Stacy, you'll scare me to death, doing that," Mom says.

"Apologies for the late delivery," Stacy says, stepping to the side.

"Hillary!" A smile explodes across Mom's face, and she rushes to pull me into a hug. "I didn't expect you back until tomorrow!"

"I took a late train in, after work."

Dad lowers the footrest on the recliner. "Welcome home, kiddo," he says, climbing out of his seat and patting me on the back. Mom's still monopolizing the hug market. "Your guy not coming with you?"

"I told you, Dad, Dalton's on tour. His family's with him in Boston this weekend."

"I still can't believe you're here and not there," Stacy says.

I shake my head and smile. "Thanksgiving weekend

has always been our family's big weekend. There's nowhere else I'd rather be."

Mom offers to make hot cocoa, but I decline. "Actually, I'm super exhausted. Mind if I just get some rest? I'm sure we have a full day planned for tomorrow."

"Of course, dear."

Another round of hugs ensues, and I thank Stacy for the ride from the train station again. "Now go see your people, Stace."

....

My old room is unchanged, except all my knick-knacks are tidied up. The bookshelf in the corner has all my favorite books, still arranged by spine color, then by height. Next to my very old (and very beloved) five-disc CD player on the top shelf is a thick black binder filled with all my old Playbills, and I turn to the one autographed by Dalton on the cover. It's crazy how things have played out.

Above the bookshelf, a bulletin board still has pictures from high school prom, college graduation, our family beach vacation, a candid photo of Grandpa and me reading new books on Christmas night, and so many moments that mattered in my life. The memories bring a smile to my face, and I can almost hear the music or smell the sea salt air—the things burned in my senses that a photo doesn't capture but still somehow releases.

A deep, dizzying yawn tells me it's time to end my walk down memory lane and get to bed, so I brush my teeth, change, and sink into the familiar twin-size mattress I've used since the tenth grade, welcoming the rest.

I love New York. I really do. But I love that here I can go for a run without having to dodge other people or pause for traffic. I haven't run in a while, but in the cold air of a late-November morning I can find my happy pace and go for miles. I run without headphones, enjoying the playlist and the sound of my feet on the pavement, hearing and watching my breath together against the quiet and still of the morning.

I follow the winding roads, first through a spattering of houses and then through open farmland, always uphill at first so the back half of my run is easier. When I reach the top of Catsback Hill, my lungs are burning. I raise my arms and interlock my fingers, resting my hands on my head. There's a wide shoulder along the road and a small pull-off spot at the top with a few picnic tables, and I head over to the guardrail to see the fields below, expanses of land dotted with barns and farmhouses and ponds. Puffs of breath escape in little white clouds; I'm panting from the climb up here.

No matter how much I love the city and its architecture and history, nothing can compare to this—to seeing for miles, having a moment alone, just you and the world. Tears prickle at my eyes, and I smile, feeling peace for the first time in a very long time.

The run down Catsback feels like a flight, and that floating on air feeling stays with me all the way home.

"Did you have a good run?" Mom asks, drying the last of the dishes as I walk in the door.

I grab a fresh muffin from the counter and sit down with a glass of water. "I did, thanks. I forgot how much I love these views."

"Little bit different from what you're used to these days, huh?"

"Just a little." A bite of warm muffin melts on my tongue. "What's on the agenda for the weekend?"

She turns away to fold up the towel and drape it over the handle on the oven door. "Oh, nothing much. Figured we'd play some games, bake some Christmas cookies, and have an early birthday party for you."

"*Mom,* you didn't."

She doesn't turn to look at me, which tells me she feels guilty and doesn't want to see my pouty face. "Everyone has been asking about you."

"Define everyone."

"Oh, the usual suspects. Gram, Aunt Janine, Uncle Rich, Nan and Pop, Wesley, Brenda…"

"That's so many people," I whine, tilting my head back, thinking through the names of family and Mom and Dad's friends who knew me from way back when, when I was a teenager who was involved in all the extra-curriculars and volunteer opportunities and the church choir. Back when I was doing things I thought I was supposed to do, before thinking about what I really wanted to do.

"What do you expect, when you disappear for six months and don't communicate with more than two of us?" Now she whips around, arms crossed, daring me to challenge her point. Of course I don't, because it's fair. "I thought it would be nice, Hillary, if we could celebrate your thirtieth with you. It's a big deal."

"I know."

"So why do you sound so ungrateful?"

I shrug. If there's one thing I've learned in my relationship with Dalton and living in New York in general, it's how to be honest, even when it's hard. Well, mostly, at least. So I do the hard thing and admit the absolute truth. "I just don't feel like I deserve to be celebrated."

"Oh, Hillary," Mom says, rolling her eyes. "Of course you do." When I don't respond, she uncrosses her arms and picks up a muffin, sitting across from me at the table.

"Listen. You had a rough year, Hillary. In fact, a rough couple of years. I know that people get to you, that you get tired of the questions about the past—"

"It's not just that, Mom. It's the *looks*. The judgment. The pity, maybe. I don't know how to describe it, but I just feel itchy whenever I'm around people here, like I can feel their eyes."

"Honey, I promise you, they're not judging you. Or maybe they are. You're a unicorn to them, independent, not rushing into some unhappy marriage or giving up her dreams to follow some cookie-cutter path. But screw it. Screw the questions and the looks. You are doing big things, kid. *Huge* things. Things people in this town could never imagine doing themselves. And you should absolutely be celebrated for that, and for the beautiful, special woman you are."

She reaches across the table and lays a hand on my arm, rubbing my jacket with her thumb. She's done the same thing to comfort me so many times, most recently after Peter and I broke up and even longer ago, when I lost out on lead parts in our school musicals or wasn't invited to the birthday party all my other friends were invited to. It draws a smile from me, and she smiles too and says, "You should also absolutely take a shower because everyone's coming for lunch."

I laugh and shove the rest of the muffin into my face, then try to hug her on my way to the bathroom, but she keeps me at arm's length. "After your shower," she laughs. "There's not time for both of us to wash up."

Stacy and Dad must have been waiting in the wings, ready to jump out and decorate as soon as I got in the shower, because the house is decked out in balloons and set up for a party by the time I'm dressed and ready.

The giant silver *3* and *0* balloons are like a punch to the gut. In fifth grade I was certain I was going to be the youngest ever published author and now here I am, a week away from this milestone, and I don't even have a first draft done. Close, but not complete.

Family and friends arrive, and I power through even the awkward greetings, and it seems most people genuinely care what I've been up to or have questions about life in New York.

Mom's got a smorgasbord set up; people grab what they want and mingle, conversing about the town, sharing updates on their own family members.

Our home is modest, for sure, so when thirty to forty people pile in and the door keeps opening and closing, I don't know who's here or where they are. Luckily the weather is mild, so a few people spill out into the three-season room off the dining room, creating a relatively connected space for all of us.

Before cake and ice cream, Stacy demands I open presents. Most of the guests pull up a chair in a circle around me while others move throughout, still socializing, not feeling the need to watch a grown woman open gifts from the floor in the middle of a friendship circle like she's turning three.

The first four cards have cash or gift cards in them, then there's a series of presents, most of which are journals or books or travel mugs. Then a bottle of wine from a local vineyard and winery, which I love, and a cold box marked *fragile,* filled with a deep-dish apple pie from Gram that promptly goes back into the refrigerator so I can eat most of it while watching old Christmas movies with Mom later on. Stacy and her husband Kirk have given me a gift card for a spa in Manhattan, and from Mom and Dad I get a silver bracelet with a dangling type-writer charm and a bouquet of gift cards to my favorite places in New York.

"Thank you, everyone, so much. Now I think it's time for cake—" I say, rising, but Stacy rests her hand on my shoulder.

"Not yet, Sis. There's one more." She nods to Kirk, who passes a box covered in children's gift wrap, cartoon tigers and pandas and chameleons wearing party hats against a yellow backdrop.

I laugh as I unwrap it because I love it so much. Inside the box is a stuffed lemming, wearing a "When in Lem-ming" shirt, showing half a dozen cartoon lemmings eating ice cream outside what I can only imagine is supposed to be our very well-known ice cream parlor. I hold it up and look at Mom.

"Is this so I always remember my roots?"

"That's not from us, dear."

I turn to Stacy, who shakes her head and bites her lip. "Don't look at me," she answers.

"Then who?" I ask, laughing.

"From me."

Whenever I tell this story, I will forever describe this as the moment I died. Seriously.

I swear my heart stops, the familiarity of the voice, here, unexpected. I turn toward it, and it's like the sea of people has parted to reveal Dalton Tremaine, standing in my parents' dining room, holding a bouquet of peonies.

I drop the lemming and scramble to my feet, then apparently forgetting about the dozens of other humans all around me I stare at him. "What are you doing here? How did you—"

"Your mom invited me."

"I slid into his DM's," Mom says proudly, and Stacy and I both groan.

"Never say that again, Mom," Stacy sighs. "I'm scarred for life."

"How about some cake and ice cream, everyone?" Mom asks as she disappears into the kitchen.

"Who's your friend, Hillary?" Gram asks.

Duh. "Sorry, everyone." I leapfrog the stack of gifts on the floor so I'm standing next to him. "This is Dalton."

"Her *boyfriend*, ladies and gents," Stacy adds from the floor.

With my hand on his back, I can feel his body move with laughter, even as I shoot dagger eyes at Stacy.

"Well, isn't he handsome," Gram says, flashing her eyebrows, assuming, apparently, that Dalton can neither see nor hear her, or not caring that he does.

"I think I love your family," he says to me as he extends a hand to Gram. "Nice to meet you."

Introductions continue as my parents prepare dessert. We answer questions about how we met, what he does, and more.

Dad carries one of the cakes my way—a layered round cake with vanilla buttercream frosting trimmed with pink dollops. "Your favorite, kiddo," he says, and I already knew it was, because of course they'd order it for me. Mom always makes sure the birthdays, the holidays—all the days—are perfect.

Everyone joins in the singing, all out of tune, except Stacy who grew up singing just like I did, and of course Dalton, who sings softly enough that he doesn't overpower the others but whose voice is smooth and expressive, even in the Happy Birthday song.

I blow out the candles and we enjoy cake—either home-made chocolate with peanut-butter icing, or my favorite, a vanilla cake with chocolate shavings folded into the batter, raspberry mousse marrying the layers. I sample both, but only small pieces, because that pie is waiting for me in the fridge.

Dalton adds a large slice of chocolate with peanut butter to his plate, refusing to try my all-time favorite. I *boop* a dot of icing on his lips, then promptly kiss it off, then keep kissing him, and Dad clears his throat.

"Oh, relax, would you," Gram says to her son. "They're young and in love." Then she turns to the two of us, eyes darting between us, and she asks, "You are in love, right?"

"Yes," I answer, at the same time Dalton says, "Very much so."

I blush and Gram winks at me, and Dalton holds my hand and tries to finish his cake left-handed.

The guests are gone by late-afternoon and Dad puts his famous meatloaf in the oven, ready to one-up my favorite desserts by throwing my favorite meal into the ring. We help clean up the party mess and play a round of Candyland with my niece and nephew, Anna and Logan.

"This looks and smells amazing," Dalton says, spreading a napkin on his lap when we sit down for dinner.

"Wait till you taste it," Kirk winks. "The James family knows how to cook."

"Well, most of us, anyway," Stacy laughs, and I kick her under the table.

Anna and Logan entertain us through most of dinner, and Kirk and Stacy talk about updates at work. They have dinner most Sunday nights with our parents, so this is a pretty standard event for them.

Of course there's interest in Dalton, hearing about the tour, hearing his side of the story about how we met.

"The way Hillary tells it, it was love at first sight, or something like that," Stacy says.

He smiles, chewing his last bite. "I don't know if that exists, but there was absolutely something there the day we met. I mean, to be able to sit with a complete stranger for hours, just talking and laughing—it was really special."

"Well, not a complete stranger, right? I mean, not for Hillary." Kirk says.

I choke on my water. Stacy glares at him.

"What do you mean?"

"Dude, you should've heard these three—" he hooks his thumb toward Mom, Stacy, and me, "when they took that last-minute trip to see you in...what was that?"

"I think you're confused, Kirk," Stacy says. Her voice matches her icy scowl.

"No, it was totally him. Hillary posted that autographed book thing in her Instagram story like twenty times, she was so excited. I can picture it, but I can't think of the name."

"How does dessert sound?" Mom asks, and bless her for trying to change the subject.

I feel Dalton's eyes on me, and I can't stand the thought of meeting his gaze, afraid of what I might see if I do. Instead, I try to use telepathy to tell Kirk to shut up.

It doesn't work.

"It's the one with the mask."

"Phantom?" Dalton asks. His voice is a dry whisper.

Kirk snaps and points. "Yes! That's the one."

"I was just an alternate in that show."

Dad chimes in, seeing the chaos unfolding, trying to protect me from Kirk's big mouth. "So they probably saw some other guy, then."

But Kirk shakes his head, completely oblivious to half the people in the room sending pretty clear signs he should drop it. "No, no. It was definitely you, man. Stacy was telling me—"

"Can we change the subject, please." Even when stern, Mom's polite. Kirk quiets.

Dalton clears his throat and doesn't even complete his "Excuse me, please" before he's on his feet, leaving the dining room.

We all glare at Kirk, who looks around the room and asks, "What'd I do?"

"Good lord," Stacy says, rolling her eyes and resting her forehead in her hands.

"You okay?" Mom asks, eyes on me.

I hang my head. "Probably not." I excuse myself from the table, hearing the whispers start behind me as I make my way upstairs to my room. He's there by the bookshelf when I reach the doorway.

"Dalton." I have no words but his name.

He doesn't respond; he just stands there at the bookshelf, in front of the pictures of my life's best moments. This snapshot would not make the bulletin board. I can feel it.

I take two steps toward him. "Dalton? Will you talk to me?"

He turns, the binder of Playbills open in his arm, turned to the Phantom of the Opera Playbill with his signature scrawled across the cover in silver Sharpie. "What is this, Hillary?"

I can't answer. It is what it looks like, but I can't admit the truth that's here, plain as day, in front of both of us.

"Hillary." His shoulders slump and he closes the binder, setting it back crooked on the top shelf. Then he looks my way again, his eyes boring into me. "You've really known? This whole time?"

Then the worst possible kind of word vomit comes out of me: excuses.

"To be fair, I-" I use air quotes around the next word, "knew that afternoon anyway."

"Jesus, Hillary."

It's a lame excuse; he has every right to be annoyed.

"Okay, fine. Yes, I knew even before that girl spoiled it."

"Why did you lie about it?"

I shrug. "I don't know. I guess at first it didn't matter, when you crashed into me. Then it felt weird to just throw it at you during conversation, so I waited. And then, you said—"

"I said I could never tell who wanted to be around me for me."

"Exactly. So at that point, I couldn't tell you, because I didn't want you to think I was just hanging out with you because of your name or your fame."

"Weren't you?"

"What are you talking about? Of course not."

"So you would've stayed—all day—with any guy who spilled your coffee all over you?"

"If they were as nice as you were—"

"Bullshit, Hil. Fresh off a breakup with a Grade A asshole, first day in a new city filled with millions of weirdos, I don't believe you would've given anyone else the time of day if they had flirted with you."

"Okay, so maybe I agreed to sit down with you because I already knew you weren't a weirdo, and because I didn't realize you were flirting with me—"

"Of course I was. But that's not the point. Do you have any idea how this feels? To know that literally from the moment we met you've lied to me?"

"I tried to tell you a million times."

"So why didn't you?" His volume climbs. I wonder how much everyone downstairs can hear.

"Because I was afraid of this exact reaction. That you'd doubt me for some reason, despite the fact that we're here and we love each other."

"Yeah, Hillary. We do love each other. And that means we *tell* each other things. In fact, you're the one who was so big on honesty since the very beginning, all the while you've been lying to me."

He turns away but quickly spins back toward me. "You know what else sucks? This book you wrote—this adaptation of my life—it feels different now. Is that why you came to New York? To stalk me for your fan fiction?"

"You're being ridiculous."

"Am I?"

"Yes." I don't want to say it. I hate that I've said it, because maybe he's not.

He goes silent, which speaks volumes.

Then, after a long moment he says, "I think I should go."

He's resolute, and when he tries to leave I block him, tears already streaming down my face. "Please, don't go."

"I need to. I can't be here right now, Hil."

"You can. We can talk through this."

"No," he repeats as I plead for him to stay. I reach for his arms, but he dodges my grasp. He's closing in on the door, which I swing closed, a last-ditch effort to keep him here.

"Dalton, please, just—let's figure this out."

He looks at the door, then at me, then runs his hands down his face. He kisses me unexpectedly, his hands pulling me toward him, and I feel our bodies move, drifting in this room that felt small when I was fourteen and even smaller now, crowded with two adults and tension and passion and hurt.

But then there's a release, when the door opens and everything can go spilling freely out.

Starting with Dalton, whose wet eyes break me as he barely whispers "I'm sorry" before rushing down the stairs.

"Thank you, everyone, for the invitation and your hospitality," he says to my family, now cleaning up after dinner, as I run after him, begging him to stay.

I throw open the front door when he closes it on my face and follow him to the driveway, then down the street to his rental car. He ignores me until he reaches the door, then turns to me. I step back, startled by the emotion that twists his face.

"You need to stop, Hillary. Let me go. I'm hurt, okay? And I need time and space to process the eighty-seven thousand different things happening in my head right now. And I can't do that here, with you. Do you understand?"

I nod, biting my lip.

His eyes linger on mine a moment longer, and I wonder if he feels the urge to hold me the same way that I feel the urge to wrap my arms around his waist and bury my face in his chest. If he feels it at all he gives no indication. Instead he takes off toward who knows where, for who knows how long.

I pass Mom on the porch, rejecting her outstretched arms. Kirk and Stacy are just inside, beyond the staircase in the living room, and their angry whispers go silent when I walk in.

"I'm sorry, Hil. I didn't realize—" Kirk says.

I hold up my hand and march up the stairs to my room, locking the door behind me.

Mom, Stacy, and Dad each make at least one appearance in the hallway, knocking, asking how I am, but I ignore all of them to curl up in a ball and cry myself to sleep.

THIRTY-EIGHT

E verything hurts.
My eyes—puffy from a night of crying.
My back—from the old mattress.
My heart—shattered and broken, irreparable.

I ache too much to run, but I need to escape. Instead, I walk in the part of town where sidewalks exist, though cracked and uneven from the root damage of the trees that have matured since their planting.

I understand the trees—planted in a space too small, growing up and wild and damaging the foundations they were expected to accommodate as they grew.

Modest colonial homes line this side of the street and festive garden flags dance in the breeze. An old Victorian sits behind a black iron gate across the road. Growing up we thought it was haunted and would fearfully avoid it. In fact, I'm not sure my feet have ever walked this length of sidewalk on that side of the street.

I look both ways, but it's a Sunday morning and most people are at church, so the roads are clear. I jaywalk and eye the Victorian as I slowly walk past. It's beautiful, different for this area, with a huge front porch hidden partially by stonework and shrubs. There's a turret on each side of the front of the home. On the lowest level of each is a bay window; the highest floors have small rectangles of glass, and on Halloween as kids we'd claim to see ghosts through them from the safety of the other side of the street.

We were never sure how the rumors started, but probably from some bored teenagers around someone's backyard campfire making up stories.

The thought takes me to a lake in West Virginia, the stories shared there. But I brush it off and walk, the frozen air burning my lungs, a pain that distracts from the hurt of losing Dalton. I consider texting him but figure that would go against his request for time and space.

Instead I walk on, past the funeral parlor and the used car lot, the Presbyterian church, the consignment shop. We truly are a single stoplight town, and at its intersection live a vintage ice cream parlor, a bank, a family-owned pizza joint, and a café, the last of which is my destination this morning.

I've brought my laptop and my journal in my backpack, and after ordering a scone and latte I claim a pleather armchair in the corner, ready to work.

I try to write, but all I want to do is create an unhappily-ever-after for my heroine. Why should she get to have it all, when I've lost so much? I have to remind myself that Dalton said he needed time and space, not that he needed forever.

Pen touches paper and recoils forty-two times before I give up, surrendering to my inability to focus, and pull my laptop out of the backpack instead.

"Still working, even on a Sunday?"

I don't need to look up to know who the voice belongs to, but I look up anyway and am instantly angry with the universe. Katie Carmine is just as gorgeous as she's ever been, and now she's glowing, though whether from the pregnancy or the mid-morning sunlight streaming through the window behind her I'm not sure.

"Hi, Katie."

"How are you, Hillary?" She lowers herself into the armchair across from mine. "Putting in some overtime, I see."

"No, actually," I tell her, gently closing the laptop lid. "This isn't work."

Katie nods. "I see. So what have you been up to? I haven't seen you around in a while."

"I've been living in New York since March, writing, working for a really great company there." She doesn't need to know all the details. "Just came home for the holiday weekend."

"Oh, very nice," she says. Then, "Did I hear you had some fancy-pants boyfriend?"

My face flushes, embarrassed and nervous, because people know my personal life and because my personal life just got incredibly messy. Messi*er*.

"I've been seeing someone, yes," I tell her, a safe answer. "But enough about me—what's going on with you? Stacy said you've got some big changes going on."

"Yes! OMG, so I'm engaged," she squeals with delight and thrusts her left hand at me, showing off the heart-shaped diamond on her ring finger.

"Congrats."

"Thanks!" Her smile falters a moment; maybe she remembers that Peter and I were dating less than a year ago. But she recovers nicely and admires her ring.

"You look great, too, by the way." And she does. She's curvy in all the ways I always wanted to be, her chest even larger than before, her hair braided in a thick fishtail, her makeup shades of gold and moss that complement her burgundy knit skirt and tan sweater. If a pumpkin spice latte was a person, it would be Katie Carmine, as she is today.

"Aw, you're so sweet, Hillary," she says, placing a hand on her heart. "You know, when I first got pregnant, I was so worried about gaining the baby weight, but ever since Chase was born I've thought, you know what, I have more important things to worry about than what my body looks like."

Spoken like someone who knows she looks amazing, I think. Then I process her words.

"Chase?"

She nods, beaming with pride. "Yep. Ever since the gender reveal we had it narrowed down to three boy names, but we waited until we saw him to name him."

I mull over the information and ask, just as the door opens, "When was he born?"

She smiles. "October fourteenth. He was due on the eleventh but came a little late."

Above her head I can see Peter, just inside the door, lugging one of those bulky baby carriers. My head is reeling, counting backwards nine months from October, spinning, knowing what that means.

I force back the tears that sting my eyes and start shoving my computer and journal into the backpack. "It was really nice to see you, Katie, but I have to go. Congratulations again."

"You don't look too good, Hillary. Are you okay?"

I mumble something—maybe yes, maybe no, maybe profanity—and weave through the maze of tables, out the door, shoving Peter's shoulder with my own as I try to squeeze past him.

Churches have just let out, and I'm stuck at the intersection, frantically pushing the button for the pedestrian walk light.

"Hillary?"

His voice is lighter than I remember.

"Go away, Peter." I push the button again.

"That light won't change for at least two minutes. Can you give me two minutes?"

I hang my head, forfeiting my fight with the light. I'm tired of fighting, so I take the defeat. "What do you want?"

"I just want to explain." There's no defensiveness in his tone. I turn to face him, to see if it's really Peter. He sounds so different, but there he is, right in front of me.

"You want to explain why you cheated on me? Want to apologize for being such a piece of shit?" By trying to hold back my tears, I've inadvertently released another emotion: rage.

"No." He's so matter-of-fact that I need him to repeat it. "No?"

"No." Peter shakes his head and says, "Listen, Hillary. I am sorry that you're hurt. I'm sorry that our relationship was so awful. We were both miserable, for a really long time."

"And you thought that sleeping with someone else would make that better?"

"You and I were no good for each other. It worked for a while, but then I didn't fit into your life. I never felt like you saw me and my needs. And I don't just mean—" he stops and dips his head toward an elderly couple passing by on their way home.

"So you found someone who did meet those needs? All of them?"

"Frankly, yes."

It's really hard to fight with someone who's so forthcoming, so unapologetic, so sensible.

"I tried so many times to end us, Hillary," he says. "But we kept hanging on. Like we were on life support but totally not there, you know? With everything that happened—"

I know he means my grandpa dying, and I don't need to hear it. "Yeah."

"I didn't want to be that guy, Hil, that dumps you at the graveside and hops in the car with the new woman. I waited. I hoped you'd be you again—the you I fell in love with. But you never came back."

His words strike me, and I cock my head. This next part is so obvious, at least to me, but maybe he's not aware. "You didn't love me."

He lowers his gaze, his piercing blue eyes hidden from mine. "Maybe not. I don't know. I thought I did, but I guess not in the 'for better or for worse' kind of way, or I would have waited longer, or adapted to who you became."

Tears wash away the rage with understanding. "Do you love *her*?" I ask, nodding toward the café, where Katie stands perched on the stoop, the carrier and a to-go bag in her hands.

He looks at Katie, then at me, and his whole face is light. It's changed, in an instant.

The excitement in his eyes is a clear indication of his adoration for his new family.

He answers, "With everything I am. Both of them."

I bite the inside of my cheek and nod. "Good. Take care of them, okay? And yourself." I turn to leave, but he says my name once more.

I stop and wipe my eyes, then meet his gaze.

"This new guy I heard about—Do you love him? Does he treat you well?"

Sometimes hard emotions come out in smiles or laughter, and my lips twitch upward with the answer. "I do. Love him, I mean. And he treats me exactly the way I deserve to be treated."

I wave to Katie and wish Peter well. Then I turn down the sidewalk so I don't have to wait for the light and walk the long way home as fast as I can.

THIRTY-NINE

eave it to Mom, the voice of reason. There's nothing that can't be solved with hot cocoa and a game of cards and a chat. Mostly she asks questions and lets me come to conclusions on my own, but she's also not afraid to throw in her two cents:

"Yes, you did change. But that doesn't mean you changed in a bad way…"

"No, what Peter did was not okay…"

"He wasn't right for you. Ever."

"This Dalton, though…"

"I still haven't heard from him." I hunch my shoulders, folded over the table where I grew up eating SpaghettiOs and hot dogs.

"It's been less than twenty-four hours," Mom reminds me.

"It sucks."

"Never said it didn't." She sips her cocoa and dumps in more mini marshmallows from the bag that sits between us, then takes a bite out of a peanut butter blossom cookie. "Let me ask you this, Hillary. And I haven't asked you this since you were seventeen, applying to colleges."

"Seventeen?" I slump forward, my arm stretching across the table, my forehead resting on it. "Ugh, that was a teen-ager ago."

"Okay, little miss dramatic." She rolls her eyes and laughs,

MEGAN BECKER

but only for a moment. Then she straightens her shoulders and places her hand on mine. "What do you want?"

Very few people ask me that question; even fewer care about the answer. But I know Mom cares, just like Dalton did when he asked me months ago. Though that conversation, overlooking the misty mountains of West Virginia, was about my dream, my perfect life, and his, too.

"I want to write. I want to be successful, making enough to get by. That's the dream," I sigh, my finger circling the rim of the cocoa mug. "Actually, I don't know if it matters what I do. I just want to be happy again. Like when I was little. And I want to be able to share that happiness with someone else."

"So start there," Mom says. "Work backward. If that's the goal, what's your journey to get there? How do you get on that path now?"

I think on her questions for a moment and tap my fingernails against the mug. "I will have to map that out, but I do know one thing."

"What's that?" she asks, slurping mini marshmallows, saving them from drowning and liquifying in the cocoa.

"I think the path begins with one of those cheesy Christmas movies."

"I was hoping you'd say that," she beams, and we carry our cocoa to the living room.

....

The map was pretty clear, once I reverse-engineered the path to my dream life.

But *clear* and *easy* are two vastly different things, and I'm grateful to have Mom and Stacy with me for support in New York, mid-December.

I've spent the last two weeks writing for hours while drinking glasses of Mark T'Wine and F. Scotch Fitzgerald at Nom Nom de Plume and working at Books Off Broadway to manage the busy holiday shopping season. What I haven't done is had a real conversation with Dalton, though he did text me on my thirtieth, just after midnight, after a show in Boston.

He also texted three days ago: Sorry I haven't called. We can talk when I get home next week. and I just texted back, *OK*.

Mom and Stacy arrive by train late on a Friday night and I usher them up to the apartment for a tour.

"It's so nice, Hil," Stacy says.

"But so small, too," adds Mom. "Think of what your imagination will be able to do when it's not trapped in a little box."

I know she's trying to help, but the words sting. I love this box, and I love the life I was building here—who I was building it with.

"I don't think it's the apartment's fault, Mom," Stacy says, waving her to the window. "Do you see this view?"

"Nice, isn't it?" I join them and slide open the door to the terrace. Snow falls above us in the darkness, disappears below us in the light, and we shiver in the cold.

"Surprisingly lovely," says Mom, who hates cities; she's always said *It's a nice place to visit, but I wouldn't want to live there,* and I imagine she is trying very hard not to say it now.

The familiar view makes a lump catch in my throat. I'm really going to miss this.

I work a bit Saturday morning while they visit Times Square, then I take them out for an early dinner and a late show. "Anything you want to see," I tell them, and of course they pick Samantha Darling's new project.

Great show, Samantha, I text when it's over. I've got her number because of her parents; she wanted to make sure I could reach her if something ever went wrong at the store.

She texts back Thanks, and a moment later, Sorry to hear about things, and I pocket my phone, her words eating at me.

What did she hear? Was it that we fought? That we broke up? *Did we break up*, and I just didn't know it yet? Regardless, no one ever says *I'm sorry* when something good is happening, so I feel more confident in my decision.

Another round of sleep, then up early for a short shift at Books Off Broadway, then a round of coffee and cocoa from Eunoia, then back to the apartment. Mom and Stacy are packed up, ready to head home, though the train doesn't leave for a few hours. They've consolidated their things into one bag, so they have a spare.

I start with the fridge, discarding anything that won't still be good in a week, while they drink their hot cocoas. Basically, Dalton will have condiments, beer, wine, and half a pack of Kraft Singles that expires in a month.

And then it's just makeup, clothing, books, and a few personal tchotchkes I've amassed in the last nine months. And, of course, a small zoo of stuffed animals. The extra bag helps; I'm able to pack everything.

"Need a minute?" Stacy asks as I survey the living room and kitchen.

"We can give you some privacy," Mom says.

"I'm fine. Almost done."

I take it all in, one last time. The hallway behind me where Dalton nearly dropped his towel. The closed door to our room, the first place we shared ourselves so openly, physically with each other. The living room, where we had that amazing night before his tour started. The terrace, where he told me he loved me.

Right here, where I'm standing now. Where we fought. Where it felt like it was ending, months ago.

I exhale, not realizing I've been holding my breath. How perfect to be back in this same spot, telling my family, "I'm ready. We can go."

I place my keys on the counter with the card I've written, and we say goodbye to the apartment and the city.

FORTY

"We can get a new mattress, you know," Mom says, for at least the twentieth time in the last two months.

I'm on my back, sprawled on the floor, pulling my knee to my chest. "It's fine."

"You look silly."

"It's these old bones," I laugh. She does too.

"So what are your plans today?" she asks, stepping over me on her way to an oversized armchair.

I close my eyes as I pull my knee closer. "I've got some work to do, but I also have a lunch date with Lindsey."

"That'll be nice," she says. "How are you liking the new job?"

"You've asked me that at least twice a week since I started."

"Well, I want to make sure you're enjoying it."

I release my knee and roll onto my stomach to look at her. "I'm loving it. I really am." It's true. Working in ad sales for our local paper has been great—it's steady and grounding, and being asked to write a few pieces for the culture and arts column has been even better.

Her smile says she knew that would be my response and she just wanted me to say it out loud, maybe for my own benefit. "I'm glad, Hillary. I just want you to be happy."

Lindsey echoes a similar sentiment at lunch.

"You deserve to be happy, Hil," she says, in town to go wedding gown and bridesmaids dress shopping with her mom, sister, and me.

"I am."

"Okaaaay." She sings the word, almost a challenge.

"Do you not believe me? I've got an awesome job, my book—"

"Your book is getting published, blah blah blah."

"Ouch, Linds."

She waves off my comment. "You know what I mean. I've heard those same talking points for a month, and I'm truly happy for you. I know that's a big deal."

"So what's the issue?"

She sits back and crosses her arms, eyeing me with a smirk. I lean back in my chair, too, arms-crossed, playing chicken.

I break first. "Seriously? Again with this?"

"I know how happy you two were together."

I roll my eyes. "*Were*, being the key word."

"Tell me again why things ended."

"He was mad at me for not telling him that I knew who he was."

She shakes her head. "I know I didn't know him very well, but that just doesn't sound like him." She takes a drink of water. "He was crazy about you, all puppy dog eyes and forced restraint."

"I don't know what to tell you. That's why he stormed out." *What were his words, when he finally called around Christmas? When he came home to an empty apartment and a goodbye letter?* "He said he was upset that I didn't tell him, and that it meant I didn't trust him, or something."

Lindsey nods, slowly, thoughtfully. "I get that."

"Et tu, Lindsey?"

"I can just imagine he was hurt that he found out the way he did. Maybe he felt like you keeping it a secret was a sign that you thought he'd leave if he found out. Maybe that's where the trust thing comes in—you didn't trust him enough to stay with you?"

"You sound like him."

She shrugs. "What I don't get though is how that's enough to break up with you. Like, I get being upset, but to just end things? Doesn't track."

I lower my gaze and drink my water.

"Wait...Hillary."

I fidget with my straw wrapper, but she reaches across the table and puts her hand on mine.

"What did you do?"

I bite the inside of my cheek. I'm happy, until I think about this. I'm fine, until I remember the end.

"Hillary. Tell me."

"I moved my stuff out of the apartment when he was in Boston and left him a note." *There. Ripping off the Band-Aid.*

She gasps, drawing attention from nearby tables. "You didn't."

I nod. "I know. It's terrible."

"Heck yes, it's terrible." People are still looking, and she lowers her voice. "What did the note say?"

"It said that I knew I screwed up and that I was sorry, and that I wished him the best."

She runs her hands down her face. "What happened when he got the note?"

Our waitress rounds the corner and asks for the third time if there is anything else she can get us. The check is paid and we've just been occupying one of her tables for the last twenty minutes, though the lunch rush has all but disappeared. Lindsey shakes her head and smiles, then turns her attention back to me.

"He called me, right away. He couldn't call me for the three weeks after the fight, but then he suddenly wanted to talk."

"Wouldn't you, if you were him?"

"Yes, I would. I did. For three weeks. And he couldn't be bothered then."

"I'm sure he needed to process—"

I shoot her a look, one that asks *whose side are you on*, and she stops.

"Sorry," she apologizes. "So what did he say?

"He said he couldn't believe that I just left, and I told him I didn't *just* leave, but I felt like I heard him loud and clear when he said nothing."

"Ouch. I bet that stung. Justifiably."

"Yeah."

"And that was it?"

"More or less," I shrug.

She settles for the less, allowing me to keep the *more* private. I'm silently grateful, because the *more* breaks my heart. The *more* ruins me.

But I'm happy, otherwise, because I have a great job, my book is getting published, and I'm rediscovering myself again, authentically.

The joy I thought I'd outgrown comes back in ice cream cones and games of Pinochle, baking cookies and drinking cocoa, reading and writing, running in the rain or frosty winter air, being surrounded by family.

He was right. Last summer—when he talked about having someone to do life with, not needing to be married, but having that family or those friends by your side—he was absolutely right. The memory stings at first, but every time I think about him the hurt eventually subsides, a little faster than the time before.

It could be the joy of seeing Lindsey try on her first dress, the happiest tears in her mom's eyes, the excitement of finding *the one*; the homemade dinner Mom and Dad have ready when I walk in the door, the laughter we share around the table with Stacy and Kirk and the kids; the look on Mom's face when she finishes reading the final draft of my book just before I submit it. This is what he meant, all of it, and I'm not alone or lonely. I'm living my perfect life, even in missing him, and I'm okay.

FORTY-ONE

Sue flits and buzzes around Books Off Broadway at a dizzying pace.

"Do you think that's enough space?" she asks, examining the open area in the corner of the store.

She and Steve have removed half a dozen display tables, replacing them with rows of chairs, a table, and a stool.

"I'm sure that is more than enough."

"I don't know about that." Samantha emerges from behind the register, phone in hand. "I've added pictures to my story, I've tweeted, and I've gotten reactions. I think you're going to pack the place."

"I think *you're* going to pack the place," I laugh.

Sue rattles off the numbers about preorders and spare copies in the back, but I can't focus.

I survey the space she's set up for the Meet the Author session and book signing for me. It's surreal to be back in New York, back in Books Off Broadway, getting ready to launch my first book and actually having an audience for it. "I can't thank you enough for all of this."

Sue shrugs. "You did the work, dear."

"I wrote the book, but you—both of you—have done so much. I really couldn't have done it without you."

It's true—I absolutely wouldn't be here without their help. Sue arranged for a meeting between me and a publisher friend of hers from a small publishing house upstate who loved the book and fast-tracked it to production. It was Sue's idea to do a signing at the store, and Samantha jumped right in to post about the book and today's event to her followers.

Somewhere along the way we became friends, I guess, and I'm appreciative of the role she's played in bringing this dream to life.

My parents, Stacy, and Lindsey arrive, passing me an iced coffee.

Beads of sweat linger above Dad's lip, reminders of the mid-May humidity. It was almost exactly a year ago that Dalton and I first kissed, said I love you, became a couple, *insert-milestone-here*.

Mom pulls me aside, her hand inside her purse. "I know this is such a big day for you, Hillary, and I really struggled with whether or not I should even give this to you."

The smile I've worn all morning flickers. "What are you talking about?"

She pulls her hand out of the bag and passes me a small box, wrapped in sky-blue paper, tied in twine.

"What's this?" I ask, but she shrugs.

I unwrap it carefully, like it's a bomb or a flower. When I take the lid off there's a pen inside, matte black and fat, with my name engraved in gold script and a nib in the same color. I've seen this pen in a magazine before—it's not cheap. There's a handwritten note, too: *Write your story. And don't ever forget who you are.*

"It's beautiful. Thank you, Mom, but you shouldn't have—"

"I didn't."

I feel the crimson rush to my cheeks, or maybe I'm ghost-white. Other than her, I've only ever told one person that I dreamed of signing copies of my first book with a pen like this.

"You alright?" she asks. "Because I can take that and throw it into the Hudson."

I feel tears welling in my eyes, the kind that hover, wet and heavy, but don't fall. "I'm good," I say, smiling. Because I am.

....

"Thanks for coming out today!" I scrawl *Get cozy & happy reading! - Hillary James* in a messy script on the title page and smile at the twenty-something woman and her mother.

It's at least the thirtieth book I've signed, all with little messages, and my hand is already cramping. There's a sea of people before me, a haphazard line of mostly women, mingling and browsing all at once.

I scribble my name inside each book with a line of gratitude or a personalized message, making small talk while I do.

What a dream come true to be here, signing books.

With a six-hundred-dollar pen in my hand. It's not the price tag—it's that he *remembered*. And that he still cared enough to send it.

The line dwindles, and as my current customer heads off for a selfie with Samantha, Sue taps my shoulder. She offers a time check and a cookie while I crack open the book that was just set in front of me.

"Thanks so much for coming out today; I appreciate you being here," I say, uncapping my pen.

"I wouldn't have missed this for anything."

I pause, not wanting to meet his eyes. Sue just told me we needed to get through the rest of the line in about fifteen minutes; I definitely don't have time to unpack all our baggage here and now.

"What are you doing here?" I ask through a gritted-teeth smile.

"I just told you—I couldn't miss your big day." He smiles gently, and his eyes are earnest and kind. Sadness fills his voice when he adds, "I see you got my gift."

I almost drop the pen. Sue swoops in once she focuses on who's in front of me. I think she says for his ears more than mine, "Dear, we really must get through the line."

"Sure," he says. "I don't want to take up any more of your time. Maybe you could sign my copy later, over dinner?"

I clear my throat and stammer. "I—I don't think that's a good idea."

"We have a lot to talk about, Hil."

"She'll be there." Samantha's next to him, grasping his elbow, pulling him aside. "We'll figure out the details later, but she'll be there."

I glare at her and turn back to the rest of the line, signing a few more copies. Steve locks the door behind the last customer. I look around and see my family and the Charles family, but no Dalton.

"Don't worry," Samantha tells me. "He's meeting you at your hotel in two hours."

We clean up and return the store to normal over the next twenty minutes, until I'm kicked out and banished back to our hotel to get ready for dinner with Dalton. The phrase *getting ready* implies there is something to get ready for, like *come-as-you-are* isn't good enough; this feels like a date.

He's already in the lobby when I exit the elevator. There's a turquoise polo stretched across his chest, tucked into tan trousers. It looks like he also "got ready" for tonight.

Instead of flowers, he's holding his copy of my book.

"You look great."

"You do, too." I say it as matter-of-factly as I can, so he doesn't think I'm flirting. "And congrats, by the way, on the nomination, and on a great run with the show." Not only has he made it back to Broadway and performed eight shows a week for months, but he's a favorite to win at next month's awards show.

He rubs the back of his neck, a bit of his "aw-shucks" West Virginia background peeking through. "Thanks."

"So, what's the plan?"

He shrugs. "Is there anywhere in particular you wanted to go?"

I could pick any of the loudest chains in the city, tourist traps with blaring music, just to avoid having to talk. Instead, my stomach gurgles its reminder that I've eaten next to nothing all day.

"There's a little place just down the block. Would that be okay?"

"Of course," he smiles. He holds the door open for me and I lead the way halfway down the sidewalk to a made-to-order pizza bar with gourmet toppings and a full bar in the back.

"Now be honest," he says, washing down a slice with a swig of beer, "did you choose your hotel based solely on its proximity to this place?"

"That wasn't the *only* reason," I smirk. The second cocktail makes everything inside warm, disconnects my mind from my body.

"It totally could be the only reason and I wouldn't even judge you," he says. "How'd you find this place?"

I tear apart two slices of my pie. "Oh, Stacy, Mom, and I just kind of stumbled across it back in—" I stop myself, hating to bring up the end.

"In December?"

I nod, and he sets his beer down on the table.

"You know, I still don't understand why you moved out."

"Oh, come on. I had to!" I laugh.

"You didn't *have* to," he says with a bit of a grin. I wonder if he finds it humorous that I apparently find it humorous. Then, more seriously, he adds, "I never asked you to leave."

My mouth, disconnected from my mind but still taking direct orders from my heart, speaks. "You never asked me to *stay*, either."

He looks wounded. "Of course I wanted you to stay, Hillary. I loved you."

My heart lurches at his use of the past tense. Past tense means it's over, for good. If he past tense *loved* me, then there's nothing to fight for now. We just *were*, and now we're not.

"It was the hardest thing I've ever done, if that helps. Packing up. Moving out."

"I'm glad to hear that."

I shoot him a look. "Thanks."

"Well, it was no picnic coming home to you being gone."

My mouth goes dry; I'm both embarrassed and indignant. I long to fight, to remind him that he ghosted me for three weeks after the argument, but I refuse to look desperate.

Instead, I sit back and cross my arms. "What are we doing here? Why did you put in so much effort to see me?"

"I told you—I wouldn't have missed your launch party for anything."

I wave away his claim. "Okay, fine. But being *there* is different from being *here*. And that pen—that was unnecessary."

"You don't like it?"

"You know that I love it. But that's not the point. Don't you think it was a bit much, considering?"

He drinks his beer and sets the glass on the table, holding its base with both hands. His mouth twists upward in a pained smile. "Don't worry, it's not like I went out and bought it after—" He clears his throat and sighs. "I bought that pen before you ever moved in."

"You're kidding."

His head moves side to side, and he examines his beer. "I'm not."

"How did you—"

"How did I know?" he asks. When I nod, he continues. "I knew you were going places. I believed in you. *Believe* in you. Present tense. Just like—" he stops himself, shakes his head again. "Forget it."

"So you bought it over a year ago?"

His head dips; it's almost imperceptible. "I did."

"Just in case I actually did it? In case I finally published something?"

He smiles, a huff escaping his nostril. "It wasn't 'in case' you did it. It was because I knew that you would."

The room spins. I'm dizzy, drunk on rum and vodka and this feeling of being seen and believed in. It's dangerous, feeling this way so close to him. I could reach across the table if I wanted to; stretch out, take his hand in mine. Slide into the booth next to him, tilt my head up and kiss him.

I shake my head and it throbs. I close my eyes and bury my face in my hands. "Why do you keep doing this?"

"Doing what?"

I search for the words and can only come up with, "Why are you still so *nice* to me?"

He laughs, but I'm not joking. "How would you like me to treat you, Hillary?"

"You should hate me."

"That's ridiculous."

"Is it?"

His eyes lock on mine. He blinks but doesn't answer.

"Seriously. After the last time we talked, I don't know why you'd care at all what I do, let alone be nice to me."

He sits back and pauses. "Can we get out of here? Just walk and talk, like we used to?"

He has to stop doing this, recreating our past, doing things like we used to.

Because there is no 'we.' No future or present, just the past. He *loved* me.

Against my better judgment I say, "Sure," and we discard our trash and emerge on the street, where the sky is dark but the sidewalks are bright, basking in the glow of neon and LEDs. The afternoon's sticky heat is gone, replaced by a warm and pleasant breeze that blows down the avenues.

"Where are we going?"

He shrugs. I'm afraid he'll reach for my hand; I've already reached for his on impulse. Maybe he's had the same thought or fear, because he shoves his hands into his pockets and walks.

I follow a step behind for two blocks. I don't mind the silence, because the alternative sucks. When we reach a red light I stop next to him, my elbow bumping his.

"Sorry," I mutter as the signal changes.

He runs a hand through his hair. I've known him long enough to know what that means: nervousness, discomfort.

We wander another two blocks and wind up back in the same park we'd ventured to our first day together. Dalton crosses the plaza and hoists himself to sit on the edge of a raised flower bed. Finally, he speaks.

"I still don't get it, if I'm being honest," he says.

"Get what?"

He sighs, and a groan transforms into words. "Why you gave up on us."

"Dalton—"

"No, I'm serious," he interjects. "I've been trying to figure it out for months. I know I overreacted in November, but what I can't figure out is why—when I called you—why you were so willing to end everything."

I lean against the same wall he sits on, and I feel small. Shoulders slumped, head hung. "I wasn't really *willing*, Dalton. It was the hardest choice I've ever had to make. But I was scared."

"Scared? Of what?" he asks. I can tell by the sound of his voice—that pained, strained pleading—exactly what I'll see if I force myself to look at him, and I know his eyes will undo me.

"I was scared that I would give up myself again, for you. That's why I moved out."

He's quiet for a moment, and he responds softly, his voice a kiss that brushes my forehead. "I understand that, Hillary. I'm talking about after."

My fingers fidget, twisting around each other. I wish I didn't have to answer. I inhale the city, stale and warm, and close my eyes. "Do you remember what you said to me in that phone call?"

In my periphery I can see his shoulders shrug. "Not verbatim. I remember asking you to stay, asking you to talk to me, if we could just see each other—"

"You said you'd leave everything behind and marry me, if that's what I wanted."

There's a certain quality that sets "stunned silence" apart from regular silence, like a tangible apprehension; the breath that's held is empty, just preceding the moment it fills with questions, and feels only head-spinning, mind-reeling shock.

I let him process, give him the time he needs to think through that night. The city serenades us as we sit.

"Was the thought of marrying me so bad?"

He's so far off-base that I laugh and finally turn to look at him. "That wasn't what scared me, Dalton. I mean, it was—it did. But what scared me was this idea that you'd give up everything you've worked for—everything that was part of your perfect life—for me. And even worse, I was scared that I'd let you."

"I don't need your permission, Hillary."

"I know you don't need it, but I'd like to think it would have been a conversation."

"Of course."

"But I don't think I would've asked you to reconsider."

"Good." He meets my eyes, a half-smile forming, and winks.

I shake my head, smiling back. "You're crazy."

"Maybe," he says, dropping his head, clasping his hands.

"Maybe?"

He shrugs again, the smile fading but the memory of it lingering on his lips. "I don't know if I *am* crazy, Hillary. I don't think it's crazy to know what you want and to go for it."

"But you want your career. You've worked hard for it."

"I do. I have. But I want someone to share it with, too. Remember?"

"I remember." The words hang in the air, stagnant until the late spring breeze blows and carries them away.

"Anyway, it's getting late, and I should probably get back. But I hope you got the closure you were looking for, if that's what you were doing tonight." I stand and step in the direction of my hotel.

"Hillary—" he pushes himself off the wall and wipes the loose gravel from his hands. "I'm not interested in closure."

A lump catches in my throat. "Then what was all of this?"

His smile flickers like a light bulb about to explode. "I wanted to have one more good night together. To be able to say goodbye better."

"Oh." It sounds like closure, but it doesn't look like it. There's hope or something like it in his eyes.

"The problem is, I don't want to say goodbye."

"I don't either." The admission tumbles out, and I don't regret it.

"Is that why you agreed to meet me tonight?"

"I agreed to meet you because Samantha made me do it."

His deep laugh greets the evening. "I didn't realize you were taking orders from Samantha Darling now."

"Well, she terrifies me, so…"

"That tracks," he smiles. "Do you remember that night in West Virginia, when we—"

I nod. "And she—" I can't finish the sentence as the laughter overtakes my body. I cover my flaring nostrils out of habit.

"Goodnight, Dalton," he says in the same way she'd said it then. "She really killed the mood."

"Well, it wasn't really her. More of what she said."

The laughter fades. Suddenly, the memory isn't so funny. "That's what scared me, Dalton. We had already been through it once before—you're not supposed to sacrifice that piece of who you are for me, and you were offering to do it again."

"But we make sacrifices when we're in love, Hillary."

In love. *Present tense?* No, present only in that memory which is now behind us.

"Not like that. You're supposed to sacrifice your Saturday afternoon to clean the apartment together, or sacrifice what you really want for dinner to go where I want to go."

He smiles again, coy and mischievous.

"What?"

"It's just funny you said that. I'd booked us a table for tonight."

I roll my eyes and shake my head. "You know what I mean."

He nods. "I do. And look, we've always talked about being honest with each other, so I'm going to be hopelessly, stupidly honest with you right now."

He pauses, just long enough for the butterflies to tickle every part of my stomach, for my toes to tingle and curl. "I want us to try again."

My eyes close and everything inside sinks and floats, all at once. "We can't just forget the past and act like it never happened."

"I'm not saying we should. I want to learn from all of it, to be better for it." He sighs; I catch my breath. "Look, Hillary, if you can tell me with one hundred percent certainty that you can never love me again, then fine, I'll—"

Something he says catches me off guard, this assumption of my feelings, and I can't stop from correcting him.

"What are you talking about? I have never *stopped* loving you."

"Really?" We're maybe five feet apart, then three, then our toes are touching. When he closes this space between us like this, my heart races. His hands graze my elbows like he's not sure if he's supposed to touch me or not. "I thought—when you said—"

I shake my head. "I know it doesn't make any sense, but I had to end it *because* I love you. Because I want you to have a full, amazing life, living your dream."

His hand slides along my jaw, cradles the back of my neck. "You're part of my dream, Hillary."

"And you're part of mine," I admit, though I'm not sure if to myself or to him.

"Then what are we doing?" he asks. A smile dares to play across his lips.

"I think," I say, our breath mingling in the inches between us, "that we're trying again?"

"That's a great idea," he says. Then his lips are on mine, tender but firm, testing waters he already knows he's willing to dive into.

His other hand skims my hip to the small of my back and he draws our bodies together as he kisses me again. My hands rocket to his chest and snake upward to his neck, his ears, his hair. I have missed every piece of him, and it feels so good to hold him again.

I could kiss him forever, just like this. Pressed up against him. His fingers clinging to me, tangled in my hair, my hands holding him tight. I could let him whisk me away, back to his apartment, pick up where we left off in August, together and happy and whole.

"I love you, Hillary," he breathes into me. "So damn much."

I bite my lip, tempering the wide smile that wants to form. "I love you too."

"I should take you back to your hotel."

"Don't you think we should talk?"

He nods. "Of course. Are you free tomorrow for breakfast?"

"I can be. Or you could stick around a little tonight—"

"I don't think we'd get much talking done."

My shoulders shake with laughter. "If you'd let me finish, I was going to say we could get a drink at the hotel bar."

His cheeks flush. "Sorry."

I kiss his cheek and wink. "I mean, we can start with a drink."

We walk, hands knotted together, back to my hotel and onto a low sofa in the lobby's lounge, talking about how this works, sipping overpriced wine.

There are still so many unknowns, but we both know without a doubt that we want to be together. We want to make it work. We want to live our dreams, which include each other.

....

The sun wakes me, warm and bright through the open shade. My head pounds from exhaustion and dehydration.

Dalton is gone.

I rummage through my bag from last night and find my phone, but the most recent message in the list is a response to the one I sent to Stacy last night, telling her not to worry, I'd be late and was getting my own room so I didn't wake her. At some point she texted back I take it your dinner went well? ☺

Dalton's copy of Check Inn For Murder is still in my bag where we'd placed it for safekeeping at the restaurant last night. I never got around to signing it.

I roll out of bed and slip on yesterday's clothes. As I pass the desk on my way to the bathroom, I see a note scribbled on the hotel's stationery.

Gone for coffee
Thought we might need it
Now sign my book
So I can read it.

—D

The box with the pen has settled in the bottom of my bag. I take it out, pick up the book, and begin writing.

FORTY-TWO

Dalton,

There's no one better,
not one man above you.
Let me put this in writing:
I'll forever love you.

—HJ

My fingers glide over the message, the ink still thick and black, the book's cover bent and its spine broken.

The apartment changes from visit to visit, gradually though, almost unnoticeable. Sometimes it's the scent of the wax melting in the warmer in the kitchen, sometimes it's a fresh arrangement of flowers. In December it's a sprig of mistletoe just inside the front door, three more at random places where we might occupy space together, and an artificial Christmas tree next to the TV, decorated in colorful lights and a few ornaments we made ourselves.

I celebrate the new year in New York for the first time, wrapped in a blanket on his terrace, craning my neck to see fireworks over the tops of the neighboring buildings. He pulls me in for a kiss and soon we fall into bed together, laughing and groping, thinking of what the new year might hold.

"Have you given any more thought to moving in permanently?" he asks as we lie there after, legs entwined, arms around each other.

I've brought the train in for one week each month, working remotely, writing here when he's busy, spending time with him when he's not. He'll take the train down some Sunday nights after his matinee, stay with my family, then ride back on Tuesdays in time for his evening show.

It's not ideal, but it works.

"I have," I answer. "But it's not time yet. I want to get this next book finished first."

He kisses my hair, a sign of understanding.

....

He surprises me on Valentine's Day. Red roses are delivered every hour while I'm at the office. At four o'clock, a singing telegram arrives. Outside of the local high school, this doesn't happen in our town. Everyone gathers around the reception area as a barbershop quartet serenades the staff.

It's a spectacle: four grown men in red and white striped vests with khakis and shallow straw hats, singing and dancing box steps in our little office of twenty people, on a holiday most of us decided long ago to loathe. I record video of everyone's reactions, then the quartet itself, knowing both Mom and Dalton will have thoughts.

The tenor, whose face has been obscured by his hat and my coworkers in front of me, begins a few bars of a solo. I pan from crowd reactions when I hear the voice, and there on my screen is Dalton Tremaine.

His hat is off, and he runs a hand through his hair as the others rejoin in their harmony. He winks at me, and a few people turn my way.

When the song is over and the applause has ended, he accepts a few individual accolades on his way to me. "Hi."

"Hi back. I thought you had to work today."

He slides backward, modeling his ensemble with his arms. "I *am* working. Clearly."

I arch an eyebrow. "You're getting paid for this?"

He shrugs and fiddles with the hat in his hands. "I mean, yeah. It's not much, but a guy slipped us two bucks for a photo op for his wife at Walmart."

"Split four ways…"

"None of that," he says, waving off the comment, his face creased with joy. "We don't nickel and dime in the quartet."

I want to kiss him and let the smile on my lips meet the smile on his, but there are still a few people milling, mingling with the rest of the group, and I don't want to engage in PDA in our lobby.

"So do you have more unsuspecting offices to serenade with your siren song today, or are you finished?"

He laughs and taps the hat back into place on top of his head. "We've got to make an appearance at dinner at the nursing home down the street, so I really should be going."

"Ha, ha, very funny. If you give me a minute I'll grab my stuff and we can head out together."

"No worries. I can just meet you at your place in about an hour or so. Unless you wanted to come to the nursing home."

"Wait—you're serious?"

He nods, then shrugs. "I wanted to take advantage of the full rental window on the costumes."

I laugh out an "I love you" just as he draws me in for a goodbye kiss. He kisses my teeth; I laugh even harder.

My parents are gone for dinner, and because he was singing at the nursing home, he didn't have time to prepare anything. Instead, he's picked up some pre-made pizza crusts, sauce, cheese, and toppings, and we make our own pizza for dinner, which we enjoy by candlelight, surrounded by roses, seated on blankets on my bedroom floor.

He sets a half-eaten slice down and leans back against the bed. "So," he says, hiding his mouth while he chews, "something exciting happened."

I set my own slice on its plate and lean in. "Something more exciting than you whipping up a barbershop quartet with my retired Geometry teacher and the mayor's son?"

He laughs. "I think so. Though that was pretty epic." He pauses for a moment and washes the pizza down with a sip of wine. "I told you I'd auditioned for another show."

"You did." My stomach sinks, because this could mean another round of touring, more time away.

"Well they called yesterday. I didn't get the part I auditioned for."

"Oh. I'm sorry." Relieved, but sorry.

"No need to be. They actually wanted me for the lead."

"Seriously?"

He nods. "Seriously. And the best part is, filming is in New York. It'll typically be Monday to Friday, though it might be long days, but ideally finished by seven each day."

"Wait—*filming*?"

He smiles wider. "I didn't want to tell you in case it didn't happen. But I'm going to step away from the stage a little, try to get a non-nocturnal schedule for myself." *For us* is implied.

I throw my arms around him with such force I nearly tackle him. "That's amazing!"

"I'm excited. And the show seems great, like it's got a few seasons in it, and it pays well, too."

"All very exciting things to hear."

"So I was thinking of upgrading some things."

"What do you mean?" I ask past the lump that rises in my throat.

"Well, I was actually thinking of getting a new apartment. Or maybe a townhouse."

"But you love your apartment. *I* love your apartment."

"Can you imagine, though, another bathroom? More space? A veranda off the bedroom; a garden out back?" He scratches his neck. "I don't know, maybe it's stupid. I just thought it would be nice to have something different, more like a home to grow into." He sighs. "Anyway, not something we have to worry about tonight."

••••••••••••••••••••••

It's early March again, and the sun warms the air bitten by winter's chill. Dalton texted me while I was on the train this morning that he was working and unable to meet me at the train station. No worries: I've had the key fob for his apartment back for months, and I'm one chapter from the end of my new novel.

I settle in, kicking off my shoes, and sit down to write. Keep me updated on your progress! He texts me.

I respond, You'll surely know when the work is done, 'cause I'll finally be ready to have some fun!

Then I push my phone aside and work on the last chapter.

At one thirty, I proudly type *The End* and giddily text Dalton. I'm actually surprised he's not here but assume he's just avoiding the apartment until I'm done so he doesn't distract me. While I wait for him to respond, I stand on the terrace and take in the sounds and sights of the city.

He texts back, Congrats! Then five minutes later, Look under my pillow.

I lock the terrace door behind me and stow my laptop back in my bag, then lift Dalton's pillow to find a journal with a glossy, rose gold cover. An index card peeks out the top, sandwiched between two pages. I turn to it; a message is scrawled in familiar writing:

Hillary—

I'm infinitely proud of you
I know this was no cake walk
Now look for me in the place
Where we first sat down to talk

—Dalton

I text him again: I love the journal. Where are you?

Follow the clue, he responds, adding a winking emoji.

I slip on my sneakers with my leggings and sweater and swap out the glasses I've been wearing since 5:00 a.m. for contacts. I dab on a little eyeshadow and add mascara to look less like death and head out the door, the journal tucked into my crossbody bag.

Eunoia is bustling with activity, even after three o'clock on a Saturday. Still, Jolie sidesteps Shan and waves me over to the pick-up area.

"Hey, Hillary. Nice to see you."

"You too." I look around again; I don't see Dalton.

"He's not here," she says, a smirk rising on her lips. "But he did ask me to give you this." Jolie slides a latte toward me. It's still hot.

"Wait—how did you—"

"Have fun," she says before returning to help Shan fulfill the line's drink orders.

I find a seat at the bar by the window and sip from the to-go lid, letting the coffee warm my hands through the paper cup. *What is he doing? What is this for?* I can't figure out what I'm supposed to do. Wait here? Go back to the apartment?

I sit a little longer in the warmth, fidgeting with the sleeve on the cup, pushing it down, sliding it back up. After the twentieth time, I see a reflection in the window and spin the cup 180 degrees, dropping the sleeve again. There's a note scribbled on the side of the cup. Not in Dalton's writing, but clearly from him:

> *There's no love story greater*
> *than the one we wrote ourselves*
> *But check out the place that has lots of them*
> *lining floor-to-ceiling shelves*

The library flashes into my mind first, but it's so far away that it seems unlikely Dalton would send me there. Instead I take off for Books Off Broadway, carrying my coffee with me as I pass other pedestrians.

Steve greets me inside the bookstore.

"Hi, Mr. Charles," I say, and we make a few moments of polite conversation. "Is Sue here?"

He shakes his head. "She's around somewhere, I'm sure, but she left me in charge for a bit. What brings you in today?"

"Oh, um," I shrug and turn the coffee cup toward him. "I was lured here through this very mysterious message. Any idea what it means?"

He brushes his hands against his pant legs and waves for me to follow him as he navigates to the register. He bends to the shelves below the counter and stands, handing me a wrapped package.

"That guy of yours is really something."

"He really is."

I unwrap the gift and Steve tosses the paper in the trash can behind the counter. This time it's a copy of William Shakespeare's *Twelfth Night*—my favorite of his works. Another index card—this one with a rectangle cut from its corner—peers out from the pages. On it, Dalton's written:

> Carry all these gifts with you
> Till we're together, you and I
> Go to our most-used entrance
> On the Line that is High

Steve passes a reusable tote bag to me. "In case there are many more stops," he says.

I thank him and head out toward the High Line. I roll my eyes, laughing, and call Dalton. "How many wild goose chases are you planning?" It's chilly outside, it'll be dark in just a few hours, and I just want to be with him.

"Probably a few more. What have you found so far?" His voice carries a smile through the line and my heart steadies. I don't know what he's doing, but clearly he put some thought into whatever it is. It's fun; I'm just tired.

"I just left Books Off Broadway."

"Oooh. Okay. You've got a few more stops then."

"Do I end up with you?"

"That's the goal." He clears his throat; his voice goes breathy.

"Alright—then I'm off to my next stop. Hopefully I'll see you soon?"

"You should. Very soon."

"Okay then. See you soon. Love you."

"Love you, too," he says, and the call ends.

I trudge through the cold to the High Line, with Shakespeare and my journal in the tote Steve passed my way. I contemplate taking a long detour to pick up more coffee but decide against it and climb the High Line steps, not sure where to even start looking for a clue.

I wander, slowly, looking on and below every bench, searching the sea of strangers for a familiar face.

"Hillary?"

There's Samantha, layered in a heavy parka and knit beanie. In her gloved hand, she holds another package.

"Aren't you freezing?" she asks.

"Very much so."

She hands me the package—a vintage hardcover of Mary Shelley's *Frankenstein*.

"You guys are so weird," Samantha laughs. "He couldn't just send flowers or something."

"Do you have any idea what he's doing?"

She shrugs. "Beats me. Where's he sending you next?"

I open the cover and find another index card, also missing a rectangular piece in the top corner.

What's waiting next for you
Is currently high above you
Go to the place
Where we first said I love you

Samantha reads the card upside down. "He isn't asking you to go out to West Virginia, is he?"

I think what she's asking is, *Was it then, when he was*

COFFEE DATES   399

supposed to be with me, that he declared his love for you? To both questions, I can confidently answer, "No, definitely not West Virginia."

"Alright, well, I'm going to go somewhere warm."

We end up walking the same direction, back toward the steps I just climbed. She heads off toward Books Off Broadway and I turn the opposite direction toward the apartment.

"Good luck, Hil," she says, pulling her coat tighter around her as she smiles and waves.

"Thanks!" I wave back, grateful to be going to the apartment so I can get a coat of my own as the sun dips further toward the horizon.

I scan his bedroom but can't find anything. Same story with the living room. I reread the clue in Frankenstein: *Where we first said I love you.* It's not just the apartment, but the terrace, specifically. I search outside, even behind the boxwoods in their planters, but nothing catches my eye. I look under the loveseat. The cushions are uneven; there's another package wedged under one of them.

This time, he's wrapped up a copy of my book, and inside is another index card.

If I had a genie
And I got to make a wish
I'd go round and round this world with you
At a place with pretty fish

I pull on my coat and the beret Lindsey crocheted for me for my birthday and ride the elevator down to the first floor. I've thrown my wallet, keys, cell, and the bag of books into my backpack for easier carrying, and I pull the straps tighter on my shoulders.

In the lobby, on my way to the door, a man in a black suit approaches me. "Miss James?" he asks.

"Yes?"

"Do you remember me?"

His face is round and kind, maybe slightly familiar looking but not unique enough for me to be sure.

"We met a few times over the last few years. Dalton asked me to give you a ride to your next stop."

"Right! Sorry. It's Jeffrey, right?"

"Yes ma'am," he says, smiling. He holds open the lobby door, then the back door of his familiar black town car.

"So where are we headed?" he asks once he's nestled into his seat up front.

"You mean he asked you to drive me and didn't tell you where?"

I catch his smile in the rearview. "He told me. But he also requested that I have you confirm."

"That sounds about right. Should be the SeaGlass Carousel."

He nods and starts driving, navigating the streets, heading southeast along the grid of New York City.

"My wife loved your book, by the way."

The comment catches me off guard. "Really? She bought a copy?"

He snickers a little, his head shaking side to side. "Dalton must've bought copies for everyone on his Christmas list. Didn't need to, though. She got a copy from her sister, too, who loved it."

I feel the heat rush to my cheeks. "Well, thank you."

"You got another one coming out soon?"

My head wobbles as my shoulders shrug. "Maybe. I just finished the first draft today."

"Can't wait. Maybe I can get a signed copy for her?"

"Of course. And for her sister, too. Anything for you, for saving me from having to walk in the cold anymore."

"Ha. Yeah, that sun goes down and you remember it's still winter, that's for sure."

A few moments later he says, "This is your stop, dear." Before I can unbuckle, he's at my door, offering a hand as I emerge onto the sidewalk.

"Thank you, Jeffrey."

Dalton's waiting outside the ticket booth, a smile rising and falling on his face in the same quick pulses of him rocking between his toes and heels.

"Hey," he says, kissing my forehead.

"Hey yourself." I wrap my arms around him. "I missed you today."

"Sorry."

"No, it's fine. It's been…it's been fun. But I'm glad you're here."

"Me too." He hugs me back and motions to the carousel. "Shall we?"

"Of course." Something seems off; he seems uneasy. "You okay?" I ask, peering up at him.

He clears his throat and forces a smile, avoiding my eyes. "Yeah. I'm fine."

We ride the carousel and he reclaims my hand when the ride is over, his eyes sparkling. "I want to show you something."

Our fingers interlock as we walk a few blocks and he asks me questions about my day.

"You really recruited some help today," I say, and he smiles. "When are you going to tell me what your master plan is?"

"Right now." He stops in front of a townhouse with a "For Sale" sign visible behind the low wrought iron gate that lines the perimeter of a small front yard.

He turns fully toward me and takes both my hands in his. "I know you said you wanted to wait until the new book was done before you thought about moving to New York full time, and I know that there's still a lot of work that goes into it after a first draft, but this place hit the market a week ago and I fell in love with it. Your first draft is done as of three hours ago, so I thought maybe we could walk through it together."

My skin tingles and my toes curl at the thought of the work he put into getting me here. "So all this running around today—it was to get me to walk through this house with you?"

"I wanted you to come here, yes." He bites his lip. "So, what do you say? Want to see it?"

"Now?"

"Yeah. The broker's inside."

I look up at the house—four stories, narrow, but picturesque and grand. "You're crazy, you know that?"

"I think so," he nods. Then he opens the gate and leads me inside.

The broker greets us but gives us freedom to roam on our own; she's already met Dalton and walked him through the home twice, so she waits on the first floor while we explore together.

I hold Dalton's hand throughout the home, taking in the craftsmanship of the railings along the stairs, the moulding around the doors, and the thoughtful upgrades and conveniences in the kitchen and living areas throughout.

"I love this bathroom," he says, leading me into the full bathroom off the primary bedroom on the second floor. There's a tile shower in the corner, built large enough for function but small enough to allow for a clawfoot tub to fit along the side wall next to it.

"It's beautiful."

"And it's not even the best part," he says, motioning with his head toward another flight of stairs. On the third floor are three more bedrooms and another full bathroom.

When we reach the open fourth floor, he says, "I think this would be a great writing studio. I mean, you can take any room you want and transform it. But I saw this up here and just thought it would be great to put in a desk right here," he says, motioning toward the window at the front of the house, "and then, back here, some bookshelves along the wall. Dad and I could build them to fit perfectly. Put in some great lights, some cozy furniture for reading—what do you think?"

I can see it all as he describes it, and it's a dream to have my own space to retreat to, away from distractions like TV and the visual reminders of the housework or chores I should be doing when I'm fully in the zone.

"It's great, it really is."

"Is there a 'but' hiding somewhere in there?"

I honestly don't know. "It's a big change."

"And that's bad?"

"Not necessarily." I shake my head, squeezing his hands in mine. "It's just big. I have to wrap my head around it."

His expression changes; his lips purse. "Do you have all of the items from your scavenger hunt today?"

We return to the kitchen island where I'd left my backpack and take the journal and books from the bag.

Dalton sets the journal aside and lays the books on the smooth granite, then stands at the edge of the counter, to my right. "Any thoughts?"

"Ha! Of course I have thoughts. The first being, I have no idea what I'm supposed to do with this."

"You'll figure it out," he smiles. It's different again though—distracted or distant, unconvincing.

I stare at the books—Shakespeare, Mary Shelley, me—then up at him. Again and again; lather, rinse, repeat.

He shifts his weight and pulls the books closer to him, reorganizing them as he does. Shakespeare, me, Shelley. He stands at the end of the list. "Talk it out," he says. "I want to hear your process."

I glance sideways at him, "Shakespeare. Me. Shelley." I pause, shrug, and say, "I still don't get it."

"You can use the index cards if you want. Though old Billy there—" he gestures toward *Twelfth Night*, "might not approve of cheating."

"You did *not* just call William Shakespeare *Billy*."

He shifts his weight again, leaning against the counter. "Oh, old Will and I go way back. Did you know I actually played Sebastian in my high school's performance of *Twelfth Night*?"

"I'm shocked," I mock, rolling my eyes. I've heard the story at least three times. His mom promised that she'd show me the DVD next time I came to visit.

But something he says stands out to me and I look at the books differently. *William Shakespeare. Hillary James. Mary Shelley. William. Hillary. Mary.* And Dalton, poised there, at the end.

My heart racing and my hands shaking, I fumble through Shakespeare and Shelley for their index cards, just to be sure. I lay them on top of their respective books and adjust them so that the missing pieces of the cards line up, sure enough, to reveal only *Will* and *Mary*.

When I shift my gaze to Dalton, his eyes are already locked on me, and his hand fidgets behind his back.

"What—" my brain tries to wrap itself around what's happening, but words spill out clumsily. "What are you doing?"

"Hillary." His voice drips sweetness and warmth, like an ice cream cake at a picnic on the sun. His free hand reaches for mine, and his thumb rubs the back of my hand.

"Tomorrow is two years since the day we met. Two years since I knew you were in my life for a reason. Two years since I knew I wanted you to be a part of it forever. You're my best friend, the love of my life. You're the kindest, most loving person I know. So I want to ask you," he says, lowering himself to one knee, sliding his hand from mine. "Will you make me, somehow, even happier than you already do? Hillary James, will you marry me?"

He holds a black box in front of him and eases open its lid. A small piece of paper pops up inside; on it he's written *page 32*, and he slides the journal to me.

On page thirty-two, he's drawn two boxes: one is labeled "yes," and the other "no."

Dalton holds up a red pen and extends it to me.

I draw a red x and turn the book to him, giddy and stupid with excitement.

"You will?" he asks, rising.

"Of *course* I will. A thousand times yes."

He kisses me and envelops me in his arms. "But you didn't even see the ring. What if it's hideous?"

"Dalton Tremaine, there could be a bent fishing hook with a worm still attached in that box and I wouldn't care."

"Oh, *now* you tell me. I could've saved a fortune," he laughs. He kisses me again and pulls away, opening the box again, removing the slip of paper that blocked the ring the first time. "Anyway, I designed this one for you."

Inside the box is a rose-gold ring with an emerald-cut diamond in the center, flanked by two baguette-cut diamonds on either side, tapering down in size to the princess-cut stones that fill the channel band.

"Wow." I don't know if any sound comes out. I'm breathless.

"Do you like it?"

"I'm so glad it's not the fishing hook."

He takes it out of the box and slides it onto my finger. We release our breath at the same time. I think he's relieved the ring fits. It's stunning. I'm still in shock.

He pulls me into his arms again; I tilt my head back and kiss him. "I know this is a really big change," he says. "And if it's too soon to think about the house, too—"

"I want it."

"You do?"

I bite my lip and nod. "I want it all. The house, you, a life together here, pursuing our dreams."

My hands twist through his hair when I kiss him again.

"I didn't even show you the best part yet," he smiles, the nerves from earlier gone. "Did you know this house is great for entertaining?"

I look around at the open floor plan. "Sure," I answer. "It looks like we could definitely have some friends over, or hang out with family if they come to visit."

"Oh, there's more," he says, practically bouncing toward a set of curtains along the house's back wall. He slides them open, revealing a garden and patio out back where nearly a dozen faces peer in at us.

Dalton opens the French door and shouts to those out in the cold, "She said yes!" Then he takes me by the hand and leads me out to the garden with everyone else.

It's still cold, but I don't mind. The excitement of the afternoon courses through my body, radiating heat throughout. Samantha, Sue, and Steve are all there. Stacy and Lindsey, Mom and Dad, too, and Olivia, Thomas, and Jordan.

Dalton's set up a reservation for all of us at a restaurant nearby to celebrate, so the Charleses lead the rest of the party there while we wait out front for a moment, soaking it all in.

We stand side by side and my hand slips into his as we stare up at the house.

"What a day," I whisper.

"That's exactly what I said when I got home after our first day together."

"You did not."

He nods. "I absolutely did. I knew that day was going to change my life."

I rest my head against his shoulder. "Who would've guessed we'd be here, two years later, just because you crashed into me and my latte."

"I prefer to say we 'met over coffee,'" he says.

I soak in the sound of his laughter, the feel of his hand around mine, the taste of his lips as we kiss under the melted sherbet sky in front of what will soon be our home.

When I first came to the city, I was running, escaping, searching. Trying to figure out who I was, trying to write.

And over the last two years—a broken heart, the most joyful moments—I did it all. I crafted my dream life.

I'm happy.

I'm writing.
I've got someone to share it with.

The End

ACKNOWLEDGEMENTS

Wow. Once I got over my desire to be the Tooth Fairy when I grew up, *writer* was all I ever wanted to be. And over the past [redacted] decades, there are many people who have helped me become just that. This book would not be possible without them:

Of course, Mom and Dad, who put up with my love of the arts since I proclaimed that I loved every song that came on the radio, who were there for the shows and concerts, who showed me what hard work and family look like. Sissy, for forcing me to play *school* as kids and getting the creativity flowing early through melted ice cream. I know your creative side is alive in you, even though you are a *numbers* person now. I love you all and wouldn't be here without your not-so-subtle shoves into the world of art.

Gabrielle Remer entered the story at just the right time to edit my "stuck spots" for me. I am so grateful for your knowledge and your eyes on the scenes and sentences I simply could not figure out. This book is better because of your suggestions. I wish you the very best things as you continue in your editing journey!

To the team at Luminare Press, thank you for bringing this dream to life. I put a lot of thought into my path to publishing, but when Melissa made "highlighter pink" happen for me, I knew I was with the absolute right team. Patricia, Kim, Melissa, Caitlin, Sallie—this book quite literally would not be here without your efforts, and I appreciate your kindness, patience, and expertise along the way.

I also owe much gratitude to Creag and the Elegant Literature community for pushing me out of my comfort zone with my writing and for building my confidence at the most critical time. I am so grateful for all that you have given me and so many new writers, and I hope you enjoy these characters as much as you enjoyed Gwen and Joey, Mel and Maddie, Sas and Etti. Thank you!

To the earliest readers of Hillary and Dalton's story, thank you. Anita, Cara, Esther, Jeff, Laura, and Mom— thank you for your support! I appreciate the time you took to read at least a few chapters, the requests for more, and the side conversations along the way that encouraged me and made me laugh (or, sometimes, happy cry).

Daily, I am blessed to be surrounded by an incredible group of women who support me along the way and let me be me. Team—you're truly the sweetest crew there is, and I'm so impressed by each of you, every day. Thanks for the coffees and cookies and conversations and cocktails along the way.

Thanks, readers! Thanks for giving these characters a chance—I love this book and hope you do, too. May there be innumerable days of perfect reading weather in your immediate future.

To Jeffrey, for reading every word thirty-seven times, for grounding and encouraging me. For being my best friend, showing me love, embarking on adventures, and for supporting the fountain pen dream. I love you, always.

To my own little artists—thank you for your excitement and for reading and writing with me. You are my reasons. Bring those dreams to life. Te amo // wuv iz tiz.

Made in United States
Cleveland, OH
19 July 2025

18669508R00246